PRAISE FOR

THE QUEEN'S VOW

"Gortner has again produced a richly detailed book that is hard to put down."

—*Historical Novels Review*

"Gortner's latest historical novel . . . is set at the beginning of the extremely popular Tudor era, but it feels fresh owing to his choice of subject and the focus on events in Spain rather than England. It should thus have strong appeal for historical fiction fans looking for a new perspective on a favorite time period."

—*Library Journal*

"Gortner avoids romanticizing and sentimentalizing and presents a believable account of a woman determined to control her own fate and shape Spain into a great country."

—*Booklist*

"A fascinating story of intrigue and power struggles with a generous helping of romance . . . Through [Gortner's] creative and spellbinding storytelling, readers [will] come to know Isabella intimately."

—*Las Vegas Review-Journal*

"An excellent portrayal of this fascinating ruler, who supported both Columbus and the Inquisition."

—BookLoons

"[Gortner's] attention to detail and ability to bring long-dead figures to life create novels that are a wonderful treat. *The Queen's Vow* shines a light on Isabella of Castile . . . shattering misconceptions. Fans of historical fiction will want to add Gortner to their must-read lists."

—Night Owl Reviews

By C. W. Gortner

THE QUEEN'S VOW

THE Queen's Vow

A NOVEL OF
ISABELLA OF CASTILE

C. W. GORTNER

BALLANTINE BOOKS TRADE PAPERBACKS

NEW YORK

2013 Ballantine Books Trade Paperback Edition

Copyright © 2012 by C. W. Gortner

Reading group guide copyright © 2013 by Random House, Inc.

Published in the United States by Ballantine Books, an imprint of The Random House Publishing Group, a division of Random House, Inc., New York.

BALLANTINE and colophon are registered trademarks of Random House, Inc.

RANDOM HOUSE READER's CIRCLE & Design is a registered trademark of Random House, Inc.

Originally published in hardcover in the United States by Ballantine Books, an imprint of The Random House Publishing Group, a division of Random House, Inc., in 2012.

Library of Congress Cataloging-in-Publication Data
Gortner, C. W.
The queen's vow: a novel of Isabella of Castile / C. W. Gortner.
p. cm.
ISBN 978-0-345-52397-6
eBook ISBN 978-0-345-52398-3
1. Isabella I, Queen of Spain, 1451–1504—Fiction. 2. Spain—History—Ferdinand and Isabella, 1479–1516—Fiction. I. Title.
PS3607.O78Q84 2012
813'.6—dc23 2012008559

Printed in the United States of America on acid-free paper

www.randomhousereaderscircle.com

Title-page and part-title images: © iStockphoto.com / © jpa1999 (border);
© Evgeniy Dzhulay (crown)
Family tree and map by C. W. Gortner

Book design by Victoria Wong

For my niece, Isabel Gortner,
and my dear friend, Judith Merkle Riley

I have come to this land and I certainly do not intend
to leave it to flee or shirk my work;
nor shall I give such glory to my enemies
or such pain to my subjects.

—ISABELLA I OF CASTILE

House of Trastámara

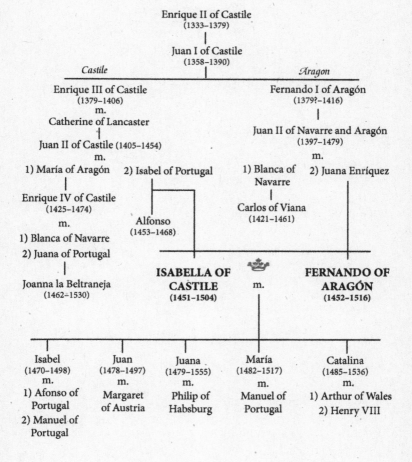

Enrique II of Castile
(1333–1379)

Juan I of Castile
(1358–1390)

Castile — *Aragon*

Enrique III of Castile
(1379–1406)
m.
Catherine of Lancaster

Juan II of Castile (1405–1454)
m.

1) María of Aragón

2) Isabel of Portugal

Fernando I of Aragón
(1379?–1416)

Juan II of Navarre and Aragón
(1397–1479)
m.

1) Blanca of Navarre

2) Juana Enríquez

Enrique IV of Castile
(1425–1474)
m.
1) Blanca of Navarre
2) Juana of Portugal

Alfonso
(1453–1468)

Carlos of Viana
(1421–1461)

Joanna la Beltraneja
(1462–1530)

**ISABELLA OF
CASTILE**
(1451–1504)

m.

**FERNANDO OF
ARAGÓN**
(1452–1516)

Isabel
(1470–1498)
m.
1) Afonso of
Portugal
2) Manuel of
Portugal

Juan
(1478–1497)
m.
Margaret
of Austria

Juana
(1479–1555)
m.
Philip of
Habsburg

María
(1482–1517)
m.
Manuel of
Portugal

Catalina
(1485–1536)
m.
1) Arthur of Wales
2) Henry VIII

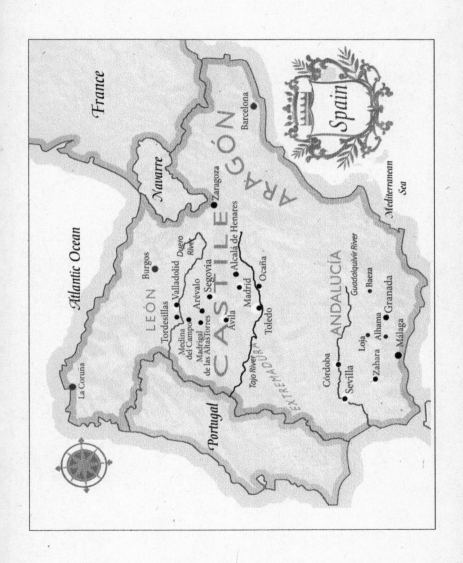

France

Atlantic Ocean

Navarre

ARAGÓN

Barcelona

Spain

Mediterranean Sea

Burgos

Valladolid Duero River

Tordesillas

LEÓN

Medina del Campo

Madrigal de las Altas Torres

Arévalo

Ávila

Segovia

Zaragoza

Alcalá de Henares

Madrid

Ocaña

Toledo

CASTILE

EXTREMADURA

Tajo River

Guadalquivir River

ANDALUCÍA

Baeza

Granada

Loja

Alhama

Málaga

Córdoba

Sevilla

Zahara

La Coruña

Portugal

THE QUEEN'S VOW

PROLOGUE

1454

No one believed I was destined for greatness.

I came into the world in the Castilian township of Madrigal de las Altas Torres, the first child of my father, Juan II's marriage to his second wife, Isabel of Portugal, after whom I was named—an infanta, healthy and unusually quiet, whose arrival was heralded by bells and perfunctory congratulations but no fanfare. My father had already sired an heir by his first marriage, my half brother, Enrique; and when my mother bore my brother, Alfonso, two years after me, shoring up the male Trastámara bloodline, everyone believed I'd be relegated to the cloister and distaff, an advantageous marriage pawn for Castile.

As often happens, God had other plans.

I CAN STILL recall the hour when everything changed.

I was not yet four years old. My father had been ill for weeks with a terrible fever, shut behind the closed doors of his apartments in the alcazar of Valladolid. I did not know him well, this forty-nine-year-old king whom his subjects had dubbed El Inútil, the Useless, for the manner in which he'd ruled. To this day, all I remember is a tall, lean man with sad eyes and a watery smile, who once summoned me to his private rooms and gave me a jeweled comb, enameled in the Moorish style. A short, swarthy lord stood behind my father's throne the entire time I was there, his stubby-fingered hand resting possessively on its back as he watched me with keen eyes.

A few months after that meeting, I overheard women in my mother's household whisper that the short lord had been beheaded and that his death had plunged my father into inconsolable grief.

"Lo mató esa loba portuguesa," the women said. "The Portuguese she-wolf had Constable Luna killed because he was the king's favorite."

Then one of them hissed, "Hush! The child, she's listening!" They froze in unison, like figures woven in a tapestry, seeing me seated in the alcove right next to them, all eyes and ears.

Only days after overhearing the ladies, I was hastily awakened, swathed in a cloak, and trotted through the alcazar's corridors to the royal apartments, only this time I was led into a stifling chamber where braziers burned and the muffled psalms of kneeling monks drifted through the room beneath a wreath of incense smoke. Copper lamps dangled overhead on gilt chains, the oily glow wavering across grim-faced grandees in somber finery.

On the large bed before me, the curtains were drawn back.

I paused on the threshold, instinctively looking about for the short lord, though I knew he was dead. Then I espied my father's favorite peregrine perched in the alcove, chained to its silver post. Its enlarged pupils swiveled to me, opaque and flame-lit.

I went still. I sensed something awful that I did not want to see.

"My child, go," my *aya*, Doña Clara, urged. "His Majesty your father is asking for you."

I refused to move, turning to cling to her skirts, hiding my face in their dusty folds. I heard heavy footsteps come up behind me; a deep voice said, "Is this our little Infanta Isabella? Come, let me see you, child."

Something in that voice tugged at me, making me look up.

A man loomed over me, large and barrel-chested, dressed in the dark garb of a grandee. His goateed face was plump, his light brown eyes piercing. He was not handsome; he looked like a pampered palace cat, but the slight tilt to his rosy mouth entranced me, for it seemed he smiled only for me, with a single-minded attentiveness that made me feel I was the only person he cared to see.

He held out a surprisingly delicate hand for a man of his size. "I am Archbishop Carrillo of Toledo," he said. "Come with me, Your Highness. There is nothing to fear."

I tentatively took his hand; his fingers were strong and warm. I felt safe as his hand closed over mine and he led me past the monks and dark-clad courtiers, their anonymous eyes seeming to glint with dispassionate interest like those of the falcon in the alcove.

The archbishop hoisted me onto a footstool by the bed, so I could stand near my father. I heard the king's breath making a noisy rasp in his lungs; his skin was pasted on his bones, already a strange waxen hue. His eyes were closed, his thin-fingered hands crossed over his chest as if he were an effigy on one of the elaborate tombs that littered our cathedrals.

I must have made a sound of dismay, for Carrillo murmured in my ear, "You must kiss him, Isabella. Give your father your blessing so he can leave this vale of tears in peace."

Though it was the last thing I wanted to do, I held my breath, bent over, and quickly pecked my father's cheek. I felt the chill of fever on his skin. I recoiled, my gaze lifting to the other side of the bed.

There, I saw a silhouette. For a horrifying moment, I thought it was the ghost of the dead constable, whom my ladies claimed haunted the castle, restless for revenge. But then an errant flicker from the lamps sliced across his face and I recognized my older half brother, Prince Enrique. The sight of him startled me; he usually stayed far from court, preferring his beloved *casa real* in Segovia, where it was said he kept an infidel guard around him and a menagerie of exotic beasts he fed with his own hands. Yet now he was here, in our father's death chamber, enveloped in a black cloak, the scarlet turban on his head hiding his mop of shaggy fair hair and enhancing his odd, flattened nose and small, close-set eyes, which gave him the appearance of an unkempt lion.

The knowing smile he gave me sent a chill down my spine.

The archbishop gathered me in his arms, marching from the room as though there was nothing of any importance left there for us. Over his thick shoulder, I saw the courtiers and grandees converge around the bed; I heard the monks' chants grow louder and saw Enrique incline intently, almost eagerly, over the moribund king.

In that moment, our father, Juan II, breathed his last.

WE DID NOT return to my rooms. Held tight against the archbishop's powerful chest, I watched in a daze as he brusquely motioned to my *aya*, waiting outside the apartment doors, and brought us down the spiral back staircase into the keep. An anemic moon in the night sky barely pierced the veil of cloud and mist.

As we emerged from the castle's protective shadow, the archbishop peered toward the postern gate, a darker square inset in the far curtain wall.

"Where are they?" he said in a taut voice.

"I . . . I don't know," quavered Doña Clara. "I sent word just as you bade me, telling Her Highness to meet us here. I hope something hasn't happened to—"

He held up a hand. "I think I see them." He stepped forward; I felt him stiffen as the hasty sound of slippers on cobblestones reached us. He let out a sharp exhalation when he saw the figures moving toward us, led by my mother. She was pale, the hood of her cloak bunched about her slim shoulders, sweat-drenched auburn hair escaping her coif. Behind her were her wide-eyed Portuguese ladies and Don Gonzalo Chacón, governor of my one-year-old brother, whom he cradled in his burly arms. I wondered why we were all here, outside in the dead of night. My brother was so young, and it was cold.

"Is he . . . ?" said my mother breathlessly.

Carrillo nodded. A sob cracked my mother's voice, her startling blue-green eyes fixed on me in the archbishop's arms. She held out her hands. "Isabella, *hija mía*."

Carrillo let me down. Unexpectedly, I did not want to leave him. But I shifted forth, my oversized cloak draping me in a shapeless cocoon. I curtsied as I'd been taught to do whenever I was presented to my beautiful mother, as I'd always done on the rare times I was brought to her before the court. She cast back my hood, her wide-set blue-green eyes meeting mine. Everyone said I had my mother's eyes, only mine were a darker hue.

"My child," she whispered, and I detected a quivering desperation in her tone. "My dearest daughter, all we have now is each other."

"Your Highness must concentrate on what is important," I heard Carrillo say. "Your children must be kept safe. With your husband the king's demise, they are—"

"I know what my children are," interrupted my mother. "What I want to know is how much longer do we have, Carrillo? How much time before we must abandon everything we've known for a forgotten refuge in the middle of nowhere?"

"A few hours at best" was the archbishop's flat reply. "The bells have not yet rung because such an announcement takes time to prepare." He paused. "But it will come soon enough, by the morning at the latest. You must place your trust in me. I promise you, I'll see to it that you and the infantes are kept from harm."

My mother turned her gaze to him, pressed a hand to her mouth as if to stifle her laughter. "How will you do that? Enrique of Trastámara is about to become king. If my eyes haven't deceived me these many years, he'll prove as susceptible to his favorites as Juan ever was. What safety can you possibly provide us, save a company of your guards and sanctuary in a convent? Yes, why not? A nunnery is no doubt best suited for the hated foreign widow and her brood."

"Children cannot be raised in a convent," Carrillo said. "Nor should they be separated at such a tender age from their mother. Your son, Alfonso, is now Enrique's heir by law until his wife bears him a child. I assure you, the Council will not see the infantes' rights impugned. In fact, they've agreed to let you raise the prince and his sister in the castle of Arévalo in Ávila, which shall be given to you as part of your widow's dower."

Silence fell. I stood quiet, observing the glazed look that came over my mother's face as she echoed, "Arévalo," as if she had heard wrong.

Carrillo went on, "His Majesty's testament leaves ample provision for the infantes, with separate towns to be granted to each of them upon their thirteenth year. I promise you shall not want for anything."

My mother's gaze narrowed. "Juan barely saw our children. He never cared about them. He never cared about anyone except that awful man, Constable Luna. Yet now you say he left provision for them. How can you possibly know this?"

"I was his confessor, remember? He heeded my advice because he feared the fires of everlasting Hell if he did not." The sudden intensity in Carrillo's tone made me glance at him. "But I cannot protect you if you do not place your trust in me. In Castile, it is customary for a widowed queen to retire from the court, but she doesn't usually get to keep her children, especially when the new king lacks an heir. That is why you must leave tonight. Take only the infantes and what you can carry. I'll send the rest of your possessions as soon as I'm able. Once you're in

Arévalo and the king's testament is proclaimed, no one will dare touch you, not even Enrique."

"I see. But you and I were never friends, Carrillo. Why risk yourself for my sake?"

"Let us say I offer you a favor," he said, "in exchange for a favor."

This time, my mother couldn't suppress her bitter laughter. "What favor can I grant you, the wealthiest prelate in Castile? I'm a widow on a pension, with two small children and a household to feed."

"You will know when the time comes. Rest assured, it will not be to your disadvantage." With these words, Carrillo turned to instruct her servants, who had overheard everything and stood staring at us with wide, fearful eyes.

I slowly reached up to take my mother's hand. I had never dared touch her before without leave. To me, she'd always been a beautiful but distant figure in glittering gowns, laughter spilling from her lips, surrounded by fawning admirers—a mother to be loved from afar. Now she looked as if she had walked miles across a stony landscape, her expression so anguished it made me wish I was older, bigger; that somehow I could be strong enough to protect her from the cruel fate that had taken my father from her.

"It's not your fault, Mama," I said. "Papa went to Heaven. That's why we must leave."

She nodded, tears filling her eyes as she gazed into some unseen distance.

"And we're going to Ávila," I added. "It's not far, is it, Mama?"

"No," she said softly, "not far, hija mía; not far at all. . . ."

But I could tell that for her, it was already a lifetime away.

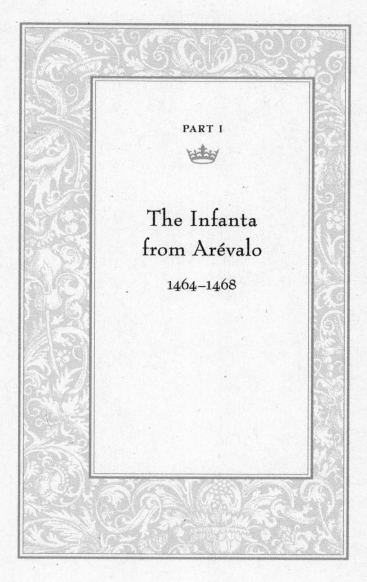

PART I

The Infanta
from Arévalo

1464–1468

CHAPTER ONE

Hold the reins firmly, Isabella. Don't let him sense your fear. If he does, he'll think he's in control and he'll try to throw you."

Perched atop the elegant black stallion, I nodded, gripping the reins. I could feel the taut leather through the weather-worn tips of my gloves. Belatedly I thought I should have let Beatriz's father, Don Pedro de Bobadilla, buy me the new gloves he had offered for my recent thirteenth birthday. Instead, pride—a sin I tried hard, but usually failed, to overcome—had refused to let me admit our penury by accepting the gift, though he lived with us and surely knew quite well how impoverished we were. Just as pride hadn't let me refuse my brother's challenge that it was time I learned to ride a proper horse.

So, here I sat, with old leather gloves that felt thin as silk to protect my hands, atop a magnificent animal. Though it was not a large horse it was still frightening; the creature shifted and pawed the ground as though it were ready to bolt at any moment, regardless of whether I could stay on or not.

Alfonso shook his head, leaning from his roan to pry my fingers further apart, so that the reins draped through them.

"Like that," he said. "Firm, but not so firm that you'll injure his mouth. And remember to sit straight when you canter and lean forward at a gallop. Canela isn't one of those stupid mules you and Beatriz ride. He's a purebred Arabian jennet, worthy of a caliph. He needs to know his rider is in charge at all times."

I straightened my spine, settling my buttocks on the embossed saddle. I felt light as a thistle. Though I was of an age when most girls begin to develop, I remained so flat and thin that my friend and lady-in-waiting Beatriz, Don Bobadilla's daughter, was constantly cajoling me to eat more. She eyed me now with concern, her significantly more curvaceous figure so gracefully erect upon her dappled gelding that it seemed she'd been riding one her entire life, her thick black hair coiled above her aquiline features under a fillet and veil.

She said to Alfonso, "I assume Your Highness has ensured this princely jennet of yours is properly broken. We wouldn't want anything untoward to happen to your sister."

"Of course he's broken. Don Chacón and I broke him ourselves. Isabella will be fine. Won't you, *hermana*?"

Even as I nodded, near-paralyzing doubt overcame me. How could I possibly be expected to show this beast that *I* was in charge? As if he sensed my thoughts, Canela pranced sideways. I let out a gasp, yanking at the reins. He came to a snorting halt, ears flattened, clearly displeased at the effort I'd exerted on his bit.

Alfonso winked at me. "See? She can handle him." He looked at Beatriz. "Do you need any assistance, my lady?" he asked, in a jocular tone that hinted at his years of verbal sparring with our castle custodian's headstrong only daughter.

"I can manage fine, thank you," said Beatriz tartly. "Indeed, Her Highness and I will both be fine as soon as we get a feel for these Moorish steeds of yours. Lest you forget, we have ridden before, even if our mounts were, as you say, only stupid mules."

Alfonso chuckled, pivoting on his roan with practiced ease for his mere ten years. His brilliant blue eyes glistened; his thick fair hair, shorn bluntly at his shoulders, enhanced his full, handsome face. "And lest you forget," he said, "I've been riding every day since I was five. It is experience that makes for good horsemanship."

"True," rumbled Alfonso's governor, Don Chacón, from his own massive horse. "The Infante Alfonso is already an accomplished equestrian. Riding is second nature to him."

"We don't doubt it," I interjected before Beatriz could respond. I forced out a smile. "I believe we're ready, brother. But, pray, not too fast."

Alfonso nudged his roan forward, leading the way out of Arévalo's enclosed inner courtyard, under the portcullis and through the main gates.

I shot a disapproving look at Beatriz.

Of course, this was all her doing. Bored by our daily regimen of lessons, prayer, and needlework, she had announced this morning that we must get some exercise, or we would turn into crones before our time. We'd been cooped up indoors too long, she said, which was true enough, winter having been particularly harsh this year. And when she asked our governess, Doña Clara, for permission, my *aya* had agreed because riding for us invariably consisted of taking the castle's elderly mules on a leisurely jaunt around the curtain wall surrounding the castle and its adjoining township for an hour before supper.

But after I changed into my riding clothes and went with Beatriz into the courtyard, I found Alfonso standing there with Don Chacón and two impressive stallions—gifts sent by our half brother, King Enrique. The black horse was for me, Alfonso said. His name was Canela.

I had suppressed my alarm as I mounted the stallion with the aid of a footstool. I was even more alarmed, however, when it became clear I was expected to ride astride, *a la jineta,* the way the Moors did, perched on the narrow leather saddle with the stirrups drawn up high—an unfamiliar and unsettling sensation.

"An odd name for a horse," I'd remarked, to disguise my apprehension. "Cinnamon is a light color, while this creature is black as night."

Canela tossed his mane and swiveled his exquisitely shaped head about to nip my leg. I did not think it a good augury for the afternoon.

"Beatriz," I now hissed as we rode out onto the plain, "why didn't you tell me? You know I dislike surprises."

"That's exactly why I didn't tell you," she hissed back. "If I had, you wouldn't have come. You'd have said we should read or sew or recite novenas. Say what you will, we have to have fun sometime."

"I hardly see how being thrown from a horse can be deemed fun."

"Bah. Just think of him as an overgrown dog. He's big, yes, but quite harmless."

"And how, pray, would you know?"

"Because Alfonso would never have let you ride Canela otherwise," said Beatriz, with a truculent toss of her head that revealed the immutable self-confidence that had made her my closest companion and confidante—though, as ever, I found myself caught between amusement and discomfort when confronted with her irreverent character.

We were three years apart, and antithetical in temperament. Beatriz acted as though the realm outside our gates was a vast unexplored place filled with potential adventure. Doña Clara said her reckless attitude was due to the fact that Beatriz's mother had died shortly after her birth; her father had raised her alone in Arévalo, without feminine supervision. Dark as I was fair, voluptuous as I was angular, Beatriz was also rebellious, unpredictable, and too outspoken for her own good. She even challenged the nuns at the Convento de las Agustinas where we went to take our lessons, driving poor Sor María to distraction with her endless questions. She was a loyal friend, and amusing as well, always quick to find mirth in what others did not; but she was also a constant headache for her elders and for Doña Clara, who'd tried in vain to teach Beatriz that well-bred ladies did not give in to random impulse whenever the urge overcame them.

"We should have told Doña Clara the truth," I said, glancing at my hands. I was clenching the reins again and forced myself to loosen my grip. "I hardly think she'll find our gallivanting about on horses appropriate."

Beatriz pointed ahead. "Who cares about appropriate? Look around you!"

I did as she instructed, reluctantly.

The sun dipped toward the horizon, shedding a vibrant saffron glow over the bleached-bone sky. To our left Arévalo sat on its low hill, a dun-colored citadel with six towers and a crenellated keep, abutting the provincial market town bearing the same name. To our right wound the main road that led to Madrid, while all around us, stretching as far as my eyes could see, lay the open expanse of Castile—an endless land dotted with fields of barley and wheat, vegetable patches, and clusters of wind-twisted pine. The air was still, heady with the fragrance of resin and a whiff of melting snow that I always associated with the advent of spring.

"Isn't it spectacular?" breathed Beatriz, her eyes shining. I nodded, gazing upon the countryside that had been my home for almost as long as I could remember. I'd seen it many times before, of course, from Arévalo's keep and during our annual trips with Doña Clara to the neighboring town of Medina del Campo, where the biggest animal fair in Castile was held. But for a reason I could not have explained, today it looked different, like when one suddenly notices that time has transformed an oft-looked-at painting, darkening the colors to a new luster and deepening the contrast between light and shadow.

My practical nature assured me this was because I was seeing the land from higher up, perched on the back of Canela rather than on the mule I was used to. Still, tears pricked my eyes and, without warning, I had a sudden memory of an imposing *sala* filled with people in velvets and silks. The image faded as soon as it came, a phantom from the past, and when Alfonso waved to me from where he rode ahead with Don Chacón, I promptly forgot I sat upon an unfamiliar, potentially treacherous animal and jabbed my heels into its ribs.

Canela leapt forth, throwing me forward against his arched neck. I instinctively grabbed hold of his mane, lifting myself off the saddle and tensing my thighs. Canela responded with a satisfied snort. He quickened his pace, galloping past Alfonso, raising a whirlwind of ochre dust.

"Dios mío!" I heard Alfonso gasp as I tore past him. From the corner of my eye I saw Beatriz fast behind me, shouting to my brother and an astonished Don Chacón: "Years of experience, eh?"

I burst into laughter.

IT FELT MARVELOUS, just what I imagined flying must be: to leave behind the cares of the classroom and studies, the chill flagstone of the castle and baskets of endless darning, the constant muttered worry over money and my mother's erratic health; to be free and revel in the sensation of the horse moving beneath me and the landscape of Castile.

When I came to a panting halt on a ridge overlooking the plain, my riding hood hung on its ribbons down my back, my light auburn hair tumbling loose from its braids. Sliding off Canela, I patted his lathered neck. He nuzzled my palm before he set himself to munching on brittle thornbushes sprouting between the rocks. I settled on a nearby pile of stones and watched Beatriz come plunging up the ridge. As she came to a stop, flushed from her exertions, I remarked, "You were right, after all. We did need the exercise."

"Exercise!" she gasped, slipping off her horse. "Are you aware that we just left His Highness and Chacón behind in a cloud of dust?"

I smiled. "Beatriz de Bobadilla, must everything be a contest with you?"

She put her hands on her hips. "When it comes to proving our worthiness, yes. If we don't take it upon ourselves, who will?"

"So it's our strength you wish to prove," I said. "Hmm. Explain this to me." Beatriz flopped beside me, gazing toward the ebbing sun. The sun fell slowly at this time of year in Castile, affording us a breathtaking vision of gold-rimmed clouds and violet-and-scarlet skies. The incipient evening wind caught at Beatriz's tangled black hair; her expressive eyes, so quick to show her every thought, turned wistful. "I want to prove we're as accomplished as any man and should therefore enjoy the same privileges."

I frowned. "Why would we ever want to do that?"

"So we can live as we see fit and not have to apologize for it, just as His Highness does."

"Alfonso doesn't live as he sees fit." I righted my hood, tucking its ribbons into my bodice. "In fact, he has considerably less freedom than you think. Save for today, I hardly see him anymore, so busy is he with his rounds of swordplay, archery, and jousting, not to mention his studies. He is a prince. He has many demands on his time."

She scowled. "Yes, important demands, not just learning to sew and churn butter and corral the sheep. If we could live as men, then we'd be free to roam the world undertaking noble quests, like a knight errant or the Maid of Orléans."

I concealed the unbidden excitement her words roused in me. I'd schooled myself to hide my feelings ever since my mother, Alfonso, and I had fled Valladolid that terrible night ten years earlier, for since then I had come to understand far better what had occurred. We were not so isolated in Arévalo that I failed to glean the occasional news that filtered over the *meseta* from the royal residences in Madrid, Segovia, and Valladolid; the subjects were gossiped about by our servants, easy to hear if one seemed not to listen. I knew that with Enrique's accession, the court had become a dangerous place for us, ruled by his favorites and his avaricious queen. I had never forgotten the palpable fear I'd felt that night of my father's death; the long ride across dark fields and forests, avoiding the main roads in case Enrique sent guards in our pursuit. The memory was branded in me, an indelible lesson that life's changes would occur whether or not we were prepared for them, and we must do our best to adapt, with a minimum of fuss.

"The Maid of Orléans was burned at the stake," I finally said. "Is that the grand end you'd have us aspire to, my friend?"

Beatriz sighed. "Of course not, it's a horrible death. But I'd like to think that, given the chance, we could lead armies in defense of our country as she did. As it stands, we're doomed before we've ever lived." She flung her arms wide. "It's the same thing day after day, week after week, month after dreary month! Is this how all gentlewomen are raised, I wonder? Are we so unintelligent our sole pleasures must be to entertain guests and please our future husbands, to learn how to smile between dinner courses without ever expressing an opinion? If so, we might as well forgo the marriage and childbearing parts altogether and proceed directly to old age and sainthood."

I regarded her. Beatriz always asked questions for which there were no easy answers, seeking to change that which had been ordained before we were born. It disconcerted me that lately I too had found myself asking similar questions, plagued by a similar restlessness, though I would never admit to it. I didn't like the impatience that overcame me when I looked to the future, because I knew that even I, a princess of Castile, must one day wed where I was told and settle for whatever life my husband saw fit to give me.

"It is neither tedious nor demeaning to marry, and care for a husband and children," I said. "Such has been a woman's lot since time began."

"You only recite what you've been told," she retorted. " 'Women breed and men provide.' What I ask is: Why? Why must we have only one path? Who said a woman can't take up the sword and cross, and march on Granada to vanquish the Moors? Who said we can't make our own decisions or manage our own affairs as well as any man?"

"It is not a question of who said it. It simply is."

She rolled her eyes. "Well, the Maid of Orléans didn't marry. She didn't scrub and sew and plan dowries. She donned a suit of armor and went to war for her dauphin."

"Who betrayed her to the English," I reminded her and paused.

"Beatriz, the Maid was called upon to perform God's work. You cannot compare her destiny to ours. She was a holy vessel; she sacrificed herself for her country."

Beatriz made a rude snorting sound but I knew I'd scored an inarguable point in this argument we'd been engaged in since childhood. I remained outwardly unperturbed, as I invariably did when Beatriz pontificated, but as I imagined my vivacious friend clad in rusty armor, urging a company of lords to war for *la patria*, a sudden giggle escaped me.

"Now you laugh at me!" she cried.

"No, no." I choked back my mirth as best I could. "I was not. I was only thinking that had the Maid come your way, you'd have joined her without a moment's hesitation."

"Indeed, I would have." She leapt to her feet. "I'd have thrown my books and embroidery out the window and jumped on the first horse available. How wonderful it must be to do as you please, to fight for your country, to live with only the sky as your roof and the earth as your bed."

"You exaggerate, Beatriz. Crusades involve more hardship than history tells us."

"Perhaps, but at least we'd be *doing* something!"

I looked at her hands, clasped as if she were brandishing a weapon. "You could certainly wield a sword with those big paws of yours," I teased.

She stuck out her chin. "You're the princess, not me. You would wield the sword."

As if day had slipped without warning into night, cold overcame me. I shivered. "I don't think I could ever lead an army," I said, in a low voice. "It must be terrible to watch your countrymen cut down by your foes and to know your own death can happen at any moment. Nor"—I held up my hand, preempting Beatriz's protest—"do I think you should exalt the Maid of Orléans as an example for us to emulate. She fought for her prince only to suffer a cruel death. I'd not wish such a fate on anyone. Certainly, I do not wish it for myself. Boring as it may be to you, I'd rather wed and bear children, as is my duty."

Beatriz gave me a penetrating look. "Duty is for weaklings. Don't tell me you haven't questioned as well. You devoured that tale of the crusader kings in our library as if it were marzipan."

I forced out a laugh. "You truly are incorrigible."

At that moment, Alfonso and Don Chacón rode up, the governor looking most chagrined. "Your Highness, my lady de Bobadilla, you shouldn't have galloped off like that. You could have been hurt, or worse. Who knows what lies in wait on these lands at dusk?"

I heard the fear in his voice. Though King Enrique had seen fit to leave us be in Arévalo, isolated from court, his shadow was never far from our lives. The threat of abduction was a peril I'd long grown accustomed to, had in fact come to ignore. But Chacón was devoted to our protection and viewed any possibility of a threat as a serious matter.

"Forgive me," I told him. "I am at fault. I don't know what came over me."

"Whatever it was, I'm impressed," said Alfonso. "Who would have thought you'd be such an Amazon, sweet sister?"

"I, an Amazon? Surely not. I merely tested Canela's prowess. He did well, don't you think? He's much faster than his size would indicate."

Alfonso grinned. "He is. And yes, you did very well, indeed."

"And now we must be getting back," said Chacón. "Night is almost upon us. Come, we'll take the main road. And no galloping ahead this time, do I make myself clear?"

Back on our horses, Beatriz and I followed my brother and Chacón into the twilight. Beatriz opted not to act up, I noted with relief, riding demurely at my side. Yet as we neared Arévalo, streaks of coral inking the sky, I couldn't help but recall our conversation, and wonder, despite all efforts to the contrary, what it must feel like to be a man.

CHAPTER TWO

The keep was deserted, an anomaly given the hour, and the moment we entered the great hall and saw that the long, scarred central table was not yet set for the evening meal, I sensed that something was wrong. Alfonso and Chacón were in the stables unsaddling and brushing the horses; as Beatriz removed my cloak, I looked at the hearth. The fire had not even been lit. The only light came from the sputtering torches on the wall.

"I wonder where everyone is?" I said, rubbing my rein-chafed hands together. I tried to sound nonchalant. "I expected to find Doña Clara in the keep with her switch and reprimands."

"Me, too." Beatriz frowned. "It's far too quiet."

I wondered if my mother had fallen ill again while we'd been out riding. Guilt stabbed me. I should have stayed inside. I shouldn't have gone out so precipitously, without leaving word.

My governess entered the hall, bustling straight toward us.

"Here she comes," whispered Beatriz, but I perceived at once that the concern etched on my *aya*'s face was not for us. If Doña Clara had initially been angered by our escapade, something more important had now taken precedence.

"Finally," said Doña Clara, in a tone that lacked its habitual bite. "Where on earth have you been? Her Highness your mother has been asking for you."

My mother had been asking for me. My heart started to pound; as if from far away I heard Beatriz say, "We were with His Highness, Doña Clara. Remember? We said we were—"

"I know who you were with," interrupted my *aya*, "impertinent child. What I asked was *where* you have been. You've been gone over three hours, in case you hadn't noticed."

"Three hours?" I stared at her. "But it hardly felt more than . . ." My voice faded as I met her grim stare. "Is something wrong? Has Mama . . . ?"

Doña Clara nodded. "A letter arrived while you were out. It distressed her greatly."

My stomach knotted. I reached for Beatriz's hand as Doña Clara said, "The letter was from court. I took it myself from the messenger, so I saw the seal. The messenger did not wait for a reply; he said it wasn't necessary. When my lady read the letter, she grew so upset we had to brew a draft of marigold and rhubarb. Doña Elvira tried to get her to drink it but she would not let anyone attend her. She went into her rooms and slammed the door."

Beatriz squeezed my hand. She didn't have to say what we both were thinking. If a letter had come from court, whatever news it brought could not be good.

"A letter now," went on Doña Clara, "can you imagine it? After ten years of silence! Of course she's upset. We've lived here for all this time with nary a summons or invitation, as if we were poor relations, an embarrassment to be kept hidden away. Only Carrillo has seen fit to send the payments promised for our upkeep, and even he, a prince of the Church, can't squeeze gold from an unwilling treasury. Why, if it weren't for our own livestock and harvest, we'd have starved to death by now. And look about you: We need new tapestries, carpets for the floors, not to mention clothes. His Grace the king knows this. He knows we cannot raise two children on air and hope alone."

Her vehemence was not unusual; in fact, her complaints of our penurious situation were so commonplace I hardly paid them heed most of the time. Yet as if she'd suddenly ripped a veil from my eyes, I saw the walls of the hall around me as they truly were, stained with mildew and draped in colorless hangings; the warped floorboards and decrepit furnishings, all of which belonged to an impoverished rural home and not the abode of the dowager queen of Castile and her royal children.

Still, it was my home, the only one I remembered. A jolt went through me when I abruptly recalled that fleeting vision I'd had on the ridge, of velvet-clad figures in a hall. It seemed I had not forgotten that distant court where my family once lived. . . .

I wished I could go to the chapel to be alone for a while, to think. Though chill and austere, the castle chapel always brought me solace when I faced difficulty; the mere act of going to my knees and clasping my hands gave me consolation and focus, even if I failed to quiet my mind enough to actually pray.

"You must go to her," Doña Clara said to me. With an inward sigh, I nodded, crossing the hall to the staircase leading to the second floor with Beatriz at my side. At the landing, we came upon my mother's head matron, Doña Elvira, seated on a stool. She stood quickly.

"Oh, Isabella, my child!" She pressed a brown-spotted hand to her mouth, choking back ready tears. Poor Doña Elvira was always close to tears; I'd never met any woman who wept as copiously or as often as she did.

I touched her thin shoulder in reassurance. She was a devoted servant who'd come from Portugal with my mother and stayed by her side throughout all our trials. She had a nervous constitution; she couldn't help the fact that she didn't know how to contend with my mother's spells. In truth, no one in the castle did, except me.

"You mustn't worry," I said softly.

Elvira wiped tears from her wrinkled cheeks. "When that letter arrived—Blessed Virgin, you should have seen her. She went wild, screaming and railing. Oh, it was terrible to see! And then she—she slammed that door and refused to let anyone near, not even me. I begged her to drink the draft, to rest and calm herself until you came home, but she ordered me out. She told me no one save God could help her now."

"I'll take care of her," I said. "Go, prepare another draft. Only give me some time first, before you bring it in." I gave her another reassuring smile and watched her shuffle away before I turned to the bedchamber door. I didn't want to go in. I wanted to run away.

"I'll wait here," Beatriz said, "in case you have need of me."

I drew a calming breath and reached for the latch. The inner lock had been dismantled some time ago, after my mother had bolted herself inside during one of her spells. She had remained sequestered for over two days. Finally, Don Chacón had been forced to break the door in.

I saw the evidence of her outburst the moment I stepped into the room. Strewn across the floor were broken vials, papers, overturned objects from flung coffers. I blinked, adjusting my eyes to the gloom before I took a resolute step forward. My foot hit something; it clattered as it rolled away, glinting dully, leaving a wet residue.

The goblet of Doña Elvira's draft.

"Mama?" I said. "Mama, it's me, Isabella."

The vague smell of mold—constant in the old castle because of the river that ran beneath it—reached me. In the darkness, familiar objects began to materialize. I discerned her sagging tester bed, the brocade curtains grazing the rushes on the floor; her loom, her spindle of yarn on a distaff in front of the shuttered window, the unlit brazier, and in the alcove, her upholstered throne, a forlorn relic under its cloth of estate bearing the impaled arms of Castile and her native Portugal.

"Mama?" My voice quivered. I clenched my fists at my side. There was nothing to be afraid of, I told myself. I had done this before. I alone had brought my mother back from the precipice time and time again. Of everyone in this household, only I had the ability to soothe her, to instill reason when her spells overcame her. Not once had she harmed me.

I heard rustling fabric. Peering at the shadows by the bed, I discerned her figure. I had a terrible recollection of the night my father died, when I thought I'd seen the constable's ghost.

"Mama, I'm here. Come out. Tell me what has frightened you so."

She warily moved forth. Her disheveled hair framed her pallid face, her long white hands kneading her gown. "*Hija mía,* he is here. He's come again to torment me."

"No, Mama. It's only the wind." I moved to the sideboard; as I struck flint to the candle there, she cried, "No, no light! He'll see me! He'll—"

Her cry was cut short when I turned with the lit candle cupped between my hands. The wavering circle of light threw the shadows higher upon the walls. "See, Mama? There's no one here but you and me."

Her greenish-blue eyes distended, searching the chamber as if she expected to find her tormentor lurking in the corners. I was about to take a wary step back when all of a sudden she went limp. Letting out a sigh of relief under my breath, I set the candle in a sconce and went to guide her to a chair. I pulled a stool beside her, took her icy hands in mine.

"I know you don't believe me," she said, her voice still holding a frantic echo of fear. "But he was here. I saw him by the window, staring at me, just as he used to do when he was alive and wanted to prove how much power he had over your father."

"Mama, Constable Luna is dead. No one is here to harm you, I promise."

She pulled her hand from me. "How can you promise such a thing? You do not know; you don't understand. No one can. But *he* does. He knows a debt of blood must be paid."

My skin crawled. "Mama, what are you talking about? What debt?"

She didn't seem to hear me. "I had no choice," she said. "He took your father from me. He was an abomination, a demon: He seduced my own husband away from me. Yet they blamed me for it. The grandees, the people, your own father—they said it was my fault. Juan told me he wished he too had died that day, so he could be with his beloved friend. And so it happened: he died. He did not even try to live, not for me, not for his own children. He preferred that . . . that unnatural man."

I did not want to hear this. It was not meant for my ears; I was not her confessor. But there was no one else; and I had to soothe her enough so that she'd at least let herself be attended. And there was the letter, the reason she'd fallen into this state in the first place. I had to find out what it said.

"Papa died of an illness," I said haltingly. "It was not on purpose. He was sick. He had a fever and—"

"No!" She rose to her feet. "He wanted to die! He chose death so he could escape me. Sweet Virgin, this is why I cannot rest, why I live day after day in endless torment. Had I not done it, Juan might have lived. I'd still be queen. We'd still be in our rightful estate!"

As if they were in the room, I heard the women's words, whispered so long ago: *That she-wolf did it. . . . She killed Luna.*

My mother had destroyed my father's friend. This was why she believed his ghost haunted her; why she kept falling prey to these terrible spells. She believed in this debt of blood she had brought upon herself.

I forced myself to stand. "It's cold in here. Let me light the brazier."

"Yes! Why not? Light the fire. Or better yet, bring in torches and set the castle ablaze. It will be a taste of what awaits me in Hell." She took to pacing the chamber again. "God in Heaven, what can I do? How can I protect you?" She whirled about. I froze, bracing myself. She did not scream, though; she did not rant or claw at herself as she had in the past. Instead she reached into the pocket of her gown and flung a crumpled parchment at me. Picking it up from the floor, I turned toward the candle. I found I was holding my breath. Silence fell as I read, broken only by the keening of the wind outside. The letter was from King Enrique. His wife, Queen Juana, had given birth to a daughter. They had christened the child Joanna, after her mother.

My mother spoke: "Enrique has achieved the impossible. He has an heir."

I looked up, bewildered. "Surely it's cause for celebration."

She laughed. "Oh, yes, there'll be celebration! They'll celebrate my demise. Everything I fought for is lost; I have no crown, no court; your brother Alfonso will be disinherited. And they will come. They'll take you and Alfonso away. They'll leave me here alone to rot, forgotten by the world."

"Mama, that's not true. This letter, it merely announces the child's birth. It says nothing about us going anywhere. Come, you are overwrought. Let us seek solace together."

I slipped the letter into my pocket and moved to her prayer bench. It was a comfort she'd instilled in me as a child, a ritual we had come to cherish; every evening we said our prayers together.

I was reaching for the mother-of-pearl box where she kept her rosary when I heard her say, "No, no more prayer. God does not listen to me anymore."

I went still. "That . . . that is blasphemy. God always listens." But in that moment my words sounded devoid of conviction and it terrified me. I felt the weight of things I barely understood bearing down, creating a chasm between us; I almost gasped aloud when a tentative knock came at the door. I found Elvira standing there with goblet in hand; she gave me a questioning look as I took it from her. When I turned around, my mother stood by her bed again, watching me. "Ah," she said, "my oblivion has come."

"It's a draft to help you sleep. Mama, you must rest now." I moved to her; she did not resist. She drank the draft and lay down on the tangled sheets. She looked so old, her eyes far too large for her gaunt face, lines engraving her once-supple mouth. She was only thirty-three, a young woman still, and it was as if she'd dwelled in this lonely fortress for a thousand years.

"Rest now," I said. "I am here; I will not leave you. Rest and all will be well."

Her eyelids fluttered. I started to sing under my breath, a nursery rhyme that all children learn: "*Duerme, pequeña mía; duerme feliz. Los lobos aúllan fuera pero aquí me tienes a mí.* Sleep, little one, sleep contentedly. The wolves howl outside but inside I am here."

Her eyes closed. She twitched once as the spell dissipated. She murmured. I leaned close to hear her words.

"I did it for you," she said, "for you and Alfonso. I killed Luna to save you."

I sat motionless at her side, plunged back to that night so long ago when we fled Valladolid. I had never pondered the events that led to our exile but now I understood the terrible secret that tore apart my mother's soul.

I watched her sleep. I wanted to pray for her; she was wrong, she had to be. God heeded us always, especially in our darkest hours. But all I could do was wonder if there might come a time when I too would be driven to this, forced to commit the unthinkable and then be haunted by my actions for eternity.

Beatriz was waiting outside. She stood as I emerged; my brother had joined her.

"I heard Mama is not well," he said. "Is it . . . ?"

I nodded. "It was bad. We must entertain her, stay close to her. She needs us now."

"Of course. Anything you say," he said. But I knew he'd prefer to stay away, to go lose himself in his weaponry and riding. Alfonso had never understood why our mother acted as she did, why her fervent embraces and gaiety could suddenly turn violent as the winter storms that howled across the plains. I had always sensed his fear of her and had done everything I could to shelter him from her fits. As he kissed my cheek awkwardly and went back down the stairs, I met Beatriz's gaze. The crumpled letter sat like stone in my pocket.

They will come. They will take you and Alfonso away.

Though everything inside me wanted to deny it, I knew it could be true.

We had to prepare.

CHAPTER THREE

The following days passed without incident, belying my tumult. I stashed the king's letter in a coffer in my room; Beatriz asked ceaselessly about it, naturally, until I could bear no more and let her read it. She looked at me in astonishment, speechless for perhaps the first time in her life. I didn't encourage her opinion; I was too preoccupied with my own troubled presentiment that we stood on the verge of irrevocable change.

I devoted myself to my mother. There were no more spells, no more outbursts; though she remained too thin and pale, pecking at her food like a bird, she welcomed the visits Alfonso and I paid every afternoon.

I was touched to discover that my brother had taken pains to learn a Portuguese song for her, which he performed with gusto even if his voice warbled. My brother was not musically inclined, yet as he sang out the native lyrics of my mother's land, I saw her face soften, recapture its faded beauty. Dressed in her outdated court gown, her fingers laden with tarnished rings, she tapped the music out on the arms of her chair, her feet silently moving under her hem as she followed the steps of the intricate dance she'd once excelled in, flaunting her skill under the painted eaves of the great *salas* where she'd been the most powerful and sought-after woman at court.

After Alfonso finished, his chin lifted high and arms flung wide, she clapped frenetically, as if she wished to impregnate the room with the rare sound of her joy. Then she motioned to me. "Dance, Isabella! Dance with your brother!" And as Beatriz picked out the song on the small, stringed *cavaquinho,* I joined hands with Alfonso, moving with studied steps, even when my brother treaded on my toes and grinned sheepishly, his face flushed with exertion.

"It's much easier to joust with *cañas*," he whispered to me, and I smiled, for in no other way did he betray his masculine pride than at times like these, preferring to flaunt his agility on horseback with the sharp stakes used for hunting rather than risk embarrassment by tripping over his own feet in front of his family. I, on the other hand, loved to dance; it was one of the few pleasures I had in life, and I had to blink back my tears of joy when my mother spontaneously leapt from her chair to take us both by the hand and whirl us around in a dizzying display.

"There," she exclaimed, as we caught our breath. "That is how it is done! You must learn to dance well, children. You carry the blood of Portugal, Castile, and León in your veins; you must never let Enrique's mincing courtiers put you to shame."

The mention of courtiers hovered in the air like a wisp of acrid smoke, but my mother didn't seem to notice her slip. She stood beaming as Doña Clara, Elvira, and Beatriz broke into applause, and Alfonso then regaled us with a show of his mastery of the sword, enacting feints and thrusts in the middle of the room while my mother laughed and Doña Clara cried out for him to be careful, lest he skewer one of our cowering dogs.

Later that night, when I kissed my mother good night after our evening devotions—for we'd returned to our daily prayers, much to my relief—she whispered, "This was a good day, Isabella. If I can only remember this day I think I'll be able to bear anything."

It was the first allusion she'd made to our shared secret since her spell. As she held me close I vowed to myself that I would do everything possible to stave off the darkness that threatened my family.

A few days later, she announced her decision to pay a visit to the Cistercian Convent of Santa Ana in Ávila. We had gone there before, several times, in fact; I'd even attended lessons with the nuns there after my mother completed my preliminary instruction in letters. It was one of my favorite places; the tranquil cloisters, the indoor patio with its fountain, the fragrant herb patches in the garden, the soughing of the nuns' robes against the flagstones, always filled me with peace. The devout sisters excelled in needlework; their splendid altar cloths adorned the most famous cathedrals in the realm. Many an hour I'd spent in their company, learning the art of embroidery while listening to the murmur of their voices.

Doña Elvira fretted that it would be too much exertion for my mother, but Doña Clara pronounced it an excellent idea and helped us pack for the journey.

"It's exactly what your mother needs," my *aya* said. "The sisters will make her feel better and getting away from this old place will prove a far more efficacious remedy than those foul potions of Elvira's."

We set out before dawn with Don Bobadilla and four retainers. Alfonso was left behind at the last minute, sulking, under the supervision of Doña Clara and Don Chacón, with strict instructions to dedicate himself to his studies, as he'd grown quite indolent. I rode Canela, who was overjoyed to see me, whickering and greedily devouring the bits of sour apple I had brought. My mother sat upon an older, more docile mare. Her veil framed her face, its creamy gossamer adding luster to her complexion and highlighting the blue in her eyes. Doña Elvira grumbled beside her on a mule, having refused to even consider riding in a litter, and Beatriz looked equally morose on her steed, scowling generally at the landscape.

"I thought you wanted adventure," I said to her, hiding a smile when she retorted, "Adventure! I hardly see what kind of adventure we'll find at Santa Ana. I rather think there'll be more poor linens and lentil soup."

Despite the fact that she was probably right, the thought of going to Ávila pleased me. While Beatriz had no doubt expected momentous change as a result of the letter, with every day that went by I felt nothing but relief that change seemed less and less likely. I knew, however, that the monotony was intolerable for my friend. As she outgrew her adolescence, transforming entirely against her will into a beautiful young woman, Beatriz became more restless than ever, though none of us dared to mention it. I'd heard Doña Clara mutter to Doña Elvira that girls like Beatriz needed early marriage to cool their overheated blood, but Beatriz seemed oblivious to any male attention, ignoring the whistling retainers who gawked at her as we passed them during our chores. At night in our rooms, she regarded the growth of her breasts and widening of her hips with visible dismay; they were manifestations of the fact that soon she'd no longer be able to pretend she was not susceptible to all that full-blown womanhood entailed.

"You could ask Don Bobadilla to take you into town," I suggested, reaching into my side-basket for the bundle of cloth containing the bread and cheese Doña Clara had packed for us. "I think Doña Elvira has some things she wants to buy. She mentioned cloth for new dresses and cloaks yesterday."

"Yes, and then Papa can take us on an insufferably slow ride around Ávila's walls," she said. "As if I haven't seen it all a hundred times already."

I handed her a piece of the soft bread, freshly baked in our ovens. "Come, don't be so disagreeable. Your face will pucker up like a sour apple." At the mention of the word, Canela pricked his ears. I patted his neck. Alfonso was right: Although mules were considered the best mounts for unwed virgins, my days of riding one were definitely over.

Beatriz grimaced as she ate her bread and cheese. Then she leaned to me and said, "You can pretend all you like, but I know you're as curious as I am about what that letter from court means. I've seen you open the coffer and look at it at night when you think I'm asleep. You must have read it about as many times as I've seen the walls of Ávila."

I lowered my gaze, wondering what Beatriz might say if I told her just how curious, and anxious, I had truly been.

"Of course I'm interested," I said, keeping my voice low so that my mother, who rode ahead with Don Bobadilla, would not overhear. "But perhaps all the king wished was to tell us that the queen had given birth."

"I suppose so. But don't forget, Alfonso was his heir first and many claim Enrique is impotent. Perhaps that child is not his."

"Beatriz!" I exclaimed, louder than I intended. My mother glanced over her shoulder at us. I smiled. "She's eating all the bread," I said quickly, and my mother gave Beatriz a reproving look. As soon as she turned away, I hissed, "How can you say such a thing? Or better yet, where did you hear such a thing that you can say it at all?"

She shrugged. "Retainers talk. So do servants. They go to the market; they gossip with merchants. Honestly, it isn't as if it were a secret.

Everyone in Castile talks of nothing else. They say the queen got herself with child to avoid having the same thing happen to her that happened to Enrique's first wife. Or have you forgotten he had his first marriage to Blanca of Navarre annulled because after fifteen years, she failed to give him a child? She claimed they never consummated their vows, but he said a bewitchment prevented him from acting the man with her. Regardless, she was sent away and a pretty new queen from Portugal was found to take her place—a pretty new queen who happens to be your mother's niece and knows that her aunt's two children could one day do to her what Enrique did to your mother."

I glared at her. "That's absurd. I never heed idle gossip and you should follow my example. Honestly, Beatriz, what has come over you?" I turned my face away, toward the approaching walls of Ávila.

An impressive wall with eighty-eight fortified towers, built centuries before to defend Ávila from marauding Moors, encircled the entire city in a serpentine embrace. Sitting atop a stony escarpment devoid of trees and punctuated by huge boulders, Ávila overlooked the province that bore its name with implacable reserve, the rugged towers of its alcazar and cathedral seeming to pierce the sapphire-blue sky.

Beatriz visibly reacted to the sight, despite her assertions of having seen it all before; she straightened in her saddle and I saw color flush her cheeks. I hoped the thrill of being in the city would dissuade her from voicing gossip and speculation that could cause us nothing but harm if we were overheard.

We rode under an arched gateway and made our way toward the northeastern edge of the city and the convent, through hundreds of people going about their business, merchants haggling and carts clattering over cobblestone. But I barely paid attention, pondering what Beatriz had said. It seemed I couldn't escape the shadow I'd hoped to leave behind in Arévalo.

The abbess greeted us in the convent courtyard, having been alerted in advance to our visit. While Don Bobadilla and the retainers saw to the horses, we were led into the common hall, where a meal had been prepared. Beatriz ate as if she were famished, even though we were in fact served lentil soup with bits of pork; afterward, she went out with Doña Elvira to persuade her father to take them into town. I stayed behind, joining my mother in the chapel for a time. Then, while she retired to discourse with the abbess, a longtime friend of hers who oversaw the convent by royal decree, I went out to wander the gardens.

Lemon and orange trees surrounded me; several nuns worked the soil in silent comradeship, briefly smiling at me as I paced the winding path, inhaling the scent of rosemary, thyme, chamomile, and other fragrant herbs. I lost all sense of time, content to bask in the sun that bathed the well-tended grounds, whose rich earth supplied the nuns with almost everything they needed, so that they never had to set foot outside their blessed walls. It felt as though the past few weeks had been erased. Here in Santa Ana, it seemed impossible that anything bad could occur, that the outside world with its trials and intrigues could ever intrude upon this place of peace.

As I neared a wall abutting vegetable patches laid out in perfect symmetry I looked toward the adjoining church and paused. Nestled in the spire high above was a latticed bundle of twigs—a nest, perched in dizzying, isolated safety.

"The stork is a good mother. She knows how to defend her young," a voice said close to my ear. I gasped, spun around. I found myself looking at a completely unexpected yet disturbingly familiar face. I remembered how he had gathered me in his arms, carried me from my father's death chamber into the night. . . .

"My lord Archbishop," I whispered. I dropped into a curtsey, in deference to his holy station. As I lifted my eyes to him, his smile exposed crooked teeth, at odds with his flushed jowls, thick lips, and beaked nose. His stare was piercing, belying the warmth of his tone.

"Isabella, my daughter, how you've grown."

My mind raced. What was Archbishop Carrillo of Toledo doing in Santa Ana? Had he come here for some other purpose, just when we happened to be visiting? Something told me it was too much of a coincidence. His presence couldn't be accidental.

He chuckled. "You look as if you've seen a ghost. Surely you hadn't forgotten me?"

"No, of course not," I said, flustered. "Forgive me. It's just that I . . . I didn't expect to see you here, of all places."

He cocked his large head. "Why not? An archbishop often travels for the good of his brethren and the sisters here have always been kind to me. Besides, I thought it would be best if I met with your mother away from Arévalo. She and I have just spoken at length; when I said I wished to see you, she told me you had come into the gardens."

"My mother?" I gaped at him. "She . . . she knew you would be here?"

"Of course. We've been corresponding for years. She has kept me informed of both your and your brother's progress. In fact, I'm surprised to find you alone. Where is Bobadilla's daughter?" His scarlet cloak with its white cross swirled around him as he looked about, a hand cocked at his brow. The nuns who'd been in the garden had slipped away; now that I was alone with him, he seemed to dominate the very air with his pungent smell of wool, sweat, horseflesh, and another, expensive musky scent. I had never smelled perfume on a man of the Church before; somehow, it didn't seem appropriate.

"Beatriz went into the city to buy cloth," I told him.

"Ah." His smile widened. "But I was told that you and she are inseparable."

"We were raised together, yes. She is my companion and friend."

"Indeed. One needs friends, especially in a place like Arévalo." He went silent, his penetrating gaze fixed on me, his hands folded in front of his rounded stomach.

Without realizing it, I stared. He did not have the hands of a prince of the Church, white and pampered and soft. Against the golden signet ring of his office, his fingers were sunburnt, scarred, his nails soiled like a peasant's.

Or a warrior's.

His dry chuckle brought my gaze back to his face. "I see you are observant as well as demure. Such qualities will serve you well at court."

At court . . .

The garden receded, like a fragile painted backdrop. "Court?" I heard myself say.

Carrillo pointed to a stone bench. "Please, sit. I appear to have alarmed you; it was not my intention." He lowered his bulk beside me. When he finally spoke his voice was subdued. "It might strike you as strange, given how much time has passed, but His Majesty the king has recently expressed interest in you and your brother. Indeed, he instructed me to ascertain your circumstances for myself. That is why I am here."

Beneath my bodice, my heart leapt. I drew in a shallow breath and tried to compose myself. "As you can see, I am well. So is my brother."

"Yes. Such a pity the Infante Alfonso could not come, but I'm told he's been remiss in his lessons and was left behind to study."

"He's not so remiss," I said quickly. "He just gets distracted sometimes. He likes to be outside, riding and hunting and caring for the animals, while I . . . I like to study more. I like to ride too, of course, but I spend more time with books than he does."

I could hear myself babbling, as if my torrent of words might forestall the inevitable. The archbishop did not react, though his gaze was attentive. Something in his steady regard disturbed me, though I did not know why. Outwardly he hadn't changed at all from my childhood memory of him—prepossessing, larger than life, but also benevolent and trustworthy; a man who had protected my mother in her time of need.

Still, I wanted him gone. I didn't want to hear what he had to say.

I did not want my life to change.

"I am proud you've both fared so well," he said, "given the circumstances. Nevertheless, our king believes your current situation should be improved. In specific, he has asked that you come to court to visit with him."

My mouth went bone-dry. I managed to say in a low voice, "I am honored, of course. But I must ask you to tell His Majesty that we cannot, for our mother's sake. We are her children and she needs us."

He sat quiet for a moment. Then he said, "I'm afraid that will not do. I did not wish to mention it, but I am aware of your mother's . . . indisposition. His Majesty is not, naturally, but should he discover it, he might consider her state too delicate to be further taxed by the care of a son and daughter entering their adolescence."

I could feel the bones in my hands as I clasped them tighter, to stop them from trembling. "We . . . we are not a burden to her, my lord."

"No one said you are. But you are part of the royal family and have lived far from court since your half brother the king took the throne.

He wishes to remedy it." He gently touched my clenched hands. "My child, I can see you are troubled. Will you not unburden yourself to me? I am a man of God. Anything you say will be held in strictest confidence."

I did not like the feel of his heavy hand on mine. Unable to stop myself, I said angrily, "For years we've lived without word or sign from my brother the king, yet now he suddenly wants us at court? Forgive me, but I cannot help but wonder at his sincerity."

"I understand. But you must put such misgivings to rest. The king has no ill intentions toward you; he merely wishes that you and Alfonso be with him at this important time in his life. You do want to see your little niece, don't you? And the queen is eager to welcome you. You'll have tutors, new rooms, and gowns. Alfonso will have a household and servants of his own. It is time for you both to take your places in the world."

He was not saying anything I hadn't considered myself since the king's letter. It seemed I had always known this day might come. Despite the tragedy that had brought us to Arévalo, far from the world we'd once inhabited, children of kings were not destined to dwell in drafty castles in the middle of nowhere.

"What about our mother?" I asked. "What will happen to her?"

"His Majesty will not deprive you of your mother forever. Once you're settled at court, he'll send for her as well. But first the Infante Alfonso and you must come to Segovia to celebrate the Princess Joanna's birth. The king wants you both present for her christening."

I looked at him. "When must we go?"

"In three days. Your mother knows; she understands. Doña Clara and her other women and servants will care for her. Your friend Beatriz can accompany you, of course, and you may write as often as you like from court." He paused; for a fleeting moment I thought I saw reluctance on his face as he stood. "I regret having troubled you but I promise I will see to your comfort at court. I want you to rely on me, for I am your friend. I've championed your mother these many years so she could keep you with her in Arévalo, but even I have my limits. In the end, I am but a royal servant and must do as the king commands."

"I understand." I stood, kissed his extended ring.

He set his hand on my head. "My dearest infanta," he murmured, and then he turned and strode off, his cloak billowing about him.

A favor, in exchange for a favor . . .

As I remembered those cryptic words uttered years earlier, I gripped the edge of the bench. I did not see Beatriz enter the open arcade by the cloisters bordering the garden, did not notice her at all until I turned and caught her sinking into a reverence as Carrillo swept past. As soon as he was gone, she gathered her skirts and ran to me. The moment she reached me, I squared my shoulders, though I felt so disoriented I thought my legs would not hold up under me.

"*Dios mío!*" she exclaimed, breathless. "That was Archbishop Carrillo, wasn't it? What did he want? What did he say to you?" She went still, taking in my expression. "He's come for you and Alfonso, hasn't he? He's taking you to court."

I stared past her to where the archbishop had disappeared into the convent. I slowly assented. Beatriz started to reach for my hands; I pulled away. "No," I murmured. "I . . . I want to be alone. Go, please. See to my mother. I'll be there shortly."

I turned pointedly away, leaving her with a wounded look on her face. It was the first time I had issued an order and I knew it hurt her. But I had to do it. I needed her gone.

I did not want anyone to see me cry.

CHAPTER FOUR

We stayed the night in Santa Ana, in the accommodations above the cloisters reserved for exalted guests; my mother had her own small chamber while Beatriz and I rested in an adjoining one. I did not say anything about my encounter with the archbishop and neither my mother nor Beatriz asked, though my friend's searching gaze followed me all evening.

The next day we returned to Arévalo in silence, my mother riding in front, talking to Don Bobadilla, her head held high. Not once did she look in my direction. The moment we reached the castle, she went to her apartments with Doña Elvira hastening behind, laden with the bolts of cloth she and Beatriz had bought in Ávila.

As Beatriz and I entered the hall, Alfonso came bounding down the staircase, his bow and a quiver of arrows slung on his shoulder. "At last," he declared, his hair tousled and fingers stained with ink. "I've been bored stiff waiting for you. Come, let's go out and shoot at the butts before supper. All I've done these past days is read. My eyes hurt. I need to stretch my muscles."

I tried to smile. "Alfonso, wait a moment. I've something important to tell you." Beatriz began to move away. I set a hand on her arm. "Stay. This concerns you, too." I led them to the table. Alfonso dropped his bow, sat on one of the hard wood stools. He frowned. "Well? What is it? Did something happen in Ávila?"

"Yes." I paused, swallowing the knot in my throat. Then I told him everything, watching his face as my words sank in. Beside me, Beatriz went still. When I was finished, Alfonso remained silent for a few moments before he said, "I don't see that there's anything to worry about. We'll do our duty, attend the christening, and then they'll send us back."

"I don't think you understand," I said, looking quickly at Beatriz. "Carrillo told me he doesn't know how long we'll be gone. It could be . . . we may not return here at all."

"Of course we will." Alfonso raked a hand through his hair. "This is our home. Enrique never cared for us before; I hardly think he'll change now." He stood. "So, are we going to shoot at the butts?"

I opened my mouth to protest when I felt Beatriz kick my foot. She shook her head. I said to Alfonso, "You go. We're tired. We'll go see if Mama needs anything."

"Fine, suit yourself." He picked up his bow and walked out; I let out a ragged sigh, turning to Beatriz. "He doesn't realize what this means. How can I keep him safe if he will not heed me?"

"He's still a boy," she said. "What do you expect him to say? Let him think it's for the best. Let him think he's going away for a visit and then he's coming back. You cannot know what the future holds. Maybe he's right; maybe it will only be for a short while. It is possible, isn't it? After all, Enrique never wanted either of you at court before."

"Yes, I suppose it's possible," I said softly. "I'm sorry about how I behaved in Santa Ana. I didn't mean to be rude to you. You are my only friend; I had no right to order you away like that."

She embraced me. "You don't need to apologize. You are my infanta. I'd go to the ends of the world to serve you."

"It feels as if that is where we're going," I said and I drew back. "I must see my mother."

"Go, then. I'll start packing." As I moved to the stairs, Beatriz added, "You are stronger than you think. Remember that, Isabella."

I did not feel strong as I climbed the stairs to my mother's rooms. Her door was ajar; I heard her voice within, chattering with Doña Elvira. I braced myself for the worst, a scene that would wrench the very stones of Arévalo apart, yet when she saw me in the doorway, she turned to the scattered fabrics on her bed to exclaim, "Look, Isabella. This green brocade will be perfect for your new court gown. It'll show off your pretty white skin."

I looked at Elvira; she shuffled sadly from the room. My mother busied herself with the cloth, pulling the rolls apart to extract a length of black damask. "And this one," she said, holding it up to herself as she pivoted to the copper looking glass. "This is for me. Widows should wear black but no one says we need look like crows, eh?"

I didn't respond. She dropped the cloth on the bed. "Why so serious? Do you not like the green? Very well, here's a lovely blue-gray. This might do nicely for—"

"Mama," I said. "Stop."

She went still, her hands buried in the pile. She did not look at me. "Don't say it," she whispered. "Not a word. I cannot bear it, not now."

I stepped to her. "You knew he would be there. Why did you not warn me?"

She lifted her eyes. "What was I supposed to do? What *could* I do? I knew it the moment that letter arrived, and I told you that day they would come. This is the price I must pay: it is my debt. But at least I will pay it on my terms. Carrillo has seen to that."

"Your terms?" I regarded her warily. "Mama, what does that mean?"

"What do you think? That worm Enrique will not take my son's place in the succession away. He will not set a bastard above Alfonso. Come what may, my son, who bears royal blood, must be king."

"But Enrique now has a daughter; she will be declared his heir. You know that Castile does not honor Salic Law; here, a princess can inherit the throne and rule in her own right. Princess Joanna will—"

My mother swerved around the bed, swift as a cat. "How can we know she is his, eh? How can anyone know? Enrique was never known for his potency in bed; all these years of marriage without a single child—it's a miraculous conception, the grandees mutter; the queen must have been visited by an angel!" She burst into derisive laughter. "No one at court believes it; no one is taken in by this farce. They all know Enrique is weak, ruled by catamites—a voluptuary who keeps infidel guards about him and whose crusade to conquer Granada was a disaster; a fool who'd rather recite poetry and dress his boys in turbans than see to the kingdom; a cuckold who looks the other way while his whore of a wife beds whichever lackey catches her fancy."

I took a step back, horrified by her words, by the malignant gloating on her face

"Outside these walls, Castile lies in misery," she went on. "Our treasury is bankrupt, the grandees wield more power than the crown, and the people sow dust and starve. Enrique thinks to buy goodwill with this child but in the end all he'll reap is discord. The grandees will not be ridiculed by him. They'll rip him apart like wolves; and when they're done, *we* will claim everything he deprived us of. He has ignored us, left us here to rot, but on the day Alfonso wears his crown, then will Enrique of Trastámara learn that he disdained us at his own peril."

I heard Carrillo's voice in my head: *The stork is a good mother; she knows how to defend her young.* I wanted to cover my ears. Her eyes seemed to burn a hole in me, smoldering with pent-up rage, with years of poisonous resentment and humiliation. I couldn't avoid the truth any longer. Because of her thwarted pride, my mother had connived to execute Constable de Luna for treason, plunging my father into a lethal grief. Her ambition had cost her everything—husband, rank, our very safety—but now she believed she had found a way to win it all back, to conspire with Archbishop Carrillo and the discontented grandees against the legitimacy of the new princess and wreak havoc upon my half brother. She did not see how wrong it was to cast such terrible aspersions, to believe the worst of the king and the queen. In her zeal to protect Alfonso's rights, she would scheme, insult, fight; even, God help her, kill.

"We must do this," she said. "*You* must do it, for me."

I made myself nod, even as to my horror I felt helpless tears prick my eyes. I refused to let them spill. I blinked them back, hardening my jaw, and as she took in my stance, I saw my mother pause, her brow furrowing, as if she only now realized how far she had gone.

"You . . . you should be ashamed of yourself," I heard myself whisper.

She flinched. Then she lifted her chin and said flatly, "I will make you a dress in the green velvet, with blue-gray trim. Alfonso shall have a new doublet in blue satin." She turned deliberately back to the fabrics, as if I had ceased to exist.

I fled the room, not stopping until I reached my chamber, banging open the door.

Beatriz turned about, startled, from where she stood packing our clothes into a brass-studded leather chest. "What is it?" she said as I stood gripping the door frame. "What happened?"

"She is mad," I said. "She thinks she can use Alfonso against the king, but she will not get away with it. I will not let her. I will protect my brother to my last breath."

RETAINERS IN LIVERY loaded our luggage into carts in the courtyard. Our castle dogs barked and loped after Alfonso, sensing, as animals do, that an inalterable change was near. Alfonso had always seen to the dogs' upkeep: He took them with him when he went out hunting or riding, fed them, and ensured that their shelter was tended. I watched him pause to pet his favorite, a large shaggy hound named Alarcón. From my position by the castle doors, I suddenly noticed how pitifully small a staff we had, compared with the impressive retinue mingling before me, sent by Enrique to escort us to Segovia.

Archbishop Carrillo had not come. He had dispatched in his stead his nephews: the marquis of Villena and Villena's brother, Pedro de Girón. While Villena was a premier noble and favorite of the king's, Girón was master of Calatrava, one of Castile's four monastic warrior orders, founded centuries ago to fight the Moors. Both had considerable power and wealth, yet there couldn't have been greater contrast between the two; indeed, the only thing that seemed to link them as brothers was their arrogance.

Slight of build, Villena had dark hair cut straight across his brow; he was handsome in a slightly sinister way, with an elongated nose and strange eyes of a yellow-green hue, all the more startling because of their coldness. He'd ridden into our courtyard with a sneer, his distaste evident as he surveyed the roaming chickens and dogs, the pigs and sheep in their pens, the bales of hay stacked by the walls and the compost heap where we threw our discards to ferment for later use in the orchards.

Riding alongside him on a black destrier that dwarfed any horse I'd ever seen, followed by men uniformed in scarlet and gold, was Girón—a giant with a red-veined face and ferociously thick beard, his beady eyes set back in a fleshy countenance, their color indistinguishable, and a mouth as foul as the compost heap. Leaping from his horse—with some agility, considering his size—he let out a loud curse, "*Miserables hijos de puta*, get moving!" and proceeded to order the retainers about with savage chops of his ham-sized hands. Standing at our side, Doña Clara stiffened.

As Villena came before us, his entire being transformed. He bowed with an exaggerated flourish over my mother's hand, declaiming that time itself dared not touch her beauty. My mother responded with a smile and a flutter of her eyes; to me, he sounded ridiculous, his gallantry uttered in an unpleasant, nasal-tinged voice. I smelled such strong ambergris wafting off his velvet-encased person I almost started to choke. Polished and urbane, his every movement a study in elegance, it was as if he had practiced for hours before a mirror, perfecting the art of falsehood. He did not pay me any mind; he barely acknowledged my presence, giving me the shallowest of bows before he turned, as if enraptured, to my brother. He regarded Alfonso with such intensity that my brother squirmed in his stiff new doublet.

Villena pivoted back to my mother to lilt, "The infante's beauty does you even more justice, my lady. No one could ever mistake him for anything but a prince of impeccable royal blood."

I resisted a roll of my eyes as Alfonso shot me a puzzled look. My mother's smile widened. *"Gracias, Excelencia,"* she said. "Would you and your brother like some wine? I've opened a special vintage just for you."

Girón had stomped up to us by then, overpowering us with the stench of sweat, leering at Beatriz before his porcine eyes fell upon me. He grinned, exposing blackened teeth. I held my breath as his paw enclosed my hand, raising it to his lips.

"Infanta," he growled. So firmly did he grip my hand, I couldn't free myself. I began to fear he'd crush my fingers like chicken bones when Doña Clara stepped deliberately between us with the decanter and goblets—her canny offer quickly distracted Girón, who released me with a grunt in favor of the wine.

Later, after Girón had drained our decanter and Villena had minced through our hall with a look that conveyed barely suppressed amusement at our, as he put it, "quaint" furnishings, they returned to the keep to oversee their staff.

It was then that my mother pulled me aside. "Villena started out as

a common page but he has risen to become one of Castile's most influential lords. He has Enrique's ear, though it seems he's been supplanted
as the favorite, and as master of Calatrava his brother Girón commands
more retainers than the crown itself. These are men to cultivate, Isabella. Grandees like these will see to our interests and fight against your
brother's disinheritance."

I stared at her. Alfonso and I were about to leave our home. How
could she expect me to absorb lessons in intrigue at this final hour? I'd
had my fill of advice from her and from Doña Clara. My head was already reeling from weeks of warnings about the corruption at court, the
licentious nature of my half brother's favorites and his queen's loose
morals; of his courtiers' intrigues and the dangerous ambition of the
nobles. The names of Castile's grandees, their familial connections and
affiliations, had been drummed into my head like a catechism, until
one evening after leaving my mother's chamber I had angrily blurted to
Beatriz that I'd never stoop to listening at keyholes or hiding behind the
arras. Beatriz nodded, replying matter-of-factly, "Of course not. Who
ever heard of an infanta of Castile acting the common spy? Leave that
to me."

Glancing at her now as she handed our valises to a retainer, I had no
doubt she was up to the task. She'd been in a whirlwind of anticipation
ever since she'd learned of our departure, going about her chores with a
skip in her step, as though we were preparing for a festival. She had
practiced her deportment (she was terrible at curtsies) several times a
day and had finally declared, much to Doña Clara's outrage, that she'd
rather learn to use a sword. The only regret she'd expressed thus far was
leaving her father; Don Bobadilla would remain behind with my
mother. I admired her pluck even as I thought she might be in for an
unpleasant surprise. It was one thing to long for adventure, quite another to find oneself plunged into it.

We stood together on the threshold of the castle waiting for Alfonso
to return from chaining the dogs so they would not follow us. He was
being stoic, but I could tell he wasn't as confident as he feigned, though
I'd taken Beatriz's advice and spared him any more mention of my private fears. Meeting Villena had been Alfonso's first experience with a

courtier; I suspected it had unsettled him. It seemed he was starting to realize the reality of what our leaving might entail.

Nevertheless, being Alfonso, he put on a brave face. "The marquis says we should leave soon if we want to reach Segovia before nightfall."

I nodded, turning to my mother, who waited on a chair, her wrap clutched about her, a ringed hand at her throat. As she stood, the rising wind tugged at her veil, revealing tendrils of silver-white at her temples. Alfonso got up on tiptoes to kiss her cheek. Her expression softened; tears moistened her eyes as she gathered him close. I heard her say, "You are an infante of Trastámara. Never forget that," and then he stepped aside for me.

I kissed her cheeks. "*Adiós,* Mama. May God keep you; I'll write as soon as I can."

She gave a terse nod. "And you, *hija mía.* Be well. Go with God."

I turned to my *aya*. I'd never known a day when Doña Clara hadn't been there to remonstrate and guide me, to watch over me and keep me from harm. But I did not expect any outward display from her, nor would she condone it from me. However, I felt her sturdy body tremble as we embraced and heard the catch in her voice when she said, "Remember everything I've taught you. Remember, you must never give in to passion. I've kept you safe for as long as I could. Now, you must prove to the world who you are."

As she released me, the enormity of our departure overcame me. I wanted to fall on my knees, plead with my mother to let me stay. But her expression was remorseless and so I went to Alfonso, itching to take his hand and never let it go.

Don Chacón, who, much to my relief, was accompanying us to court, led us to our waiting horses. After he helped me mount Canela and took his place in the entourage, Girón grunted from his destrier: "That's a pretty toy horse. But it's a long ride to Segovia and we've no time for tender hooves. Wouldn't you rather ride up here with me? There's plenty of room on my saddle."

"Canela is sturdier than he looks," I retorted and took up the reins. "He's a gift from the king, as well."

A shadow darkened Girón's face. He reeled away from me and

shouted at the retainers to move. As we lumbered out of the gates, Alfonso rode to my side. I resisted the urge to glance back, fixing my gaze ahead, when all of a sudden Alfonso's dog Alarcón broke free from its tether and bounded forward, letting out a determined bark.

Villena raised his whip. Alfonso cried, "No, don't harm him!" and the marquis glowered, spurring his horse to canter forth, leaving Alfonso to order, "No, Alarcón. Go back!" He flung out his arm toward the castle. "Go back home!"

The dog whimpered, sitting on its haunches. Alfonso looked at me; this time, he couldn't hide the bewilderment in his eyes. "He doesn't understand. He thinks we're leaving forever. We're not going away forever, are we, Isabella? We are coming back, right?"

I shook my head. The time of sparing him was past. "I don't know."

Though neither of us looked back again, we both knew Alarcón remained seated at the castle gates, watching forlornly as we disappeared onto the desolate plain.

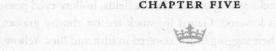

CHAPTER FIVE

We had not traveled further than Ávila before, and as we left the high *meseta* behind, Alfonso's melancholy began to lift, engaged by the change in scenery and his natural curiosity for anything new. The ochre expanse that we had grown up with slowly gave way to a lush landscape dominated by clusters of pine, majestic gorges, and stream-drenched valleys and meadows, where packs of deer bolted in a lightning dash of russet, causing my brother to strain in his saddle.

"Did you see that stag? It was huge! There must be excellent hunting here."

"The best," drawled Villena. "Our king wishes to personally introduce Your Highness to the diversity of our hunting. Boar, hind, bear: he chases them all. His Majesty is a master of the hunt." As he spoke, he glanced at his brother, who was eating something; Girón groused, "Yes, he likes to hunt all right. He's an expert with his quiver."

Villena's chuckle carried a nasty undertone; I sensed something unspoken pass between him and his brother, some deceit, but I kept my smile on my lips as Alfonso exclaimed, "Bear! I've never hunted bear before!"

Around us, the landscape unfurled like verdant tapestry, studded with fortresses of dun- and russet-colored stone. I knew many of these castles were owned by the Castilian grandees, first erected as bulwarks during the Reconquista, the centuries-long war against the Moors. Now, with the infidels pushed back to their mountainous realm of Granada, these castles remained as potent symbols of the immense power held by the nobility, whose wealth and number of vassals eclipsed those of the king.

But as we passed through hamlets huddled under the castles' shadows, where corpses of bandits hung from gibbets, their hands and feet

severed, I began to feel a strong unease. In the fields, hollow-eyed peasants toiled with eyes lowered. Gaunt livestock fed on thorny grasses,
ribs poking against their sagging hides, covered in filth and flies. Yellow-
skinned children worked beside parents; even old people in tattered
clothes sat on doorsteps carding wool, or trudged with loads of kin-
dling. Palpable despair hung over them, as if every day was an eternity
in a life that held no joy, no comfort, no peace.

At first I thought the plague had affected this part of Castile. Rumors of the dreaded sickness had always prompted us to bolt Arévalo's
gates and remain inside until the danger passed, so I did not know what
it actually looked like. When I ventured to ask why these people looked
so miserable, Villena said, "They're starving, like all their kind. Laziness
is the disease of the *campesino*. But these are not times of plenty; taxes
must be paid. Those who do not—they know the price they'll pay."

He motioned to a nearby gibbet, where a decaying body festered.
"We do not tolerate sedition in Castile."

Girón guffawed. I stared in disbelief. "But we've just ridden through
acres of untended land. Why can't the poor plant there and earn their
keep?"

"Your Highness has much to learn," said Villena coldly. "That untended land, as you deem it, belongs to the grandees. It is for their
pleasure, not for some peasant to tear up with his hoe and oxen and
parcel of snotty brats."

"All that land? It all belongs to the nobles?"

Before Villena could reply, Girón spat, "It should be more. We
wouldn't have to use our own retainers to guard these rat-hole towns had
we not been forced to compromise, because the king said we received
their rents." He hit his chest with his fist. "I said no, let them fend for
themselves; but I was outnumbered by those cowards on the Council."

I felt heat rush into my cheeks and turned from his contemptuous
face. Beatriz arched her brow at me, as if to say these were matters we
could not possibly understand. But I understood. I remembered what
my mother had said of the grandees' unquenchable greed and of my
half brother's willingness to do anything to keep them at bay. She had
not exaggerated; evidently, the kingdom had been given over to them.

Never had Arévalo seemed as distant as it did in that instant. I almost cried out in relief when I finally caught sight of the dusky eastern ridges of the Sierra de Guadarrama in the distance, framing Segovia's sunset-lit spires. The city lay draped in hill-cuddled splendor behind fortified walls, carved by the Eresma and Clamores rivers, and guarded by the proud alcazar on its promontory. As we approached one of the five city gates, I saw scaffolding covering the thrust of the alcazar's oblong keep, the Torre de Homenaje.

Villena said, "My lord the archbishop has prepared lodgings for you in the *casa real* near the alcazar." He sighed with dramatic weariness. "With the king's habitual restoration projects and the grandees' retinues, I regret there is no extra room in the castle itself."

I hid my relief, even as I noticed Beatriz's pursed lips, betraying disappointment that we'd not lodge in the very center of the court. I was tired from the journey and my troubled thoughts. Unlike her, I preferred to collect my thoughts in a place apart, before we were thrust into court life.

We entered the clamor of a city twice as large as Ávila and three times as populated. The streets were narrow, cobblestoned or mud-packed; the ringing of our horses' shoes echoed against the close-set buildings as Beatriz and I rode behind Alfonso. Villena, Girón, Chacón, and the retainers surrounded us. The smells of horse droppings, smoke, cooking food, foul tanneries, and forgers mingled in the dense air; it took all my concentration to keep Canela from prancing nervously at the din of shouting passersby. The retainers opened a path before us, using halberds to disperse anyone who impeded our way. Some of the townsfolk stopped to stare as we rode past, whispering to each other behind their hands.

What were they saying, I wondered; what did they see? An adolescent girl whose hair was coming loose under her veil and a young boy, the grit of the country under his nails—that's what they must see: two innocents, brought into a world where they did not belong.

I glanced at Villena. He rode with ease, his gold-edged cloak wrapped about him, his chin lifted as if to avoid the stench of the street. As though he sensed my scrutiny he turned his pale yellow stare to me. We rode under a stone-lace Mudéjar gateway into the royal palace, where Carrillo waited in the courtyard, a frown worrying his brow.

"You're late," he said as we dismounted. "His Majesty has asked that the infantes attend him tonight." He gave me a hasty smile. "My dear, you must be quick. We're expected in the alcazar within the hour."

"I hope we have time to bathe," I whispered to Beatriz. She started to whisper back when a thin man of medium stature emerged from the palace. He wore a simple black velvet doublet of mid-length and impeccable cut, slightly flared at the waist to show off his elegant legs in embroidered hose. Bowing before us, he spoke in a courtier's modulated voice. "I am Andrés de Cabrera, governor of the alcazar of Segovia. I have the honor of escorting Your Highness to her apartments."

He immediately made me feel at ease. With his solemn features, receding hairline, and deep-set brown eyes, he reminded me of Pedro de Bobadilla, Beatriz's father, though Andrés de Cabrera was many years younger. Beatriz also reacted to his presence, her face brightening as she said, "We are most grateful for your assistance, Don Cabrera."

"It is my pleasure. Please, come this way." It was only then that I realized Alfonso wasn't with us. I glanced past the servants collecting our belongings to see Carrillo taking my brother in the opposite direction. Carrying Alfonso's personal coffer, Don Chacón trudged obligingly behind.

Fear coiled in me. "Where is my brother going?" I asked. Though I tried to sound calm, I heard the ragged edge in my voice.

Cabrera paused. "His Highness has his own rooms, of course." He offered me a gentle smile. "Do not worry, Your Highness. You'll see him at the banquet."

"Oh." I forced out a chuckle. "Of course, how silly of me."

It made sense; Alfonso must live as befitted his rank now that we were at court. He'd no longer be just a few doors away; we could not meet up at a moment's notice. But the suddenness of our separation clung to me as we moved away from the palace and into the labyrinthine *casa real* next door, Beatriz close at my side. We passed under fluted arcades that opened onto citrine patios, our heels clicking on the polished floors of jasper and emerald-tiled *salas* dripping in painted alabaster lace. After the noise of the city, the silence was luxurious, enhanced by the diamond-clear trickle of water in unseen fountains and the soft rustle of our skirts.

I was doubting that I'd ever be able to find my way around this place on my own when we entered a spacious room with fluted windows—framed by carved wooden jalousies—that opened onto an expanse of garden. From somewhere nearby I heard the muted roar of a beast and gave a start. "What is that?"

Cabrera smiled again. "His Majesty's leopards; they must be hungry. It's almost time for their feeding."

"Leopards?" echoed Beatriz, in astonishment. "The king keeps wild animals here?"

"Only two," said Cabrera. "And I assure you they're well caged and fed. In his forest lodge of El Balacín in the foothills, he has many more lions and bears, as well as big strange birds from Africa, and an assortment of other creatures. His Majesty is a great lover of animals; here, he usually oversees the leopards himself, but tonight that duty falls on me."

"And does he use these animals to hunt?" I asked, wondering how close these exotic leopards were to my rooms. "I've heard he is quite fond of hunting."

Cabrera frowned. "On the contrary, His Majesty rarely hunts and never with his own animals. He abhors bloodshed; he's even forbidden the corrida in Segovia."

"No bullfights?" Beatriz glanced at me; she had heard Villena tell Alfonso that Enrique wanted to show him the pleasures of the hunt. Apparently, the marquis had misled us. It made me wonder what other untruths he and his uncouth brother had told us, though I was secretly pleased to hear that Enrique disliked bullfights. I did, too, intensely; I had never understood how anyone could find delight in the blood and pandemonium of the arena. Though I'd been raised in a rural area where animals were regularly slaughtered for sustenance, it seemed unnatural to me to turn a creature's suffering into a crowd-pleasing spectacle.

"Are Alfonso's rooms far from us?" I asked, unclasping my cloak.

"Not too far," answered Cabrera. "His Highness will reside in the alcazar, which is rather crowded at the moment. My lord the archbishop thought it best if you resided somewhere more private. However, if you do not care for these rooms, I could try to secure apartments closer to the infante's. Alas, they will be smaller. All the large rooms are currently occupied by the grandees who have come to see the new princess."

"No," I said, "do not trouble yourself. These rooms suit me fine."

He stepped aside as two men brought in our clothes chests and set them on the tiled floor. "You'll find a basin of fresh water and cloths on the stand by the window, my lady. I regret that a hot bath is impossible, given the hour, but tomorrow I'll have one drawn for you."

"That would be lovely." I inclined my head. "Thank you. You are most kind."

"No need to thank me, my infanta. It is my honor to serve you. Please, do not hesitate to call upon me should you require anything. I am at your disposal." He bowed. "You, too, my lady de Bobadilla; I am, of course, also at your service."

As he left, I was amused to see Beatriz flush. "Such a nice man," she said, "but I didn't tell him my name, did I? How did he know?"

I didn't answer her. I was not thinking of Cabrera, whom I sensed was someone we could trust, but of Villena. "Beatriz, why do you think the marquis misled us? First he said the king was a master of the hunt, which isn't true according to Don Cabrera, and then he said there were no rooms for us in the alcazar. Such petty lies; I hardly see the point."

"Petty on the surface, perhaps." She unlaced my outer gown, removing it to leave me in my hose and shift. "But he won Alfonso's attention with the first lie and effectively separated him from us with the next. And Cabrera also said that *Carrillo* had decided to lodge you here, for privacy's sake. Might it not be less for privacy and more because he too wants to keep you and Alfonso at a distance?"

I did not relish this astute assessment. As I went to wash the grit from my face and throat with the lavender water in the basin, leaving Beatriz to rummage through the chest for my gown, I pondered what else I knew. If Carrillo and Villena sought to keep Alfonso and me apart, when they knew my brother and I had grown up together, it was either out of cruelty or for more sinister motivations. We'd just arrived; did they seek to draft Alfonso into their schemes already? And were they working together?

I took up a towel, about to tell Beatriz my thoughts when a clamor came from outside. Before I could move, the door flew open and a group of women swarmed in.

I had not undressed in front of anyone save Beatriz since my tenth year. Not even Doña Clara had dared intrude on me without knocking, and I stood dumbstruck as the women flittered into the chamber like fantastical birds, their words unintelligible to me in my stunned state. My new court gown, made from the green velvet bought in Ávila, was snatched from Beatriz and passed around. One of the women made a disapproving cluck. Another laughed. As their mirth penetrated my ears, Beatriz grabbed the gown from them.

"It *is* new," I heard her declare, "if you please, and of course it has matching sleeves. I was just looking for them when you so rudely barged in."

She glared. I focused on the women. My breath caught in my throat.

They all were young, dressed in gowns unlike any I'd ever seen, with low-cut bodices that almost exposed their bosoms and frothing skirts of glittering fabric, their cinched waists enhanced by a multitude of dangling silk purses and ornaments. Their hair was curled into elaborate coiffures concocted with flimsy veils, combs, and threaded pearls or coins; their mouths were rouged, their eyes lined in thick kohl. Some had a decidedly dusky cast to their complexions, denoting Moorish blood; the ones Beatriz faced were dark-eyed beauties with milky skin and sharp white hands.

The lady whom Beatriz had taken my dress from—green-eyed and clad in curve-hugging scarlet—shrugged. "*Está bien.* If this is all the Infanta Isabella has, we can make do." She turned to me with an apologetic air. "I'm afraid we've no time to find a suitable gown but we can fetch accessories to make this one more appealing."

My voice issued hoarse. "And who . . . who might you be?"

She paused, as though no one had ever asked her such a question before. "I am Doña Mencia de Mendoza, lady-in-honor to Queen Juana. I am here for whatever you require."

I nodded, gathering my composure as best as I could, considering I was standing barefoot in my stockings and chemise. "I don't require anything at the moment, thank you. There's no need for any fuss."

Mencia de Mendoza widened her eyes. "It's no fuss. The queen sent us specifically to attend you. It is her express desire that you be well cared for."

"The infanta is in my charge," said Beatriz. "I assure you, she's *very* well cared for."

"Your charge?" Mencia laughed. "But you're hardly out of the nursery yourself!"

"I am fifteen," Beatriz said. "Out of the nursery long enough to know my duty, my lady. As Her Highness just informed you, *we* do not require anything."

Mencia's smile faded; her black-lined eyes narrowed.

I said quickly, "My lady de Bobadilla and I are most grateful to Her Grace, but I've no desire for accessories; my tastes are simple. And I'm unused to so many attendants and would prefer that my lady de Bobadilla serve me alone, if you please."

Mencia's expression did not betray further displeasure, though I detected tartness in her voice as she executed a curtsey. "As Your Highness wishes." She glanced pointedly at Beatriz. "You should become accustomed to being part of a larger household; you're under the queen's care and Her Grace likes to surround herself with women of culture."

With these words, she herded the others out, leaving Beatriz and me alone.

"The nerve!" Beatriz fumed, turning to the chest. She found the sleeves and proceeded to dress me as I stood immobile. "Who does that Mencia de Mendoza think she is? Women of culture—did you see the paint on her face? Harlots wear less. Oh, if Doña Clara were here she'd have a fit. Can it be the queen lets women like those attend her?"

I repressed a shudder as she laced up my outer gown and affixed the draping sleeves lined in velvet. "She's not just any woman," I said. "The Mendozas are one of the noblest families in Castile; Mencia is the daughter of a grandee."

Beatriz snorted. "Is that so? Well, I've never reprimanded a grandee's daughter before." She turned me around. Taking a brush from a case, she stroked my waist-length, chestnut-gold hair to a rippling sheen; my hair was one of my secret vanities, though I had tried to subdue it, having been advised by the nuns in Santa Ana that a woman's tresses were Satan's ladder.

"There." Beatriz stepped back. "Let's see what Mencia de Mendoza has to say now. I vow there's not a girl at court with skin as unblemished or hair as golden as yours."

"Vanity is a sin," I reproached with a smile, as she changed into her own sedate black gown, coiling her hair at her nape moments before a rapping at the door preceded Carrillo.

At the sight of him, I straightened my spine. Though I knew he would look after us as promised, for our welfare was bound with his, I had no doubt he'd manipulated my mother into conceding our release, promising something he had no right to offer. He was a powerful man, ruthless; and we were now beholden to him. I must be careful, in both my actions and my words. I must feign acquiescence so I could better watch over my brother. Fortunately, I had the feeling Carrillo didn't expect anything else from me anyway.

He regarded me. "I was informed that you disdained the attentions of the queen's own ladies, though they were sent here to attend you. Is this true?"

"Why, yes." I injected concern in my voice. "Did I make a mistake? I hardly saw the need for ten to accomplish what one can do just as well."

Beatriz shot me a sarcastic look but Carrillo, to my relief, only let out an indulgent laugh. "You certainly weren't raised at court; that much is clear. Doña Mencia complains that your clothes are fit only for the poorhouse but I think you look rather charming, even if the gown's style is a little outdated."

"It was made by my mother. I am proud to wear it."

"Good." He nodded vigorously. "Pride is good, though not too much of it, eh?" He wagged his finger, encircled by its gold ring. "We don't want you starting out on the wrong foot." He winked at Beatriz. "And you apparently excel at protecting our infanta and making enemies, little Bobadilla. Exercise more care with whom you insult, yes? Doña Mencia holds the queen's favor and I don't have the time or inclination to arbitrate feminine quarrels."

"Of course," I said, stopping Beatriz's protest. "It will not happen again, my lord." I set my hand on his arm. "I believe I am ready."

With a smile, I let him lead me out to my first meeting with the king.

CHAPTER SIX

Within the great *sala,* countless beeswax tapers melted above us in hanging iron candelabra, lighting up the gilded stalactites of the ceiling, which shimmered like an iridescent sky. Along the upper edge of the walls, painted statues of Castile's early kings frowned; below their pedestals hung wide tapestries of wool and silk, the vivid hues reflecting like liquid across the polished floor. The air throbbed with conversation, with laughter and firefly flashes of brilliantly clad courtiers, everything scented by myrrh and perfume and incense.

I knew the alcazar's history. During the glacial winters in Arévalo, Beatriz and I had entertained ourselves reading aloud from the *Crónicas,* which related stories of the kings and queens who had lived and died within these walls. Like Castile's other fortresses, the alcazar of Segovia had been built as a Moorish stronghold before it was wrested away during the Reconquista. I'd expected to feel awe inside the historic castle where my ancestors had dwelled. What I did not anticipate was the sudden emotion that overcame me, like the awakening of something dormant in my blood. I had to focus my eyes on the dais at the hall's end, with its empty throne, to keep from gaping as Beatriz was.

Carrillo approached us and told Beatriz to step aside. He took me to the dais. The courtiers drew back, staring at me for what seemed an impossibly long moment before heads lowered in deference. I could almost hear their thoughts—"Here she is, the half sister of the king"—and fought to ignore the sensation that I was being appraised by hungry predators. I caught sight of Mencia in her scarlet gown, standing close to the marquis of Villena. When his smile bared teeth, I looked away to the tables set against the walls in preparation for the evening banquet, each weighted with jewel-rimmed platters sprouting minarets of Andalucían oranges, cherries from Extremadura, sugared almonds, dates, figs, and apricots—a veritable orchard of delights, piled with such abundance it seemed almost sinful, a profligate waste.

Carrillo bowed before the dais, declaring in his booming voice, "The Infanta Isabella!"

I curtsied to the floor, hiding my discomfiture. Why did he address an empty throne?

Then I heard a soft voice inquire, "Can this be my little sister?" and I peeped up to see a large man in black, reclining nearby on a mound of silk tasseled cushions, a plate of delicacies at his side, attended by a veiled figure in a gown. Lined up directly against the wall behind him stood a regiment of Moorish sentries, sheathed scimitars at their hips, their pantaloons and turbans making them look as if they'd just arrived from Granada.

"Majestad," I murmured.

My half brother Enrique rose. The last time I'd seen him I had been a child and had not marked how tall he was. Now he seemed to loom over me—an odd, misshapen man, his head, crowned with a red, Moorish-style turban, seeming too large for his gangly body, his shaggy gold-red mane falling in lank strands from under his turban to his concave shoulders. He wore a black-and-gold embroidered caftan; I glimpsed the curling tips of red leather slippers on his strangely dainty feet.

I stared at him, forgetting myself. I'd heard it said he resembled my father but I barely recalled the dead king who had sired us and searched in vain for any familial resemblance.

"You . . . you are pretty," said Enrique, as if he'd not considered my appearance until this moment. I met his mournful amber-hued eyes, slightly protuberant and heavy-lidded. With his flat nose, rounded cheeks, and fleshy lips he was not comely; only his impressive height lent him distinction. And while tunics in the Moorish style were part of every Castilian's wardrobe, especially useful for keeping cool during the summer months, my mother had only allowed us to don such garb in the privacy of our rooms. I could imagine what she'd say if she had been here, to see the king dressed like an infidel on our first night at court. But Enrique's timorous smile beckoned me closer; as I leaned to kiss his hand, adorned with the signet of Castile, he suddenly pulled me into an awkward embrace. He smelled musky, like an unwashed animal. Sensitive as I was to odors, I did not find his unpleasant, though I supposed it was not how a king ought to smell.

"Welcome, sister," he said. "Welcome to my court."

Around us the courtiers broke into fervent applause. Enrique kept my hand in his as he turned with me to face the hall. "Where is my brother the Infante Alfonso?" he called out, and from within the throng of courtiers my brother emerged, hand-in-hand with a sturdy youth. Alfonso was flushed, a telltale sign he'd been imbibing undiluted wine—something forbidden to him until now. Evidently whatever regrets he'd had at leaving our home behind had been subsumed by the excitement of our new surroundings. I didn't see Don Chacón anywhere, either, though usually he was not far from Alfonso's side.

"Look who's here, Isabella." Alfonso nodded toward his companion. "It's our cousin Fernando from Aragón. We're sharing a room, though all he's done so far is ask about you."

Fernando bowed before me. "Your Highness," he said, a tremor in his voice, "this is a great honor, though I doubt you remember me."

He was wrong; I did remember him, or at least I knew of him by name. He was the last person I'd expected to find here, at my half brother's court, however.

Our families shared Trastámara blood through our ancestors, but enmity and rapacity had led Castile and Aragón to wage war against each other for centuries. The kings of Aragón zealously guarded their smaller, independent realm, constantly at odds with France and suspicious of Castile, though never enough to disdain alliances of marriage, in the hope of one day putting an Aragonese prince on Castile's throne.

A year younger than I, Fernando was, like Alfonso and me, born of a second marriage, in his case between his father, Juan of Aragón, and Juana Enríquez, daughter of the hereditary admirals of Castile. Fernando was also heir to Aragón since his older half brother had died several years before. While I was acquainted with the facts of Fernando's family and his bloodline, I'd not heard anything particularly interesting about him or his kingdom; indeed, I knew almost nothing other than the fact that in my childhood, his ever-scheming father, King Juan, had proposed Fernando as a spouse for me.

As I now gazed upon this prince who was my distant cousin, I thought he had a disconcertingly attractive countenance, with a strong nose and clever mouth, and shining brown eyes fringed in thick lashes that any woman would envy. His left eye was slightly smaller, with a peculiar slant to it that lent his face an impish cast. He was short yet robustly built for his age, and his thick dark hair was straight, cut bluntly at his shoulders. I was especially taken by the olive cast of his complexion, turned bronze by the sun. I imagined he spent most of his time outdoors, like my brother, but while Alfonso shone pale as alabaster, Fernando looked almost swarthy, like a Moor, his person exuding irrepressible vitality. Though they couldn't have been less alike, I did not wonder that my brother and he behaved as if they were old friends, for in spirit they appeared to have much in common.

I started as I realized his gaze was equally intent on me. I said softly, "How can I remember you, cousin, when we've not actually met until now?"

"I've heard so much about you," he replied, "I feel as though we've known each other our entire lives."

Though he was only twelve—a boy, in truth—for some inexplicable reason, Fernando of Aragón left me strangely breathless.

At my side, Enrique said, "Fernando has come to help us celebrate the birth of my daughter. He'll be standing in for his father tomorrow, as King Juan suffers from cataracts and could not make the journey. It is my hope we can look forward to a newfound rapport between our realms. There's been too much strife, though we share the same blood."

"Indeed, Your Majesty," said Fernando, without taking his gaze from me. "Rapport we must have, now that the French spider knocks at our gates."

"Foreign policy from the mouths of babes," exclaimed Carrillo with a guffaw. But Enrique replied somberly, "He speaks the truth. Neither Aragón nor Castile can afford war with Louis of France. Peace, indeed, we must have."

Fernando turned abruptly to me. "Will Your Highness dine at our table?"

I faltered, looking at the king. Enrique smiled. "I don't see why not—" he started to say before his voice cut off, his entire posture stiffening.

Curious, I followed his gaze.

A woman was gliding toward us, her head held high. Courtiers lining the aisle to the dais dropped into obeisance as she passed. She moved with rhythmic grace, a ruby-and-gold belt girdling her slim hips, the hem of her ivory velvet gown encrusted with jeweled tracery. Following behind her were the women who had tried to attend me earlier in the *casa real*.

I didn't have to ask who she was. I too bent my knees into a deep curtsey.

"Enrique!" chided Queen Juana. "I had no idea our guests had arrived. Why did you not send word? I was just seeing our *pequeñita* to sleep." As she spoke, she bestowed a dazzling smile upon Alfonso, who went red as flame, before turning her attention to me.

Never had any woman looked less as if she had just been at an infant's bedside. In fact, it was almost impossible to believe she'd ever given birth. She was slender as a wand, impeccably coiffed, her lustrous dark auburn hair coiled at either side of her face, threaded with seed pearls. She had a flawless complexion highlighted by powder and rouge. Her eyes in particular were stunning, black as onyx and wide-set, her lashes thickened with kohl to enhance their luster. She looked like a perfect piece of painted statuary.

"Rise, my dear," she said. "Let me see you. So grown up," she purred. "Why, you're practically a woman. And here we expected a little girl in braids."

As she kissed my cheek, her cloying scent of attar of roses smothered me. I flinched and started to draw back; her stare cut through me like a blade, cold appraisal in her eyes.

The sound of pages dragging the tables forth for the meal intruded; Enrique said, "We were just discussing our seating arrangements. Isabella wishes to dine with her brother and Fernando. I did not see any reason why she shouldn't—"

"Absolutely not," interrupted Juana. "She must dine with my ladies, as is proper. You did say she'd be under my care, yes?" She extended a long-nailed hand to Enrique; he recoiled. "Stop that," he muttered. She shrugged, taking me by the arm to steer us to the nearest table.

"Wait," Enrique said.

She paused.

"I believe Isabella and the infantes should dine with me tonight."

"But Beltrán de la Cueva is dining with you tonight, remember? You promised——"

"I know what I promised. But I am the king; I am entitled to change my mind. Beltrán de la Cueva is a subject. Let him dine with my other subjects, as is proper."

I felt her fingers dig into my arm. "Enrique, is that wise? You know how quickly Beltrán takes offense and you did promise to show him favor tonight."

"I don't care if he takes offense." Enrique replied stonily, but I had the impression he did not relish confrontation of any sort, much less with his wife. "My family is here for the first time since I took the throne. They'll dine with me tonight. I command it."

She let out a terse laugh. "Why, yes, of course! No need to command, my dear. But there's hardly room on the dais for all of us. Would you have us dine on cushions like Moors?"

Enrique's voice hardened. "I said, Isabella and the infantes. You may eat wherever you like. That way, you can save a place for Beltrán de la Cueva, whose dignity you are apparently so intent on preserving."

She froze. I could not tell if she was horrified or enraged.

"I'll dine with Her Highness," piped Alfonso. "That way, she can be near family, too."

Enrique glanced at Alfonso. "You've been well brought up, my brother. If Her Grace agrees, then by all means, dine with her."

Alfonso looked eagerly at the queen. All he saw was a woman in distress; he was too young, too inexperienced to perceive what was painfully clear to me. She had borne a child after years of barrenness yet Enrique treated her without any respect or affection. Was it true then, what Beatriz had told me on the ride to Ávila? Was there doubt at court about the child's paternity? Did even my own half brother doubt the child was his?

"How can I resist such gallantry?" She smiled with brittle coquetry at Alfonso before she flicked a hand at her women and they proceeded to the nearby table.

As the sentries removed the throne and set up a table on the dais, I glanced at the archbishop. His bushy black brows were knotted in a scowl, his stare fixed on the queen as she ostentatiously sat my brother at her right side, flanked by the ladies. The open contempt in his stance startled me; for a second, his jovial mask had slipped and I glimpsed something hard and much darker beneath it.

"If Your Majesty will excuse me," he said, turning to Enrique, "I have some urgent business to attend to."

My half brother gave an absent nod. Carrillo inclined his head to me and without another word strode away. I couldn't help but think his sudden departure was due to his obvious dislike of the queen; I stared after him, not hearing Beatriz sidle up to me until she whispered, "I've something I must tell you."

"Not now," I said. "Find Don Chacón. I don't know where he is and Alfonso should not be left alone with the queen and her ladies for too long."

I took my seat on the dais beside Enrique, and Fernando took his place at the king's opposite side. I found I was trembling. It must be fatigue and hunger, I decided; by this hour in Arévalo I'd have long since dined, recited my devotions, and retired. But as the first courses of roast boar in artichoke hearts and venison sautéed in a Rioja sauce were set before us, I could barely eat a full bite. All my attention was focused on covert observation of the queen, as she consumed goblet after goblet of wine until bright pink punctuated her face; she was leaning to Alfonso, caressing his cheeks and murmuring in his ear. At the table next to them, the marquis's brother Pedro Girón sat alone, tearing into a haunch of venison with his bare hands. Bloody juice ran down his chin as he gestured brusquely for a refill of his goblet. Villena was nowhere in sight. Had he followed Carrillo out?

"This must all seem very strange to you," said Enrique suddenly, and I started, turning in my chair to face him. "All this excess: I'm told you did not have nearly as much in Arévalo. Indeed, I understand you, your brother, and your mother have led a frugal life."

"Yes, we did. But we managed well enough. Frugality can be a blessing."

"And I notice that you prefer water," he said, glancing at my goblet, which I'd covered with my hand to stop the page with his ubiquitous decanter. "Do you not drink wine?"

"Wine often gives me a headache, even when I dilute it." As I spoke, I saw Fernando lean in, looking past Enrique at me with disquieting intensity.

"I too dislike wine," said Enrique. "I'll only drink it on state occasions. There is much clean water in Segovia; it comes from the sierra, fresh and cold. It used to flow through the aqueduct during Roman times but now the aqueduct is in disrepair. I've always meant to have it fixed." He paused, gnawing his lower lip. Then he said abruptly, "I wish to apologize to you. I did not see to you or your brother's welfare as I should have. It's not that I did not care. Being a king . . . it's not what you'd think. I understand our father so much better now than I ever did when he was alive."

I met his gaze. "What do you mean?" I asked softly.

"Our father once told me, he wished he'd been born common, so he wouldn't have to bear the weight of the world on his shoulders." Enrique gave me a sad smile. "I often feel the same these days."

It was a very strange thing for a king to say. Monarchs ruled by divine right; they were answerable to God. Being born to such a position was a great privilege, not a curse one should wish away. All of a sudden I thought of the last time I'd seen Enrique, the odd smile on his face as he'd watched me kiss our father, his eager incline over the moribund body. Had I only imagined it was eager? What if he'd been anxious, instead? To a child, one can look much like the other and Enrique did not seem like a man who had ever desired to be the center of attention.

"That is why I am glad you're here," he went on. "Family should be with each other and we've had so little time together. You agree, don't you? You are happy to be here?"

Without realizing what I was about to do, I set my hand on his. My fingers looked white and delicate against his hirsute, freckled skin. "I am happy to see you. And Segovia is beautiful. I just need time to adjust. As you say, all this is still quite new to me."

I saw Fernando nod, his approving smile bolstering my confidence. For some reason I cared about his opinion. I had the feeling he expected nothing but the best from me.

"What can I do to make you feel more at home?" Enrique sounded troubled. "It's your mother, isn't it? You did not want to leave her. You miss her."

I hesitated, unsure what to say. I did miss the comfort of my little room in Arévalo; I missed the dogs barking at night, the clatter of servants setting the table in the hall under Doña Clara's baleful eye. But did I miss my mother? I honestly could not say.

"I offered to bring her here as well," Enrique told me, his voice anxious, "but Carrillo advised me against it. He said she'd exert too much influence, as mothers often do, and that Alfonso must learn to stand second in line to the throne now."

I did not betray my alarm at his words. Did my mother know she might have been invited to court? Or had Carrillo misled her because he had his own, hidden reasons for separating us from her side?

I met Enrique's eyes. There was no guile there, only an earnest desire to please; and all of a sudden I wanted to tell him everything. He was my father's firstborn; we were brother and sister, family. We should protect one another, not be used against each other like pawns on the archbishop's chessboard.

But I didn't know what to say. Later, I told myself. I would tell him later, should anything happen. No, *before* anything happened. Surely I would hear of any plots; Alfonso would be their centerpiece, and Carrillo would require my brother's cooperation. Alfonso would tell me; he would not betray Enrique any more than I would.

The servants removed our soiled knives and trenchers, set down silver bowls of rose water for us to clean our fingers and linen serviettes to dry them. From the gallery, musicians struck up viols and lutes; as music floated over the assembly, courtiers abandoned their seats and servants rushed in to dismantle the tables, clearing the floor.

My head ached. I'd had enough for one day. But Beatriz had disappeared and so I turned back to Enrique. I would make conversation until I found an opening to request leave to retire.

Enrique had leaned back in his chair and the beautiful veiled figure who'd been attending him earlier slipped onto the dais to rest hands on his shoulders. The half-veil covered the figure's nose and mouth but revealed beautiful dark eyes, the lids heavy with kohl and powdered with gold. The figure whispered in his ear.

"Yes, my sweet," murmured Enrique, "in a little while. I must seem to care about the diversions here for a bit more, yes? Be patient and rub my back. I ache terribly."

The figure removed its veil. I froze. I sensed rather than saw Fernando rise and come around the table to me. "Your Highness, may I have the honor of this dance?"

I couldn't move.

The painted boy dressed as a Moorish odalisque smiled at me with languid indifference, his hands caressing the king. A groan came from Enrique; he said drowsily, "Go, Isabella. Dance with Fernando. You're young and there is much amusement to be had."

Fernando took my hand, the pressure from his fingers obliging me to stand. I couldn't feel my legs, scarcely registered my surroundings, until I was on the floor, assuming my position for the dance. Courtiers surrounded us; the music swelled. As we commenced the elaborate choreography of the Castilian seguidilla, I kept my gaze on Fernando, feeling as if he were the only thing that could keep me anchored right now.

I didn't know how I managed the intricate footwork—heel-to-toe, turn, dip the head, and heel-to-toe again—but somehow I weaved my way through the paces until I was curtseying with the other ladies and Fernando stood before me, chest out, shorter and by far the youngest of all the men, yet emanating a pride that made him seem years older.

"For someone who was raised away from the court, you dance well," he said, his breath coming fast. "Everyone is watching."

"They . . . they're watching me?"

He nodded. "They are. And none more intently than Beltrán de la Cueva."

I looked around to see a striking man in crimson velvet staring at me, sweat on his brow. Beltrán de la Cueva stood next to the queen, with whom he'd just danced. His mane of thick fair hair rippled to his broad shoulders like sunlit copper; his nose was finely sculpted, his lips full, and his high cheekbones complemented by a red-gold beard, a rarity in a court of mostly clean-shaven men. He was almost too beautiful, this royal favorite, whose right to dine on the dais I'd unwittingly usurped. He held the queen's hand, though the dancing was over; his smile was indolent, seductive; his piercing emerald-green gaze so intimate I felt as if I dared not look away.

Queen Juana saw me; with a glare she cupped Beltrán's chin with her other hand and turned his face to her. She murmured; he laughed aloud—a brash laugh, full of confidence.

"They say she's besotted with him," Fernando murmured, bringing my gaze back to him. "They say he gives her what the king cannot. That is why they call her child la Beltraneja, the daughter of Beltrán."

I'd heard similar calumny from my mother and Beatriz, had seen enough by now to suspect that anything was possible. But I raised my chin anyway, for I'd not condone such open defamation of my half brother's consort.

"You forget of whom you speak. Whatever they may say, she is still our queen."

"And you," he replied, "mustn't let your emotion show so clearly. Your face gives you away. At court you must learn to dissemble if you are going to survive."

His blunt words cut through me. I took a step back. "I thank you for your advice and for the dance. But I fear it is late. I must retire."

He went pale. "I did not mean to offend—"

"You did not," I interrupted. "Good night, cousin." I extended my hand. He bowed over it, his lips warm as they grazed my skin. He lifted his eyes to me; I saw a mute appeal there but before he could say anything else, I turned to the dais. It was empty, the table with its mess of napkins being dismantled by pages. As I searched the nearby environs, Beatriz shoved her way through the crowd to me, my cloak in her hand. I glanced back at Fernando; he still regarded me with a stricken look.

"Did you find Don Chacón?" I asked as Beatriz clasped the cloak about me.

"No, but I asked Andrés de Cabrera and he did. The marquis of Villena had ordered Chacón to stay put and unpack. But he's coming now to fetch Alfonso."

"If he can find him," I said. The air had turned thick with laughter and smoke; courtiers swayed drunkenly while couples slinked into the shadows. I'd never seen such brazen behavior, the women shoving down their bodices to reveal their flesh, the men fondling them, without shame. When we came to the hall doors I glanced toward the arcade and caught sight of Alfonso sprawled on pillows, being plied with a goblet by Girón. A woman knelt at their feet, her bodice completely unlaced to expose her nipples. Her hand was sliding up Alfonso's leg.

I let out a horrified gasp; Beatriz gripped my arm to detain me from marching over to them. As she steered me into the corridor I saw with relief that Chacón strode toward my brother, his expression thunderous.

Cabrera waited with four of the formidable Moorish sentries and a torchbearer. "I'm afraid the alcazar is not safe at night," he explained when he saw me looking at the sentries with confusion.

"Not safe? But I am the king's sister; how can his palace not be safe for me?"

Cabrera regarded me sadly. "I regret many here do not recognize his authority or the law. I would never forgive myself if harm should befall Your Highness."

I looked at Beatriz; her grim expression warned me not to protest further. I pulled up my hood as Cabrera led us into the alcazar hallways, where inebriated courtiers sprawled in the corners, decanters at their sides. The acrid smell of spilt wine clogged the air; members of the grandees' retinues—identifiable by the distinctive badges on their sleeves—lolled by the light of candles stuck in wax on the floor. They leered at us; one cupped his groin and called, "Come over here, *hermosas,* and play with this." The others guffawed, adding their own lewd suggestions.

The sentries shifted closer; we quickened our pace. It was as though the hallowed splendor of this fortress had fallen under a midnight curse. I heard moans, grunting; I saw hounds roaming everywhere, snarling, as couples rutted in the alcoves like beasts.

Finally, we were moving through empty arcades to emerge outside, under the expanse of the spangled night sky. Cabrera unlocked a stout wooden door in a high stone wall. We encountered sudden silence, the air redolent with moisture—a stretch of fragrant garden abutting the *casa real,* the same garden my new rooms overlooked.

We'd not come this way earlier. Under other circumstances, I would have delighted in the display of early spring blooms, in the delicate fountains and tiled pathways that reminded me of the Convent of Santa Ana. But I could scarcely pay attention; my entire being was overcome by an urgent sense of peril. Only after Cabrera had seen us to our apartment, lighting the candles and leaving the sentries posted outside our door, did I vent my emotion.

"We cannot stay here another day! I will speak with Enrique tomorrow; even he must understand that under the circumstances this is no place for me or Alfonso."

"Say whatever you like but I'm afraid he will do nothing." Beatriz met my stare. "He left the hall as soon as you and the prince went to dance. He had his . . . friend with him."

I stood utterly still.

"What I was trying to tell you earlier," she added, lowering her voice, as if unseen ears listened from the woodwork. Never in Arévalo had we felt the need to conceal our words. "I overheard courtiers talking; they say the queen hates Alfonso and you because of the threat you pose to her daughter. They say she'll keep you both prisoners, do anything she can to see you removed from the succession. And if she fears you so much, if she'd go to such extremes, then perhaps the rumors are true. Perhaps this child of hers is not . . ." Her voice faded into wary silence; I had reprimanded her on the way to Ávila for this very discussion, but this time her intimation hung over us, inarguable in its malevolent logic.

I shut my eyes. I heard the caged beasts roar nearby, imagined the hedonism overtaking the alcazar and the corruption seething underneath. I saw again the painted youth fondling Enrique, that horrifying glimpse of Girón and Alfonso; and as I recalled Beltrán de la Cueva's smile and the queen's jealous glare, I felt suffocated.

What if the queen had played the wanton to save herself? What if this newborn princess was illegitimate, the by-blow of the queen and Beltrán de la Cueva? If so, then the disaster my mother predicted would come to pass; if Enrique made a bastard his heir, it would be an affront to his divine right to rule. He would divide the realm, anger the grandees, and invoke chaos. He would invite God's wrath upon Castile—and upon all of us.

You're at court now. Here, you must learn to dissemble if you are to survive.

"What shall we do?" Beatriz whispered and I opened my eyes. She stood with her hands clasped, pale with worry. I had to be strong, for her and Alfonso. I had to see us safe.

"Whatever we must."

CHAPTER SEVEN

Ispent an uneasy night, plagued by a dream in which I found myself walking endlessly down a dark corridor. Ahead an arched doorway beckoned, flooded with bright winter light, but as hard as I tried I could not reach it.

I awoke gasping, tangled in my sheets, Beatriz at my side. She huddled in the bed with me, both of us so unsettled that we had clung to each other even in our sleep. When I told her about my dream she said it was a premonition that my future held both promise and danger. For an otherwise practical soul, she had a superstitious side—the legacy, she claimed, of her converso heritage. I shrugged aside her talk of portents; those of Jewish descent might favor such things, but I did not. I had my faith in God; I must trust in that alone to guide me.

When we peeped out the door, the sentries were gone and cool May sunshine softened the gardens beyond. Cabrera brought us a breakfast of warm bread, fresh fruit, and cheese; a bath was drawn by a maid supervised by an elegant elderly woman who identified herself as Doña Cabrera, Andrés's mother. Beatriz and I gratefully luxuriated in hot rosemary-scented water, splashing and giggling like the girls we were.

But once we donned our gowns and went to assemble under the gilded, coffered ceiling of the Sala de los Reyes in the alcazar, my worries returned. I had no idea what to expect from today's event and was inordinately glad to catch sight of Fernando. His presence reassured me, as did his quick smile when I passed him on my way to the dais. Of everyone at court, only he seemed normal, unfettered by secret agendas or intrigue.

Alfonso had already arrived. He waited on the dais with the royal family. He looked tired and pale, no doubt from all the wine he'd imbibed the previous night, his blue-and-gold embroidered doublet and jaunty feathered cap offsetting his chalky complexion. Close beside him stood Archbishop Carrillo, who gave me his usual warm smile—only now I found myself regarding him with more wariness, knowing that he might have deliberately contrived to keep our mother from coming to court with us. I found the calculating serenity of his eyes unsettling, as if he were looking through me into a future only he could see.

The princess lay in Queen Juana's arms, swaddled in trailing lengths of pearl-studded white velvet. Juana thrust the baby at me after I curtsied, obliging me to kiss her soft milky cheek; little Joanna was sleeping, and for a moment I melted at the sight of her. Surely such an innocent creature couldn't be the cause of any tumult.

"You shall be her godmother," Juana informed me, with a smile as artificial as the carmine color of her lips. "We've had a gift made especially for you to bestow on her during the festivities tonight—a silver baptismal font, with her name inscribed on it. After all, how would it look if the godmother came empty-handed?"

I muttered my gratitude, turned from her sharp eyes. If she felt any shame at what she had allegedly done, she did not show it; and I found myself now doubting the sordid rumors I had almost believed just hours before. In the cold light of day, it was inconceivable that she, a Portuguese princess, sister of that nation's current king and relative of my own mother, would go as far as to risk the very crown on her head.

I took my place beside Alfonso. Enrique sat on his throne, looking uncomfortable in a gem-encrusted coronet and mantle. He had stubble on his face; his eyes were shadowed, red-rimmed. He did not look at me. Instead he nervously eyed the assembly as his herald intoned the words of the patent conferring upon baby Joanna the royal title of princess of Asturias, which made her heir to the throne.

Castile's Cortes, the parliamentary body composed of representatives from each of the kingdom's important provinces, had to approve the new succession by vote, but as the grandees approached the dais to kneel and swear to uphold the princess's rights, their faces were like granite, and they uttered their oaths in monotones, imbuing the occasion with a funereal air.

"Where are the counts of Alba, Cabra, and Paredes?" I heard the queen hiss to Enrique as the last of the queue of grandees made their obeisance. "Where are the Andalucían grandees, Medina Sidonia and Cádiz? Are we to be insulted by them? They were summoned weeks ago; they should *all* be here to honor our daughter."

Enrique's chin sank deeper into his ermine collar. When Alfonso's turn came, Carrillo reached out and I thought for a heart-stopping moment that he would hold Alfonso back. But he simply patted my brother's arm, as if in reassurance. Once Alfonso recited the vow and stepped aside, it was my turn. I knelt before Enrique's pained gaze and said, "I, Isabella de Trastámara, infanta of Castile, do solemnly swear to uphold the Princess Joanna as the legitimate first heir to the throne, barring all others."

The words were like ash in my mouth. I did not know if I believed them or not, if I had just committed a sin by acknowledging this child whose paternity was in doubt; but as I returned to my place I was overcome by relief. My mother might rail when she heard of it; the nobles might continue to grumble and courtiers to spread vile conjecture, but the deed was done. Little Joanna was now Enrique's heir unless the Cortes said otherwise. We'd done her homage. We had sworn an oath. We could not go back on our word.

Leaden silence ensued.

Enrique stood, his raiment lending him an awkward regality. I thought he might speak but instead he turned on his heel and strode abruptly from the dais. From the crowd stepped his companion of the night before, now clad in a simple doublet and hose. Together they left through a side door, prompting the rest of the assembly to quickly disperse.

Fernando stood alone, looking at me.

I turned to Alfonso. "Come, brother. We could use some fresh air before the afternoon meal."

Alfonso made as if to move when Carrillo said, "I regret it, but such pastimes must wait. His Highness has important duties to attend to. Don't you, my prince?"

Alfonso sighed. "Yes, I suppose so. Go ahead, Isabella. Maybe we can meet later?"

I nodded. "Of course." While I disliked the possessiveness in the archbishop's manner, all I could do was trust that Carrillo would see that Alfonso's best interests were served.

Still, as I kissed my brother's cheek I whispered, "Do not promise anything."

Alfonso started. I drew back with ease, smiling at Carrillo, who beamed right back. Then I moved to the steps of the dais, where my young cousin from Aragón waited.

Fernando held out his hand. "Let us walk together, Isabella."

WE WENT INTO the garden, Beatriz and Andrés de Cabrera trailing discreetly behind.

The day was still cool, but the promise of summer could be felt in the warming breeze, glimpsed in rosebuds unfurling on thorny stems. The path under our feet sparkled with quartz; at intervals were benches inlaid with painted tiles, depicting the heroic deeds of our early kings, each of whom had fought to reclaim Castile from the Moors.

At my side Fernando walked with measured steps. I did not want to be the first to break our companionable silence; I was happy to enjoy this respite, to be outdoors and take in the air. But as we neared a fountain and Beatriz turned away with Cabrera to afford us some privacy, I heard Fernando clear his throat.

"I wish to apologize for last night. I did not mean to offend you."

I regarded him. I sensed that despite his youth, he was not accustomed to asking forgiveness of anyone, much less a girl. As Juan of Aragón's sole heir, Fernando must be quite indulged, though I didn't think he'd enjoyed much in the way of material luxuries. His fustian doublet and leather boots appeared clean but well worn, and there was a mended spot on the knee of his hose, though the stitches were so perfect, it was almost unnoticeable. I wondered if his mother, the Castilian queen of Aragón, had repaired it. The work denoted an expert hand and only royal women or nuns had time to perfect the art.

"I told you, there's no need for apology. I was not offended."

"But I shouldn't have spoken thus of the queen," he said.

"No, you shouldn't have." I adjusted my skirts, sitting on one of the stone benches near the fountain. The sunlight shimmered on the trickling water; in the murky depths, tiny colored fish darted. I looked up to meet his eyes; in the light, they were gorgeous, a deep brown with a hint of molten honey in their depths, the slight tilt at their corners enhancing their luster. One day, he'd melt hearts with a mere glance. He was already irresistibly handsome and he was not yet a man.

Without warning he said, "I leave today for Aragón."

My heart gave a disappointed start. "So soon?"

"I'm afraid so. I've received news from my father. My mother . . . she needs me." His mouth quivered; as I saw his eyes moisten, I shifted aside on the bench to make room. "Sit, please," I said, and he perched beside me, his body tense, as if he feared giving rein to his emotion. I waited for him to regain his composure. When he spoke again, his voice was subdued, with only the faintest tremor.

"She is very ill. The physicians don't know what is wrong. She keeps getting weaker. She was always up before anyone else, always the last to retire; she ran our entire court. And as my father has grown increasingly blind, she helps him with all his affairs. But Papa says she collapsed a few days after I left and now she's asking for me."

I could see the struggle on his face as he tried to contain his sorrow. I wanted to embrace him, comfort him, but that would have been most improper; as it was, I shouldn't be alone with him at all, even though Beatriz and Andrés de Cabrera were somewhere nearby, lending us the illusion that we were chaperoned.

"I am so sorry," I finally said. "Losing a loved one must be very hard."

He nodded, the bones of his jaw clenching under his skin. He turned to me. "You lost your father; you know better than most the pain it can cause."

"I was only three when my father died. I scarcely knew him."

He regarded me with unsettling focus. "Are you always so honest?"

"I've never found a reason to be otherwise."

"Then you'll not take my advice to heart, about the need to dissemble at court?"

I paused, considering. "I do not like to lie."

"I did not mean you should lie. But you also mustn't be so direct about your feelings, not here. It is not safe, nor wise. There are dangers here that you do not understand."

"Are you telling me you know my brother's court better than me?" I said. I intended to put him in his place but as I heard myself speak I realized how naïve I sounded. He knew I'd been raised far from court; and that he, a prince of our ancestral foe and sometimes ally, had a perspective that, by reason of my upbringing, I lacked.

Yet he didn't seek to assert his superiority or take offense at my words. Instead, he leaned to me and said in a hushed voice, "This unrest over the succession is only going to worsen."

"Why would you say such a thing? My brother has an heir. Surely that is not cause for unrest."

He looked at me with almost painful reluctance. "You know what I mean."

"Yes," I replied dryly. "It would seem we're back to unseemly rumor again."

"It is not just rumor. Many of Castile's nobles are deeply discontent with the king and his choice of an heir. They do not trust Beltrán de la Cueva or the queen; they believe the right to inherit belongs to your brother Alfonso—"

I cut him off. "I've heard this before. Would you subject me to it again?"

"Forgive me." He reached out and grasped my hand. I let out an involuntary gasp. "But I must warn you before I go," he said, "for it affects the very future of these realms."

"And did your father, King Juan, instruct you to convey this message?" I asked.

He flinched. "I would never be my father's mouthpiece. I only want to help you, so you may protect your throne."

"Throne?" I repeated, with some asperity. "Which throne do you refer to, pray? My niece is princess of Asturias, Castile's heir; should anything, God forbid, happen to her, my brother stands next in the line of succession. He will wed, sire children of his own. They will rule after him. I shall never be queen."

"But you will! It has always been my father's most earnest desire that you and I should wed. You will be queen, Isabella—queen of Aragón, my wife."

I stared at him.

"It is a good match," he added, his fingers tightening on mine. I'd never felt such warm hands. "I know Aragón is smaller and not as powerful or as rich as Castile, but we have many blood ties. We can bind our realms closer together, restore peace between them." He paused, gazing at me. "What do you say? Would it not please you to marry me?"

Of everything he might have said, this was the one thing I was not prepared for. Meeting his ardent gaze, I managed to utter, "But you are a boy, I a maiden—"

"No!" His voice rose. "I am not a boy. I'll be thirteen next year; I've been knighted, bloodied my sword in Aragón's defense. In my kingdom, I am already a man."

It was a boastful claim, the very sort I'd expect from someone like him. Yet as I looked down at our entwined hands, they seemed to be separate strands of silk from the same skein—mine so white and slim, his square and brown, yet both of near-equal size, with the same unblemished texture of our shared youth.

Why did he evoke such feeling in me? He was blunt and arrogant, too forthright for all his advice about dissembling. I hardly knew him at all. But if I was honest with myself I couldn't deny that envisioning him as my spouse was not unappealing. All my life I'd been told that one day I must wed for the good of Castile. I never thought I'd have a say in who I would marry but that didn't mean I did not wonder what kind of husband fate had in store for me, that I did not nurture the same dreams as any other girl. Our world was full of old, fat kings; it was only normal that I should be drawn to the promise of this brash young prince.

But of course I wouldn't tell him that. I would never compromise myself. He was leaving today for his kingdom. Who knew when, or even if, I'd ever see him again?

I withdrew my hand. "Fifteen is the marriageable age for an infanta in Castile. If you want an answer, come back then and I shall give it—after you've petitioned my brother the king for my hand," I added, preempting him. "Now, let's not spoil the rest of our time together." I smiled, to ease the look of wounded pride on his face. "Come, let's walk more. You can tell me about Aragón. I've never been and I would see it through your eyes."

He lit up at the invitation, launching into a detailed account of his homeland as we strolled, his voice resonant with pride as he described its domains, which spread from the rich lands of northern Huesca to the azure waters of Valencia in the south; he made it all come alive, so that I could see the imposing serrated mountains of Aragón changing from violet to blue under glacial Pyrenean winds, the deep gorges that hid valleys so lush that fruit trees grew wild, and arid steppes where herds of cattle and sheep grazed. I saw the walled capital of Zaragoza at the mouth of the Ebro River, its lacy Aljafería Palace and the alabaster altarpiece of the famed Basilica; and the merchant city of Barcelona, inhabited by the wild Catalans, who begrudged Aragón's dominion over them. I tasted the stew made of crabs believed to prevent illness, and the famous *pata negra* ham served in the city of Teruel. I learned of the Aragonese people's courageous fight against the ceaseless encroachment of the vulpine French and of their centuries-long struggle for control over the distant, sun-baked realms of Sicily and Naples.

"At one time, we had most of southern Italy under our rule," Fernando said. "We had the duchies of Corsica and Athens, too. We were masters of the Mediterranean."

I was familiar with the breadth of my native kingdom of Castile and León, naturally, but he mesmerized me with this revelation of Aragón's holdings abroad, where enterprising seafarers sought riches in distant lands, hauling back coffers of spices, gemstones, and silks, as well as the coveted mineral alum, for which merchants paid fortunes, used to fix dyes in cloth.

"You're like the Romans," I breathed. "You have an empire."

"And we fell like them too!" He laughed, showing off a gap between his front upper teeth that I found inexplicably charming. "You see, our treasury has never been as full as our ambitions, and maintaining such far-flung holdings takes money—lots of it."

He paused, turning somber. "And since the loss of Constantinople to the Ottoman Turk, we face a grave threat from the infidel. That conquest leaves all of Europe vulnerable. This is how the Moor first overtook us centuries ago; it could happen again. The Turks could use Granada as a gateway, just as the Moors used Gibraltar."

I shuddered at his vision of the infidel swarming in a dark wave over us, even as I marveled that he could know so much, about so many things. I'd never given any thought to the cataclysmic fall of Constantinople, one of Christendom's most venerated cities, though it happened two years after my birth and had shaken our faith to its core. My knowledge was limited to illustrated histories of Castile, to troubadour poems and romantic parables such as *The Book of Good Love*. I'd never looked at our world as Fernando did, from a vantage that did not make us the center but rather a piece of its entirety. The very act of hearing him left me exhilarated, as though I stood on a galleon plying foam-flecked waters toward uncharted shores. . . .

Fernando sighed. "And now with that spider Louis XI threatening Aragón's northern border we must maintain a ready army. Troops also cost money, more than you can imagine. The nobles won't summon their retainers without coin, and vassals won't fight without adequate rations. My mother was the best organizer we had; she knew exactly how to economize at court so we could . . ." His voice faded. He looked away. "I can't believe I just spoke of her as if she were already gone."

"I'm certain you did not mean it," I said.

He returned his gaze to me. "It's too easy to forget my pains with you at my side."

I paused. We'd reached the arched cloisters that circled the palace; without realizing it, we'd walked twice around the entire garden. When we first entered it I had thought it large, a veritable maze. Now, with his words swimming in my head, it felt cramped, a man-made creation of idealized hedges, unnaturally pruned trees, and symmetrical paths that went nowhere.

"Isn't that your friend?" he said, and I looked toward the cloisters to see Beatriz seated on a stone bench next to Cabrera. He was gesticulating, talking with more animation than I'd yet seen him display, while she gazed at him in silent, rapt attention.

Fernando chuckled. "Some might say he's too old for her, but she seems not to mind."

I immediately bristled at his innuendo. "Whatever do you mean?

Don Andrés de Cabrera has been nothing but kind to us. I hardly think he has any designs on . . ." But now it was my turn for my words to drift away as I looked closer and noticed the manner in which Beatriz held herself, a definite coquettishness to her cocked head and wider-than-usual stare, as though Cabrera was the most fascinating man she'd ever met. Though I stood in plain sight, only a few paces away, she had not even noticed me.

I stifled a giggle. It *did* look as though she was entranced by him. . . .

At my side, Fernando breathed, "I must teach you to dance."

My mirth evaporated. "Dance? But we danced only last night. I know how to do it quite well, thank you."

"Oh, you do, yes, beautifully, but you don't know any of the dances of Aragón. You must learn one so you'll have something to remember me by." He grasped me by the hand before I could protest, steering me toward the tiled area near the fountain.

I tried to pull away. "No," I said, and I heard a frightened breathlessness in my voice. "Someone . . . anyone could see us."

"Who?" He chuckled, glancing over his shoulder to the cloisters. "They wouldn't notice if we fired a cannon. Come, it's only a dance."

"No, really; I mustn't. Not here, in the garden. It's . . . it's not proper."

He went still, his gaze fixed on me. "Do you always take yourself so seriously?" he asked. Though his question could have been offensive, I knew at once by his tone that he didn't intend it that way. He was honestly curious.

"Of course," I replied, with a defensive lift of my chin. "I'm an infanta of Castile. I must always remember that."

He arched a brow. "Always? Can't even an infanta have fun now and then?"

"I hardly think dancing in the garden can be deemed—" I started to retort, but he ignored me, humming under his breath as he paced to the tiled area. He assumed position.

He had gone mad. He was actually going to do it. He was going to dance.

"This dance," he said, raking his hair from his brow, "is one the peasants perform after the harvest, to celebrate nature's bounty."

And a peasant dance, no less, of pagan origin! I should walk away. This was unseemly. *He* was unseemly. But I couldn't. I remained locked in place, riveted by his sturdy, confident body as he threw back his shoulders, arms akimbo, and with a loud trill from his lips, leapt up and crisscrossed his legs in swift, razor-sharp precision.

"It symbolizes the sheaving of the wheat," he called to me, as he swirled about, while still executing the amazing kicks and leaps. "Come! I'll show you."

He held out a hand, beckoning. I couldn't believe what I was doing even as I moved toward him. There could be courtiers watching us from the palace windows, scandalized; anyone passing through the cloisters might see. By now, I was certain Beatriz had been alerted and was at this very moment watching, openmouthed, as I reached for Fernando's hand and felt his hot fingers enclose mine.

He was sweating, his grin wide. "Those skirts will trip you," he said, raising an eyebrow at my gown.

I froze.

He leaned to me. He whispered, "Be brave, Isabella."

My throat had gone dry. With a few deft movements, I bent over, gathered up my trailing skirts and tied them to the side of my calf in a knot. I looked at him.

"You've done that before," he said, his gaze roving with unmistakable insolence over my ivory-hosed ankles. I did not like my bony ankles; they made my feet look too big.

"Contrary to what you may think about pampered infantas," I replied, with enough tartness in my voice to bring his eyes back to mine, "I did grow up in a working castle, with livestock. Mud and muck were a daily hazard. And I have few dresses to spoil."

He bowed, moving next to me, one arm sliding about my waist. "It's easier than it looks," he murmured, so close I could smell the salt of his skin. "Just follow me."

At first, I almost fell, so fast and sudden was his leap, followed by that complicated leg movement. I clumsily managed it the second time, to his clap of encouragement; then, as he again hummed his wordless tune, which reminded me of the piping of goatherds on a windswept cliff, he took my hand in his, turned me so we faced each other, and said, "To the beat of three, we leap together, kick, swivel, and do it again."

"Impossible," I said, as I braced myself, closing my eyes to better catch the nuance in his tune. When I heard the lilt and felt the pressure of his fingers tighten, I caught my breath. I jumped, kicking my legs back and forth. As we touched the ground, I turned with him so quickly my headdress almost flew off. And then I lost all sense of myself, of what was proper and what was not. With my blood beating in my ears, I heard my laughter burst from me like a long-captive bird set free, and we did it again.

Then we stood panting, hands entwined, as the water in the fountain splashed its applause. The throbbing in my ears subsided as Fernando met my gaze. A cloud drifted overhead, veiling the sun. In the interplay of sudden shadow and light I saw how he might appear years from now, in adulthood, when his cheeks grew more angular, his brow broader, but still with those lively eyes and that exuberant air. I had the sense that however how old he became, his smile would never change.

"You're blushing." Removing his hand, he lifted it to my face. "You've such fair skin, white as the moon. . . ."

I did not move. I let his fingertips graze my skin, welcoming the tendrils of heat he sent spiraling through my veins, until everything inside me tingled.

A cacophony of bells rang out from the cathedral, heralding midday and sparing me a response. Behind me I heard a clatter of footsteps. Fernando stepped back. Turning, I saw Beatriz hustling to me, her reddened cheeks making her look as flustered as I felt. Cabrera stood by the bench, a bewildered expression on his face. Could it be they had not seen us, so engrossed in each other that only the bells had alerted them to propriety?

"My lady, please forgive me." Beatriz dipped into one of her awkward curtseys. "Time got away with me. Are you finished walking? Have you been waiting long?" Her questions were hasty, but I detected the mirth in her voice, indicating that while she may have been otherwise entertained, she had indeed seen us.

"No," I said, wondering if my delight was as transparent as hers, "not long. . . ." As I spoke the haze of the dance dissipated, like scented smoke or a lovely dream. I wanted to grasp it in my hands before it slipped away, encase it in nacre, a rare pearl. For a moment, I felt as though I hadn't an obligation in the world, a single worry or fear or doubt.

For a moment that was quickly escaping me, I had been free.

"I'm afraid we must go," I said softly to Fernando. "We are due to hear Sext and then we must change for the banquet. Will I see you in the hall later?"

"I regret to say, no," he replied. "My servants must be wondering where I've gotten to; we were due to leave long before Sext. The trip to Aragón will take at least two days."

"Oh." I forced out a smile, despite my disappointment. "Thank you. It's been a delight, cousin. I do hope we will meet again."

"As do I, my infanta." I did not miss the emphasis he placed on "my" as he bowed over my hand. Beatriz jabbed me; I shot a glare at her. Fernando said to her, "My lady de Bobadilla, a pleasure," and she curtsied, simpering, "An honor, Your Highness."

He looked into my eyes. "I will write."

And before I could utter a word he strode back through the garden toward his rooms, as though he'd trod upon the unfamiliar winding paths a hundred times before.

I watched him disappear into the palace; I had to curb the urge to call out to him, to tell him he was right. I had liked the dance, very much.

"He pleases you," Beatriz said.

I nodded, feigning nonchalance. "He's rather entertaining, for a boy."

"He won't be a boy for long. And he's bold, for one so young."

"Indeed, and you appear to have enjoyed your chat with Don Cabrera."

I took satisfaction in watching her flush deepen, even as she tossed her head and said with a flippant air, "Cabrera? Bah. He means nothing to me."

AFTER SEXT, WE returned to our rooms and hastily changed into our court gowns. As we returned to the alcazar, I mentioned to Beatriz that

I could see how we'd need a more extensive wardrobe, given the amount of functions we apparently were expected to attend. But the idea of asking Mencia de Mendoza or the queen for assistance, especially after I'd so impulsively turned it away already, was not pleasant to contemplate.

"Perhaps we could ask Andrés—I mean, Don Cabrera—for his mother's help," Beatriz said. "She's been so kind to us. I'm sure she'd be happy to oblige."

I nodded. "Indeed, and maybe she can also help us make the gowns. With the right patterns, I can do well enough. Your stitches, however, are about as hopeless as your curtsey."

She scowled. "As if anyone cares what I wear."

"Don Andrés de Cabrera seems to," I replied.

She set her hands on her hips with an indignant air. "Are you going to tease me about him all day? If so, please let me know now so I can ignore you."

"Such a temper you have." I kissed her cheek. "Forgive me. I promise, I'll not mention it again."

"Good. For there's nothing to mention: I found him entertaining, is all." She winked at me and we both choked back our giggles as we entered the hall, the floor strewn with rosemary-scented rushes crunching under our feet.

I made my way to the dais, where Alfonso was already seated beside Enrique and the queen. Juana's snide regard as I breathlessly assumed my seat made me think I'd best watch my time more accurately from now on. Thus far, I appeared to always be running late.

The queen wore a purple velvet gown designed solely to display her perfect cleavage; clasped about her throat was a shimmering diamond-and-pearl necklace that caught the light with fiery luster. Catching me staring at it—for I'd never seen such magnificent jewels—she touched it knowingly and purred, "Do you like it?"

"It's very beautiful." I did not add that it also looked incredibly expensive.

"A token from Enrique, to celebrate our daughter's birth." She cast an indulgent smile at the king before she returned her gaze to me. The cordial exasperation in her tone barely masked her contempt. "Isn't that the same gown you wore last night? Isabella, my dear, you really must allow me to see to your wardrobe. You should appear as befits your rank at all times. This isn't Arévalo; at court, appearances are very important."

It was as though she had thrown cold water on me. How did she know I'd just been worrying over this very issue? For a moment, I remembered how Fernando had looked at me as we danced in the garden, the admiration in his eyes. He hadn't seemed to care what I was wearing.

Enrique gave me a timorous smile. "Yes, Isabella, do let Juana help you. She knows all the latest fashions."

"And," she added, with a hint of malice in her honeyed voice, "I can also give you some of my older jewelry to wear. Every princess must have pretty jewels, yes?"

I averted my eyes. "Your Highness is most kind. I'd be honored."

"Of course you would." She turned her attention to the hall as servitors entered with the first dishes. I assumed she and Enrique must have settled whatever differences they'd had the day before, because she laughed and whispered with him as if nothing untoward had occurred. I also noted that her handsome dance partner from the previous night, Beltrán de la Cueva, dined with her ladies and was paying conspicuous attention to Mencia de Mendoza. In the light of day, he was even more striking, his rich azure doublet slashed in the Italian style, the sleeves and collar of his shirt peeping through gores rimmed in tiny diamonds. But the queen acted as if she didn't see him at all and I soon became preoccupied by Alfonso's unusual silence.

Finally, I asked him how his day had gone.

"Fine." He jabbed a piece of roast venison with his knife.

"You don't sound fine." I eyed him. "What's wrong? Are they making you study too hard? If you want, I could ask Archbishop Carrillo to let me help you—"

His voice flared. "You don't understand anything, Isabella. You're just a silly girl."

Enrique glanced at us. I tried to force out a smile, though I was hurt by my brother's unexpected attack. He'd always been carefree, rarely given to moods. All of a sudden he seemed like a stranger and I found myself fighting back a horrifying surge of tears. The last thing I wanted to do after being called a silly girl was to cry like one.

"Now, Alfonso," said the king, betraying that he'd overheard us. "I'm sure Isabella is just concerned for you and—"

A loud bang of the hall doors preceded the marquis of Villena, accompanied by his gigantic brother Girón and six of their retainers. As they stalked toward us, the hiss of Girón unsheathing his sword sounded like a serpent in the sudden silence.

Alfonso went rigid; under the table, I felt him grip my knee. Enrique likewise froze on his throne. When the grandees came before the dais, the queen let out a frightened yelp and Beltrán de la Cueva leapt from his chair.

Villena smiled. Girón swerved on the queen's favorite, narrowly missing him with the broad swing of his sword.

"Whoreson," spat Girón. "Get one inch closer and I'll skewer you alive and feed you to my dogs."

Cueva was unarmed; no courtier by law was allowed to bear weapons before the king. He stood panting, realizing too late his mistake. Girón made a menacing gesture. As Mencia and the ladies scrambled out of the way, Girón delivered a resounding blow to Cueva's face with his fist that sent the favorite sprawling across the table, cutlery and goblets and platters smashing to the floor.

The queen wailed. The Moorish sentries rushed from the wall, scimitars in hand, to form a barrier before the dais. Enrique gripped the armrests of his throne.

"What . . . what is the meaning of this, my lord marquis?" he quavered.

Villena pointed to Cueva, who was sodden with spilt wine and food, his face already showing a massive bruise. A weeping Mencia helped him to his feet. Courtiers had backed away, some of them running to the far doors as though they anticipated a conflagration.

Villena's voice rang out. "You'd give that prancing fool the mastership of Santiago, the highest military order in Castile. After everything I have done for you, you'd accord him an honor that by all rights belongs to me!"

"How dare you——" shrieked Juana but she was cut off by Enrique.

"You forget yourself, lord marquis. I am king here. I honor whomever I please."

"Honor who pleases your Portuguese whore is more like it," said Villena. Icy hatred gleamed in his yellow-green eyes as he and Enrique stared at each other. There was history between them, tortured and shared—history I knew nothing about. But I could not believe any grandee, no matter how offended, would dare behave like this before his sovereign.

"She's not yours," Villena said. "That babe you have made your heir is not yours. I thought you didn't know, but now I see you do. You must, for only a knowing cuckold would bestow titles on his wife's man-whore."

"Yes," added Girón, spraying spit as he eyed the sentries, his fist clenching his sword as if he longed to lunge at the impassive Moors. "You can hide behind your infidel filth all you like, but in the end God's truth *will* prevail!"

For a terrifying instant I thought Enrique would order his sentries to cut the marquis, his brother, and their men down; but he only stood there, trembling, his bewildered expression revealing he couldn't believe any of this was happening.

"Do something," Juana hissed at him. "Arrest them. They are lying; it is treason."

"Is it?" said Enrique coldly. She recoiled. He looked at Villena. "You have my leave to depart this court if you no longer agree with my policies. But let me warn you, treason will not be tolerated, no matter how righteous you may think the cause."

"I'll remember that," said Villena. With a mocking bow, he turned and made his way out. Girón brandished his sword again at Cueva, whose bruised face drained to sickly white. Then the marquis's brother trudged out, barking lewd comments at a group of terrified court women huddled by the doors.

The sentries remained in position; Enrique uttered something in their native tongue and they retreated in unison, like well-trained hounds. I had no doubt that if he had ordered it, they'd have killed Villena and Girón without hesitation.

Juana swept from the dais, her ladies rushing to join her as she left the hall. Standing dazed and alone, Cueva looked imploringly to Enrique, who turned away. Only then did I notice Archbishop Carrillo bustling into the hall from a side entrance, concern visible on his florid features, Cabrera and several of the palace guards in his wake.

"Your Majesty," he said, "I've just been informed. It's an outrage! Villena goes too far. May I—"

Enrique whispered, "Take them away."

Carrillo motioned. "Come, my children. Quickly."

Alfonso and I stumbled from our chairs; Beatriz emerged from the watching courtiers to join us. As Carrillo led us out, I saw Enrique crumple upon his throne, burying his face in his hands as though he'd been delivered a mortal blow.

In the passageway, Carrillo directed Cabrera to take us to our apartments. "See that they stay inside tonight," he said, and something in his voice, a dark edge, made me look at Alfonso, standing by the archbishop and his guards with a frightened cast on his face.

Cabrera began to herd us away; I heard the clanking of the sentries' armor as they moved with Carrillo and my brother in the other direction.

Then Alfonso cried, "Isabella!" and I reeled about. He ran to me, throwing himself into my embrace. "I'm sorry," he gasped. "I didn't mean it. You're not silly. It's just that I . . . I am so scared."

"Why? What is it, Alfonso? Why are you afraid?" As I spoke, I looked past him to where Carrillo stood impatiently, hands at his hips, his white robe flowing to his booted ankles, slightly parted to reveal a black tunic underneath, his broad waist encircled by a leather belt thicker than my arm, from which hung a sheathed sword.

He also was wearing a weapon at court. A man of God, garbed like a warrior. I had the sudden image of him roaring with bloodlust on a battlefield, swinging his broadsword as he cut off heads, and my heart started to pound.

"Stay here with us," I said to Alfonso. "Please, don't go with him."

My brother shook his head. "I cannot. I promised I would do my duty. I'm sorry, Isabella." He kissed me gently and returned to Carrillo. I stood still, as the light from the high windows filtered in dusty shafts around me, watching the archbishop set his arm across my brother's shoulders like an oak beam, guiding Alfonso away.

I wanted to run after them, make Alfonso swear to me that he'd not do anything to risk his life.

But I already knew that nothing I said or did could change what would occur. He was right: I was only a silly girl, without any influence; without any power to decide the course of our lives.

At that moment, I knew it would be a long time before I saw my brother again.

TWO DAYS LATER, as Beatriz and I huddled in our candlelit room and listened to the leopards in the king's menagerie snarl in discontent, Cabrera came to us with news.

"Archbishop Carrillo has left court. He took the infante with him, claiming your mother entrusted Alfonso to him personally. The king has issued a demand for their return but no one knows where they've gone. Carrillo has many holdings, much support among his vassals. He could be anywhere. I'll do everything I can for Your Highness, but. . . ."

"I must also fend for myself," I finished, forcing myself to smile. With Carrillo and my brother gone, this gentle man and Beatriz were my sole friends at court.

Cabrera reached into his doublet, removed a folded parchment. Silently, Beatriz slipped on her cloak. "We'll leave you alone to read it," she said, following Cabrera out.

I stared at the missive for a long moment before I broke the wax seal bearing the bars of Aragón. I slowly unfolded the crisp paper.

It was just six words:

Be brave, Isabella. Wait for me.

CHAPTER EIGHT

As spring gave way to fiery summer, word spread throughout Castile, carried by vendors to outlying provinces and cities, where goodwives scattered it like seed among vassals, who hastened to convey it to the lords in their castles. By autumn, everyone had learned of Alfonso's abrupt exit from court and of the marquis of Villena's rebellion, which made the doubts surrounding Princess Joanna's legitimacy gossip for public fodder.

I did not hear from my brother or Carrillo, nor did I dare send any letters. Though I dwelled in my apartments in the *casa real*, where I disposed of a small household, paid for by the king and overseen by Doña Cabrera, I was closely watched, my freedom circumscribed. Any excursion I wished to take outside the gates required both royal approval and the appropriate escort of guards.

Beatriz informed me of all the court gossip; through her, I learned that Villena and several other grandees had gathered in the northern city of Burgos, from which they had issued the declaration of an alliance formed in defense of my brother's rights. The threat of civil war loomed over Castile like clouds awaiting the first roll of thunder, and not a day went by that Juana was not overheard haranguing Enrique to send an army against the rebels.

She did not mind her words even when I was present one morning, seated in a corner of her rooms, trying to make myself as small as I could.

"Carrillo is behind this," she cried to my flustered half brother. "He has found his instrument of revenge and he intends to use it against you. You should never have let him take Alfonso away. You should have stopped it while you had the chance!"

"Juana, please." Enrique stood before her with his red wool turban crunched in his hands. "Alfonso is only a child. How can he possibly pose a threat to—"

"That child, as you call him, could turn this entire realm against us! God in Heaven, are you so blind that you cannot see the truth? Villena and Carrillo are at the head of this so-called alliance; they schemed together to make a scene at court so they could steal Alfonso away. You must put an end to their treason before it's too late!"

Bowing his head, Enrique muttered that there was no evidence of treason and thus there was nothing he could do. Then he shot me an apologetic glance and promptly fled to his forest refuge of El Pardo in Madrid, as he so often did, leaving me behind to contend with his queen's thwarted rage.

"I'll not abide aspersions cast on my daughter, who is Castile's rightful heir," she declared, stabbing her ring-laden finger at me. "If Carrillo dares join that parcel of traitors in Burgos, it will cost him his head— and your brother's, too. I'd pray extra hard if I were you, for I'll see every last one of them dead before they take my child's inheritance!"

I shuddered at her threats, even as I felt embarrassed for her. She strode about in her garish gowns, arms akimbo, swearing vengeance in language as crude as any tavern maid's. Her very vociferousness, her insistent display of the cradle at every court event, where the poor babe cried and coughed as the soot from the torches trickled onto her coverlets, seemed to me the bravura of a coward in a gale.

Everywhere I turned, courtiers gathered to whisper; everywhere Juana looked she must have seen the same. Even Beltrán de la Cueva's betrothal to Mencia de Mendoza had not quelled the gossip; on the contrary, everyone now said if his title as master of Santiago had not been reward enough for his efforts in the queen's bed, marriage into the powerful Mendoza clan must certainly be, seeing as he was nothing but an upstart with only his good looks to commend him, while Mencia was the noble-born daughter of a grandee.

Juana's reaction to this sordid speculation was to force my outward compliance, as though my public humiliation could bridle wagging tongues. She made me walk behind Joanna at every function to emphasize my lesser standing at court and sit and dangle silver rattles over the cradle for hours in her rooms while she played dice with her women. I soon realized that while she might badger everyone in public about her child's rights, in private she cared nothing for little Joanna. Not once did I see her hold the babe if there wasn't an audience present, and Joanna always grew fretful when the queen was near, as if she could sense her mother's indifference. I pitied the little girl and tried to give her my affection, even as I sensed a trap slowly closing in around me.

In April of 1465, I quietly celebrated my fourteenth birthday. It was now one year since I'd seen my brother. The blooms of the almond trees scattered; the earth soaked up Castile's fervent sun, and Joanna took her first tentative steps, graduating from cradle to lead strings. As soon as the weather turned warm enough, Beatriz and I began to steal away to the gardens whenever we could, eager to escape the stagnant court and the queen's sour face.

Joanna cooed and scuttled about on fat feet, trying to grab fistfuls of butterflies as her nursemaid held her upright in her reins. We went to view the sleek spotted leopards in their walled enclosure, a perfect replica of their native habitat, right down to the dismembered deer haunches buzzing with flies under drifts of leaves. After Joanna exhausted herself and her nursemaid rocked her to sleep, we sat under the arcade on the stone benches, chatting about inconsequential things.

Cabrera often joined us. He'd been true to his word, keeping watch over me as best he could. He saw to it we always had enough candles and extra covers for our beds, and his mother oversaw my rooms and acted as my honorary matron, assisting us with our wardrobe, for despite the queen's promise she'd not provided me with a single gown and we soon outwore the few we'd brought. In those tense days, I came to look upon Cabrera as a surrogate uncle, with his broad tanned forehead, intelligent brown eyes, and his trim figure always impeccable in unadorned black velvet. He was friendly but never forward; he had consummate tact. But I did not fail to notice how Beatriz flushed whenever he addressed her and how his eyes, in turn, lingered on her. She had turned seventeen, a strikingly beautiful and exceedingly independent young woman. I sensed she returned Cabrera's affection, even if she couldn't yet admit it. I did not tease her or pry, as I'd promised, but the thought that she might have found love was one of the few joys I had, and a coveted gift I could only hope to one day find myself.

I had not heard from Fernando again, though I'd poured out my fears to him in a spontaneous letter, which Beatriz dispatched in secret. At first, his silence hurt me more than I had expected. I thought we had shared something unique, a kinship he treasured; he had said he would write, yet thus far I had only his one brief note. I was ashamed that I had been so forward with him, that I had let him affect me so much that I'd confessed more of my inner thoughts than I might otherwise have done. But I must have shown my disappointment somehow, for one day in early June Beatriz came to me in the gallery to declare, "I've just spoken to Cabrera about the situation in Aragón. I'm afraid to say, it's not good."

I looked up, startled, from the book in my hands. "What is wrong? Is Fernando . . . ?" I couldn't finish. I actually couldn't even begin to imagine it.

Beatriz gave me a contemplative look. "I thought as much. You've been moping about for weeks since we sent that letter."

"I have not," I retorted at once, but of course I knew I must have been. Otherwise, she'd never have gone so far as to question Cabrera in order to obtain some news for me. I sighed. "You're right. I was worried."

"You had reason to worry." She sat beside me, her voice subdued. "He's gone to war, Isabella. The French have invaded those contested borderlands of Catalonia; apparently, Aragón and France have been dueling over the right to those territories for years. Fernando is leading the army because his mother is still very ill, and his father will not leave her side. Plus, apparently, King Juan is—"

"Going blind," I interrupted softly. "We heard he had cataracts, remember? It's why Fernando was here for the christening, in his father's stead."

She nodded. "Yes, you see? It's not that he's forgotten you. He's fighting for his kingdom. That is why he has not written back. But I'm certain your letter arrived, and I'm certain that he will respond, as soon as he is able."

I bit my lip, looking down, away from her knowing gaze. "We must pray for his safety," I murmured. "He is so young, to be at war. . . ."

"Indeed, and while we're at it, we should offer up a few prayers for you, as well."

"Me?" I lifted my gaze sharply. "Why would you say that?"

She sighed. "Because Cabrera also told me that the king has arrived unexpectedly from Madrid and has asked to see you."

"Me? Do you know why?" My anxiety coiled like rope about my throat, cutting off my breath. I'd not seen Enrique in months; he avoided the court whenever possible, preferring to remain far from the queen and her remonstrations.

"I don't know why. Cabrera wants to tell you himself." She stood and retreated to the gallery entrance. Andrés de Cabrera stepped from the shadows, bowing low.

"Your Highness, please forgive me. I do not mean to intrude, but I . ... I felt you should be warned. The queen is in a rage. Enrique met with Villena and his league a few days ago, unbeknownst to her. They gave him an ultimatum and . . ." He paused, as if uncertain whether to continue.

"Whatever it is," I said, "I must know. I cannot walk into the lion's den unprepared."

"Yes, of course. You must. It seems Villena demanded that His Majesty sign a document which officially declares the princess Joanna is not his. Villena also demanded that Beltrán de la Cueva be stripped of all rank and the mastership of Santiago conferred on Villena himself. . . ."

I stood still, waiting, my breathing shallow.

"His Majesty refused to sign," he went on. "Instead, he asked that all grievances be settled through a special gathering of the Cortes. Villena agreed, but as soon as the king left he went back on his word."

Everything around me grew distant, blurred.

"He marched with his army to meet Carrillo, your brother, and your mother in Ávila. They deposed the king in effigy before a crowd, crowning Alfonso in his stead." Cabrera met my eyes. "His Majesty is beside himself. Circulars have gone out in Alfonso's name. Many strategic cities, including Zamora and Toledo, have declared in Prince Alfonso's favor. We are at war, Your Highness: civil war. Castile now has two kings."

The world went black. I felt my knees give way; I might have fallen had Beatriz not rushed over to take me by the arm. She guided me to the window seat, where I sat and closed my eyes, praying for strength.

Here it was at last, the moment I had been dreading since Carrillo took Alfonso from court.

With my heart in my throat, I went to the royal apartments. I found them submerged in shadow, curtains drawn against the light. Enrique sat on a chair under his cloth of estate, his head lowered. Behind him stood Beltrán de la Cueva, clad in gold and scarlet. His eyes stayed fixed on me as I approached; standing nearby was Pedro de Mendoza, bishop of Sigüenza, Beltrán de la Cueva's new brother-in-law—a slim man with the same keen dark eyes as his sister. He was considered the most ambitious ecclesiastic in Castile after Carrillo.

Enrique looked up at me, pushing strands of his dirty shoulder-length hair from his face. His eyes were red-rimmed, sunk in shadow; he seemed to have aged years, his cheeks gaunt under an unkempt beard. I smelled his musty odor as I knelt before him.

"Your Majesty," I said softly, "forgive me."

Enrique let out a sigh. "So, you already know."

"Yes. Don Cabrera told me and I am stunned. I never expected my brother to become involved in this terrible affair. But I am sure he is innocent. He never meant to offend you."

"As if we believe that," said Juana. I had not seen her in the shadows of the alcove and I turned, startled, as she stepped forth. She was dressed in a dramatic black-and-silver gown that cleaved to her figure, her topaz eyes livid, her hair wild about her shoulders. "So meek and pious on the outside," she sneered, "so charitable, like a little nun. But I know better; you're a viper at heart, just like your brother. Better you'd both been strangled at birth."

"Juana, *basta*," said Enrique. "I called for Isabella so I can hear what she has to say."

"Why?" The queen shook aside Bishop Mendoza's restraining hand. "What can she possibly say that will make any difference now? Carrillo and Villena have defied you; they've gathered an army and crowned Alfonso as king in your place. She will plead for her brother's life, of course. You must not heed her. You must imprison her until the time comes to marry her off to some foreign prince, so she can cause no further mischief."

My mind reeled. I still found it impossible to believe that Alfonso would willingly seek to vanquish our brother, who, for better or worse, was our anointed king. But as I heard the menace in the queen's voice, I knew she would not rest until she saw my brother dead and me sent far from my home.

"Juana." Enrique enunciated carefully, in a terse voice I'd never heard him use before. "Alfonso is not my enemy. Yes, he did wrong in letting them set a crown on his head, but I was told the matter went far beyond his limited ability to control it. Evidently he had to go through with it, for fear they might otherwise do him harm. I will find out later who exactly is to blame for this, but for now I wish to ascertain what *my sister* Isabella thinks."

His emphasis of my status as blood kin didn't go unnoticed. The queen threw up her hands in a fury, whirling to Mendoza. "See? He does not listen to me! He does not consider me worthy of counsel, yet he'd heed this—this mealymouthed creature, though she no doubt is in league with her traitor-brother. I warned him this would happen, but he said no, they're my family, they love me, they will never harm me. Let Carrillo care for Alfonso and Isabella can stay here at court. Well, look at how that worked out! Look at how his loving family serves and obeys their king!"

"Enough!" Enrique barked. "Out, all of you. I would be alone with my sister."

Beltrán de la Cueva went to Juana and led her out, but not before she cast a vicious glance in my direction. Mendoza murmured, "Be gentle with her, my lord. Remember, she is still an infanta."

Then I was alone. I could not look my half brother in the eye as he left me there on my knees, in silence; before this moment, he'd refused to allow any ceremony between us. I had never felt the danger of my situation as acutely as I did in that moment. I feared I'd be thrown into a prison cell while an army was dispatched to kill Alfonso. I'd be disgraced, our name dishonored. Alfonso would go down in history as a rebel traitor to his half brother, and I'd find myself either forced to take the veil or wed abroad, sent from Castile forever.

Then Enrique sighed again—a drawn-out sound of such sorrow

that I looked up. His protruding eyes were wet with tears; his voice quivered as he said, "Swear to me that you knew nothing of this. Swear to me you did not participate in this infamy by word or deed."

"I swear," I whispered.

He regarded me for a long moment. "She wants me to imprison you. She says you and Alfonso are the spawn of a she-wolf who has always wished to see me dead. Is it true? Do you want your brother to be king of Castile in my place?"

My throat closed in on itself. I could not tell him of the years of poison heaped on him by my mother or of my own conflict as his sister, torn between love for Alfonso and loyalty to my king. I searched for a response but found only roaring emptiness, until without warning I heard myself say, "You are my sovereign lord, anointed by divine right to rule. I would never dare question God's will."

He flinched, as if my words were barbs. "It seems you're not quite as innocent as they say. Even you recognize who has rights—and who does not."

I regarded him. I scarcely felt the ache in my knees as I watched him rise, pace to the window. He drew aside the drapes, flooding the room with the stain of a dying afternoon sun. "Do you think she is mine?" he said suddenly.

Fear surged in me. "She . . . ?" I echoed, though I understood what he asked.

He did not look at me; his voice was low, as if he spoke to himself. "Juana vows she is but I'm not convinced. I never was. And if I'm not certain, how can I ask others to be? How can I plunder my own flesh and blood for a child who may not be mine?"

A mirthless chuckle escaped him. "All it takes is one time, she said. And we had it, that drunken night with Beltrán, which is when she believes she conceived. But there were two of us that night in bed with her. How can I know whose seed took root?"

He turned back to me; I saw the torment on his face, the doubt. He did not know the truth any more than I did; he did not know what to believe. As my breath burned for release in my lungs, he bowed his head. His next words were so hushed that I almost didn't hear them.

"But of course none of it matters. Because of what our brother has done, now I must wage war for her sake." He lifted his gaze to me. "And Alfonso may die for it."

"Please," I said, "please, do not harm him. He is only eleven. He doesn't understand the gravity of what he's done."

Enrique nodded. "No, of course not. How could he? That is why I wanted him at court with me; I thought if he came to know me, he'd think twice before he betrayed me. This is my fault as much as anyone else's. I let Carrillo take him even though I've known for years that the archbishop despises me and would do anything to see me overthrown, including using my own brother as his weapon. But Alfonso still did it. He let them set a crown on his head, a crown he has no right to wear."

He lifted his hand, indicating I could rise. "Is there anything else you wish to say?"

My voice was ragged; I could no longer disguise my anguish. "I beg you, my lord, do not go to war yet. Let me go to him. I'll return to Arévalo, send word from our mother's house. He will come. I know he will, and I will persuade him to repent. I will bring him in person to court to beg your forgiveness on his knees, before everyone."

He shook his head with regret. "I know you would do as you say, but I'm afraid it's too late. I will not see you punished for your brother's misdeeds but I do command you to leave the *casa real* for rooms here in the alcazar. Beatriz can still serve you but your household will henceforth be overseen by Mencia de Mendoza, who will ensure your continued compliance. Do you understand me? Your future is in my hands, Isabella. You must not do anything to force me to act against my conscience."

I assented, lowering my face, my tears threatening to break free.

"And you'll have no further communication with your mother. She is to be deprived of Arévalo and sent to reside in a convent. I do not trust her anymore. She has abetted these treasons of Carrillo for too long."

He extended his hand. I leaned over it, kissed his signet ring. I got to my feet and backed away, step by step, until I found myself in the corridor. Then I was moving with Beatriz, past the knowing looks of courtiers who turned to each other to whisper even before I had passed.

Whatever Enrique might feel for me as a sister, I was still under suspicion of treason, and desperately afraid.

CHAPTER NINE

In the alcazar, I took up residence in apartments linked by a short passageway to Juana's. Paneled in gilded wood and tapestry, with floors of alabaster tile, their luxury belied the fact that they were a prison. I no longer enjoyed spontaneous escapes to the gardens or visits to the cathedral; I wasn't allowed anywhere without an escort of women, hand-picked by the queen and headed by Mencia.

Every day they threatened me with reminders that if I should be found abetting the rebels in any way, I'd be thrown into a dungeon. I might have been flattered that they thought I could be in possession of such power, given my circumstances, had I not been so anxious for news of the war. I knew the king had appointed Beltrán de la Cueva to lead the royal forces and that several of Castile's nobles, including the marquis of Santillana and the powerful duke of Alba, had answered Enrique's summons for their vassals to defend him.

But weeks went by without further word from the outside world, for Juana had all correspondence routed to her secretary. Finally throwing caution aside, I set Beatriz to eavesdropping in the galleries and querying Cabrera. She discovered that the royal army had gathered in Tordesillas by the confluence of the Duero and Pisuerga rivers. A bloody skirmish ensued with the rebels; the king and Alfonso escaped, but many others died.

Prayer was my consolation. Juana had denied me my own confessor and made me attend Mass with her, where she barely hid her boredom while her women gossiped and ignored the flustered chaplain reciting the service. As soon as Mass ended, she and her ladies would return to flitter about Juana's rooms to polish and paint their nails, pluck each other's brows, brush their hair, and try on various veils, slippers, and other baubles which Juana ordered by the dozens from Segovia's merchants. I'd never despised her more than I did in those moments, when she behaved as though men were not spilling their blood in defense of her child—a child she might have conceived in sin.

Every afternoon after I'd been released from her tawdry displays, I went to the stone chapel in the keep and beseeched God to aid all those who fled their war-torn farms and villages. I prayed for the poor and hungry, the sick and frail, always the first to suffer. I prayed for my mother, evicted from Arévalo; for Fernando, of whom I'd not had news in months; but most of all, I prayed for Alfonso, plunged into danger because of the ambition of others.

The arrival of winter achieved what my prayers could not, forcing the warring factions to a stalemate. Enrique returned to Segovia, looking gaunt and pale; he barely acknowledged me during the lackluster Christmas festivities, departing the court upon the conclusion of the Feast of the Kings to gallop off to his hunting lodge in Madrid, where he remained, "attended by his catamites and smelly beasts," Juana mocked.

Sequestered in Segovia, I grew thin, restless. I had to sit with Juana and her ladies during their silly entertainments, as the queen drank too much wine and danced the night away with gallants in skin-tight hose, making eyes at Beltrán de la Cueva even as he lolled in a chair with his wife at his side. I couldn't forget what Enrique had said about how he had shared a bed with Juana and Beltrán. As I watched Juana draw her hand suggestively down some courtier's muscled arm, her carmine lips parting in invitation, I had to dig my nails into my palms to stop myself from leaping to my feet and marching out.

As soon as the snows thawed, the war resumed. Beatriz learned from Cabrera that various cities, including Toledo, still supported Alfonso. Toledo was Carrillo's archbishopric, the oldest and wealthiest in Castile; its stance prompted many of our grandees to side with the rebels. Enrique was losing ground but I lived in daily fear that word would come of Alfonso's death. In a place deep within my soul I still believed God would strike down those who sought to depose their rightful monarch.

I began a fast, thinking the time-honored ritual of the holy would offer the comfort I needed. Beatriz implored me to eat, saying I could not afford to waste away, but I drank only water for weeks, until one frigid March night when she abruptly shook me awake.

With a finger at her lips as a warning, she threw my cloak about my shoulders and led me past the sleeping chambermaid in the passage, through the alcazar into the icy night. Crossing the great plaza we came before the cathedral.

Cabrera stood waiting. I'd not seen him in months and had missed him. But he did not give me the opportunity to say so; drawing me into the cathedral's cavernous interior, he whispered, "We've little time. The prior of the Monastery of Santa Cruz has asked to speak with Your Highness; he says he has important news to impart. But you must be quick. Should the queen discover I let you meet him, she will deprive me of my post."

I nodded, shivering. What was so important that the prior of Segovia's oldest Dominican monastery should want to see me in the middle of the night? It was so cold I could see my breath like frost, my footsteps echoing eerily as I moved toward the elaborate wooden choir. Votive candles flickered before Our Lady of Sorrows, catching the crystalline tears on her flesh-colored cheeks and the glint of the gold dagger hilt protruding from her velvet-swathed breast. The scent of old incense permeated the air, a rich, smoky fragrance that not even the chill could dispel.

I almost failed to see the figure waiting in the shadows, his long veined hands folded across his white robe, his black cloak falling from his stooped shoulders. He was thin and tall, with an ascetic's ageless angularity. His brooding eyes were of an unusual gray-blue hue, offsetting his broad flat nose and thin lips. As he inclined his tonsured head, his voice issued low and cultured—the voice of a man of strict restraint, who has dominated the unruliness of the flesh.

"Your Highness, I am Fray Tomás de Torquemada. It is an honor to meet you."

I drew my cloak closer about me. "I was told you wished to speak to me?"

He nodded. "Forgive me; you must be cold. Come, we can sit by the candles. Though their light is feeble, the proximity to our Holy Mother will warm you."

I perched beside him on a pew. He was silent for a long moment, his eyes fixed on Our Lady's grieving face. Then he said, "I understand you've lived in Segovia for almost two years now without a private confessor. However, when I offered my services, I was denied."

"Oh?" I was taken aback. "I did not know this. No one told me."

His gaze shifted to me. He did not blink. Power emanated from him, even in his stillness. "How could you? I petitioned the king. But he was not concerned with the welfare of your soul. Quite the contrary, judging by his actions; yet despite all their attempts, it appears you have held steadfast against their corruption. Your heart is pure."

I did not feel the cold anymore. I felt . . . recognized.

"Yet your trial is hard to bear," he added. "You are young, untried; one of lesser faith might have given in by now, surrendered to licentiousness and luxury, succumbed to temptation, even if it meant losing God's grace."

I looked at the marbled floor. "It . . . it has not been easy," I said softly.

"Indeed. And yet you must stay pure, for much will still be demanded of you. You must rely on the conviction of your faith, knowing that even in our darkest hour God does not abandon us. You must trust that He will not suffer a false king to rule over Castile."

I looked up. The blues of his eyes were lit as if by inner flame. It was the sole sign of emotion in a face otherwise schooled to sculptural impassivity.

"How do you know this?" I asked. "How *can* you know?"

He sighed. "Doubt is the Devil's handmaiden, sent to lure us into perdition. Enrique IV has forsaken his own throne; he hides away even as his realm falls prey to godlessness. Our Church is riddled with rot; monks and nuns abhor their holy vows in pursuit of worldly sin; heretics are free to practice their foul rites; and the infidel raids our southern lands with impunity. Discord and anarchy flourish, for our people are like sheep without a shepherd. The king knows all this and does nothing to abate it. He has turned his face from his duty and embraced his own weakness. And now he would set a bastard over us, usurping the succession of the one who can bring us salvation. Whatever else you think, my infanta, never doubt that the king is doomed."

I'd only ever heard my mother speak like this of Enrique and a part of me resisted it, for I didn't want to see my own half brother in so tarnished a light. Yet despite my efforts I recognized in Torquemada's stark appraisal my own sense of Enrique as a lost soul, a man unable to bear the burden of his crown.

"He is still my king," I said at length, "appointed by God and our Cortes to rule. Would you have me disavow my solemn duty to him as his sister and subject?"

Torquemada raised a brow. "I would have Your Highness do only what your conscience dictates. Your brother the infante fights to save Castile from damnation and God will strengthen his arm. But while he fights with the sword, you must fight with your will, for they would soon send you far from this realm. The queen has entered into secret negotiations to wed you to her brother, King Afonso of Portugal."

"Afonso!" I exclaimed, before I could contain myself. "But he's a widower already! And he has a son by his first marriage, an heir. How can such a union benefit me or Castile? I'll be his second wife; whatever children I bear will have no rights unless his first son happens to die and . . ." My voice faded as the realization sank in. "The queen: She is determined to exile me."

"She'll certainly try," Torquemada said. "She must invalidate your claim to the succession first, for with you out of the way, few will dare deny her bastard child. Yet you are the true daughter of Castile; in you runs the ancient blood of kings. And should your brother Alfonso fail, you must be prepared to take up his banner, for you are next in line to the throne. God needs you here."

I looked at my hands, twined in my lap, then back at him. "What can I do?" I whispered. "I have no power. The king can wed me to whomever he wants. He's warned me as much. My future, he said, is in his hands."

Torquemada's eyes glittered. "You are not without power. That is why I am here: to remind you of who you are. Tonight, I will absolve you of all prior oaths, so that you may live henceforth in virtue, following only the dictates of your heart."

He knew I had sworn an oath to uphold Joanna; that I was bound by filial duty to obey my king. Yet, like me, he knew Joanna might not be legitimate, that even as my half brother plunged Castile into chaos to uphold her claim, he too doubted her right to the throne. I had suffered endless doubt, questioning myself and everything around me. Was this austere man the answer to my prayers? Had God sent Torquemada to me to show me the truth?

I slipped from the pew to my knees, my hands clasped before me. "Bless me, Father," I said, "for I have sinned . . ."

Tomás de Torquemada leaned close to hear my confession.

I EMERGED FROM the cathedral to find the moon skulking behind icy clouds. Beatriz and Cabrera hastened to me from the portico. I thanked Cabrera, promised I'd keep this meeting a secret, and returned with Beatriz to my rooms.

As we tiptoed in, I almost laughed aloud when I realized a weight had been lifted from me; I no longer felt afraid. I did not care if Mencia or Juana herself discovered I'd disobeyed them. I had been relieved of the turmoil that had gnawed at me since Alfonso declared himself king. I even felt hunger, for the first time in weeks; I was ravenous for simple hearty fare, like the food I used to enjoy in Arévalo.

I embraced Beatriz. "I know this was your doing," I said, "and I love you all the more for it. You are my dearest friend. Should you ever wish to ask my leave to marry, you shall have it, by my solemn word."

She drew back. "Marry? Desert you? Never!"

"Never is a very long time. Now, do you still keep that bread and cheese in the window seat? If so, go fetch it."

She rushed to retrieve the food; we sat in bed and ate to our heart's content, whispering and scattering crumbs for the mice that scampered in the corners. She did not ask me for any details of what had transpired in the cathedral, and I did not offer any.

But we both knew I was prepared for battle.

👑

MY CALL TO arms came a few months later.

In that time, I'd endeavored to spend fewer hours in the chapel and more in the alcazar library—an astonishing, neglected room with a high scarlet-and-azure vaulted ceiling and shelves crammed with ancient texts, tomes, and folios. I lamented my rudimentary education; I'd never had occasion to master Latin or Greek, the languages employed by scholars, and was thus barred from reading many of the books. What I could find in our Castilian vernacular I devoured, including the statutes of Alfonso X, the king who had been known as El Sabio, for commissioning his famous *Partidas,* which were the basis for our current legal system. I also read other translated works from King Alfonso's time, including Arabic fables and his *Mirror of Princes,* a multivolume treatise instructing monarchs in the ways of proper governance.

In between fevered bouts of reading, I was drawn again and again to a brass spherical globe of the known world standing in a corner, its glimmer dimmed by dust and age. I was mesmerized by its depiction of the Ocean Sea—a vast space of water which no man had dared to cross. Many believed nothing existed past the edge of the Ocean Sea, that terrible monsters lurked in its depths, waiting to hurl unsuspecting ships into a void. But others believed unknown lands existed far beyond our own. Tales of these distant shores and of the adventurers who sought them fascinated me; I couldn't read enough of the chronicles of Marco Polo, who had opened a route to the Orient, now lost to us since the fall of Constantinople, or of the Portuguese prince known as Henrique the Navigator, who had funded intrepid expeditions to Africa.

When I read of these valiant men willing to risk everything for the promise of discovery, I forgot I sat alone with a musty book, an inexperienced girl who had never even seen the sea. I lost all sense of self and time, and became a man forged of salt and driftwood, permeated by spindrift and attuned to the siren's call, with endless blue all around me. Such books proved to me that we have courage inside us we do not recognize until we are put to the test; their words roused in me a fervor I hadn't known I possessed.

By the time Enrique returned to Segovia, following another confrontation with the rebels, I felt I was ready for anything he might demand of me. But as soon as I was called into the Sala de los Reyes, where the gilded statues of our ancestors looked down imposingly from their niches, I espied the lean figure of Villena at Enrique's side.

Then I realized how little of the world I truly understood.

I stared in disbelief at Villena's sardonic face, his entire person perfumed and disdainful, as though he hadn't spent the last twenty-six months agitating rebellion in Alfonso's name. I was astonished that he still lived. Treason such as his deserved death.

Enrique appeared uncomfortable as I curtsied before him. After asking how I fared, he blurted, "We've found the means to end this infernal conflict."

"That is good," I answered, keeping my tone reserved. I pondered his use of "we." If he and Villena were no longer at odds, was the war over? If so, where were Carrillo and Alfonso? I focused on ensuring that my expression remain impassive, despite my confusion, having finally understood the value of the advice Fernando had given me on the night of my arrival to court.

"We are relieved by Your Highness's cooperation," drawled Villena, "for you are instrumental to our success."

I kept my eyes on Enrique, who shifted on his throne. He shot a glance at Bishop Mendoza; the bishop looked pained, unable to meet my eyes when Enrique ordered, "Tell her."

Mendoza cleared his throat. I had taken a wary liking to him, ever since he tried to calm Queen Juana during our confrontation following the revelation of Alfonso's complicity with the rebels. Though he was Mencia's brother and a senior member of one of Castile's oldest and most rapacious noble families, Mendoza was, by all accounts, devoted to his office, a man of piety and reserve who had always treated me with respect.

"We believe . . ." he began. Discomfort creased his brow. "That is to say, we think . . . it nearing Your Highness's birthday, and with the revenues of the towns of Trujillo and Medina del Campo to be delivered to you upon your fifteenth year, as stated in King Juan your late father's testament, that it would be incumbent for you . . . that is, for us, to—"

"God's teeth," spat Villena. "She needn't be treated as if she has a choice!" He turned to me. "The king would end this crisis. He proposes two matches—one between his daughter, Princess Joanna, and the Infante Alfonso, to be ratified upon the princess's fourteenth year, and another between yourself and my brother, Pedro de Girón. These marriages will bring accord and . . ."

The roar in my head drowned out his voice. I recalled Pedro de Girón as he'd been the last time I saw him, a leering giant with his sword, swinging at Beltrán de la Cueva as if the blade were nothing but a toy.

Enrique averted his eyes from me as I said haltingly, "I . . . I will not give my consent."

Villena let out a crude laugh. "You are mistaken if you think we need it."

I lifted my chin. "By the same will that bequeaths those towns to me on my fifteenth birthday, my father ordained that the Cortes must grant its approval before I wed. Has the Cortes been consulted about this proposed match with your brother, my lord?"

Silence fell. Torquemada had told me this in anticipation of the Portuguese alliance; now I wielded it in the desperate hope that a man like Girón would never gain the Cortes's approval to wed me, no matter how powerful or wealthy he was.

Enrique gaped at me. Villena snarled, "Who has she been talking to?" He spun to Mendoza. "Is it true? Do we need the Cortes's approval to wed her?"

Mendoza regarded me pensively. "I believe she is indeed correct. By the terms of King Juan's will, the Cortes must approve any proposed alliance that involves the infantes. Even His Majesty had to request it when he sought to marry his second queen."

"It cannot be! You told me this could all be done without fuss," Villena hissed to Enrique. "We agreed: I gain the mastership of Santiago and the marriage for my brother, and you get Alfonso. I abandoned Carrillo for this! Now he and his rebel wolves are baying for my head, and this chit of a girl dares stand in my way?"

"I am an infanta of Castile," I reminded him. "Did you think to barter me like cheap coin for your vanities?"

"Enough." Enrique was trembling. "I told you, you must do as I say."

"You asked me not to do anything to force you to act against your conscience," I said, "and I have not. Yet now you ask me to go against my own conscience, to violate the terms of our father's testament so my lord the marquis can have a title he is not entitled to, one which by all rights belongs to my brother, the Infante Alfonso."

Enrique's mouth worked. He stared at me as if he suddenly didn't know who I was. Then he said, "How dare you? You do not rule here. I can't bear this anymore. You and your brother. Carrillo. The grandees. All of you want me dead, so you can take everything I have." His voice increased, growing shrill. He lunged to his feet. "I will have peace! And if it means you must wed Girón, then you will!"

I stood immobile, horrified. His eyes bulged, his hands curled before him like claws. I started to protest again but before I could utter a word, he bellowed, *"Get out!"*

Behind me, the hall doors banged open. Footsteps raced toward me; I couldn't move, frozen by the hatred and fear that I saw twisting the king's face. All the bravery I thought I had found in the library, all the daring and strength, seemed to desert me as I realized that he had lost all control of himself. He was desperate, capable of anything.

Beatriz tugged at my sleeve. "My lady, please. We must go."

Spittle flecked Enrique's chin. He stood there, glaring at me, and I forced myself not to take my eyes off him. I had to engrave this moment in my memory, so that I would never again weaken, never doubt or forget that in the end, it was he who had forsaken me.

"You will do it," he said. "You will marry Girón. If you do not, you will regret it."

Those were the words I needed to hear. I curtsied, sinking almost to the floor.

Villena sneered, setting his slender hand on Enrique's shoulder. The king shuddered. I was reminded with a cold jolt of the moment from my childhood, when I'd seen Constable Luna do much the same to my father.

I knew then, without a doubt, that nothing could save Enrique from his fate.

CHAPTER TEN

We were ordered to the alcazar of Madrid—a cramped stone fortress with suffocating staircases, crumbling battlements, and mildewed walls. Despite its adequate furnishings, it was devoid of the lavish embellishments of Enrique's beloved Segovia, to which he'd devoted all his attention and money. The king let it be known via a circular posted throughout Castile—intended, no doubt, to test the rebels' sincerity toward the proposed peace—that I'd been moved to Madrid for my own protection, the freedoms of the court being not conducive to an impressionable virgin about to be wed.

The queen, forced to move with me, now disdained my presence and forbade me from seeing Joanna. Even Mencia stopped pretending she was supposed to serve me, and Beatriz and I were left to the mercy of a chambermaid named Inés de la Torre, whom Mencia employed to spy on us. But out of pity or necessity, or perhaps both, Inés allowed herself to be bribed to our side instead, content to fetch our food, turn down our beds, and clean our rooms for a few extra coins and then deliver to Mencia only the most banal reports of our activities.

I was severed from everyone and everything I cared about—save Beatriz. Desolate over my impending marriage and her own separation from Andrés de Cabrera, one evening she seized the old bread knife and cried, "If that monster dares touch a hair on your head, I'll plunge this blade into his black heart!"

I had to laugh, reminded of the time when she'd claimed she wanted to lead a crusade. "Come now, you know that dagger barely slices our cheese. We cannot fight like knights if we have no swords."

"Then, what *can* we do? Wait to be bartered off like slaves to Moors? Because you have to admit, being Girón's wife is tantamount to slavery."

"I did not say we should not fight. We just need other weapons," I said, echoing Torquemada. "Like lions, we must use our hearts."

"Lions also have teeth," she grumbled, but she joined me at the makeshift altar we'd set up, with a small marble image of the Virgin of the Sagrario, patroness of La Mancha, who hears all our sorrows.

I should have felt solace entrusting my fate to Our Lady. I didn't. I was secretly terrified at the mere thought of having to bed Villena's brother. I kept thinking of Fernando, wondering what he would do, what he would say, when he heard I'd been forcibly wed to another. He had seemed so certain we were destined for each other; now, at this dreaded hour, I wished it were so with all my heart. The thought of the bestial Girón taking Fernando's place was so intolerable I felt I might welcome death first.

I finally wrote to tell Fernando what was happening, determined that he would not think I had forgotten him. Ironically, in Madrid we found it easier to send clandestine correspondence; an eager page besotted by Beatriz conveyed my letter to Segovia, and Cabrera forwarded it by courier to Aragón without anyone being the wiser.

But Fernando did not respond. I waited for days, weeks; I wrote again, two, three, five letters, until my quill went blunt and my remonstrations, churning like dark water in my head, turned bitter. I knew the war against France persisted, but could he not send one brief missive?

Be brave, Isabella, he had said. *Wait for me.*

Yet it seemed he had stopped waiting for me.

I returned to my prayers, doubling my vigil. I did not shift when Mencia swept in to declare that Girón had left his castle and was on his way to Madrid, bringing with him three thousand lancers and a new bed for us to share. I did not look at her as she laughed spitefully and told me I'd best prepare myself, for she'd heard Girón was a rough lover; I did not let myself doubt that somehow, some way, I would be spared. Beatriz fretted over me. I knew I wasn't eating enough, that I was too thin and too pale. She told me I would get sick; she wondered how I could possibly think my demise was the answer.

"Let me kill him," she implored. "One thrust is all I need."

I ignored her until the April morning he was scheduled to arrive.

When I moved to stand from my cushion before the altar, the chamber swayed in nauseating circles around me. I staggered to the mullioned window, cracked it open for air. Outside, I saw a horde of storks, circling the forbidding keep.

I gasped. Beatriz rushed to me, convinced I'd found a way to squeeze myself through that narrow opening to fling myself onto the flagstones far below. I could not tell her what I felt, for I had no faith in omens or superstitions; I'd never put store in the myriad fortune-tellers and soothsayers who plagued the court like vermin.

Yet in that moment, I sensed it. I knew my prayers had been heard.

I finally made myself eat and let Beatriz bathe and fuss over me; Mencia came in to taunt.

"He'll be here," she said. "He stopped in Jaén overnight and had a late start, but he'll be here, have no doubt. A man like him, granted a royal prize like you——why, he'll crawl here on his hands and knees, if he has to."

"Get away from our sight, demon." Beatriz held up crooked fingers to ward off the evil eye. Normally, I'd have chastised her for such foolishness but I just sat and waited. My deliverance would come; it already winged its way to me, fleet as the stork.

By nightfall, Juana herself appeared in my chambers. "Girón has taken ill," she informed me as I sat on my chair, calmly sewing an altar cloth. "His departure from Jaén was delayed, but as soon as he recovers, the wedding will take place."

I lifted my gaze to her, unperturbed.

"It will," she spat, "even if I have to see you wed at his bedside!"

I slept soundly that night, without dreams. I awoke later than usual to discover Beatriz already dressed, staring out the window.

"Beatriz?" I asked.

She turned about slowly, a hand at her throat. "You knew," she said. "You never spoke a word but you saw those storks and you *knew*. Why didn't you tell me? Why did you leave me to worry?"

I raised myself on my elbows. "Knew what? What on earth are you talking about?"

"Girón. He is dead. He had a sore throat, fever; he took to his bed and never got up. They say he saw storks the day before he died, flying overhead. He feared it was an omen and asked his retinue what they thought. They told him it had to be a good omen, for the storks flew toward Madrid. But it wasn't good. The storks were a harbinger of his death."

I crossed myself. "God have mercy on his soul," I murmured. I rose from bed, wrapping my robe about me. I went to her. She had tears in her eyes; taking my hand, she raised it to her lips before I could stop her, kissing it fervently.

"Cabrera is right," she whispered. "Torquemada told him that God Himself watches over you. He has a special plan for Isabella of Castile."

I drew my hand away. A sudden chill ran through me. "Don't say that. I . . . I don't like to hear such things. Girón perished of an illness. There is no divine plan at work here, just an everyday, average death." Yet even as I spoke, relief and gratitude filled me. I had won. I had thwarted both Juana and Villena.

"Can you honestly say God had nothing to do with this?" said Beatriz.

I frowned. "Of course He did. God has everything to do with everything, but I am no more special than any of His children. I am mere dust, as are all mortal beings. Do not make out this terrible act to be part of some grand plan, because it is not. It cannot be. I would not have any man, even one as base as Girón, die because of me." I turned from her searching eyes. "Now, please fetch my breakfast. I am hungry."

She left me standing by the window. I gazed at the sky but the storks were gone. They often nested in towers throughout Castile. I'd seen an empty nest in Santa Ana, on the day I met Carrillo and my life changed forever. I had seen the flock the day before, as Girón took to his deathbed. Yet they were only birds, creatures of the air, beautiful, yes, but without souls. They could not be messengers of divine will. It was pagan even to consider it.

And yet the idea began to take root in my mind.

What if God did have a plan for me, after all?

THE CIVIL WAR between my brothers resumed with brutal intensity. Girón's death had shattered both Villena's aspirations and his credibility; having failed to secure a royal link through me and despised by the rebel movement he had once espoused, he hid at court at the king's side, insisting on his own Moorish guard any time he dared venture outside. The proposed alliance between Joanna and my brother also fell apart, and Alfonso's supporters seized numerous provinces, until all Enrique had left was a handful of minor loyal cities and his Segovia.

The land was charred, the harvest devastated, and our people crushed. Such trade as existed had been disrupted, the coinage so debased by Enrique's frantic approval of new mints for funds that merchants would only accept payment in kind for goods. Every day, Beatriz brought me a new anecdote of the realm's suffering, and every day, I wondered how long Castile could hold out before the earth itself began to crumble away into a chasm.

In August 1467, four months after my sixteenth birthday, Alfonso's army was spotted within a few miles of Madrid. Queen Juana flew into a panic and hurried us back to Segovia's alcazar. While Enrique, Villena, and their men went out to meet the rebel forces, the city bolted its gates and the cathedral bells ceased to toll, leaving Juana to pace her rooms like one of Enrique's leopards in its cage, waiting for word of the battle's outcome.

She had heeded Mencia de Mendoza's advice to send little Joanna to safety in the Mendoza fortress of Manzanares el Real, lest the rebels take Segovia. I was outraged by the intimation that Alfonso might harm a child but remained expressionless on my stool, my hands folded in my lap as I watched the queen. She had insisted I attend her.

Suddenly, she whirled to face me. "Our cause is just and God is on our side. I tried once before and was overruled by that pompous idiot Villena, but not this time. The moment Enrique returns with your brother's head in a sack, I *will* see you wed to my brother King Afonso." She held up a finger, as if to halt an objection I had no intention of presenting. "And don't dare cite the Cortes to me. I don't care whose approval you think we need. I'll drag you to Portugal myself, in chains. I'll see you married and sent far from this realm—forever."

Beatriz half-rose from her seat, glowering. Juana glared at her in return before she ordered her ladies, "Fetch your instruments! I will have music, dancing! This is a time of victory over our enemies. We must celebrate it."

Beatriz looked at me. I stared forward. The women feverishly strummed their lutes as Juana twirled about in her brocade, glistening with jewels, as if she were still the envied center of the court's attention. I marveled that she didn't feel my hatred for her, that it didn't turn her into a pillar of salt. I could taste brine in my mouth, feel it coursing in my veins, for now I understood how devoid of compassion she truly was. My brothers drew swords against each other at this very moment on a battlefield, the flower of Castile's manhood lying dead around them. Many more would be wounded. And what did our queen do?

She danced.

I would have walked out if I could. Instead I sat and endured, repeating under my breath a plea to Saint Santiago, warrior-patron of Spain, for our deliverance.

It came within hours, conveyed by Mencia herself, who rushed in with her coif askew on her head and her hair unraveling about her face. "The people forced the gates open! The battle is done. The king and Villena have fled. Segovia is lost!"

Juana froze midstep, fingers outstretched as if to grasp the last chord of music. Then she released an unearthly howl and flew at me. I leapt to my feet, kicking back my stool; she would have fallen on me had Beatriz not planted herself between us. Before I could move, she had seized Juana by her wrist.

"Touch her," Beatriz said coldly, "and I'll see to it that King Alfonso drags *you* to Portugal in chains."

Juana was panting; I could see her teeth from where I stood behind Beatriz, by my overturned stool. Mencia said urgently, "Your Grace, please, there's no time. We must leave now. Once the rebels arrive, who knows what will happen to us?"

Juana was staring at me. She pulled her arm from Beatriz. "You stay," she said in a strangled voice. "Stay here to welcome them, you treacherous bitch."

"We never had any intention of leaving," replied Beatriz. She stayed in front of me like a shield as the queen gave me one final, searing look.

Then she and her women hastened out. Within minutes, the apartments were silent. It seemed as if a hush had fallen over the entire alcazar, all of Segovia; over Castile itself.

"We must go up," I finally said.

Beatriz gave me a puzzled look. "Up?"

I grabbed her by the hand. "Yes, up to the battlements—to watch them enter!"

THE HEAT ENVELOPED us like steam from a cauldron, undulating across the stretch of dry plain visible from where we stood on the keep. I saw sunlight flare on armor as the meandering line of bedraggled standards, horses, and men lumbered into view, moving toward the city. Putting my hand to my brow, I strained to see past the haze of dust kicked up by hundreds of hooves and feet.

"Can you see him?" Beatriz asked anxiously. "Is Alfonso there?"

I started to shake my head, standing on tiptoes and peering further over the waist-high wall. And then I caught sight of him—at the head of his army, his hair an unmistakable disheveled white-gold. Behind him rode Carrillo in his red cloak.

Together with Beatriz, I raced back down the staircase into the alcazar, my skirts clutched above my ankles as I ran through the empty corridors, forlorn and echoing *salas,* down into the courtyard, where I came to a breathless halt in time to see my brother ride through the gates with his battle-worn men.

The courtyard was crowded with citizens who'd come to seek refuge, terrified for their safety now that a rebel army was in the city. As my brother dismounted, they went in unison to their knees. As he looked about, I too dropped into obeisance. When he strode toward me, I caught my breath.

He was fourteen—broader of shoulder but still slim of hip, graced by our Trastámara height. His features had become more angular, an amalgam of the strong traces of paternal ancestry and lithe beauty of our mother's Portuguese blood. Clad in a dented, blood-spattered breastplate, his sword sheathed at his side, he was like an avenging archangel come to life, and my words of greeting turned to dust in my throat.

Beatriz let out a cry of joy and ran to embrace him. Slowly, he swiveled about to peer at me, still on my knees. *"Hermana,"* he said, his voice cracking, "is that you?"

I took his extended hand and let him raise me to my feet. I started to kiss his hand, in respect for the kingship he now claimed, but his arms, lean and hard, came about me and suddenly I was in my brother's embrace. A sob of relief escaped me.

"I'm here," he whispered. "I will see you safe. We're going home, Isabella."

CHAPTER ELEVEN

Arévalo's castle seemed impossibly small and bleak; I had forgotten how isolated from the rest of the world our childhood home was. Still, I felt only relief as Alfonso and I rode toward it, accompanied by Beatriz and Alfonso's ever-loyal governor, Chacón, as well as several other attendants. Luckily, my brother insisted on disposing of the large contingent of advisors he had lived with the past three years.

Carrillo had not been pleased by my brother's decision to return to Arévalo. He'd lectured Alfonso that his duty was to stay in Segovia and oversee the ousting of Enrique from his last vestiges of power. While our half brother and Villena remained at large, Carrillo warned, Alfonso's victory was not complete.

But to my surprise and great pride, Alfonso refused. "Enrique has suffered enough," he told Carrillo. "He's now an exile in his realm, obliged to seek sufferance from his few remaining vassals. I'll not humiliate him further. I want a stalemate decreed between us for the next six months. Tell him if he agrees to meet with us to discuss terms, I'll not seek further reproof. In the meantime, I will escort Isabella to pay a long overdue visit to our mother, who must be worried for us."

He would not be dissuaded, not even when Carrillo—now choleric and sweating in the alcazar's council chamber—thundered back with a litany of all the things he himself had neglected in order to dedicate himself heart and soul to Alfonso's cause.

"Then you mustn't neglect anything further," replied my brother. "Go attend to your see in Toledo and whatever else needs attending. We'll meet again in Ávila, after Epiphany."

He left Carrillo openmouthed, grabbing me by the hand and taking me from the chamber. When he muttered under his breath, "We could use some time apart. The man is a tyrant," I laughed out loud for the first time in as long as I could remember.

Only one deed marred our departure from Segovia. By the time Beatriz came to warn me and I'd rushed into the gardens to intervene, it was too late. Enrique's beautiful leopards, which had languished during the years of war, cared for by loyal Cabrera to the best of his ability, lay dead in the pen, pierced by arrows. Alfonso stood over them with his bow in hand; as I reached the fenced wall, breathless and in anguish to see the spotted, bloodied bodies sprawled at his feet, he looked at me, his expression disconcertingly blank.

Cabrera stood nearby, ashen, clearly affected by the animals' senseless death; yet when I started to remonstrate, he shook his head. Without his needing to say a word, I understood this was my brother's sole act of vengeance, the only way he had found to vent his rage and grief over an adolescence spent fighting for an inheritance that was his by right. Though he had shown mercy to Enrique, through the leopards he had sent a message our half brother could not ignore.

I turned away. But it took weeks before I could close my eyes and not see the dead leopards or feel the pain that had driven Alfonso to such an act.

And now we were home. Arévalo had been restored to my mother, who had returned from her cloister in Santa Ana. As we rode under the gatehouse, the servants came out to greet us with tears, their faces marked by time and the uncertainty they'd lived through.

I almost cried myself as Doña Clara held me close. *"Mi querida niña,"* she said, "look at how beautiful you are—a woman grown, so like your mother."

She put her dry, gnarled hands on either side of my face. She had aged visibly; she seemed much frailer than the domineering *aya* I remembered from childhood.

"How is she?" I asked.

She shook her head sadly. "Doña Elvira died while we were in Santa Ana. The poor dear caught a fever. She went without pain, but of course your mother was devastated. She's not yet recovered, though she's eager to welcome you. She's waiting now in the hall."

A knot filled my throat. "Take me to her," I said. I left Beatriz in the arms of her father, Don Bobadilla, and Alfonso grinning as his favorite hound, Alarcón, leapt up to lick his face, and I walked into the castle, where, despite the recent occupancy by Enrique's vassals, nothing seemed to have changed.

When I saw my mother standing by the greenery-filled hearth, I had a vivid recollection of those times when I'd approached her in dread of her spells. A remnant of that fear clung to me, prickling along my nape. But in September's saffron light spilling through the hall's windows my mother looked beautiful, dressed in her outdated court velvets and tarnished gems. Only as I neared her did I see the febrile glitter in her eyes, a sign that she had required one of her calming drafts, and she was too gaunt, her collarbones marking her skin under her chemise, her ruby bracelets dangling from brittle wrists.

"Hija mía," she said, with an absent smile, as I kissed her cheek. She did not seem to hear my greeting, her gaze focused past me to the threshold, where Alfonso laughed with the man-servants who'd cared for his dogs.

She said, "See? Didn't I tell you that Alfonso would avenge us? Look at him: My son is king of Castile. At long last, our place has been restored. Soon we can take up our estate at court and leave this horrible castle forever."

She spoke in pride, and when Alfonso came to her and she fervently embraced him, he made no mention of any hardship. After supper, we sat before the hearth, I at my mother's side and Beatriz at her father's, Doña Clara knitting in the background, as Alfonso regaled us with tales of chivalric valor worthy of El Cid, describing how he had fought Enrique single-handedly, embellishing their skirmishes into an epic struggle. My mother leaned forward in her chair, clapping her hands to emphasize her delight at the vanquishing of the man she held responsible for our woes. As night fell over Arévalo, she became visibly exhausted and Alfonso escorted her to her rooms. She clung to his arm, as though she were a child.

I remembered how he'd once stayed as far from her as he could. I sat in contemplative quiet as Beatriz and Bobadilla bid us good night, leaving me with my *aya*. At length she said, "Alfonso has made her happy. Some mothers want nothing more than a son they can depend on."

"He didn't tell her the truth," I replied. "He didn't tell her what really happened or what might yet happen. Alfonso isn't king of Castile yet."

"You and I know that, but she doesn't need to; she wouldn't know what to do with the truth anymore." Doña Clara set aside her yarns. "You, on the other hand, appear to thrive on it. That inner fortitude you showed as a child has made you into someone she can no longer influence or control. Be grateful you've escaped her at long last. Better she look to your brother now for the respite she needs from this vale of tears."

She forced herself to her feet with an aged person's groan and trudged to the hall sideboard, unlocking one of the doors to remove a leather-and-brass casket. She set it in my lap. It was surprisingly light, despite its armorial appearance.

"The Jews make these, to store important documents and money," she explained. "I bought it for you in Ávila when the letters started to arrive."

"Letters?" My hand poised over the lid.

"Yes." She met my gaze. "Go on, open it. See for yourself."

I couldn't contain my gasp when I saw the pile within, tied with ribbon. "There must be a dozen, at least!"

"Twenty-four, to be exact; I counted each one. Whatever you said must have impressed him. Once they started coming, they never stopped. He sent them by courier to Santa Ana." She chuckled. "It must have cost him a fortune to use a private messenger to cross Castile. He's determined, this prince of Aragón. I'll leave you to read them. No doubt he has quite a lot to say."

Alone in the hall, I cracked the seal of the first letter in the pile. His unrefined handwriting leapt at me in the flickering candlelight, the entire page covered with words:

My dearest lady,

When I received your letter, it was all I could do to not abandon my land and my father's fight against the wolves of France to run to

your side. I am unable to sleep, to eat; all I do is think of you, fighting off your own wolves in your brother's court, who seek to quench
your spirit. Yet as I cannot be there to draw my sword for you and
strike at the hearts of all who wish you harm, I can only tell you that
I know in my soul that you are much braver than even you realize.
You must withstand this marriage they propose for you, for with
God's grace you and I must meet again and discover if we are bound
by the same fate. . . .

I went completely still.

Fernando had not forgotten me. This was his reply to my anguished
letter sent more than a year earlier from Madrid as I awaited Girón's
arrival. Somehow, Fernando had known he couldn't risk sending it to
me directly, so he dispatched it to my mother's cloister instead. And he
had not stopped. I read his other letters, the candles guttering low as
night deepened, Alfonso's hound slumbering at my feet. I was astounded by how closely the prince of Aragón had watched over me
from afar. He was apprised of every event in my life since we'd last seen
each other, even amidst his own trials, which he related with an unvar-
nished candor that only illustrated his inner strength.

His mother had died, finally, after a long and terrible illness. Barely
had he and his father found time to grieve for her before they were
plunged into war once more with the perfidious French. Though not
yet fourteen at the time, Fernando had led an army against King Louis
to defend the contested border counties of Roussillon and Cerdagne,
rousing his men to incredible bravery against the invading forces. Severely outnumbered, he lost the battle. Now, with Aragón's treasury in
arrears and the people in near-revolt, with the French gnawing at the
kingdom like the ravenous wolves they were at heart, Fernando had to
fortify his borders and guard against further incursions, all while contending with his father's crippling blindness, which had in effect, if not
title, left him the ruler of his embattled realm.

"We've summoned a Jewish physician," he wrote,

trained in the Moors' healing arts, of which we have heard marvels.
It is said this physician once cured a caliph of Granada of the same

ailment my father suffers—indeed, that he can perform miracles with the removal of cataracts. He has expressed confidence that Papa's eyesight can be improved; however, it is a dangerous procedure involving four separate surgeries with needles, and I worry. My father is past his sixtieth year, weakened in heart and soul by my mother's passing. Yet he insists it must be done. He says he will not be an old blind man on the day that you and I wed.

I smiled as I read this; it was so like him. Indeed, every line of every letter conveyed the same unswerving belief that in the end, he would prevail. And at the bottom of each letter, as if to emphasize this fact, he ended with the same words:

Be brave, Isabella. Wait for me.

It wasn't until I'd read the last letter that I realized I'd spent the entire night immersed in his words. Already the darkness lightened around me; the candles had gone out, except for the last one flickering by my side, which I'd relit several times, singeing my fingertips in the process. As it dissolved in a pool of molten wax, I sat with the casket on my knees and closed my eyes, imagining the laughing, exuberant boy I'd met so briefly in Segovia. Now he was a man I did not know, so how could I feel as if he were such an integral part of me? No matter how much I tried to tell myself I was foolish and overly sentimental to entrust my future to a confident promise, an irresistible smile, and a spontaneous dance, in truth that was what I had done. He had taught me something about myself. He had shown me I could trust my own instincts and carve my own path. And instinct told me that despite the distance between us and the many challenges we faced, there was no one in this world better suited to share my life.

Come what might, Fernando of Aragón and I were destined for each other.

CHAPTER TWELVE

The snows came early, drifting from leaden November skies, covering the *meseta* in a cold white mantle. I'd always loved the start of winter, forgetting that the creeping chill would eventually turn so bitter it would seem to freeze my breath in my lungs. This winter was especially poignant. Though it might seem as if we'd escaped danger to return to the safety of our former life, it was an illusion I feared would be dispelled sooner than anyone thought.

Still, we reveled in our freedom, saddling the horses every day to ride out with Don Chacón, who told us of how he'd stayed steadfast at my brother's side, despite Villena's efforts to discredit him.

"Archbishop Carrillo is a man I can respect," said Chacón, his black eyes fierce in his bearded countenance. "After all, as a priest his task is to supervise the infante's well-being. But that marquis is a devil; he did everything he could to corrupt Alfonso. I even caught him trying to sneak into Alfonso's bed one night. You've never seen a man look as surprised as he did when he tripped over me on my pallet, dagger in hand."

I glanced at Beatriz. After what we'd witnessed at court this revelation about Villena was not surprising. I'd suspected he exerted some type of intimate hold over Enrique; now, I knew what it was.

Chacón went on. "His Highness said it wasn't the first time, either. Villena and his brother Girón both apparently behaved like boy-loving Moors whenever the mood overtook them. Disgusting, if you ask me; who needs further proof that they are damned?" He spat on the ground before he paused, flushing. "Your Highness must forgive me," he muttered. "I've grown unaccustomed to the company of ladies, it seems."

I offered him a reassuring smile. "I understand. Your loyalty to my brother is commendable, Don Chacón. He is fortunate you were there to watch over him."

"I would die for Alfonso. As I would for Your Highness. I will always put you and your brother first, before all other considerations."

As he cantered forward to catch up with my brother, who was busy hunting, Beatriz said, "Do you still doubt Girón was struck down for his evil ways?"

"No." I watched my brother veer his horse, Chacón close behind. Alfonso swiftly raised and shot his bow, catching a startled hare in midleap. "But that doesn't mean the evil died with him. Villena is still alive and he controls Enrique entirely."

"Is this why you've been so quiet of late? Are you worried for Alfonso?"

"How can I not be?" The hare twitched as Alfonso lifted it by its hindquarters, trickling beads of scarlet onto the cold white ground. "Castile still has two kings."

Beatriz eyed me, much as she had on the day we'd learned Girón was dead. I turned from her questioning gaze to pat Canela, who was eager to stretch his muscles after having spent too much time, like us, pent up in Segovia's alcazar. "*Brr!*" I said. "Come, Beatriz, I'll race you back. Last one there has to pluck the pheasants for supper."

Beatriz cried out that it wasn't fair, for I had the faster horse, but she took the challenge anyway and we streaked onto the plain toward the huddled township and castle, laughing aloud, the wind biting our cheeks and billowing our skirts.

For a brief time, I forgot that out there, somewhere, Enrique must be plotting his revenge.

THE NATIVITY ARRIVED with howling winds and snowstorms so blinding they turned the world beyond our gates into an impassable white void. Inside the icy castle we piled logs in the hearths, exchanged homemade gifts, and played games and music to pass the time. Shortly after Epiphany, my mother had one of her spells—the first she'd exhibited since our return. She insisted she heard ghosts wandering in the passageways, and one night fled barefoot in her shift onto the battlements. She might have frozen to death had Doña Clara not been awake and followed her out. Still, it took all of our combined persuasions—and Chacón's brute strength—to force my mother back inside. By then she was blue with cold, her feet and hands frostbitten.

After that, we restored the outside lock on her door and I stayed in her rooms on a cot, in case she awoke in the night. Though I hoped the spell would pass as it usually did, instead she grew worse. She fought us as we cured her hands and feet, saying she deserved to lose her limbs for her sins, growing so agitated we had to force calming drafts down her throat. Afterward, she sat in silence and stared at nothing, while I coaxed her into taking mouthfuls of broth, lest she starve.

Her withdrawal must have reminded Alfonso of our childhood, when he had shared a house with a mother he could not understand. He began to escape outside as often as he could despite the wind and snow, mending the animal pens, keeping the stables clean and warmed with braziers, and brushing and exercising the horses. As soon as the weather improved, he resumed his hunting, sometimes from morning till dusk, returning laden with early spring quail, partridge, and rabbit.

In April, I turned seventeen—a quiet birthday, like so many before. My mother had not left her rooms in months, oblivious to the birdsong heralding the long-awaited thaw. To keep busy, I supervised the cleaning of the entire castle. I set the maids to beating dust from our faded tapestries and carpets, boiling our linens in thyme-sweetened water, and airing our musty clothes. I had every floor scrubbed; even the privies did not escape my attention. I worked right alongside the servants, despite Doña Clara's admonition that I'd chafe my hands, and collapsed exhausted into my bed every night, too tired to dream.

A courier came in June, bearing word from Carrillo. Though misfortune had dodged Enrique all winter, leaving him to wander Castile on his horse and seek refuge from whoever would open a door to him, with the advent of spring he had resurfaced in Madrid, where he refused to concede defeat. He had sent Queen Juana into semi-captivity in a remote castle when he discovered she was pregnant by a lover and he relayed to Carrillo that he now believed Joanna was not his child. He was willing to name Alfonso heir, but only if Alfonso refuted any right to call himself king while Enrique lived. To bolster Enrique's stance, Villena had bribed most of the grandees back to the king's side and circulated pamphlets among the people declaring that Alfonso had illegally usurped the throne. Carrillo warned it was only a matter of time before everything collapsed; he was on his way to escort Alfonso to Toledo, where they could plan their defense.

Civil war loomed once more but this time, I would not be left behind. When Carrillo arrived with his retainers, I stood with Beatriz in the courtyard, our saddlebags packed and our horses ready. The archbishop scrutinized me from under his heavy brows, astride an enormous destrier that dwarfed my Canela. Carrillo's stout cheeks were rubicund from the June sun, his forehead dripping sweat under a wide straw hat like those peasants wore to till the fields.

"I suppose this means you're accompanying us?" he said without fanfare, as though we'd seen each other the previous week.

I nodded. "From now on, wherever my brother goes, so must I."

He guffawed. "Yes, Arévalo's no place to hide. I hear Afonso of Portugal is still eager for your hand. He's even offered Villena a country in Africa if you consent. We can't have them marrying you off to that conniving fool."

I didn't dignify him with a response. I had no doubt he'd have married me off to the conniving fool without compunction if it would secure Alfonso's throne. In his eyes, I was just another infanta to be used. I turned from him to embrace Doña Clara.

She held me close. "I'll see to your mother," she whispered, "I promise."

Mounting Canela, I followed Alfonso out.

A LAVENDER TWILIGHT tinted the sky around the walls of Ávila, our first stop on the road to Segovia, when young Cárdenas, one of Carrillo's favored pages, who hailed from the southern province of Andalucía, appeared on the road. He'd been sent ahead to the city to ensure that our lodgings were ready; he now materialized on his pony like a phantom, his face bone-white as he uttered terrifying words: "Plague has struck Ávila. We must turn away."

My heart started to hammer. The dreaded pestilence had made an early appearance this year; it was usually a bane of autumn. Carrillo barked orders at his retainers, ordering us to the nearby township of Cardeñosa, where we'd spend the night before departing at first light.

"We will eat and drink only what we carry," he said as we dismounted, saddle sore and weary. "Anything else could be contaminated."

Alfonso grimaced. "Who has ever caught plague from soup? I'm not going to bed on nuts and dried rabbit after riding all day. Find someone who can serve us a proper meal."

Carrillo sent men ahead to seek out lodgings; the town mayor eagerly offered his own house, and there he served us a late supper of fresh-caught trout, cheese, and fruit. It was the best he could manage on short notice and we were grateful for it. Exhausted, we retired to our quarters, where Beatriz and I stripped to our shifts and fell fast asleep.

Urgent knocking at our door startled us awake. It was Cárdenas. The archbishop wished to see me at once, he said. I threw on my soiled clothes and yanked my hair into a net, following the fair-haired page downstairs. Through the windows of the hall where we'd dined last night, I glimpsed dawn gilding the horizon.

Carrillo waited at Alfonso's door. I took one look at his face and my knees weakened. He opened the door without a word. Inside, motionless on the bed in his shirt and hose, was my brother. Chacón knelt at his side; at my entrance, he looked up. The anguish in his eyes tore at me.

"I found him like this," he whispered. "He went to bed as usual, teasing me that I'd be cold in my cloak on the floor. But when I tried to wake him, he didn't respond. He . . . he doesn't seem to hear me."

I couldn't take a step forward. I strained my gaze toward Alfonso, seeking out the telltale buboes of plague, my throat so tight I could barely breathe.

"There are no sores," Chacón said, sensing my fear. "He has no fever. If it's the pestilence, I've never seen it manifest like this."

I forced myself to move to the bed. Alfonso was so still he resembled a sculpture; I was certain he must be dead. I dug my nails into my palms, bending over him as Beatriz whispered anxiously from behind me, "Is he . . . ?"

I nodded. "Yes, he's breathing." I touched his hand; his flesh was chilled, as though he had slept outside. I looked at Chacón in bewilderment. "If it's not plague, then what can it be? What is wrong with him?"

"Show her." Carrillo's voice was inflectionless. I watched Chacón pry open my brother's mouth, exposing a blackened tongue. I could not contain my gasp. And as I turned to meet Carrillo's relentless stare, I already knew what he would say.

"This is Enrique's doing. Your brother has been poisoned."

BEATRIZ, CHACÓN, AND I took turns sitting vigil at his bedside. Helpless, we watched as a local physician, summoned by Carrillo, bled Alfonso. The blood ran sluggish; the physician sniffed it several times before muttering that he found no evidence of poison. My brother's tongue was swollen but no longer black; this sole sign of improvement was belied by his increasing stiffness, as if his life were leaving him in slow, inexorable stages.

After a full day and night, I was swaying with exhaustion on my stool and Beatriz finally insisted I go to the hall to eat something with Chacón, whom I'd sent out earlier. But I did not get farther than the passageway before I heard her cry out.

She stood trembling by the bed. As I came to her side, I saw Alfonso staring at us, his eyes vivid blue in the marble pallor of his face. His mouth hung open; from deep within his throat came a choked gurgle. Black fluid burst from his mouth and his nose; his body jerked in a spasm, his face contorting.

Then he went still.

"Blessed Virgin, no," whispered Beatriz. "No, please. It cannot be."

I felt a strange calm, almost as if I had gone numb. I knew my brother was gone but I took his wrist anyway, as I'd seen the physician do, to check his pulse. Then I quietly cleaned his face of the vile fluid and folded his hands across his chest.

"I love you, Alfonso," I whispered as I kissed him for the last time. My hand quivered only slightly as I closed his eyes.

"You must tell the others," I said to Beatriz. "His body must be prepared."

She retreated. I went to my knees to pray for his immortal soul, for he had not received Extreme Unction before death. I didn't weep, though I had expected the grief to plunge me into an abyss. He had not yet reached the end of his fifteenth year—a beautiful prince imbued with endless promise, cut down in the very prime of his life.

I had lost my beloved brother. My mother had lost her only son.

Castile had lost its hope.

Yet as I knelt by his deathbed, hearing the clamor echoing in the hall—the cries of his servants and Carrillo's ranting disbelief—all I could think was that I had become Castile's new heir.

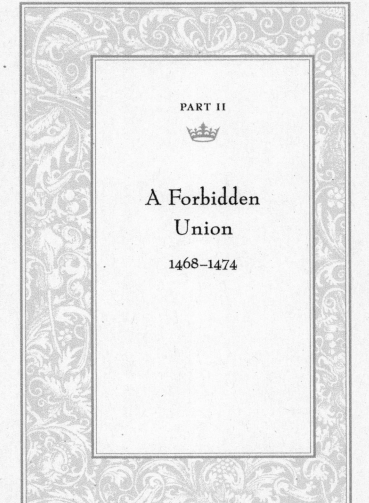

PART II

A Forbidden
Union

1468–1474

CHAPTER THIRTEEN

P*rincesa*, you must answer me. They are here again. They are waiting."

The abbess's voice reached me as if from across a vast divide. I slowly
turned from where I knelt before the altar in Santa Ana's chapel; I'd
gone there every day since my brother's funeral, searching for a peace
that eluded me.

I saw in her firm stance that this time, she would not take no for an
answer. I'd decided to seek refuge in the Convent of Santa Ana in Ávila,
despite Beatriz's terror of the plague and Carrillo's demand that I fulfill
my duty. I saw my brother's corpse conveyed to the Franciscan monastery in Arévalo, veiled his body as the monks chanted the Vespers for
the Dead. After he was entombed in a temporary niche and I paid for a
funerary monument to be built, I proceeded to the castle to break the
news to my blank-eyed mother. She turned away, walking back into her
chamber without a word. I knew her grief would come later, plummet-
ing her into an inconsolable abyss, and I left orders with Beatriz that my
mother was not to be left alone, not even when she slept, lest she do
some harm to herself.

As for me, I did not care that Ávila was quarantined, so desperately
did I need to escape. As it turned out, the sick were in the poorer sections of the city and the sisters welcomed me with open arms, aware as
only nuns can be that in those days of tumult and grief what I most
needed was a place of solitude, where I could reflect.

Immured behind bolted gates, I donned the white of mourning,
refusing all privileges to live as the nuns did, beholden to the daily toll
of bells. The numbness I'd felt at my brother's passing soon gave way to
visceral grief. I kept remembering him as he'd been when we were growing up in Arévalo, fascinated by the natural world around him; as a

youth enraptured by the hunt, who had a gift for soothing horses and dogs; and, finally, as the rebellious lost prince he would now forever be.

Eventually, acceptance sank in. The realization came that I must find a way to live, and this was my hardest challenge. Yet as the raw pain faded, I lay awake every night pondering what to do, fighting back near-paralyzing fear at the thought of Carrillo seeking to wield his power through me or of Enrique amassing an army to take me down while Villena and the other grandees plotted to destroy me.

I had read enough of our history to know that if female succession was not forbidden in Castile as it was in Aragón, no one actually believed a woman capable of ruling. The few who had succeeded had encountered relentless opposition, sacrificing everything to retain their tenuous power. In the end, none had lived a happy life; all had paid a price for the right to call themselves queen.

Was this what God required of me?

The question burned in my mind. If I forsook my right as Enrique's heir, agreeing instead to uphold the oath sworn to Joanna as princess, I would condemn Castile to chaos, to the rapacity of those like Villena. They would set Joanna on the throne after Enrique's death and marry her off to some prince they could manipulate, ransacking the realm as if it were their private larder until there was nothing left. But if I chose to fight then I would brand Joanna with the stigma of illegitimacy for the rest of her life. I'd face the same forces that had turned my brothers into enemies, that had already cost Castile so much.

Neither choice would give me happiness. Yet after a month of prayer and private turmoil, after repeatedly denying entrance to the lords who came to the convent doors every week to request audience with me, I finally came to one inescapable truth.

What I wanted did not matter. Not when so much was at stake.

I looked at the abbess, who'd cared for me with such tenderness, never once advising me yet always affirming by the manner she addressed me—*princesa*, a title reserved for a recognized heir—what she believed I must do.

"I will see them today," I told her and she nodded, turning away to prepare the room where I would meet my fate. I genuflected and stood.

On this day I would truly become the princess—but only on my terms.

FOUR MEN WAITED in the receiving room above the cloisters: Carrillo was one, along with Bishop Mendoza, whom I was grateful to see, and a secretary at the table armed with quill and paper. Though Mendoza served as advisor to Enrique, I had not forgotten his kindness toward me. The fourth occupant was none other than Villena, doused in expensive musk and wearing gold-slashed black velvet, his sulfuric eyes alight, as though he were about to receive a reward. Did he actually think I'd be happy to see him, after everything he had done?

Carrillo bustled over to me. "We are so pleased to see Your Highness in good health," he said, bowing over my hand. His deference took me aback; as I watched the others bow, all of a sudden my confidence vanished. I was not sure I could assert myself before these men, after having been disregarded for so long.

"We were concerned," said Villena, his solicitous tone at odds with his cold stare. "We feared Your Highness might neglect her obligations indefinitely."

I recalled the afternoon when he and Girón had stormed into the *sala* in Segovia to menace Enrique, and I knew that he hadn't come to ascertain whether I'd enter the fray. He was here to gauge my readiness and discover any weaknesses as well as any strengths. No doubt he'd already relegated me to another arranged marriage; I could envision his sneer as he informed me as much. After all, once I was summarily disposed of the road lay open to whatever ambitions he nursed. He had a son, I recalled. Perhaps he had already started to plot a way to wed the boy to Joanna? It was the next logical step, if he had, in fact, bribed someone in Cardeñosa to slip poison into my brother's cup. . . .

At this thought, my hands clenched at my sides. My words burst from me: "I would never neglect so sacred an obligation as my duty, undeserving as I am. I have not taken this time to indulge but rather to reflect on the events that led me to this pass. Though I mourn my late brother the Infante Alfonso as only a devoted sister can, I tell you now that I've searched my conscience and believe with all my heart that while King Enrique lives, no other can stake claim to his crown. Perhaps if Alfonso had had better counsel, he might have realized the same and this realm would not have been sundered by tyranny, nor its people forced to suffer so much. And Heaven itself would not have seen fit to show its displeasure with these actions, which I believe lent a hand in Alfonso's demise."

I paused for breath. Carrillo had recoiled from me, but I saw the subtle approval in Mendoza's gaze and the smoldering fury in Villena's.

I continued before anyone could stop me. "And so I ask you now, my lords, with all due humility, return this kingdom to my brother Don Enrique and restore peace to Castile. I am content with the title of princess of Asturias, heiress to the realm, may our sovereign King Enrique long reign over us."

It was done. I stood with my chin raised, amid deafening silence. Mendoza was the first to speak. "Your Highness is wise beyond her years. Is it truly her wish that we convey these sentiments to our king?"

"It is," I replied.

He nodded, turning at once to depart. The secretary—with my words on his parchment—hastened out behind him. Villena bowed curtly and followed. I felt assured that Mendoza would do his utmost to convey my true messages to Enrique and not twist my words into another nefarious scheme, as Villena's devious mind might.

Archbishop Carrillo stared at me with narrowed eyes before he let out an acid chuckle. "That was excellent. You almost convinced me. A diplomat could not have done better—you have bought us the time we need to devise our strategy."

I moved to the chair vacated by Mendoza's secretary, sitting with composure as Carrillo extracted a clutch of papers from his satchel and dropped it on the table before me.

"Here are letters from various cities, promising to support your bid for the throne. Segovia remains undecided, of course; but I'm sure that once you declare your intent it will follow suit. Your brother's cause was just and—"

"I have declared my intent," I said, without looking at the letters.

He snorted. "To that fool Villena, perhaps, but of course you'll not leave undone what we've struggled these past four years to attain. Alfonso cannot have died in vain."

"Alfonso died because God did not allow him to live." I stood abruptly, facing him. "He was struck down because he sought the throne of an anointed king. It was God's judgment; I, my lord Archbishop, will not incur the same."

His mouth tightened. I had a sudden recollection of the day he'd come upon me in the gardens of this convent, of how indomitable he'd seemed. I had been afraid of him then, and I still was, in some ways; but I had learned by now that it would serve me nothing to show it. Carrillo would feed on my fear. His entire existence depended on my subservience.

"Are you telling me you *meant* what you said? You would actually throw everything away to suit some girlish notion of divine wrath?"

"Call it what you will. I will not lie; I will not be the cause of further strife. If I am to succeed to the throne, I must do so in good conscience, not by the blood of innocents."

"Conscience!" He banged his fist on the table. "What about Enrique's conscience, eh? What about the lies he's told, the falsehoods he's promulgated? He took you from your mother to lock you away at court, elevated a bastard to the succession, and may have had your brother poisoned. Would you leave his harlot queen to steal what is rightfully yours?"

I glanced at his clenched hand. For a paralyzing moment I remembered a scene from my childhood, a chilling memory of a man behind my father's throne, reaching over to touch his shoulder. . . . And then I recalled Carrillo himself, setting a hand on Alfonso's shoulder as the world broke apart around us, steering him away from me, toward revolt, insurrection, civil war, and chaos.

Toward death.

I did not want to end up like my father or my brothers—a puppet ruler, prey to the shadows lurking behind me. Yet that could be my fate, if I did not choose my path carefully from this day forth. Every step I took could lead me to glory or tragedy; every choice I made had a consequence. My fate was in my hands.

"You forget with whom you speak," I finally said. "I am the heiress of Castile now, and as such, perfectly capable of making my own decisions." I had already turned to the door when I heard him say through clenched teeth, "If you refuse to espouse our cause, how do you expect me to protect you? For heiress or not, they *will* come after you; they'll force you into marriage with Portugal and exile you for the rest of your life. You'll never rule here, not if they have their way."

I took a long moment before I turned back to him. "If you want to protect me, then negotiate a treaty with Enrique that secures my rights. I want to sign it in person with him, so no one can accuse me of treason. You can also help me set up my own household, separate from the court. I do not wish to reside there."

His scowl indicated he'd not anticipated taking orders this day. "Anything else?"

I paused, hearing Fernando's voice in my head, as clearly as if he stood beside me.

Be brave, Isabella.

"Yes." I looked the archbishop in the eye. "You say they will force me to marry against my will. What if I stipulate in my treaty with Enrique that both the Cortes and I must first approve any match suggested for me?"

"Approve?" He scoffed. "It's never been seen before, a princess deciding whom she should wed. Political necessity, not personal desire, dictates the foundation of royal union."

"I wouldn't dare argue the point," I replied. The calmness of my voice surprised me, for my heart was galloping in my chest. For the first time, I voiced aloud what, until now, had been only a secret possibility. "Political necessity is of course my primary consideration. As such, who better to be my spouse than the prince of Aragón?"

Carrillo's eyes widened.

"He is ideal," I added. "We're nearly the same age and share the same blood. He is a fellow Spaniard, not a foreigner who will yoke Castile to his realm. He is a warrior already, one who has led armies in defense of his kingdom; he would protect me, as I could protect him. With Castile and Aragón united, France would think twice about attacking and I would have a leader for my armies, if the need arose. I may not be permitted to don armor or take to the battlefield, but I wish to be respected as if I can. And surely he is worthy to——"

"Not here," Carrillo interrupted. "No Aragonese was ever deemed worthy in Castile, not for the position you would raise him to."

My smile faded. "I deem him worthy. That is enough. Or do you think like the rest of them?"

Carrillo went silent, considering. "If I did," he said at length, and I almost thought I saw a mordant smile tugging at his mouth, "would it make any difference? You appear to have made up your mind." He held up a hand, preempting me. "As it happens, I do not disagree. In fact, it is an excellent choice. King Juan has wanted such a match for years, as everyone knows, and Castile would benefit, if the prince himself is of equal mind . . . ?"

"He is," I said. "I know it."

"Then why delay?" Carrillo said softly. He inclined his head. "We'll add the stipulation you suggest to the treaty and send King Juan a private letter. Let fate take its course."

As he bowed, I resisted the laughter that threatened to erupt from me.

I could hardly believe it, but I'd just issued my first order as Castile's future queen.

CHAPTER FOURTEEN

Nobody knew why the four stone bulls of Guisando had been erected. They were older than recorded history, pagan and aloof, mute symbols of a time when Castile was a fragmented and unconsecrated land.

I found them fitting, nonetheless, the ideal witnesses to my first political triumph, if such it could be called. The bulls were situated a few miles from Ávila in a windswept valley, where covert ambush was impossible. On a balmy September morning, only two months after my brother's death, this is where I met with Enrique to seal our new accord.

As I rode toward the king, I felt perspiration pool under my elaborate gown, trussed and jabbed in a hundred different places by the excessive finery Beatriz had insisted I wear. She'd returned to me along with the chambermaid Inés de la Torre, who had disavowed her prior allegiance to Mencia and begged entry to my service. I saw no reason to refuse her; Inés had never actually betrayed me and I certainly had need of another pair of capable hands. As Beatriz pointed out with her usual candor, no other lady had volunteered to serve me, not with my future still so unsettled. Moreover, we needed Inés's skills as a seamstress. My gowns were too tight because I'd been dining on good convent fare and staying on my knees all day; I required an appropriately regal costume for my meeting with Enrique. Together with Inés, Beatriz set herself to letting out the seams of my purple velvet banded in silver filigree and adding a few panels of embroidered silk, along with new green satin sleeves trimmed in pearls. Over it, I wore a short cape lined in ermine—the unmistakable mark of royalty. I left my hair loose under a jeweled bonnet and caul; even my Canela was elaborately harnessed in a gilded halter and tooled leather bridle bearing my initials.

It was all for show, because in truth, I could barely afford the clothes on my back after having paid for Alfonso's obsequies, alongside the regular sums that went to the maintenance of my mother. But everyone kept saying I must present the proper image. The treaty Carrillo had hammered out with Enrique would, allegedly, provide me with enough income hereafter.

But I still felt ridiculously overdressed when I spied Enrique among his retinue, wearing a plain black tunic without a trace of finery to distinguish his person. He had aged; deep lines now scored the corners of his eyes, as if he'd been squinting too much in the sun, and his unkempt beard was liberally threaded with white. Nevertheless, he sat astride a magnificent white stallion—his sole concession to luxury—and he faced me without any outward sign of trepidation or fear.

I ordered Carrillo to halt. "You go and greet him. I'll follow behind with my attendants."

"No," hissed the archbishop. "Let him greet you first."

I shot him an exasperated look, tired of his insistence that we should always appear to hold the upper hand. I dismounted with the aid of a groom, and walked alone across the rocky ground to where Enrique waited. I resisted glancing at Villena and the other grandees who flanked him, certain I'd receive nothing but contemptuous looks in return. The last time Castile had had a queen was over two hundred years before, and she had not fared well.

To my relief, Enrique strode to meet me. "Hermana,"he murmured. He leaned close to kiss my cheek, exuding a pungent odor of horseflesh, sweat, and unwashed skin. "I was deeply saddened by Alfonso's death," he said, "but I am overjoyed to see you after so long."

His speech sounded rehearsed. I drew back as politely as I could, offering a wary smile in return. Now that we were together again, the memory of everything that had happened between us surged up in me, along with all the accompanying corrosive doubt. How could I ever trust this strange, malleable king, who had allowed so much to go wrong in his realm and led armies against his own brother, to defend a child he now assured everyone was not his?

"I am happy to see you, too," I finally said, acutely aware of his curious regard. I'd forgotten how much I must have changed as well. During my last two years at court, he had barely seen me, and I was no longer that impressionable young girl he must recall. At that moment, I was finally grateful for Beatriz's determination to outfit me in rich cloth; to Enrique, I must look as though I were about to assume his scepter and mount his throne.

A little fear, I had come to learn, went a long way toward instilling respect.

He pawed the ground with his boot, as if he'd stepped in something distasteful. His mouth turned inward, even as he said, "I am glad you've chosen to be obedient. As my heir, I will recognize you above all others, granting you the cities of Ávila, Medina del Campo, Escalona, and . . ." His speech faded. His expression assumed a pained uncertainty.

"Huete, Oviedo, Molina, Olmedo, and Ocaña," I prompted. "As well as the means to maintain my household in any of those cities where I deem fit, and the right to refuse any marriage proposals that do not meet with my express desire and the Cortes's approval." I quoted directly from the settlements outlined in our treaty and he blinked in owlish surprise. "Yes," he muttered. "Of course. Whatever you say."

"I want only what we agreed upon. I ask for nothing more."

The skin under one of his eyes twitched. Alarm crept through me; I suddenly heard the wind as it brushed over the hulking, lichen-spotted bulls, rustling the stunted pines nearby and snapping at the dark cloaks of the watching nobles.

Enrique had averted his gaze. I beckoned to Carrillo. As the archbishop marched to us with the treaty pinned to a portable desk held by Cárdenas, Villena slithered forth to assume his place beside Enrique, like an oily second shadow.

"If we are still in agreement . . . ?" rumbled Carrillo, making it clear that he'd prefer to throw the desk with the treaty aside and brandish his sword.

I looked directly at Enrique. My mouth went dry. For an impossibly long moment, he did not move, did not speak. Then, to my relief, he took up the inked quill.

"I hereby declare the succession of this kingdom for Doña Isabella my sister," he intoned, "who, by this document, will now be known as princess of Asturias and is thereby entitled to all properties, rents, and customs pertaining to said title. She is my sole legitimate heir, to be named queen after my death, as this document shall attest and as I shall see declared throughout the realm by proclamation and ratified by the official gathering of the Cortes."

He bent over the desk to scrawl his signature across the page. Villena produced the signet seal of Castile, stamping it in red wax and affixing it to the document.

"And I, Isabella," I said, when the quill was handed to me, "for the peace and repose of these realms, do hereby declare that the king my brother should have his title for as long as he shall live, while I, for the present, am content to be known as princess of Asturias, sole heiress of Castile."

I too signed.

While the seals dried and the ink was sanded, Enrique and I embraced, and then each of the grandees knelt before me to offer their oath of allegiance. I kept smiling, even as I reflected that by this one act, Joanna had been officially declared a bastard, barred forever from the succession. How much harder would Queen Juana's hatred against me burn, once she learned of this? What would little Joanna think of me, the aunt she had trusted, when she grew old enough to understand exactly what I had done to secure my place?

It was for Castile, I told myself; for our peace and safety, for the memory of my dead brother, and for the royal blood in my veins, which was unsullied by the taint of adultery.

I refused to brood, returning to Ávila at Enrique's side to dine in the convent and celebrate our newfound accord. But in the back of my mind I kept seeing Alfonso, looking at me as he stood over the bloody corpses of the king's leopards.

👑

I ESTABLISHED MY household in the provincial city of Ocaña, in central Castile. It was not a major township; a dusty walled settlement on the edge of the *meseta*, Ocaña boasted a plaza, a parochial church, and crumbling Roman ruins. All in all, the city had barely two thousand inhabitants, but I needed money and its rents were the first I could draw upon as princess, while I waited for the creaking bureaucracy of the royal secretariat to implement my new status. Moreover, while not

as ancient as Toledo or celebrated as Segovia, Ocaña was situated in
such a manner that I could travel to either city once the Cortes assembled, yet it remained far enough away that I needn't guard my every
word. Here, there was no threat from eavesdropping courtiers eager to
curry favor with Villena or the king.

The city staged a lovely parade to receive me, bringing out its best
statue of the Virgin, dressed in blue velvet and lace, to bless my new
home—a gracious three-story mansion with exposed timber-beamed
ceiling and tiled rooms. The gallery opened onto an enclosed interior
courtyard with a fountain, surrounded by ceramic pots overflowing
with greenery. I appointed Chacón as my head steward; Beatriz became
my maid of honor, with oversight of my chambers, while Inés de la
Torre was named my lady-in-waiting. And Carrillo's seventeen-year-old
page, Cárdenas, with his large green eyes and thick blond curls, became
my principal secretary.

Thus did I settle into my first household as princess of Asturias.

Beatriz started visiting Segovia on a regular basis, to requisition tapestries, silverware, and other suitable furnishings for our home. I suspected she and Andrés de Cabrera had been corresponding in secret, a
suspicion soon confirmed when she returned one evening to inform me
that Andrés had finally asked for her hand in marriage.

"And you said . . . ?" I replied, hiding the sharp pang that pierced
me at the thought of losing her.

"I told him it was too soon. Maybe later, when Your Highness has
less need of me."

"Beatriz, I'll always have need of you. If you love this man as much
as he obviously loves you, then you must stop making excuses and follow your heart."

She regarded me with unabashed yearning. I'd never thought I
would actually see this day, when my stalwart friend could look so forlorn. I had to curb the urge to tease her when she added, "But we'd have
to reside in Segovia. He's still governor of the alcazar and overseer of the
royal treasury, though that devil Villena has tried more than once to
oust him from his position solely because of Cabrera's loyalty to you.
And how could I move so far away from you?"

"I daresay it won't be easy for either of us," I said softly, "but we'll manage." I clasped her hand, adding with a wink, "Besides, having you near the treasury could be a blessing. Who knows when the day will come when I have urgent need of it?"

She laughed. "Andrés will guard it with his life for you!" She embraced me, releasing the tears I had tried to hold back. "Perhaps it will be your turn next," she whispered. "I am sure that Fernando has not forgotten you."

As she went to write to Cabrera, I turned to the window, suddenly pensive. It had been two months since Carrillo had sent our proposal to Aragón; all we'd received in return thus far was a formal communiqué from King Juan, whose eyesight had been restored by the perilous surgery Fernando had written about. While he'd expressed keen interest in exploring the proposed union, he had not committed to anything definite. Carrillo assured me the delay had to do with my dowry arrangements. Aragón was perennially short of funds, and to wed a princess of Castile was no trifling matter. I hadn't liked the way Carrillo sniffed as he said this. I couldn't have cared less what Fernando brought to our marriage, providing I had his person, but Carrillo insisted on formalities being observed.

Fernando had also written to express his condolences over Alfonso and detail his ongoing struggle to regain the Pyrenean counties that Louis of France had usurped. But to my disappointment he made no mention of marriage. This was proper, of course, as the negotiations had to go through our appointed representatives, but still his omission hurt me far more than I'd expected. His letter seemed stilted and without his usual exuberance—almost as though he were reluctant—when I'd thought his very words would have leapt off the page in joy that I had finally broached the subject of our future together.

I began to fear something was amiss, so much so that I wrote to Fray Torquemada in secret to request his advice. After all, I was breaking my own treaty agreements with the king, because I should have first asked his leave before I even considered a marriage with Aragón. I had to know if I was making a grave error in judgment, if I had offended the Almighty by conspiring to woo Fernando behind Enrique's back.

Torquemada replied that he had already absolved me of all prior vows of obedience to the king because of Enrique's own misdeeds. He advised me again to trust in my faith to guide me.

My conscience absolved, I considered summoning Carrillo from his residence at Yepes to demand an explanation for the delay, but I didn't want him to know how much I had come to depend on this betrothal. I did not want anyone to think I nurtured romantic notions about a prince I'd met only once—notions I found hard to admit even to myself.

I thought of Fernando often, especially in the hours of the night. I wondered what he looked like now, how he fared, and if he ever thought of me. I had no illusion that he remained innocent of carnal knowledge. Men were not held to the same standard as women. While I didn't relish the idea of him bedding others, I told myself I could endure it, if I was assured he would be faithful to me once we were wed.

Once we were wed . . .

It had become my litany, my beacon of hope, but as time passed without word from Fernando I began to doubt. Situations changed, and as Carrillo had said, political necessity, not personal desire, dictated the foundation of a royal union. Perhaps, as heiress of Castile, I was destined for a more important match than the penurious heir of Aragón, no matter how appealing he might be to me personally. Perhaps I should be seeking a prince who had enough power and riches to both protect my inheritance *and* help me subdue my enemies.

Yet even as I considered it, I knew I couldn't envision being anyone else's wife. Rich or poor, Fernando was everything I needed: Persistence like his could forge nations, and I could rely on his strength, his courage, and his refusal to let anything, or anyone, stand in his way. I could still remember the way he'd beckoned me by the fountain, his daring whisper. In an instance of apparent frivolity, he had offered me a precious gift, one that had sustained me through the tumultuous passage of these years, through danger, fear, and hope.

And, most important, he would be my ally, not my master. He would share my vision of the future yet not seek to relegate me to the background. He understood that I must reign in Castile in my own right, as he must in his realm of Aragón. He would be my king-consort here, just as I would be his queen-consort there. Together we could unite our realms, yet remain independent, never forced to prove that one of us was stronger.

Fernando had taught me how to trust myself.

And now, God willing, we would trust in each other.

☙

IN OCTOBER 1468, Beatriz wed Andrés de Cabrera in Segovia. The ceremony was attended by all the prominent members of the court, as well as the king himself, as he wished to honor his loyal servant.

Beatriz looked radiant in a velvet dress of forest green, the color of constancy. Her abundant dark hair was wreathed with fresh flowers under a long silk veil, and my own rope of gray pearls—my wedding gift to her—was clasped about her throat. At her side Cabrera beamed so wide, it seemed the sun shone through him. His happiness caused me a moment of uncharitable envy, for I realized that my Beatriz, my childhood companion and lifelong friend, now belonged to him.

I observed Enrique during the festivities in the alcazar. I'd not seen him since the signing of our treaty at Guisando, and I found his odd darting glances at everyone but me, as well as his overall dishevelment, troubling. He looked as though he hadn't bathed in weeks and his anxiety was evident in the ceaseless drumming of his fingertips on the table. Villena was at his side, sleek and overdressed as ever, murmuring who knew what deviltry into Enrique's gullible ears.

When the tables were pulled back for the dancing, the marquis's reptilian gaze locked on me from across the dais with unmistakable intent. I froze. Would he actually have the temerity to ask me to dance? I'd hoped to use the distraction in the court to approach Enrique and ask about the Cortes, whose assembly, though promised at Guisando, had not yet materialized. Carrillo had refused to come with me to Segovia to discuss this very thing; instead he roared into Ocaña only hours before our departure, after having sent several bristling missives, to shout at me that it was all a ruse and Enrique never meant to gather the procurators together to legally declare me heir.

"If you go," he warned, "they'll take you prisoner. I've heard that that whore Juana gave birth to another bastard and is trying to wheedle herself back into Enrique's good graces. She escaped her captivity to find refuge with the Mendozas and now seeks rapport with Villena because he has the king's ear. If you go to Segovia, you will regret it."

I had paid him little attention for I was not about to miss my beloved friend's wedding. But as Villena sidled up to me on his high-heeled shoes, I braced myself for the worst. While he held Enrique's favor, I had to contend with him, but I would never let him bully me again, no matter what. The Cortes *must* be summoned. I would not accept anything less than a definitive date for an answer.

"His Majesty would have a word with Your Highness," Villena informed me in his irritatingly nasal voice, after a bow that was so cursory it bordered on insulting. "It is a matter of some urgency. Would tomorrow morning suit?"

I assented; relieved he'd made no move to escort me to the floor. "Naturally. Tell His Majesty I am at his disposal."

"That," he replied, "remains to be seen." Before I could respond he walked back to Enrique. As they whispered, Enrique looked at me for the first time that day.

The mistrust in his eyes chilled me to my bones.

I COULDN'T REST that night. I paced my rooms in the alcazar while poor Inés looked on, not knowing what to say or do to soothe me. She and I had not yet established a rapport, and though she served me with devotion, she was not my Beatriz. All she could think to do was brew endless drafts of chamomile, which, instead of producing their intended drowsiness, obliged me to pass water every half hour.

The walls of this gilded cage, where I had spent so much lonely and anguished time in my youth, seemed to close in around me. I kept seeing Queen Juana's malicious smile in my mind, hearing Mencia de Mendoza's triumphant laughter. Carrillo's words repeated in my head like the dread roll of an execution drum: *They will take you prisoner.*

Why had I come here, when I knew what Enrique was capable of? I should have given Beatriz my gift in Ocaña, explained I could not see her wed in person. She would have understood; no one desired my safety more than she. But instead I'd disdained Carrillo's warning. With habitual obstinacy, I'd refused to consider even for a minute that Enrique might go back on his word. Now I was trapped in his alcazar, just as I'd been during Alfonso's rebellion, with only Cárdenas and Chacón to protect me. Carrillo was miles away; even if I sent word now, by the time he cajoled his allies to action, it would be too late.

I would be captive once again.

By the time dawn crept over the horizon, I was ready to bolt from Segovia in my shift. I made myself take slow deep breaths as Inés dressed me. I chose a sedate blue velvet gown with draping canary-yellow sleeves and had Ines coil my hair into a tourmaline-studded net. Over my shoulders and bosom went an opaque silk partlet, edged in black lacework. The regalia afforded me a sense of protection as Cárdenas and Chacón escorted me to the private *sala* where Enrique awaited me.

As we neared the oak double doors set below an elaborate arabesque, I said to Chacón, "If I do not come out in an hour, send Cárdenas to the archbishop's palace at once."

Chacón nodded, and Cárdenas's beautiful green eyes fixed on me in adoration. I knew he would run barefoot to Yepes, if necessary, to alert Carrillo, and I felt a measure of relief that I was not without friends.

I entered the room to find Villena and Enrique waiting for me. There were no others present—no guards or attendants or hovering secretaries. I straightened my shoulders as I came before them. The very fact that I had been summoned here and they had cleared the room of prying ears and eyes indicated I was about to be dealt an upset.

"You have deceived me," Enrique declared, without preamble.

I met his gaze, recalling how quickly and irrationally his suspicions could escalate. "Deceived you?" I said, feigning calm. "How so, my lord brother?"

"You lied to me. You said you would obey me in all matters, but then you went behind my back to seek betrothal with Fernando of Aragón. Please, do not try to deny it. We intercepted several of your letters, though after we read them we resealed them and let them go on to King Juan." He tapped a finger on his throne's gilded armrest. "You are evidently very committed to the prince and I too, as you know, am fond of him, but, of course, I cannot allow it. You will not marry anyone without my permission."

Standing behind the throne, Villena smiled.

I stood silent, stunned. They had found out. How naïve I had been! I should have known they would be watching me like hawks. What would they do now? How could I escape whatever trap they had prepared for me?

When I finally spoke, I sounded hoarse. "I regret to have caused you distress, but by the terms of our treaty I do retain the right—"

"No." Enrique cut me off. "You have no right save that which I see fit to give you." He regarded me with an icy composure that was far more disconcerting than his previous flares of temper. He'd obviously been waiting a long time to enact this revenge; he was wilier than anyone had supposed. He had fooled us all.

"That treaty of ours," he continued, "was a farce, a grave insult to my dignity. I should have arrested the traitors and beheaded the lot. They left me a beggar in my own realm, forced to seek terms with those who abused my trust. I was humiliated."

This time, I could not stop myself from taking a step back as he stood, looming over me with his shoulders hunched, so immense he seemed to fill the room.

"Your brother should have died on the scaffold," he said. "He escaped my wrath but you, beloved sister—you shall not, not if you dare defy me again."

I couldn't take my gaze from him, not even when I heard Villena drawl, "The king was forced to sign the treaty of Guisando under duress. Princess Joanna, his child by his queen, is by right of birth the true heiress of Castile."

I said to Enrique, "So now you once again believe she is your daughter?"

He bit his lip; he'd not forgotten his confession to me years ago. But before I could exploit the advantage, Villena added, "But we are willing to keep you in the succession if you agree to marry where we deem fit."

"We?" I turned to him in stony disbelief.

"Yes." Villena tripped to a side table and took up a red leather portfolio. He brandished it in my direction. "Your Highness shall wed Afonso V, king of Portugal."

While his pronouncement was not unexpected—the queen had espoused this match for me before—it felt as if I'd been kicked in the stomach. Enrique had taken the path he knew I was least likely to accept, which meant there could be no doubt he sought revenge. Captivity would have been preferable; at least in a prison, I could hope for rescue. But marriage to the Portuguese king, often called El Africano for his seafaring exploits, brother to Queen Juana—it was exactly what Carrillo had warned me against. I would be a prisoner for life, barred from inheriting Castile, while Villena turned the realm into his private trough.

"No." I spoke before I knew it, a sudden core of strength taking shape inside me. "Absolutely not. Though I owe fealty to my king, I can never consent to such a match."

"Who are you, to speak thus?" spat Villena. "If we say you'll wed King Afonso, then you will. By all that is holy, either you obey us or you will suffer the consequences."

I met his stare. "By all that is holy, my lord, *you* are not my king."

"But I am." Enrique stared hard at me. "I am your king and brother; and I say you will do this. In fact, I command it."

I regarded him in silence. I saw nothing in his stance to denote any loss of control brought on through weeks of manipulation by Villena. Enrique was treating me as if I were one of his helpless creatures in his menageries, though I suspected he would have felt more for a captive animal's suffering than he did for mine.

In that moment my last remnant of affection for him, which I'd tried so hard to retain, which had kept me from assuming Alfonso's cause and inured me to Carrillo's disdain, was extinguished. I saw only a man unworthy to rule this ancient realm and I was not afraid anymore. Not of him.

"I will consider this request, as it comes from my king," I said, ignoring Villena. "Now, by your leave, may I depart for my house in Ocaña? The air here does not suit me."

Villena started to bark something but Enrique held up his hand. "No," he replied, without looking away from me. "Let her go. Send an escort with her to Ocaña. I believe she can just as easily consider my orders from there."

"Sire, she will try to escape," said Villena. "Remember, she is a liar; like all women, she has Eve's own cunning. Keep her here, under guard, until spring, when we are due to negotiate the terms of our Portuguese alliance—"

"I will not escape," I interrupted, keeping my gaze fixed on Enrique. "You have my solemn word as your sister."

He returned my stare for a long moment before he gave a curt nod. I sank to the floor in a curtsey. If they thought they'd cajoled me into submission, so be it.

For I would never let them seize control of my fate.

CHAPTER FIFTEEN

Villena undertook my escort to Ocaña, along with two hundred armed men. I kept my head high as we entered the city, where the people had gathered to welcome me back, the women and children with bouquets of autumn flowers and the men with their caps doffed. Their spontaneous cheers sputtered and faded when they saw me surrounded by pikes and helmets; their surprise soon turned to outright alarm when they found themselves playing unwilling host to Villena's posse, who would remain in Ocaña to ensure I did not flee.

Villena may not have dared to set his men in my palace but he'd managed to lure Mencia de Mendoza back into service. I found her waiting in my rooms the moment I entered. As she swept into a curtsey, she announced that she had been appointed my matron of honor by the king, now that Beatriz resided in Segovia with her husband.

Inés scowled. Our adventures at court had finally created a bond between us and her spine was rigid at the sight of the woman who had first hired her to spy and whom she had turned against in order to serve me.

"You will not attend my lady in her bedchamber," she announced. "That is my duty."

Mencia's lips pursed. She was about to say something no doubt disagreeable about her noble status and Inés's utter lack thereof, when I stopped her cold. "You will see to our supper now, Doña de la Cueva." My deliberate use of her married name and the order to perform a menial task did not go unnoticed; with another, stiffer curtsey, she stormed off.

"Sweet Mother save us," said Inés as she unfastened my cloak. "Why is she here?"

"The same reason she first sent you to me: to spy, of course." I went to my oak desk, wondering if Mencia had already rifled through it. Before I had left for court, I'd hidden a portfolio with copies of my letters to Fernando and his replies, as well as copies of the archbishop's correspondence with King Juan of Aragón, and my own with Torquemada; it was all in a secret compartment under the bottom drawer. To my relief, I saw that Mencia had not yet found it. But now that she was here, nothing in my palace would remain private for long.

"Inés," I said, and she turned to me, alert. I handed her the portfolio. "Give this to Cárdenas. Tell him to hide it in the stables." I allowed myself a smile. "I believe Mencia thinks of herself as too much of a lady to go digging in horse muck."

Inés left. Alone in my chambers, I paced. What was I going to do? What *could* I do? With Villena's men scattered throughout the city and Mencia in my house, how was I going to elude their trap? Villena had returned to Segovia, but only after threatening me with an unpleasant end if I dared leave Ocaña for any reason. Winter approached; nothing of import could transpire while the winds and snows blew, but by March, at the latest, they would meet with the Portuguese. They could conclude their arrangements within days and immediately have me sent for. I could find myself betrothed to King Afonso before my eighteenth birthday, in April.

I dug my nails into my palms to stop myself from spiraling into useless rumination. I would not let it happen. I must escape. I must elude them and find a safe place. Enrique and I were now at war; it might be undeclared but war it was, nonetheless.

For, no matter what my half brother threatened, I would wed no one but Fernando.

IT WAS A moonless night, frigid and hushed as March nights in Castile often were, the land still dormant under the grip of winter.

Inés had told me Chacón would bring Carrillo through the city gates in disguise; a nervous chuckle escaped me when I heard this. However would Chacón manage it? Surely the archbishop was the most recognizable man in the realm—a formidable figure in his signature crimson cape, his sword strapped to his waist. I couldn't envision him going anywhere unperceived. But the letters we'd exchanged through Cárdenas, who'd braved freezing gales to slip in and out of Ocaña with the stealth of a hawk, had assured me Carrillo would find a way.

Now I waited, walking back and forth across the worn floor, nervously eyeing the door which might bring me my escape—or my doom.

Over the last five months, while Cárdenas carried my covert missives and Ines waged a domestic battle with Mencia, the number of guards about my palace had increased like locusts. It soon began to look as if Villena had dispatched a veritable army to Ocaña. When I was denied permission to visit my mother in Arévalo for Epiphany, I finally ventured to ask Mencia *why* there were so many soldiers in the streets—indeed, outside our very gates.

She replied with a feigned air of indifference, "I believe there's been an uprising in the south, led by the rebel marquis of Cádiz. His Majesty and Villena must travel to Andalucía to contend with him. Naturally, their utmost concern while they are gone is Your Highness's continued safety."

"Naturally," I said dryly, but inside me, hope flared. Cádiz was a notorious troublemaker, a temperamental grandee with vast swaths of land in Andalucía and a lifelong enmity for his rival, the duke of Medina Sidonia. Together, these two southern nobles had wreaked more havoc than the Moors had. Their quarrel could upset the precarious balance of power in the region, and such a threat to the realm's stability would preclude meeting with the Portuguese. With Enrique and Villena gone for at least a month—for Sevilla was much farther away from Castile than Portugal—the timing was perfect for me to carry out my escape.

Carrillo must have felt the same, for within days Cárdenas brought word from the archbishop. My valises were packed with essentials; Ines took them to the stables to hide them under the straw. We then spent several anxious weeks pretending to go about our daily activities, overseeing the house, embroidering, reading, and retiring shortly after nightfall to save candles—all of which was calculated to drive Mencia into a state of desperate boredom. When Ines reported that Mencia had taken up with one of the soldiers, a brawny youth with whom she stole off to frolic every night, I had to stifle my rather unseemly delight.

"And she's a married woman," Inés sniffed. "Common harlots have more scruples."

I told myself that the circumstances were extraordinary and Mencia's lack of scruples could not matter to me, not when her distraction could serve my purpose; and so I feigned utter indifference to the love bites on her throat and her satisfied leer.

Tonight she was once again absent, having slipped out the moment she heard me close my bedchamber door. Inés had hurried downstairs to open the gates; we could only pray that the soldiers who usually patrolled our area had chosen to get out of the cold and seek diversion in one of the plaza taverns. The notches in the candle on my sideboard showed it was past two in the morning. Surely the sentries would not still be outside the palace at this late hour—

I paused, hearing footsteps on the stairs. I went still. The horrifying thought that it was Villena's men made my blood run cold. Word could have leaked out that I was writing to Carrillo; they were undoubtedly watching him in Yepes, as much as they watched me here. After all, they'd discovered my letters to Aragón. *Dios mío,* what if they had come to arrest me now?

I stifled my gasp when the knock sounded on my door. Then I heard Inés whisper, "My lady? My lady, it is us," and I unlocked the bolt to reveal her in the corridor, along with two large figures dressed in long hooded capes.

I sighed with relief as they strode in. Both wore Franciscan habits under their cloaks and I immediately recognized one of the men as Chacón. When the larger man tore back the cowl covering his face, I smiled. "Welcome to Ocaña, my lord Archbishop."

Carrillo snorted, his thick brows drawn together in his habitual frown. "I told you they'd try to do you some harm." His gaze raked my chamber. "God have mercy, it's like a pauper's den in here. Is this the best they could find for the next queen of Castile?"

I found it amusing that after nearly a year of absence, he remained irascible as ever. "It was quite suitable," I said, "until Villena decided to fill it with informants."

"Villena is a snake," he growled, as though the marquis no longer shared any blood of his. "I'm going to cut him into pieces as soon as I see you settled in your proper state."

I glanced at Chacón; my steward explained, "Just before we left Yepes, his lordship received warning through my lord the Admiral. Villena actively plots to—"

"Treason!" blasted Carrillo, making me wince. "That mincing lap-dog nephew of mine dares to accuse me of treason! Well, here I am! Let him come arrest me, the shit." He guffawed. "That is, if our Andalucían friends Medina Sidonia and Cádiz don't make mincemeat of him first. Or better yet, throw him over the walls of Málaga for the Moors to have their pleasure with."

"My lord," said Chacón sternly, "Her Highness is present."

Carrillo paused. His florid cheeks turned redder. "Ah, yes. Forgive me. I'm a crude old man, lacking in refinement."

I inclined my head. "It is late. Perhaps we should . . . ?" I let my words linger; I had no idea what their plans were, but even I knew traveling friars did not go about with armed escorts, or, for that matter, refugee princesses. Their disguise wasn't going to facilitate my escape.

As I searched the archbishop's expression, my heart sank. "You're not taking me with you."

Carrillo paced to the sideboard to pour a goblet. He did not appear pleased that my decanter contained only fresh, clear water. It was one of my whims; whenever clean water could be found (and there was plenty of it in cities with working aqueducts) I insisted it should take the place of wine in my chambers. I disliked how wine affected men's reason and watched in amusement as Carrillo drank with a grimace. "It's not advisable," he said, setting his goblet down. "Not yet. Too many of Villena's men are still roaming about, not only here, but all over Castile. That bugger seems to have eyes in the back of his head. And the situation with Aragón isn't resolved yet. There are still several important details to work out."

"Such as what?" I contained a surge of irritation. "You told me King Juan was outraged that Enrique sought another alliance for me. I thought he'd decided to favor my cause and send a representative to us with Aragón's full capitulations, formalizing the betrothal."

Carrillo nodded. "He did, yes. We have his capitulations, but I'm not yet satisfied. We've the issue of your dowry yet to settle and the papal dispensation of consanguinity to procure, as you and Fernando are second cousins; not to mention the manner in which you'll assume the throne. Castile must always hold precedence over Aragón; we cannot afford to be embroiled in their realm's ceaseless feuding with France or to deplete our treasury in their defense. Such issues take time and—"

"I don't care about dowries," I interrupted. "As for the dispensation, surely His Holiness the pope will not refuse us. And as to how I will assume the throne, we can settle that at a later date. God willing, I'm not going to become queen anytime soon."

The corners of Carrillo's mouth turned downward. He said in a flat voice, "After everything he has done, you would still grant that spineless worm his right to the crown?"

"He is our king; he has that right until the day he dies. I'll not wage war on him as Alfonso did. But neither shall I consent to whatever arrangements he sees fit to make for me." I paused, regarding Carrillo with impatience. "I thought I had made it clear that all I want is to marry the prince I've chosen and reside in a safe place without Villena spying on me."

"Then I suggest you move outside Castile," he retorted. "For if you insist on upholding Enrique's right to the throne, there'll be no safety in this realm for you, not once you marry Fernando."

My pent-up rage was growing so hot I could practically feel it scalding my throat. I could not believe he had come here merely to chastise me. Was he so arrogant he thought he could browbeat me like a child into doing his will? If so, he was making a grave mistake.

Chacón and Inés had gone still, watching the archbishop and me face each other like combatants. Then Carrillo released one of his dramatic sighs. Reaching into his habit pocket, he removed a messenger's leather cylinder.

All of a sudden I was holding my breath.

He gave an uneasy chuckle. "No harm in waiting a little at first, eh, just in case Your Highness should happen to change her mind."

I exhaled through my teeth. Taking the cylinder from him, I went to my desk and opened the lid, tapping out a rolled parchment with dangling seals. I scanned its long paragraphs, barely registering the convoluted clauses, the agreements and counter-agreements detailing the minutiae of status that underpinned every royal union. Instead, I looked at the bottom of the page. There, scrawled in the handwriting I had come to know so well, was: *Yo, Fernando de Aragón.*

He had signed our betrothal. He still wanted me.

I could not move. The moment I signed this paper, there would be no turning back. Though I had no desire to usurp his throne, Enrique would see this as a declaration of war; he had forbidden me to seek any arrangement without his leave, and once he heard of my defiance, his retaliation would be swift. I was about to risk everything for a prince I had not seen in years—my place in the succession, my future as queen, perhaps my very life.

My hand paused over the quill in my ink pot. "And the dispensation . . . ?" I asked.

"It will be here by the time of the wedding. King Juan and I have already requested it from Rome." Carrillo regarded me with unblinking eyes. Chacón and Ines were like statues by the door. It seemed as if the entire palace held its breath, the quiet so profound I could hear a dog barking somewhere in the fields outside my walls.

I closed my eyes, invoking my memory of Fernando as I'd last seen him, in Segovia, his brown eyes earnest as he took my hand. *We can bind our realms closer together, restore peace. . . .*

I took the quill and inked it, carefully inscribing *Yo, Isabel de Castilla* at the bottom of the page.

It was done. For better or for worse, I was betrothed to Fernando.

I turned to Carrillo. "What of my living arrangements? Under the present circumstances, I can hardly remain here anymore."

"No, you cannot." He came to the desk, sanded the ink and blew it off. "I think Valladolid is the best place for you. The city has expressed its loyalty to you and we have trustworthy friends there. We'll travel first to Madrigal and rest overnight. Hopefully, Fernando's grandfather the admiral will have summoned his forces by the time we arrive. Valladolid is his domain; he'll see that you're protected there while we send the betrothal agreement to Aragón."

"I see." I fought back a smile. I should not have doubted him; petulant and calculating as he could be, no man knew better than Carrillo how to mount a defense.

He cleared his throat. "As I said, I saw no harm in waiting first. If you'd elected to go to battle for your throne, instead of to the altar, the admiral's forces would have been just as useful."

"Indeed," I replied, "if you had your way."

He met my gaze. "Instead, Your Highness has hers. Now, let us pray it doesn't bring all of Castile down about our heads." He rolled up the document for return to the cylinder. "I suggest you fetch your cloak. No time like the present to make your escape."

THE SADDLED HORSES were waiting; after Cárdenas assisted me onto Canela, I pulled up my cloak's fur-lined hood and cast a lingering gaze upon my palace. I'd not lived here long, but it was the first place I had called my own, and I did not want to leave it. I was weary of not being at home anywhere. Since I'd left Arévalo, I had felt like a lost soul in my own country.

At my side Inés said, "I'd give anything to see Mencia's face when she returns from her rendezvous to find our rooms empty and us gone."

I glanced at her; as her smile lit up her eyes, I found myself abruptly on the verge of laughter as well. "We can only hope it'll prove as upsetting to her as she's been to us." I took a last look at my palace. "After all, it's just walls, chairs, tables, and beds. We can always buy new ones."

We followed the men out. The streets were deserted. A light rain drifted from the black sky. As we approached the city gates I had to remind myself that no one expected me to make my escape, certainly not today or at this hour. Villena had ordered the town surrounded and, to his mind, made enough noise to frighten a cornered princess and her attendants into submission. His guards would be lax, thinking me well in hand. But if anyone did try to detain us, Carrillo had warned me to break into a gallop and not stop until I reached Valladolid.

Three sentries were posted in a makeshift shelter by the gates, huddled with a wineskin over a smoking brazier. They looked up with ill-humored frowns as we neared.

"Didn't we just let you in?" one of them said suspiciously, looking at Chacón.

My steward replied, "You did, and now we are leaving. As we explained, this lady's father is gravely ill at our monastery and he has asked to see her."

The sentry glanced past Cárdenas and Carrillo at me and Inés. I lowered my head, avoiding his stare. "I see two ladies. Are both their fathers dying in your monastery?"

Carrillo growled, "The lady has a maid with her, of course. Or haven't you ever seen a lady with a maid before, you ignorant son of a swine?"

I tightened my hold on my reins as I saw the sentry's face harden. It was not the right thing to say, I knew at once. By asserting his authority, Carrillo had only managed to insult the man and rouse suspicion.

"Look here," the sentry said, "I just follow my orders. His lordship the marquis of Villena commanded that these gates stay closed from sunset to sunrise. I let you in once, against my better judgment—"

"You were paid," interrupted Chacón, "and quite well, as I recall."

"To open the gates once." The sentry exchanged a wink with the others, whose leather-gloved hands had dropped to their swords. It would be hard to draw the weapons from the scabbards; even I knew that much. The cold tended to make blades stick. Still, a pitched fight in the middle of the night by the gates wouldn't do us any favors, nor was I looking forward to riding over these men, and possibly risking injury to our horses.

"Now, if suitable arrangements can be made I'll gladly open the gates again," the sentry added, and though he sounded jovial in his thievery, I detected the threat underneath. Unless we complied, he was not going to touch those bolts, and, what's more, he was likely to call for reinforcements.

Without warning, I kicked my horse forth and came before him. He stared up at me, startled and momentarily confused. I reached upward, and ignoring Carrillo's stifled gasp, pulled back my hood. The sentry went still, except for his mouth, which gaped wide as if he suddenly found himself short of air.

"Do you know who I am?" I asked quietly.

He nodded, still without moving. I couldn't tell whether he was truly so astonished he'd yet to formulate a reaction or already gauging this sudden twist in the situation, weighing the potential benefits and drawbacks.

"You should raise the alarm," I said, "but as your future queen, though, God willing, it be many years hence, I know you will not. And in return, my good man, I shall not forget how you helped me on this night." I reached into my saddlebag, retrieved and dropped a velvet purse at his feet. It clinked satisfactorily as it hit the cold ground.

The sound startled him into movement. He quickly bent over and retrieved it; a leer spread across his face when he drew back the purse's cords to peer inside. He glanced over his shoulder at the others, who stood regarding us with wide eyes. "That's more like it," he said, and he made a little flourish toward me before barking at his men, "Go on, you heard the lady. Open the gates."

The bolts were drawn back; we rode out quickly, into the dark open countryside. As soon as we had cleared the walls, Carrillo said testily, "That was hardly the moment to go and prove your rank. We could have been arrested."

"Yes, we could have," I replied. "But we weren't. And the story will spread, hopefully right to Villena's ears, of how I eluded his snare. Let him shiver in his boots, for a change."

Chacón let out a rare gruff laugh. Ines whispered to me, "Were those your jewels?"

"Yes," I whispered back. "As I said, we can buy new ones."

And we spurred forth, to Valladolid.

CHAPTER SIXTEEN

Situated in the north-central part of Castile, Valladolid was a beautiful city on the Pisuerga River famous for rich wines, fertile croplands, and the splendid Gothic Church of Santa María the Ancient, with its thick Romanesque tower.

I took up residence in the palace of the Vivero clan, a grandee family loyal to the admiral. I was saddle sore from our three-day trip over treacherous back roads and through woodlands; we'd avoided any thoroughfares where royal patrols were likely to be searching, as we were under no delusion that my disappearance would go unreported. Mencia would have doubtless raised the alarm as soon as she returned to our deserted palace. But we depended on the fact that while messengers were dispatched to Enrique and Villena in Andalucía, and their outraged responses returned, we would have enough time to send our own embassy to Aragón with the signed betrothal documents. Within a few weeks at most, Fernando would be in Castile; he and I would wed. And not even Villena, for all his wiles, could sunder those whom God had joined.

I had barely settled in when Fernando's grandfather Don Fadrique Enríquez, Lord of Medina and Admiral of Castile, came to see me. In the painted *sala*, he bowed over my hand—a short, trim man with a completely bald pate and a kindly myopic gaze, dressed in the somber black damask favored by the kingdom's elite. As one of the most powerful grandees in the land, the admiral had remained aloof from the internecine struggles of the court, because his eldest daughter had been Fernando's mother, Juan II of Aragón's beloved queen, and that made him a target of Villena's ceaseless machinations.

I took one look at him, and I knew he did not bring good news. I also noted that he appeared taken aback to see only Ines at my side. As a rule, a princess usually had a retinue shadowing her every move.

"My lord the Archbishop Carrillo has taken up lodgings in the Convent of the Agustinas," I explained, as the admiral was too polite to voice his concern. "He's been busy with various matters pertaining to the betrothal." I motioned to two high-backed carved chairs set before the greenery-filled hearth. "Have you broken your fast yet? Shall I fetch bread and cheese? We have fresh figs, as well."

He shook his head. "No, no, Your Highness. Thank you. That will not be necessary."

I smiled as he perched on the chair. I was prepared for almost anything, given the circumstances, and still when he spoke I had to stop myself from flinching.

"King Enrique has issued a warrant for your arrest. He claims you left Ocaña against his command, though you promised you would not. His men have been instructed to take you to the alcazar of Madrid, where you'll be imprisoned. He plans to make his way back from Andalucía as soon as he can raise his siege on Cádiz's city of Trujillo."

I focused on maintaining my composure. Was my lot in life never to know more than a few days' respite from pursuit?

"Your Highness has nothing to fear as yet," the admiral went on, misinterpreting my silence. "Between us, the archbishop and I have more than eight hundred men at our disposal. Villena's soldiers will not easily apprehend you. But I thought you'd want to know that the king is apprised of your actions and has every intention of stopping you." He lowered his voice, despite the fact that we were quite alone save for Inés. "It goes without saying that he has declared numerous times that your union with Fernando of Aragón is strictly forbidden, and should you disobey him, he will consider it an act of treason."

It was a shock to hear the words, though I couldn't reasonably claim I hadn't expected this. "Yes," I said quietly, "thank you. I am indebted to you for your diligence."

"Oh, it's not diligence that brought me here," he said, with sudden levity in his tone. He rose and moved to where he had deposited his cloak. From it he withdrew a shallow case covered in azure velvet. As he handed it to me, his smile deepened, enhancing the laugh lines at the sides of his eyes.

"A birthday gift," he said. "From my grandson, His Highness of Aragón."

Nestled within the case upon a lining of snow-white satin was the most magnificent ruby collar I'd ever seen. The blood-rich tabled stones exuded light as if tiny suns shone in their depths, and from the gold links in between each stone dangled large pink-gray pearls.

"It's . . . breathtaking," I said, in awe.

"And rather convenient," piped Inés. "Her Highness was fresh out of jewels, as it turns out. It'll come in quite handy for the wedding."

As I saw the admiral's smile fade, I closed the case. "I would prefer to thank Prince Fernando in person for his gift, but I see by your expression that I'll not have that pleasure quite as soon as I hoped."

He released a troubled sigh. "There are complications. The French have overrun the city of Girona. By virtue of his position as heir, Fernando must head the defense." From his doublet he removed a sealed paper. "He asked me to deliver this to you."

I took the paper in disbelief. Complications? I understood Aragón was besieged, but what was I supposed to do in the meantime? How was I to survive? Surely Fernando must realize I could not hold out indefinitely, that even now Enrique and Villena were moving against me, against us.

"You'll naturally want to read the letter in private," said the admiral. He bowed. "By your leave I'll now go pay my respects to Carrillo. Perhaps later, we might dine together?"

I nodded, hiding my distress. "Yes, of course. I . . . I would be honored."

"The honor is all mine," he replied, with a gallantry that went straight to my heart. "Your Highness must not lose faith. My grandson will find his way to you, even if he has to cut through every man in the French army to get here."

Inés accompanied him out. Alone in the *sala*, I cracked the letter's seal. His calligraphy leapt at me, stark black on the paper, ink splotches denoting frustration with a poorly trimmed quill.

My dearest Isabella,

    Your embassy has arrived and I now know that that which I've dreamed for so long, which I once thought might never come to pass, is a reality. We are to be man and wife. I cannot describe in words the joy I feel or my impatience to be at your side. But as my lord grandfather has by now told you, Aragón faces another ordeal, and I cannot desert her. My father is still brave even in his advanced years and would send me to you regardless, but what kind of man would I be, what kind of husband could you hope to expect, if I abandoned my realm to indulge my desire? I know you would never do such a thing, so therefore neither must I. God is on our side; this time, I shall defeat Louis and his French spiders, and take wing to where you are, Until then, know that not an hour goes by when you are not in my heart.

    Be brave, Isabella. Wait for me.

There was no signature; there was no need. I let my tears come. I let them fall down my face and wash away my disappointment, my fear and anxiety and corrosive doubt.

    I would wait. I would wait even if I had to lead an army myself. Fernando and I were destined for each other; we would find a way to be together, no matter the odds.

    And once we united, nothing would part us, save death.

I CELEBRATED MY eighteenth birthday without fanfare. The news from Aragón had dampened my spirits and rumors came almost daily of some new menace to my person. Nothing concrete had materialized thus far but we knew Enrique's southern exploit was not going well and, for the moment, threats were all he could issue. His men in Castile were disinclined to march into Valladolid to engage the admiral's forces. But I had no doubt that as soon as the situation in Andalucía resolved, Villena and his wolves would come after me.

    In late September, after a sweltering summer that dried up the Pisuerga's tributaries and charred the harvest in the fields, I received word that my mother had fallen ill with fever. I'd not seen her in over a year and so I decided to go to Arévalo. Carrillo protested that it was unsafe for me to leave Valladolid, as neither he nor the admiral could vouch for my safety if I took to "gallivanting about Castile," but five months of near-daily contact with the archbishop had worn my patience thin. Retorting that I hardly planned to undertake a progress of the realm, I insisted on preparing for the trip.

Yet just as I planned to depart, the long-awaited royal delegation arrived. By now, word of my betrothal to Fernando had become widespread; indeed, one of my first acts of defense had been to proclaim it via circulars in every major city, to demonstrate that I'd done nothing wrong and had nothing to hide. Now I had no other option than to make good on my declarations of innocence and agree to receive Enrique's men.

I had donned gray velvet and the rubies of Aragón, their weight lending me comfort as the lords strode in. Carrillo and the admiral flanked me. I clenched my teeth at the unexpected sight of Villena; a surreptitious glance at Carrillo revealed that he likewise hadn't known the marquis would be present. His expression turned so dark, I thought he might leap on Villena and throttle him with his bare hands, then and there.

I preempted him. "My lord marquis," I said, my voice ringing loud and clear, "I sincerely hope you've come to request our forgiveness. Otherwise, let me warn you that we'll not take kindly to words such as those you've used against us in the past."

I basked in the pallor of his face. I had used the royal plural on purpose and he'd not anticipated it. *Bien.* I was determined that he find me a future queen, not the helpless infanta he had so often bullied.

Then he sneered, whipped from his accompanying groom's hand an impressive-looking document, clattering with an assortment of seals.

"Herein is Your Highness's amnesty," he declared. "Due to unforeseen trouble in the south, His Majesty cannot be here in person but out of respect for your shared blood, he offers a full pardon for your rebellious acts, should you in return renounce your illegal and unsanctioned betrothal with Fernando of Aragón."

"Miserable cur," Carrillo spat. "You're not fit to lick her boots—"

I held up a hand, detaining him. I stepped forward, glancing markedly toward the admiral. Don Fadrique inclined his head; he stood among sixty armed retainers, proof of the men I now had at my command.

Villena said, "Do you think to intimidate the king's representative? I come with the full power of the crown. I could have Your Highness arrested this very hour."

I halted a mere pace from where he stood, so close I detected the nauseating smell of his expensive musk, a hint of sweat underneath. I looked past him to the lords in his posse, many of whom I'd met or seen in my years at court. I hid a start of surprise when I recognized the queen's former lover and Mencia's husband, Beltrán de la Cueva. He had grown older, his lithe beauty coarsened, but his eyes were lucent as ever; as he averted his gaze, I could see his discomfort with the role he'd been compelled to enact.

The realization gave me strength. Villena might think to wield power over me, but I suspected these lords would not be here willingly, given a choice. Rapacious as they could be, few liked seeing a woman harassed, and as usual, Villena had made no effort to befriend the very men he now relied upon to support his dirty work.

"Arrest me, then." I returned my gaze to Villena. "But before you do, you must tell me before these lords what I am accused of; even the lowliest serf in Castile deserves that right. By the terms of the treaty I signed with His Majesty, it was agreed I would not wed without his consent, yes, but that he in turn would not force upon me a marriage not of my choosing. He broke our arrangement first by seeking alliance for me with Portugal. Therefore, I suggest we submit our disagreements to the Cortes and let them decide."

Villena's feline eyes turned to slits. "There will never be an assembly of the Cortes while the king lives," he hissed. "Never! You've forfeited your right to call yourself heiress of Castile. If you dare embark on this marriage with Aragón, it is doubtful how long you may live. The king will not tolerate sedition. Unless you obey, you *will* pay for the consequences of your actions, as will every man who supports your unseemly defiance."

I blinked. His spittle had struck me in the face. Meeting his burning eyes, I said, "You will one day have cause to regret those words, my lord marquis."

I walked purposefully to the far doors. Villena shouted at me, "You are the one who'll have cause to regret, Doña Isabella!"

I did not turn back. I heard Carrillo bark, "Get out now, before I slice the fleas from your fur," and then the ensuing uproar, a clash of dissent that could not, fortunately, escalate past heated words, seeing as the admiral's retainers were there precisely to impede it.

The moment I closed the door behind me, I sagged against the wall, my heart hammering. Inés came to me, cloth in hand. "Here, let me clean your face." As she dabbed the marquis's spit from my cheeks, I heard the muted clamor of the admiral's men escorting the king's delegation out. Moments later, Carrillo banged the door open; he was flushed, furious, and all the more invigorated for it. The man seemed to thrive on discord.

"That royal catamite dared to warn me that he'll return with an army to tear down these walls. Hah! I'd like to see him try. Those high and mighty lords all looked as though they wished the earth would swallow them whole." He gave me an admiring grin. "You've won the day. You showed them what a true ruler is."

"I'm not a ruler yet." I looked past him to where the admiral stood on the threshold, his expression far less enthusiastic. He understood the situation we faced; he knew as well as I did that this time, we could not afford to disregard Villena's threats. When he next came, he would indeed have an army and a warrant for my arrest.

"I can't delay anymore," I said, looking back at Carrillo. "I must send word to Fernando. Whatever else he does, he must come to me before it is too late."

CHAPTER SEVENTEEN

Night hung sultry over the indoor patio, where lemon-scented torches burned to discourage insects. I paced the arcade-enclosed square, unable to sit indoors.

After nearly two weeks, I had finally received word that Fernando was on his way. He'd slipped over the border between our realms with a few trusted attendants, all disguised as common carters. Cárdenas, whom I'd sent to Aragón with my letter, was among those who accompanied him. Thus far, Fernando had eluded Villena's patrols; I knew this because the count of Palencia had sent a missive that my betrothed safely reached that castle. Fernando departed the next evening for Valladolid, taking advantage of the cover of the night, and over the last two days we'd heard nothing more.

Castile crawled with royal informants. Enrique had given Villena full permission to ransack the treasury and hire as many spies as he could, to ensure that Fernando never made it across the border. But Andrés de Cabrera and my spirited Beatriz had refused the marquis access to the alcazar, even though their actions branded them traitors. Thus thwarted, Villena began bribing funds from the less scrupulous grandees in exchange for flagrant offers of land and castles. Now he had hirelings stationed on every road and in every township, all on the watch for the prince of Aragón and his entourage.

Of course no one was searching for a carter and muleteers, Ines assured me, but I envisioned the worst. Princes could let themselves be known by any number of unwitting actions—the use of gold in a place where base copper was the rule; a careless request to a servant, when he should have had none. Even the way he walked and talked could reveal his superior rank. If Fernando let his guard down even for a moment, and one of Villena's men noticed, it would be the end of him, of us. Villena had the king's order to arrest Fernando for entering Castile without leave, with intent to marry a princess forbidden to him.

I paused in my restless ambulation, lifted my gaze to the moon, high in the star-spangled night sky and wreathed in cloud. The horrible heat of summer had not abated, though it was already October. The tawny Castilian wheat—essential for our bread—had withered; everyone was predicting widespread starvation. As if that were not enough, the Black Death had erupted in Ávila and Madrigal, killing hundreds. I'd sent for news of my mother in Arévalo but had not heard back, which only increased my fear that she and her elderly attendants would suffer from lack of supplies, due to the plague shutting down vital commerce. Portents abounded, prompting market-square prophets and doomsayers to take to the streets to herald the beginning of the Apocalypse.

God, they claimed, was displeased.

It couldn't be because of me, I kept telling myself. I did not embark on this marriage for my own selfish purposes and I had not asked Fernando to abandon Aragón for me. No, I had asked him to come because we were out of time and options; only he could help me save Castile. Together, we would be that much stronger and better equipped to withstand Enrique. My half brother could cry treason all he wanted, but once Fernando and I were wed, it would force Enrique to seek terms, lest he find himself at war with both the rebellious grandees in Andalucía *and* the entire kingdom of Aragón.

And yet guilt gnawed at me. Fernando had left behind a sick, old father and a horde of French soldiers clamoring to devour his realm. He risked his very freedom, perhaps even his life, to honor my request. Had I been too impetuous? Perhaps I should have waited, manned the walls of my palace and dug in like a mole to withstand winter. Villena was indolent, for all his bombast; he'd hardly have roused himself to besiege me with the months of bitter cold so near. . . .

Around and around the patio I went, circling in my own personal purgatory. I'd even written a belated letter to Torquemada, begging him for guidance. He had reminded me of what he'd imparted the night we met in Segovia:

> Much will be demanded of you. You must rely only on the conviction of your faith, knowing that even in our darkest hour the Almighty does not abandon us.

Inés appeared in the arcade, out of nowhere. "My lady," she said, "he is here."

I paused, staring at her as if she spoke nonsense. "Who is here?"

"The prince. He is in the *sala*. They arrived a few minutes ago. He is asking for you." She recovered my gossamer wrap, left crumpled in a corner. As she draped it about my shoulders, I passed my hands over my disheveled coiffure in a daze.

"You've been bitten," chided Inés. She wet her finger, cleaned the smear of blood from my throat. "I told you to use the oil of lavender when you're outside at night. Skin as fair as yours attracts mosquitoes." As she spoke, she guided me into the palace. My heart was beating so fast I felt as though I might faint. Suddenly we were at the doors of the *sala;* the flickering light of the candelabra dazzled me.

I paused, blinking.

There were several figures in the room—men with goblets in hand, as well as Doña Vivero and a cluster of her women friends, all talking in groups. The house dogs sprawled on the tiles near the hearth. I noticed Carrillo, red-faced, blustering to the recently arrived papal nuncio; nearby, I saw with relief, was my dear Chacón, who had gone to meet Fernando halfway. With him was intrepid young Cárdenas, his face tired as he sat on a window ledge and petted one of the hounds. He looked up; as his wide grin broke across his face and he stood, the hall's occupants turned as if on cue to regard me.

They bowed low. I remained frozen on the threshold, as if the expanse of floor before me had become an impassable sea. The admiral stepped forth with a broad-shouldered man in a leather doublet and thigh-high, mud-spattered boots. His forehead was ample, offset by tousled chestnut hair; his sun-bronzed complexion so dark in the room's dim light that at first I mistook him for a Moorish guard, the type En-

rique liked to keep about him. For, while he wasn't tall, he exuded undeniable power; his muscular body moved with a confident stealth that
reminded me of Enrique's leopards.

As he came before me, I caught a hint of mirth in his eyes, which,
by some alchemy of the light, gleamed like sun-shot amber. His hand
was strong, veined; I felt its callused warmth as his fingers grasped mine.
He raised my hand to his lips. The shadow of a beard patterned his
cheeks; it felt rough against my skin.

"What?" he said, so low only I could hear him. "Do you still not
remember me?"

I saw the boy now, shining out of his expressive eyes, but in my
anxiety and worry, in the anticipation leading up to this moment, I'd
somehow forgotten that years had passed. He was a man of seventeen
now, not that audacious youth who'd proposed to me in the alcazar
garden.

"I . . . I didn't recognize you," I heard myself say.

"So it seems." His smile widened, revealing his slightly crooked
teeth. "Now that you do," he said, "do I please?"

"Yes," I whispered. "You do." His fingers tightened over mine, as
though he sought to impart a secret, letting loose a cascade of sensation
inside me.

"As do you, my Isabella," he said. "You please me, very much." His
smile widened. "I have our dispensation. My father and Carrillo got it
for us only a day before I left Aragón."

"Dispensation . . . yes, of course. Thank you." I was barely paying
attention, all too aware of the others watching us; of Inés's soft giggle
and Cárdenas's proud stare, as if he'd carried Fernando here on his back.
But they were part of a vague backdrop I barely registered; the sounds
of their presence muted, like the susurration of a distant river.

Though we stood in a crowded hall for this first public meeting,
witnessed by dozens of eyes and ears, it was as if Fernando and I were
alone in our recognition that without each other, life could only be an
incomprehensible labor.

"They're waiting for us," he said, rupturing the spell.

I nodded, withdrew my hand from his. Together we turned to the
hall and everyone raised their goblets. They drank a toast, began to ap-

plaud. The noise rushed over me in a deluge, so loud that I swayed. I felt Fernando's hand come to rest on the small of my back.

I knew then that, no matter what the future held, with him at my side, I could face anything.

OVER THE NEXT four days the palace seemed to explode with cheer, as the banns went out and loyal grandees and their retinues came from all over Castile to attend us. Fernando and I couldn't find the time to be alone, surrounded as we were every minute, but now and then, as the days progressed, we'd catch each other's eyes across the crowded hall and in those moments the intimate knowledge that we had at last found each other passed between us, warming my entire being.

On the eve of the wedding, Inés and I frantically worked to put the finishing touches on my gown. Money was in short supply, as always, and we had spent the past few days wearing out our eyes and fingers as we sewed my raiment.

The door opened. At first, I was so tired I thought I must be dreaming when I saw Beatriz walk in. Then, as she stood there with her hands on her hips, a broad smile on her face, I slowly came to my feet. I was stunned. I hadn't expected her, not at this late hour. I knew the situation in Segovia was extremely tense, with Cabrera caught between Villena's exigencies and his habitual lifelong loyalty to his royal office. I had assumed Beatriz would not wish to risk more enmity falling upon her husband by attending my forbidden union.

As I took her in my arms I whispered, "You shouldn't have. It's too dangerous."

"Nonsense," she scoffed. She drew back. "As if Villena and the entire royal guard could have stopped me! I wouldn't miss this for anything." She was rounder, rosy-cheeked; while still disarmingly beautiful, she had a new serenity about her. Marriage evidently suited her. She unfastened her cloak. "Now, give me a spare needle and let me help you. Ines, look at that sleeve—it's a mess! Did no one teach you to properly hide a seam?"

We sat up all night, laughing and sharing confidences, as we had in our childhood. The months of separation dwindled and vanished, until

I clasped her hand and confessed, "I could not imagine this day without you," and rare tears glistened in her eyes.

She helped me dress that morning, just as she had so many times before when we were young girls. She wove silk flowers in my waist-length hair and arranged the gossamer, gold-threaded veil. She and Inés accompanied me into the hall and stood behind me as I joined Fernando, who'd been titled king of Sicily by his father especially for the occasion. Carrillo read aloud the papal dispensation sanctifying our marriage within the degree of consanguinity, but just before my turn came to recite the vows I froze in a moment of paralyzing panic.

What was I doing? I was defying my king, threatening everything I cherished. I risked being branded a traitor, endangering my very future as heir—and all to marry this man I did not know.

Sweat broke out under my azure brocade gown. Fernando stood rigid beside me in a high-collared matching doublet trimmed in gold; as though he sensed my doubt, he slid his gaze to me. And he winked.

Relief washed over me, cool as rain. I had to repress the urge to laugh as the nuptial rings were slipped on our fingers and we made our way to the open balcony overlooking the courtyard. People had been gathering there since dawn, with banners and bouquets of autumn flowers. When we appeared, they waved them at us, men hoisting children on their shoulders to better see us, wives and daughters clasping hands, gnarled widows and grandmothers peering upward and smiling.

"Their Royal Highnesses Isabella and Fernando, prince and princess of Asturias and Aragón, and king and queen of Sicily," trumpeted the heralds.

The sky arched over us, a vault of unbroken cerulean; the air was redolent of roast meat from the banquet being laid out inside the palace hall. I gazed upon the hundreds of anonymous faces beaming at us, their tribulations momentarily set aside in their zeal to share our moment of joy, and euphoria swept through me.

"We do this for them," I said, "to bring them justice and honor. To give them peace."

Fernando chuckled. "Yes. But there will be time enough to care for them. Today, wife, we do this for us," and before I realized his intention, he turned me to him, and in full view of our court and future subjects, he kissed me with unrestrained passion—our first real kiss as a married couple.

His mouth was warm. He tasted of an indefinable spice and the tang of claret. His body was chiseled, incredibly strong; his arms enveloped me like muscular wings, sheltering and all-encompassing, making me want to melt inside their embrace. I—who had never before experienced that urgency of the flesh which poets so often exalt—felt such heat inside me that I let out an involuntary gasp. Again he chuckled, only this time his mirth was saturated with unmistakable intent, and I felt him harden where he pressed against my thighs.

When he finally drew back, his kiss still tingled on my lips and the entire room seemed to sway. From outside came lewd whistles and hearty applause.

"You're blushing," he said, and I bit the inside of my lip, hard, forcing myself to feel the pain rather than my searing desire. I glanced over at the spectators in the hall, all of whom, including the servitors and pages, had paused to watch us.

"Must everything we do be witnessed for posterity?" I muttered.

Fernando threw back his head and laughed—a bold, hearty laugh that made me wonder at his apparent indifference to propriety. Again, I was reminded of the fact that he was still a stranger to me and I breathed deeply, pushing my misgivings aside. He was a man, and men liked to display their prowess, both on the field and in the bedchamber. It was only natural that he'd want to stake his claim on me.

And I couldn't deny that I enjoyed being claimed as his.

As we moved to our garland-festooned dais, I met Beatriz's knowing eyes. I wished I could sneak off with her. All of a sudden I had a thousand urgent questions. From the way Fernando had kissed me, I was certain he had carnal experience, and I didn't want to prove a disappointment, though exactly how I might evade this possibility eluded me. It was disconcerting. I was required to be a virgin; indeed, it was this one aspect that princes prized above most others in a bride. Yet now I found myself worrying that I'd not be able to properly satisfy my prince in the ways he might have become accustomed to.

My appetite vanished, despite the rich platters of roast piglet, duck, and heron drenched in plum and fig sauces. I kept looking at Fernando's square hands as he cut into his meat or raised his goblet. Though he abstained from wine, opting instead for cider, he displayed a healthy appetite and he laughed boisterously at Carrillo's insistent muttering in his ear (the archbishop, as our most esteemed advisor, sat to his left) and smiled at everyone who approached the dais to offer felicitations. He didn't appear as though *he* were contemplating our upcoming nuptial night with any trepidation, while in my head it loomed large as a shuttered gatehouse into an unknown world.

During the last course, however, before the dancing began, I suddenly sensed a shift in his mood. Setting his goblet down, he turned to me. His regard was so direct, so sober, in a hall where the flushed faces of our guests testified to their liberal intake of wine, that I thought for a moment I'd done something to displease him. I couldn't think what it might be; I'd been as occupied as he was, entertaining the grandees at my side with small talk and feigning interest in every anecdote or remark thrown my way.

Before I could speak, his hand fell over mine. "You mustn't fear," he said. "I promise you, I will kick them out, every last one. There'll be no witnesses in our chamber but us." He paused, a gleam in his eye. "I think the display of the sheet afterward will be more than enough evidence to satisfy."

I dared not look away, even as I wondered if anyone at our table had overheard him. I didn't know whether to be mortified or relieved as he drew me from my seat, leaving the ravaged trenchers on the soiled tablecloth to open the dance. We were only expected to perform once before being accompanied to our bedchamber, but as the music swelled, cocooning us in its invisible bubble, I remembered the first time we had danced. It now seemed a lifetime ago; then we'd been little more than children, strangers in a strange court. I had rebuffed him for his impertinence, not knowing that he had in fact foreseen our future struggles. Now we were husband and wife, about to embark on our new life together, and I found myself reveling in my newfound right to clasp his hand openly, and knowing that at long last, I was his. I forgot my trepidation over the upcoming nuptial night, enjoying the chance to indulge my passion for dancing, in which I'd had so little occasion to enjoy. I noted that despite his own travails in Aragón, Fernando had evidently not neglected his courtly training, for he danced with ease and exuberance. And the sudden kiss he bestowed me as we turned toward the courtiers caused a loud crack of spontaneous applause.

I must have flushed to the roots of my hair, especially as we were swept upstairs by the cajoling crowd right after, ushered into separate rooms first, where our attendants waited to prepare us. Before entering his chamber, he glanced over his shoulder at me and I saw only that same unimpeachable confidence in his smile.

Beatriz and Inés had laid out my embroidered linen shift and damask robe; as they divested me of my gown and veil, careful to not dislodge the flowers in my hair, I couldn't bear the silence any longer.

"Well?" I demanded, glaring at them. "Isn't one of you going to say something? Or will you let me go into that bedchamber like a lamb to the slaughter?"

Inés gasped. "It's Your Highness's wedding night, not a crucifixion! And what can I possibly tell you? I am a virgin." She glanced markedly at Beatriz, whose lips pursed, as if she fought back a smile.

"What is it Your Highness wants to know?" Beatriz said.

"The truth." I paused. My voice dropped to a whisper. "Will . . . will it hurt?"

"Yes. At first, it usually does. But if he is gentle with you as he should be, after a few times it won't hurt so much. And after a few more times . . . well, I'll leave it to you to decide." Beatriz couldn't restrain her smile anymore; it curled the corners of her mouth, as it had when we were young and she'd committed some mischief.

I almost began to laugh myself. I suddenly felt ridiculous, dreading the bed in which I must lie, after everything I'd gone through to get there. I lifted my chin, turned without another word and marched down the short passageway to the nuptial chamber, where the crowd had assembled outside the door. I ignored them, entering the candlelit room, which was dominated by a large brocade-draped tester bed. Fernando stood next to it, with his small entourage of gentlemen.

He glanced up, goblet in hand. He wore an open robe of muted red cloth; I could see the muscles of his bronzed chest under the loose lacings of his knee-length under-chemise. I knew without seeing it that his goblet now contained wine. I could smell it in the air, a rich Rioja mixing with the scented beeswax of the tapers in the candelabrum.

He looked at me in silence, his focus so intense that even the eager speculations of those gathered at the door came to a halt.

"Out," he said, without taking his eyes from me. "All of you."

Beatriz quickly came forward to help me with my robe, but I waved her aside. She guided Inés to the doorway instead, where she confronted the stubborn few who had remained, believing it their right to witness my deflowering, for such was the barbaric custom in every court in Europe. With an indignant wave of her hand she saw them out and clicked the door shut behind her.

Fernando and I were finally alone.

I found it difficult to believe he was actually my husband. What he lacked in stature he more than compensated for in presence and vitality; with his strong nose and penetrating eyes, well-shaped mouth and broad forehead, I thought him possibly the most handsome man I'd ever seen. I reached this conclusion with a detachment that surprised me, considering the circumstances. My heart did not flutter. My palms did not sweat. I felt none of the agitation I'd experienced earlier, as if now that the moment was here, impervious calm had conquered the tumult I should be experiencing.

Men and women had been doing this since time began, and as far as I knew, no one had died of it.

"Would you like . . . ?" He motioned toward the pewter decanter and extra goblet on the sideboard. "We were expected to drink from one cup together, in bed. Naked."

"I know." I smiled faintly at this reminder of what he had spared us. "But I don't like wine. It makes my head ache."

He nodded, set his goblet aside. "Mine, too. I almost never drink, but tonight it seemed necessary." He paused. His hands, empty now of the goblet, hung awkwardly at his sides, as if he didn't know what to do with them.

"Why?" I asked.

He frowned. "What?"

"Why did you think it necessary? Are you nervous?" The question was out before I realized it. As soon as I spoke, I wondered why I had said it. As if any man would admit to being nervous on his wedding night!

"Yes," he said quietly, startling me. "I am. I've never felt like this, not even before going into battle." He parted his chemise, showing me more of his chest. It gleamed like brown satin, tight curls of dark hair caught in the cleft between the muscled broadness. "My heart races," he said. He stepped to me. "See?"

I lifted my hand, set it on his skin. He was right. I could feel how fast it beat.

"I can't believe you are mine," he whispered, echoing my own thoughts. He looked directly into my eyes as he spoke, for without our shoes, we were almost of equal height. I had a sudden memory of our hands entwined; of how I'd thought they resembled separate strands of silk off the same skein. . . .

"*Tanto monta, monta tanto,*" I whispered, and he blinked.

"What?"

"It is to be our saying. It means, 'We are the same.'" I paused. "Did you not read it? I made it part of our prenuptial agreement, our Capitulations."

"I did read the Capitulations, yes," he replied, a husky timbre in his voice. "But to be honest, I didn't pay much attention. All I cared about was that they made you mine." His hands came up to either side of my face and he drew me against him. "All mine," he whispered, and his mouth covered my lips, drenching me with an abrupt blossoming of sensation, like a field of fiery petals unfurling within me.

He guided me to the bed, his tongue probing, his fingers scattering my clothing, tugging a lace here, undoing a ribbon there, until I felt my shift fall with a whisper about my ankles. The brazier heat of the room flushed my pale skin to rose.

He worshipped me with his eyes. "*Eres mi luna,*" he whispered in my ear. "You are my moon. So white. So pure. . . ."

Though I knew deep inside me that I wasn't his first, that no man could know how to touch a woman like this his first time, I let myself believe we were both innocents. I surrendered to the garden of pleasure he sowed in me, my body growing taut, moist, desperate for his, until I was hearing myself gasp from the exquisite sensation of it all.

When I felt him enter me, the pain Beatriz had mentioned was so sharp it tore away my breath. But I did not let him see it. I wrapped my legs tighter around him and urged him to plunge faster, deeper, even as the spoils of my virginity seeped beneath us, reddening the sheet.

Afterward, as we lay entangled, my hair tousled across his chest, he asked, "Was I too rough?" I shook my head, though I ached. He chuckled, his hands roving over my curves, lazily at first, then more quickly, with increasing ardor. I saw desire flare again in his eyes and I lay back to welcome him once more. Even if it hurt, I told myself, it might hurt less the more we did it.

And as he shuddered and gasped, the heat of his passion easing that raw pain inside me, I heard him say: "Give me a son, my moon. Give me an heir."

CHAPTER EIGHTEEN

I had thought of myself as a woman.

I had imagined what being a woman entailed and had strived to fulfill those exacting requirements. But in the weeks that followed our wedding, as October was swept away by the first November snows, as fires crackled in the hearths while outside an arctic wind enshrouded our palace, I realized I'd not begun to experience what being a woman meant.

Nestled in furs in our creaking bed, we explored the realm of the flesh like two ravenous children with nothing else to do. I imagine now that the servants and my ladies went tiptoeing about the icy corridors, attending to their duties with stifled giggles as they were regaled by the sounds emanating from our room, where we luxuriated in oblivion. We had to eat, of course, and this we did, from platters we picked over with our fingers, feeding each other cold chicken in pomegranate sauce and sliced cheese on figs, marveling that no food had a flavor as rich as the taste of each other's skin. I lay back laughing as Fernando hopped barefoot across the freezing floor tiles to throw more wood on the fire, then rushed back to bed, naked and cursing, jumping beside me with hands and toes like ice.

"Stop it!" I cried as he wrapped himself about me, his chilly fingertips probing. But soon enough I was arching against him as he tangled those hands, hot as cauldrons now, in my hair and plunged to fill me again with his seed.

Epiphany came and went in a blur. We held a celebration for our household, paid for by a loan from Carrillo, and right after the Masses and exchanging of gifts, we retreated back to our cocoon, sheltered from the howling storms that turned all of Castile into a wasteland. Nothing intruded on our idyllic isolation, our *luna de miel;* we were content to bask in it, to see and be only with each other, to pretend the entire world had paused.

But of course the world had not paused, and eventually we had to get out of bed to send a carefully crafted letter to my half brother. Carrillo had informed us that the moment Enrique learned of the marriage, he had lifted his siege in Andalucía and returned to Castile, riding in dead quiet the entire way; not even Villena had succeeded in cajoling him out of his dark silence. My letter, composed in bed between bouts of lovemaking, with both of us chewing the edges of our quills and spilling ink on each other, implored his understanding. It was our first joint effort as husband and wife, intended to promulgate our official new status while emphasizing our continued fealty. Still, when we sent it by courier, I worried that Enrique had already decided on retribution and that nothing we said or did could change his mind.

With winter upon us, we could do nothing but wait and see. After a time, Fernando and I graduated from the bed to the hearth and began to explore our common interests. We discovered that we both liked chess and cards and had an abiding passion for riding. I was surprised to learn that while he enjoyed the hunt, he too detested bullfighting; he deemed it a "barbarity" and agreed we should never allow the corrida to be held in our honor. Excessive ostentation unsettled him too, for he too had been raised in an impoverished court, where every coin mattered. Most important, he shared my preference for erring on the side of optimism, to seeing the world in terms of what could be achieved rather than what had been lost. He was overly confident and disliked opposition, and in those early days I was content to let him express himself without interference, watching him stride about our chamber declaiming his vision for our future, while I sat by the fire and darned his hose and shirts.

"Arrows and a yoke," he said, his eyes alight. "That will be our device: *flechas* for Fernando and *yugo* for Isabella—our symbol, surmounted by our *Tanto Monta*. It's the perfect device for a future king and queen of Castile, don't you agree?"

I smiled and held up his darned shirt, watching him slip his lean arms into its sleeves and hiding a pang of sudden fear as I glimpsed his body's silhouette through the frequently washed and repaired cloth.

Sensing the change in me with the uncanny perceptiveness he often displayed, Fernando cupped my chin, raised my face to his.

"What is it?" he murmured. "What makes my moon sad?"

"You know," I replied.

He faltered. "Enrique," he said at length, and I nodded.

"He still has not replied to our letter. How long do you think he'll make us wait? We have no money, Fernando. As princess I was supposed to be given possession of various towns, but so far, nothing has been done. All of this—" I motioned to the room around us, encompassing the palace with my words—"is being paid for by Carrillo. We depend on him for everything."

"But we requested your due in our letter. Surely Enrique will not deny us the means to live according to our rank. It's not as if we require much."

I sighed. "You do not know him. This silence of his disturbs me. I fear he prepares some kind of a trap for us."

"But we are married now and you are his declared heir. What can he possibly do?"

I shook my head, reaching into the basket at my feet for another of his linens. "I don't know. But whatever it is, we must be cautious. We must not let him win."

I saw in the firm cast of his jaw that Fernando wasn't likely to let anyone get the better of us. But not even he could have expected Enrique's answer when it finally came, conveyed by none other than Carrillo himself.

Bundled in heavy wool, exuding the chill of the rain-drenched February afternoon, the archbishop flung the parchment onto the table in our *sala,* where Fernando and I took our meals informally, alongside our servants.

"From the cretin and his degenerate," Carrillo snarled, snatching the goblet of hot cider Cárdenas was quick to offer. Carrillo unraveled the layers encasing his bulk, until he stood, steaming, before the fireplace. He took a long draft, eyeing us as Fernando reached for the parchment. As he read, all color drained from his face.

A pit opened in my stomach. "What does it say?"

He looked up. For the first time since we'd exchanged vows, I saw him hesitate. "Isabella, *mi amor* . . . it's . . . I don't want you to—"

"Just tell her," interrupted Carrillo. "She understands the risk she took." He grabbed the paper from Fernando and read aloud: ". . . thereby, I do not recognize Doña Isabella's marriage to Prince Fernando as legal or canonically binding, seeing as the dispensation used to solemnize said union is false. Furthermore"—he lifted his voice against my gasp—"my sister has willfully disobeyed my royal authority, blah, blah, blah."

Carrillo dropped the letter onto my lap. "In other words, he defies the marriage and may seek to disinherit you in favor of Joanna la Beltraneja; at the very least, he'll try to wed her to a foreign prince who'll lend him aid, seeing as he and Villena have wasted their resources on that idiotic siege in Andalucía."

I sat perfectly still. I heard Beatriz's knife clatter to the table as she rose in haste to attend me. Summoning my strength, I gripped my chair arms and came to my feet. The parchment slipped from my lap to the floor. Fernando was immobile but Carrillo gaped as I turned, and without a word, walked out. Beatriz and Inés followed close behind me. I did not look at the staring servants, though I did catch the complicit, troubled glance that Fernando's treasurer, Luis de Santángel, cast in Fernando's direction. It was like a stab in my heart, for it proved that Fernando had confided his dilemma to others, even as I had been left unaware.

I felt as if I were suffocating as I climbed the staircase to our rooms. I closed the door on my women's worried faces, turning the key in the lock before I tugged in desperation at my bodice, trying to ease its bone-hard edges so I could fill my lungs with air. I slid in a heap against the door, hands pressed to my breast. I closed my eyes, drawing in shallow breaths. Eventually, the knock came at the door.

I knew who it was even before he said, "Isabella, please. Let me in."

I heard Beatriz murmur something and I heard Fernando's curt reply. He knocked again, harder this time. "Isabella, open this door. I am your husband. We need to talk."

The anger in his tone made me consider leaving him to stew, but I didn't want any more scandal, so I stood and turned the key. I moved into the center of the room as he entered, slamming the door shut again on Beatriz.

"You knew," I said, cutting him off. "When? Before or after we said our vows?"

He met my stare. The skin under his left eye twitched as it did when he was upset.

"Well? Are you going to answer me?"

"Give me a moment," he retorted.

I took a step to him. "Why would you need a moment? It's a simple question."

"It's always simple with you, isn't it?" he said tersely. "Good or bad, black or white, saint or sinner—that's how Her Highness Doña Isabella sees the world."

I halted, taken aback by his contemptuous tone.

"But I do not." He paced to the decanter on the sideboard. Contrary to his avowed abstinence, I'd discovered that Fernando in fact enjoyed a little wine at night, in private, and I'd instructed Inés to make sure there was always some ready. I wondered now, as he filled his cup, what other surprising discoveries I was fated to make about him.

"I see all the shades of gray in between," he said. "I see that men are both bad and good, that we're capable of great evil and great sacrifice. I know, as you do not, nothing in this world is ever as simple as we think."

I considered him. "You are undoubtedly right," I said at length. "I do not know a great many things. But a dispensation from His Holiness is either legal or it is not. And according to the king, the one your father and Archbishop Carrillo procured for us is not."

"My father is not to blame. He did request the dispensation from Rome, repeatedly, but that pompous ass Pope Pius kept delaying. He finally sent it, as you yourself saw, but he insisted it would only be valid *after* we wed. How was anyone to know—"

"Pope Pius has been dead for five years," I interrupted. "Pope Paul should have issued the dispensation." I saw him wince. "But you've answered my question, at least. Evidently, you knew the dispensation was falsified even before we said our vows."

"Isabella." He drained the cup and came to me, taking my hands in his. "*Dios mío,* you're like ice," he murmured.

I withdrew my hands. "I do not like being lied to."

He let out an impatient exhale. "What were we supposed to do? Tell me. You wrote to say you were in danger, that Enrique plotted to wed you to Portugal and you needed me in Castile, without delay. But Aragón was at war with France; we had nothing with which to bribe the pope, who'd already accepted offers from Villena to refuse us the dispensation." He paused, searching my eyes. "Yes, it is true: Villena sent envoys to Rome to thwart us. But my father has friends in the Curia and our own Cardinal Borgia from Valencia finally sent us the dispensation, backdated to Pius's last year of life."

"And the signature . . . ?"

Fernando averted his gaze. "Carrillo had other papers with Pius's handwriting."

"So a man of the Church forged a late pope's name." I turned to the window. Outside, heavy rain mixed with sleet obscured my view of the city. "And now you and I are accused by my brother the king of living together in sin, our marriage invalid in the eyes of God."

"It's not invalid." Fernando did not move, but I detected a hint of imploration in his voice. "Carrillo has assured me, we are legally and canonically, under the saints and Church and God Himself, most firmly wed."

"Do not blaspheme." I stared, unseeing, out the window.

"The dispensation is just a technicality. We are related, yes, but by distant kinship; it's not as if we're brother and sister. Royal couples with far more shared blood than ours have done worse."

"Is that what it is to you?" I turned to him. "A contest to see what we can get away with?"

"No, of course not. I only meant that—"

"Because to me, it is a grave matter indeed. We require a dispensation; whether or not it's a technicality is beside the point. A pontiff's name and signature were falsified; we must make it right. We must request another—one that is legal and binding."

"And so we shall." He finally moved to me, clasping my hands again, more firmly this time, so I wouldn't pull away. "I promise, I'll write to

Cardinal Borgia myself. But now is not the time. We have more serious issues to deal with."

"What could be more serious than the validity of our union? Enrique accuses us of a graceless state so he can put the queen's illegitimate child on the throne in my place." My voice rose, despite my efforts to control it. "Because of you, your father, and Carrillo, my entire claim to Castile could be in jeopardy!"

"So is our safety," he said, and I went still. "You left before Carrillo could tell us the rest of his news. Villena has lured the grandees into an alliance against us. We are the enemy, Isabella—you and me. We cannot stay here. Valladolid sits on a plain and as such, we are defenseless. My grandfather has offered us his retainers as protection, but we must take refuge in a castle with a moat and walls thick enough to keep the king's men out."

I looked into his eyes—those revealing brown eyes that I'd begun to know so well and suspected could never lie to me, regardless of what his lips said. I found no deceit.

"Where can we go?" I whispered, shuddering at the thought of another hurried and secretive departure, another rush through the night to a fortified structure. It seemed as if all I'd done since Enrique had come into my life was flee him.

"Carrillo says the castle of Dueñas will suffice, for the time being."

"Dueñas," I echoed, dejected. "But that's miles away from anywhere."

"Yes, but Carrillo's brother is lord mayor of the town. We'll be safe there." He went quiet, caressing my hand before he ventured, "Am I forgiven?"

I nodded. "But you must never lie to me again, Fernando. Promise me."

He leaned to me, murmured against my lips, "I promise."

I was warmed as ever by his touch, by the desire that flared between us, but as we returned to the *sala*, I had the disquieting sensation that we had offended God in our zeal to wed. Though I did not know what trials awaited us, I feared we would be sorely tested.

And already, I sensed a new life stirring inside me.

CHAPTER NINETEEN

Inés hovered at my chair, one of her reliable herbal drafts in hand. "Doctor Santillana says you must drink it. Chamomile helps with the vile humors."

I grimaced. "I'm with child. Vile humors are normal. All chamomile will do is constipate me, and that's the last thing I need."

I waved her aside and stood awkwardly, my hand on my jutting stomach. I was in my seventh month and I felt as if I were about to give birth at any moment—my feet and ankles swollen, my digestion in an uproar, and my temperament uneven at best. The entire experience had caught me off guard; I'd expected to remain active and energetic up to my confinement. After all, I was just nineteen, and the midwife had coarsely assured me that girls my age bred "like cows in the field."

So far, that had not been the case. Along with my other ailments, I'd been plagued by insomnia, and my appetite seemed to be the only part of me that hadn't undergone some bewildering transformation. Fernando kept telling me I was beautiful, that I resembled a lush Madonna such as those being painted in Italy, but I wasn't convinced. While vanity had never been integral to my well-being, I'd begun to secretly fret that my figure would never recover from its distorted shape, molded by the unseen being now kicking at my insides with obstinate determination.

A boy, the midwife had said: it must be a boy; this naturally made Fernando all the more attentive and had prompted a torrent of premature congratulatory gifts from his father in Aragón. Carrillo shared the sentiment; every time he came to visit, armed with the latest news and money to pay our expenses, he never failed to remind me that a boy would turn the tide in our favor. No matter how much damage Enrique inflicted, if I gave birth to an infante, all would change. A boy could inherit Castile *and* Aragón. Our son would be the first king to rule both realms.

"A male heir to succeed us," I muttered, "while Enrique has nothing but that child everyone calls la Beltraneja." I leaned against the windowsill of my chamber to peer through the uneven panes. "The entire country will flock to our standard. . . ."

"My lady?" said Inés, not hearing me from where she busied herself at my coffers.

I turned about with a sigh. Poor Inés had borne the brunt of my enforced cloistering in what I'd come to call "our prison of Dueñas." With my activity curtailed, Fernando often went out with his men all day to hunt, braving the unseasonably humid autumn to hunt the deer, rabbits, and other creatures whose meat we needed to survive winter.

Beatriz had reluctantly returned to Segovia. With Enrique back in Castile, the pressure exerted on her husband by Villena to release the treasury had increased, and Cabrera needed her at his side. Unfathomably, Enrique had developed a liking for Beatriz; she was the only one capable of dissuading him from surrendering to Villena's mad demands, such as sending an army against me. I knew by her letters that she'd single-handedly persuaded Enrique to leave us alone for the time being, citing my pregnancy as reason for him to show his forbearance. However, though she might have succeeded in forestalling his official denial of my status as his heir, not even she had been able to stop him from refusing me income and reducing us to poverty. I worried that as soon as my child was born, he'd do far more than that.

"Did my letter leave yet?" I asked, pacing back to my upholstered chair and the pile of poor linens I'd taken to making, to help the numerous widows and beggars in the town that had sheltered me, many of whom suffered privations because of the prolonged instability in the kingdom.

"Yes, Cárdenas took it to Segovia himself this morning." Inés paused, regarding me. "My lady, it's not my position to say anything, but do you really expect His Majesty to respond? This will be the sixth letter you've sent in as many months."

"I know." I sat. Those few steps across the room had exhausted me, to my chagrin. "But I dare not stop. Even if he ignores them, if I keep sending letters reiterating my loyalty to him as my king and brother, perhaps he'll not go any farther than he already has."

"He's not the problem, though," countered Inés, and I paused, looking at her.

"Indeed," I said softly. "He is not. Villena holds complete sway. While that man has Enrique's heart and ear, the most I can hope for is reprieve from—"

An abrupt cramp snagged my breath. I gasped, my hands dropping instinctively to my belly. Another spasm overcame me. It couldn't be. I was only in my seventh month; I had still two left. . . .

The third cramp was strong enough to cause me to gasp. Warm liquid started to seep down my thighs; as the gush wet my hem, I said to Inés, "Go, quickly. Fetch the midwife. She was wrong. I'm going into labor—now."

I SCARCELY REMEMBERED the next fourteen hours. The midwife and her crones hovered about me as I reclined, groaning, upon an open-seated birthing stool in an overheated chamber smothered in herbal vapors and the sourness of my own sweat and urine. I had asked that a silk veil be placed over my face, so no one could see me grimace. The pains were strong but not too much so. I was still in a state to consider my dignity. I began to recite prayers to the Virgin who succors women in their hour of delivery, but as the time passed and the pain squeezed me in an inescapable vise, my prayers fractured, replaced by breathless pleas. I had never felt such agony; I would have given anything to revert to my previous, pregnant misery. By the middle of the night, as I stared at women whose faces had blurred into one anonymous visage, all urging me to "push," I finally understood that I might die. I scarcely had any strength left to breathe.

It had always been with me, in truth—that unseen specter at my heels. It was the bane of our sex, thrust upon us by Eve's sin. Women died every day in childbed, be they commoner or queen. I'd given the matter some contemplation when I said my daily devotions, thinking to prepare my immortal soul; but it adopted a visceral intensity in those hours as I struggled to expel the child in my womb, my shrieks sounding in my ears like the keening of a demented animal.

Then, miraculously, as the second morning in October broke over Dueñas, I opened my mouth, and instead of a bellow, I was overwhelmed by a shuddering sigh of vast release that was almost like pleasure. I looked down between my splayed, bloodied thighs to see the midwife capture a slimy body that did not resemble anything human. I managed a whisper through my parched lips: "*Dios mío,* is it . . . ?"

The women crowded together. I heard water splash, heard the slice of a blade, and a resounding slap. Inés, drenched in perspiration and looking as if she'd gone into labor herself, swabbed my forehead with a cloth as we stared toward the black-clad women.

They turned to us. I gripped Inés's hand so tightly that she bore the bruise for days afterward. The midwife, who'd decided she must have erred in calculating my time of conception, came to me and extended the naked mewling infant in her gnarled hands.

"A girl, Your Highness," she said dryly, "perfectly formed, as you can see."

At her unwilling entrance into the world, my little daughter promptly let out a wail that went straight to my beleaguered heart.

Fernando was ecstatic; as soon as he ascertained that I was well, he turned his attentions to little Isabel—named in honor of my mother—proudly taking her in his arms to show her off in her swath of velvets to all our household.

"She's perfect," he whispered to me at night, when he snuck into my rooms, defying the prohibition that I must not receive him until I'd been churched, cleansed of the stain of childbirth by a priest's blessing. He sat on the bed with Isabel cradled between us, her little fists curled at her face, and he regarded her in rapt silence, as though she were the most precious thing he had ever seen.

"I thought you'd be disappointed because she's not a boy," I finally said.

"My father is disappointed" was his reply. "So is Carrillo. In fact, our lord Archbishop acts as though this were a personal failure, moping over the Salic Law in Aragón that forbids a woman's succession and predicting catastrophe."

"Such a ridiculous custom, Salic Law," I exclaimed. "How can it be right to exclude half the children born to a royal couple? If I—a woman—am considered capable of inheriting the crown in Castile, why shouldn't our Isabel be equally so in Aragón?"

He smiled. "I am happy. She's healthy and we are still young. We'll have sons."

I gave him a sharp look, peeved by his apparent indifference. "Yes, of course," I said. "Only pray, let me recover from this child first."

His chuckle awoke Isabel. She blinked, her gorgeous big blue eyes focused on him for a moment before she drifted back to sleep. Overwhelming ferocity filled me as I caressed her warm, delicate cheek.

"I'll not let them do her harm," I said. "I don't care how disappointed everyone is, they will not make her feel unwanted." I lifted my gaze to him. "Is there any word from court? I imagine Enrique is beset with relief, even as Villena plans his next attack. Because of this Salic Law, we're as vulnerable as ever."

Fernando's eyes glittered. "Not quite," he said enigmatically. He leaned to me, silencing my question with a kiss. "You've been through an ordeal few men would willingly undergo. Let me shoulder the war for now, while you look after our daughter, yes?"

He left me before I could stop him. I wanted to rise from my bed at once but fatigue overcame me as I snuggled closer to my babe. Though we now had a robust peasant wet nurse, selected for her good teeth, placid temperament, and unassailable constitution, I secretly nursed Isabel in private, easing the ache in my milk-swollen breasts and giving her a reputation for being a finicky eater who nonetheless seemed to grow overnight. I was content to stay with her, cocooned and apart, and let the cares of the world drift by. It was the only time in my life when I'd enjoyed the luxury. And with the winter snows blanketing Dueñas, I could pretend for a time that I was not an embattled princess fighting for her rights but rather an ordinary mother, enraptured by her first child.

And so it went. I oversaw every aspect of Isabel's rearing and refrained from asking Fernando any questions when he came to dine with us, though I knew he spent hours closeted with Carrillo. I once overheard him and the archbishop through the hall door, shouting at each other; that same day, Fernando came banging into my chamber with a hot flush to his face, declaring Carrillo a high-handed mule who thought too much of himself and too little of everyone else.

"If he dares quote those blasted Capitulations to me one more time, I vow I'll not be responsible for my actions! Whatever happened to our *tanto monta* that he dares say I must respect his wiser counsel?"

I went to pour him a goblet of cider, warm in its decanter by the hearth. "We did agree to honor him as our premier advisor as part of our prenuptial agreements."

"So he keeps reminding me." Fernando drank. "I should have read those so-called Capitulations more closely."

I had a moment of apprehension. Carrillo was used to getting his way. He had always believed in his own preeminence, even when guiding Alfonso. But Fernando was not some pliant prince he could dictate to; in my husband ran a streak of willfulness that more than matched the archbishop's. I did not want them to end up at each other's throats, not when we still awaited a reply to my countless, increasingly indignant letters to Enrique.

"Perhaps I should start attending these meetings," I said. "I'm well acquainted with our Capitulations and—"

"No." He slammed the goblet down so hard it startled Isabel in her cradle. She began to cry. I rushed to her, picking her up and glaring at him. His jaw set. "Let me handle Carrillo," he said, and he marched out, his shoulders squared with resolve.

I rocked Isabel, murmuring endearments; from the corner where she sat on an upholstered stool, quietly mending one of my skirts, Inés raised a questioning brow.

The next morning I donned my best day gown of gray wool, coiled my hair in a gilded net, and entered the hall to find Carrillo and Fernando facing each other across the table, while Admiral Fadrique and Chacón stood to one side, looking decidedly uncomfortable.

"You know nothing of how we do things here in Castile," Carrillo was saying, his big features tinged scarlet with ire. "This is not the backwaters of Aragón, where you can overtake cities whenever you please."

Fernando rattled a paper at him. "Look here, old man! This is from the lord mayor of Toro himself; he has *invited* us to overtake his city.

What more do you need, eh? Should we send for engraved proclamations? Will that suit your bloated sense of pride?"

"We need the princess's approval," snapped Carrillo, and as I saw Fernando's fist clench over the paper, I stepped over the threshold.

"And here I am, my lords, so you may request it."

The admiral's face brightened with relief; Fernando, I saw at once, was furious—but he contained himself because he had no other choice. Because of our prenuptial agreement, in which he'd agreed to uphold Castile's superiority over his realm, Carrillo had him in a stranglehold. My instincts had been correct: He needed me here, though he'd never admit it.

I sat at the table, strewn with discarded papers and quills. "What seems to be the issue?" I asked, regarding them placidly.

Con blandura, I reminded myself. With a soft touch, almost anything can be accomplished—even with men as fiery as these two.

Carrillo bowed. "Your Highness, alas, I'm sorry to disturb you, but it seems His Highness and I are not in agreement over—"

"The issue," interrupted Fernando, setting the paper before me, "is that my lord the archbishop seems to think we should refrain from asserting our rights, though it's as plain as the nose on his face that Enrique and Villena are losing ground—valuable ground we should be taking full advantage of."

"Oh?" I perused the paper. As its implications sank in, my heart quickened. It said that Enrique was seeking to affiance Joanna la Beltraneja to the Portuguese, and had brought the queen herself to Segovia to swear before the altar that the child was his. I looked up in disbelief. "I . . . I am to be deprived of all rights as princess. He has officially disinherited me."

"Read further." Fernando tapped the paper. I tried to focus. Through the pounding haze that overcame me, isolated words jumped out. None made sense. I finally had to whisper: "I cannot read this. Tell me, what does it say?"

Fernando shot a look at Carrillo. "It means that in disinheriting you, Enrique has made his last blunder. The realm is in an uproar; from Vizcaya to Jaén, and every city in between, the people cry out against your disinheritance and take to the streets." His voice quickened. "Ávila has thrown Villena's henchmen out; Medina del Campo vows to fight for you to the death. They say Joanna la Beltraneja is the by-blow of an adulterous whore and that you are Castile's sole successor. The people want you, Isabella—this paper is an invitation from Toro to enter the city. We've received dozens like it from all over Castile, pledging to open their gates to us."

"Bribed is more like it," sniffed Carrillo, "with promises we cannot keep."

"Bribed?" I looked into Fernando's fervent eyes. "How? We've nothing to offer."

"Only the promise of peace, justice, and prosperity," he replied. "It's just as we discussed, remember? This is our *tanto monta*, come to pass. The cities know what we can offer them because I've sent personal delegates to tell them so. They cannot abide the starvation, the feuds, the debased coinage and arrogant grandees any longer. The king is despised and we are their only hope for righting the kingdom. This is our time. We must seize it."

"With what?" Carrillo flung up his hands. "Stewards, pages, and grooms?" He brayed laughter. "Yes, why not? Let's send Chacón here to claim Toro in your name!"

"I'll lend support," said the admiral quietly. Carrillo froze. Fadrique stepped to us—a small, confident figure in elegant dark velvet. "I promised Your Highness my retainers and I can summon more. We can take Toro and Tordesillas, certainly."

"What of the others?" retorted Carrillo. "What about Ávila? Medina del Campo? Segovia? Will you take all those cities with your retainers, my lord? I hardly think even you, head of the powerful Enríquez family, can summon that many men."

The admiral acknowledged this with an incline of his bald head. "Indeed. But I understand the marquis of Mendoza will assist us, and the duke of Medina Sidonia in Sevilla has also offered support. Surely between us we can gather enough of a show of force to make the king think twice about putting his decrees into effect."

"The marquis of Mendoza will assist us?" Carrillo turned slowly to Fernando. "But the Mendozas have always supported the king. How did you . . . ?"

"Easily." Fernando smiled. "Like every grandee, my lord of Mendoza has an expensive lifestyle to maintain. In exchange for my offer of a cardinal's hat for the marquis's brother, the bishop, along with a significant stipend, Mendoza was more than willing to accept our terms."

"Cardinal's hat . . . ?" Carrillo stared at him in stunned disbelief, his face chalk-white. "You . . . you promised that mealymouthed Bishop Mendoza a prize that is mine by right?"

"I did not promise anything." Fernando's voice was cold. "Cardinal Borgia of Valencia did. He also promised to send the dispensation *you* failed to obtain, sanctioning Her Highness's and my marriage. So, as you can see, she now has no reason not to take a stand."

Carrillo met Fernando's stare, his eyes bulging. *"It is mine!"* His roar reverberated through the *sala*, causing the hounds dozing by the fireplace to leap up, growling. "Mine!" He thumped his meaty fist on his chest. "That cardinalship belongs to me. By ecclesiastical law, it should be conferred on me. I am a lifelong servant of the Church in Castile. I am the one who has supported and fought for Her Highness's cause these many years!"

He was panting, spittle spraying from his lips. I resisted the impulse to beg for civility. All of a sudden, it was as though everyone else in the room had ceased to exist to Fernando and Carrillo as they faced each other like combatants. The rest of us had become part of the backdrop, no more significant than the tapestries and candelabra and snarling dogs, spectators to a battle of wills between the man who'd dominated my life since he had first approached me in Ávila and the husband to whom I had given my heart.

Fernando did not move, did not take his unblinking gaze from Carrillo. He let the throbbing silence between them crack open like an abyss and then he turned to me and said, "My grandfather and I believe a condemnatory letter is in order. If you publicly reject the king's actions and reiterate your injured stance, it should be enough to gain the cities' loyalty. We do not need an army, though we will gather it. Your letter posted on every church door and in every plaza will be sufficient. *Con blandura,*" he added, with a smile. "Isn't that what you always say?"

He had come to know me better in our year of marriage than Carrillo ever had. He understood, as Carrillo never would, that I abhorred the senseless chaos of Enrique's reign, that I'd prefer to maintain some semblance of outward peace, even as we paved my inexorable path to the throne. I did not want the people of this realm to suffer any more than they already had. I did not want death and destruction dealt in my name.

I nodded, feeling Carrillo's stare boring into me. "Yes, that is what I say." I turned my eyes from Fernando to the archbishop; a pang of sympathy made me want to offer him comfort, for he suddenly appeared so old, so tired. I'd never marked before the broken veins in his face, the watery eyes, the sagging jowls, the dull silver in his thinning mane. He'd been a figure of such tireless brute strength for so long, I'd failed to recognize how time had begun to weigh on him.

"I will do everything I can to ensure your contributions, ecclesiastical and otherwise, are recognized," I told him. "Rest assured, you remain one of our most trusted advisors."

He met my eyes for a long moment. I couldn't read anything in his expression; it was as though something inside him had closed, shuttering his face. It frightened me, his sudden blankness. Before, he had always shown his emotions openly to me.

Then he turned and walked out. No one called him back; even as I started to move to go after him, I felt Fernando's hand on my sleeve.

"No. Let him go," he murmured. "We don't need him anymore."

I heard the archbishop's heavy booted footsteps fade down the corridor. The dogs whined, settling back on the frayed carpet by the fire. The admiral waited for us to speak, his face averted. Chacón gave me a stalwart look, one that reflected my own realization that everything had just shifted on its axis.

After a lifetime of his influence, all of a sudden I was free of Carrillo.

I turned to Fernando. "I need a fresh quill and ink," I said quietly, and I resumed my seat, drawing a clean sheet of paper near.

I had made my choice.

From now on, Fernando and I alone would steer our course.

CHAPTER TWENTY

My letter went out, claiming that *"if by passion and ill advice Enrique were to deny my rights as heir, it would be a great insult and disgrace to the realm. God will hold the king responsible for this great evil, while my lord the prince and I will be blameless."*

It was a brazen pronouncement, the closest I'd ever come to insinuating that Enrique endangered the kingdom. And in the months that followed, it generated the very reaction Fernando had predicted. Cities and townships which previously supported Enrique, or remained neutral, posted my letter and came over to our cause, hanging banners from their walls with our entwined initials and declaring: "Castile for Isabella!" When I protested to Fernando that I did not wish to appear as though I sought to usurp Enrique's rights, he laughed.

"What rights? Ávila, Medina del Campo, and six other cities are already for us, and I'm off tonight to throw Villena's officials out of Sepulveda, at the town's own request. If matters continue as they are, by Epiphany all of Castile will be ours."

He was in his element, donning his chain mail and breastplate to rally the admiral's retainers and the forces sent by Medina Sidonia from the south into effective infiltration units that could scale walls, unlock gates, and overpower royal garrisons in the dead of night, with only the moon to illuminate their way. By mid-1472, we held more than half of Castile's fourteen major townships in our grasp, and by the beginning of 1473 we were confident enough of our safety to finally leave Dueñas for a grand new residence in Aranda de Duero, near Valladolid. Once we were established in our palatial estate, even the most recalcitrant grandees, who had opted to bolster Enrique and his villainous favorite, began to send us covert pledges of support—"no doubt," remarked Fernando acidly, "because they know that if they do not, I'll tear their castles down about their ears and put their heads on spikes, to boot."

Though I would never admit it out loud, this statement, more than anything else, proved Carrillo's unwise comment that Fernando did not understand the ways of Castile. To harass the grandees was pointless, even dangerous. Pride and ambition were two sides of the same coin to these lords who had badgered, cajoled, and ignored their sovereign for centuries. They must be enticed, brought to heel without realizing it; otherwise they'd bite like the feral dogs they were at heart. I had seen it throughout my childhood, witnessed firsthand the chaos that Enrique had sown in trying to appease the grandee factions, the internecine intrigues and alliances that had tied him up in knots and turned him into a mere figurehead who must bend to the strongest wind.

Therefore, while Fernando assumed charge of our military affairs that year, I undertook the diplomatic—suffering endless hours of penning letters until spots danced before my red-rimmed eyes and my fingertips bled. I answered every missive I received personally. I did not miss an opportunity to inquire after a sick family member, congratulate a birth, or offer condolences on a death, determined to make myself known to these arrogant lords who could as easily defeat us as defend us. With my Isabel close at my side, playing with her toys or napping in her upholstered cradle by the fire, I worked harder than I ever had before, for I knew that these seemingly small gestures of recognition on my part, these simple exchanges of information and pleasantries, might, in the end, sway the grandees to my side when I most had need of them.

And as I worked, I could imagine Enrique's despair, helpless once more as he watched his kingdom turn against him. Even Villena, it seemed, had fallen ill from the distress of watching his edifice of power and lies crumble. While I did not rejoice in physical suffering, I did take satisfaction that at least with Villena indisposed I was finally at liberty to visit my mother without fearing apprehension by the marquis's zealous patrols. Time had fled by; and between my labors and caring for my child, I had been remiss in attending to my mother's needs. Though I had sent money and letters to Arévalo whenever I could, Doña Clara's replies had been slow in coming and her unrevealing, dutiful tone made me suspect that matters in the household were not as they should be.

I had hoped Fernando would join me in visiting Arévalo, as he had not yet met my mother, but he was unexpectedly called to Aragón by his father to welcome a delegation sent by Cardinal Borgia, carrying our long-awaited dispensation. The cardinal wished to convoke a peace conference between Aragón and France, and peace was something we desired. If Aragón could find some way to stave off its much larger and aggressive neighbor, it would free up men for our ongoing struggle in Castile. Still, it was our first official parting since our marriage and Fernando could be gone for months. I knew I'd miss him terribly, though I endeavored not to show it. I packed his saddlebags full of clean shirts I had sewn with my own hands, kissed him goodbye, and made my own plans, thinking that if I kept occupied, time would pass more quickly and hasten his return.

Not knowing in what state I would find Arévalo, I reluctantly left my Isabel, who was almost four years old, in the care of attendants in our new residence. Inés and Chacón accompanied me, along with an escort of soldiers, in the spring of 1474. It was an uneventful trip but my fears regarding my childhood home were not unfounded; I found the castle more desolate and threadbare than even I recalled, with the animals crowded in filthy stockades and the smell of mold and smoke permeating the hall. My mother was gaunt, shockingly aged, her conversation meandering down blurred pathways between past and present, as if time were a river without any end. She spoke of Alfonso as though he were still alive but failed at moments to recognize me, staring at me with a vacant gaze that twined like barbs about my heart. Doña Clara, whose hair had turned snow-white yet whose presence remained forceful as ever despite her advanced years, informed me that my mother rarely left her apartments anymore, not even to go to her beloved Convent of Santa Ana. Travel in such unsettled times was ill advised and expensive, Doña Clara remarked, and money had been sporadic at best, dependent on what I sent, as Villena had cut the household allowance from the treasury in retaliation against me.

"Some days all we have to eat are a chicken, lentils, and a few on-ions," Doña Clara said, as I inwardly seethed at the fact that even firewood—never abundant on the arid *meseta*—had required strict ra-tioning, the hall so cold in the dead of winter that meat could be hung from its rafters without spoiling. "But we persevere, *mi niña*. What else can we do?"

As I sat embroidering with my mother, glancing at the brittle fingers worrying her needle through the cloth, shame choked me. I couldn't keep her any longer in this deplorable state, no matter how limited my own means. She was becoming an invalid before her time, crippled by inactivity and these harsh living conditions she'd been obliged to en-dure. At the very least, new tapestries, carpets, braziers, and cloth for garments must be purchased; the castle must be cleaned from keep to cellar. While Chacón went to work with the soldiers, repairing the di-lapidated stockades and replenishing the storehouses with game, I swal-lowed my pride and wrote to Carrillo. We'd not seen each other since his abrupt departure from Dueñas despite my various conciliatory mis-sives, which he'd disdained like "a petulant sixty-year-old child," as Fer-nando put it. Now, I abased myself in order to obtain the funds I needed; and something in my plea must have softened his heart, for one evening as we prepared to dine, Chacón strode in to announce that a visitor was requesting admittance at the gate.

"At this hour?" exclaimed Doña Clara, whose existence had become so insular she viewed any intrusion as a potential threat. The other el-derly ladies exchanged apprehensive looks; they had all experienced Vil-lena's belligerent officers barging in to harass and intimidate.

I instructed Chacón to invite our guest in; we had fresh rabbit stew and a dried apple-and-carrot salad in almond milk, and what six can eat, eight can share. But as the small cloaked figure walked in and reached up to remove its cowl, I could not contain my cry. I dashed into a welcome embrace, to the astonishment of those seated around the table.

"How can it be?" I whispered, holding my dear friend close. "How can you be here?"

"Carrillo, of course." Beatriz drew back with a smile. "He asked me to give you this." She pressed a leather purse stuffed with coins into my hand. "And to convey these tidings: Villena is dying of a stomach tumor and the Portuguese alliance for la Beltraneja has fallen apart. The king annulled his marriage to the queen and sent her into a convent. He is sick of conflict. He wishes to personally receive you in Segovia."

I DEPARTED ARÉVALO in the coppery haze of autumn. I had not wanted to show my eagerness by leaping at Enrique's offer of a truce; instead, I composed a cautious reply that indicated I was overseeing my mother's care and requested the release of those long-delayed funds due to me, as a gesture of his sincerity. Then I waited. The money came quickly, sure sign that Villena must indeed be on his deathbed. But Fernando advised me by letter that I should not go near Segovia until we knew for certain that the marquis had succumbed to his ailment, lest it all be an elaborate ruse to entrap me. It was sound advice and so I waited, summoning my Isabel to join me in Arévalo, while with my new funds I proceeded to refurbish the castle.

Beatriz assisted me, regaling me with details of how Carrillo had hidden away from everyone to sulk in his palace in Alcalá, until one day, without warning, he made a brash move and appealed to the king, seeking to reinstate himself in the royal favor.

"He'd heard Villena was ill and that Enrique wandered the country-side between Segovia and Madrid like a lost soul, unable to reconcile himself to the impending loss of his favorite." Beatriz arched her brow; she had never dissembled her feelings and was not about to feign lament now at the end of Villena. "Enrique agreed to see him and to-gether they hatched this reconciliation with you."

I eyed her as we measured the tester on my mother's bed for new curtains. "And I suppose you and Cabrera had nothing to do with it?"

"I didn't say that. In fact, we had a great deal to do with it. My hus-band was the one who took Carrillo's letter to the king, after it sat un-opened for months on a pile of neglected correspondence as tall as the alcazar itself. And once he persuaded Enrique to receive the archbishop, I went to work." She paused for effect. "I told Enrique that if he recon-ciled with you, he would restore peace to Castile, like 'a tree whose dried branches have turned green again and will never wither.'"

"You said that?" I had difficulty repressing my smile. "I never took you for a poet."

"Anything for my lady" was her tart reply, and as our eyes met, we burst into laughter, startling Isabel in the window seat.

"I have missed you so," I said, wiping tears of mirth from my eyes. "I do not know how I've survived all this time without you."

"But you have," she said. "You have a beautiful little girl, and this one"—she made a good-natured moue at Inés, who unfurled the new damask—"to look after you now, not to mention that proud warrior-prince of yours, who defends you with shield and sword."

"Yes," I agreed softly. "I am indeed blessed."

Though lovely as ever, my Beatriz had grown plump in her married state; she too, I could see, was happy, but it occurred to me that after all this time, she'd not yet conceived. I doubted the fault was hers. Though it was commonly believed women were to blame for childlessness in a couple, her robust health showed in the bloom of her cheeks and the sparkle in her eyes. Perhaps it was because Cabrera was older, I reasoned. Maybe just as happened to women in their middle years, men lost their potency after a certain age.

"What are you thinking?" she asked, breaking into my reverie.

"Only that I am very happy we are together," I said, and she gave me one of her discerning looks, as if she could see right through me. But she did not say anything, swooping over instead to twirl a delighted Isabel in her arms. My daughter had taken to Beatriz at once, dubbing her Tía Bea, and I saw in Beatriz's adoring gaze that she too had formed a deep attachment to my child. A better mother would not be found; even with her severely aged and ill father, Don Bobadilla, who was now confined to bed in the castle and not long for this earth, she showed a stoic patience, always ready to attend him no matter how late the hour. I hoped that despite the odds, perhaps she might yet bear a child.

Finally, in early November, shortly after we buried poor Don Bobadilla and Beatriz went into mourning for him, word came of Villena's demise. My most formidable foe, who had hounded me since my brother's death and betrayed or deceived nearly every person he had come in contact with, was gone. He had died in great pain, eaten alive by his stomach ailment, but I found it difficult to summon any compassion for him. With Villena dead, no longer did I need to worry that his malicious tongue and elaborate schemes would turn Enrique from his better judgment. At long last I was free to seek rapport with my half brother and put an end to the succession crisis in Castile.

I dispatched the news to Fernando with due urgency. It would take at least two or three weeks for him to receive the letter and respond, so after I bid my mother farewell in her newly garrisoned abode, I brought Isabel to Aranda de Duero before making the return trip to Segovia with Beatriz. Despite my newfound confidence, I would not entrust my daughter to that court.

As the alcazar loomed into view, stark and pointed as a fang against the leaden winter sky, I was beset by sudden unease. I'd not stepped foot in Segovia since I had left the city seven years earlier; I had no fond memories of the time I'd spent in captivity in that fortress's arabesque interior. Now here I was again, a grown woman and mother in my twenty-third year, about to enter it again.

I turned to Beatriz, saw in her steady gaze that she understood. "Do not worry," she said. "Andrés has prepared everything with Rabbi Abraham Señeor. You will be safe."

I had met the rabbi during my previous stay here. He was an erudite Jewish scholar whom Enrique had always favored, despite the antagonism leveled against him by Villena and others who disliked Sephardic influence at court. Don Abraham was Enrique's head tax collector; he'd also offered invaluable support to Cabrera in his struggle to keep the treasury and crown jewels safe. If the rabbi was involved in my reception, I could indeed be assured of protection, and so I nodded, turning Canela in to the main courtyard, where hundreds waited to receive me.

A light snow began to drift down, dusting the plumed caps and sumptuous velvets of the courtiers as they dropped into obeisance. Canela's hooves struck the cobblestones with a metallic ring that echoed around the courtyard. As I gazed uncertainly upon the anonymous sea of figures, fear rippled through me. What if Beatriz was wrong? What if despite all assurances to the contrary, Enrique had summoned me here to take me captive?

Then, I caught sight of the lone figure standing in the court's midst—a pillar of black with his signature red turban.

I would not have recognized him without it. As Chacón assisted me from my saddle and I approached, I concealed my dismay at the king's extreme thinness. He was jaundiced, sharply etched cheekbones showing under his skin. His mournful eyes were dull, sunk in bruised shadows, bearing testament to his grief. He had the haunted look of a man who has seen the depths of misfortune and I blinked back the sting of tears as I curtsied before him, taking his extended hand with the signet ring and raising it to my lips.

"*Majestad,*" I said, "I am deeply honored to be in your presence again."

Enrique did not speak. I glanced up, trembling, wondering why he had not bidden me to rise. Had he summoned me here only to humiliate me before his court? His amber eyes were fixed on me, unabashedly wet; as tears seeped down his face, mingling with the wet snow dripping from his turban, his mouth quivered. He did not speak because he could not. His emotion, held so long in check, threatened to overcome him.

I did not wait for his leave. I stood and enveloped him in my arms, not caring what any of the courtiers or grandees thought. All that mattered in that moment was that he and I shared the same blood. We were family, brother and sister.

"*Hermano,*" I said, so low that only he could hear me, "I am so sorry."

I felt his stifled sob. His emaciated body melted against mine. And he finally whispered with childlike bewilderment, "No, it is my fault. Mine. I am cursed. I destroy everything I touch. . . ."

WE RODE CEREMONIOUSLY on horseback through the streets, to demonstrate our reconciliation to the people. They responded with ear-shattering enthusiasm, waving pennons and shouting acclaim, as the skies turned dark, torches were lit, and the snow dissolved into sodden drifts.

In the alcazar, we dined in the great gilded *sala,* seated together on the dais overlooking the polished floor and crowded tables as if nothing had happened between us, as if the years of strife had never been. He had youth attending to him, as always—handsome boys with soft eyes and perfumed hands, to proffer his plates, fill his goblet, cut his meat. His Moorish guard stood stationed behind him with their scimitars and aloof expressions; only the extravagant red flash of his much-maligned queen was missing to complete this bizarre regression to the past.

But not everything was as it seemed; I could sense that something profound had changed in Enrique. Though he sat enthroned as king, with me, his acknowledged heir, at his side, he seemed removed from the surroundings. He looked upon his court, upon the grandees and lesser nobles who drank his wine and ate his food, who feigned subservience even as they gauged us with the intensity of predators, and he exuded only weary indifference. It was as if he were witnessing a pantomime that held no meaning for him anymore.

Finally I requested his permission to retire. I was exhausted, in body and spirit; and as I kissed his cheek, he murmured, "Tomorrow we'll talk, yes? We have so much to discuss, so much to do. . . ." His voice drifted off. His expression grew even more unfocused, as if the coming days presented an ordeal he was not sure he could face.

"We have time," I said. "My lord husband is not yet here; it could be weeks before he's able to depart Aragón. There is no need to rush. Let us enjoy our reunion first, yes?" Even as I spoke, my heart went hollow. All of a sudden, I wished with a profound desperation that Fernando were here with me. I longed to see his face, touch his hands; I needed to know that he would be my bulwark against whatever intrigues I would have to endure.

I saw in Enrique's haunted expression that he had felt the same about Villena.

He gave me a faint smile. "Yes, why not? Let us enjoy ourselves." He reached for his goblet, drank its contents down in one gulp. As his cupbearer hastened to refill it, I had no doubt that—judging by the yellowish taint to his skin—Enrique would drink himself to a stupor that night. That he'd been doing just that since Villena's death.

Unexpected regret rose in me as I made my way through the crowd. Ines caught up with me at the doorway and as we were escorted to my apartments—those same overdressed rooms once held by Juana—I could not help but wonder if I was in part to blame for Enrique's piteous state. Perhaps if I'd been more dutiful, less prone to stubbornness or contest; perhaps if I had offered him the compassionate love of a sister, rather than revolt and defiance, none of this would have come to pass. Maybe he would have turned to me for guidance instead of placing his trust in the rapacious marquis, whose death had cast him into such despair. . . .

Inés's gasp startled me to attention. She stood frozen in the apartments' audience chamber, staring at the spectral figure that seemed to hover above the painted tile floor, made even more incorporeal by the few lit candles, which cast more shadow than light.

He inclined his tonsured head. "Your Highness, forgive my intrusion." His voice was low, almost muted; in the gloom, his pale eyes were opaque, like the eyes of a wolf.

"Fray Torquemada." I set a hand over my pounding chest. For a terrifying moment, I'd thought he was an assassin disguised in the habit of Santo Domingo, Villena's final act of revenge. "You gave us a fright. I did not expect you here, at this hour."

"As I said, forgive the intrusion. What I have to tell you is of the utmost importance." His unblinking stare apparently unnerved Inés; her hands trembled as she went about lighting more candles. In the brightening room, Torquemada looked too pale and thin, like an anchorite who had not seen the sun in weeks.

I motioned Inés into the bedchamber. I should not be alone with a man who was not my husband and, had he not been of the cloth, I would have dismissed him regardless of the importance of his message. But he had acted as my confessor, advised me during my time of doubt over my betrothal, and I was in no danger. No matter whose apartments he visited at whatever hour, his celibacy would never be in question.

Still, to emphasize the unsuitability of his presence I did not assume a seat, nor did I motion him to one. Instead I said, "Your news must be urgent, indeed. I've only just arrived. Had you waited, I assure you I would have found a proper place and time for us to speak."

"There was no time to wait," he replied. "God has sent me to you now because your moment is almost here. Soon you will hold the scepter in hand and your glorious purpose will be revealed."

A shiver crept down my spine. He spoke like one of those odious soothsayers who often skulked about court with their numerous talismans and claims of fortune-telling.

"Please," I said, "speak plainly. I am tired. It has been a long day."

He took a step toward me. I was stunned to see that his feet were bare under his robe's ragged hem, tinged blue from cold, clotted blood on his toes. He must have walked to the alcazar from the monastery without sandals. I shivered again.

"God gave you Fernando," Torquemada intoned. "He heard your implorations and He granted you the earthly passion you so desired. He gave you the strength to overcome all obstacles, to vanquish all foes; but in return you must vow to serve Him. You must do Him honor first, above all other considerations. He demands it of you as His earthly queen."

He paused, his words reverberating with eerie resonance in the closed room. I swallowed against a throat that was suddenly parched. Why was he saying this to me? Was he here to accuse me of some lapse in my devotions?

"I assure you, I do serve Him. Every day," I said. "I'm but a frail servant and—"

"You'll be more than a servant," he said, and I resisted the urge to recoil as he bent toward me, his eyes seeming to smolder in his otherwise cadaverous face. "You cannot deny that you too have seen the mark of Satan upon our wretched king. Enrique IV is doomed; already death creeps into his bones. He has offended the Almighty with his perversities, turned his face from the righteous to embrace his venal sin. But you"—he took another step to me, so close I could smell old candle smoke on his person—"you are His chosen one. In you, His light and wrath burn bright. Only you can guide these realms from the clutch of the Devil and restore our sanctity. Only you can wield the sword that will cut out the heart of evil that plagues these domains."

I had gone immobile, unable to look away from him. "It is treason to predict the death of a king," I heard myself say.

"I do not predict." He lifted a bony finger, as if to chide me. "I am dust, as is every man, even a king. He will die and you will rule. And you must vow to cleanse Castile of corruption, to root it out no matter where it may dwell and cast it into the abyss, by your immortal soul."

"What corruption?" I whispered, though I already knew and dreaded the answer. "What . . . what do you mean?"

He stared into my eyes. "Heresy. It lurks everywhere. It has permeated the very rocks and water and soil of this land: It hides in the child who laughs, in the woman at the fountain, in the man on the donkey who passes you on the street. It is in the very air you breathe. It is in the false Christian, who takes the Holy Wafer and spits it out to indulge his abomination, who pretends to revere our Church yet secretly Judaizes with his creed. They are the festering sore in Castile; they are the diseased limb you must amputate and burn to purify the one true faith."

He spoke of the conversos, the Jews who had converted to our faith. There were thousands in Castile, many of whom had accepted Holy Baptism during the mass conversions of 1391, following a horrific wave of anti-Sephardic violence. They had wed Christians, raised their children as Christians. Beatriz and Andrés de Cabrera were of converso ancestry and so were many of the realm's most noble families. Purity of blood was an abstract idea, something that few in our land could claim to possess.

"Are you asking me to persecute my people?" I said, incredulous.

"It is not persecution when it is done in God's name. They are unclean and false. They defile the Church with their forked tongues. They pretend to venerate our Holy Virgin and the saints but they lie. They always lie. They must be exposed, dealt with. Eliminated."

I forgot myself, letting out a brittle laugh. "But they're more than half the realm! I bear converso blood in my own lineage; so does Fernando in his. Indeed, you yourself, Fray Torquemada, are a descendant of conversos. Are we all false, then?"

His face hardened. In a voice sibilant with an emotion darker than rage, stronger than hatred—an emotion I didn't know how to identify because I had never felt it and hoped I never would—he replied, "Let me prove to you just how false they are."

I regarded him in laden silence. Then I raised my chin. "You are impertinent. I am not yet queen, nor, God willing, shall I be for many years hence, as it would mean the loss of my sole surviving brother. Yet even if I were crowned tomorrow, the last thing I'd condone is the persecution of my subjects."

"It is your duty." His eyes were cold. Flat. "You must not let heresy flourish under your rule. God has granted you a great privilege; with it comes great responsibility."

How dare he remind me of my obligations, after everything I'd undergone to protect my very right to fulfill those obligations? In that instant, I wanted him out. He repulsed me with his vehemence, with his outrageous effrontery. I'd just returned to Segovia; Enrique was bereft, ill; I was alone, without proper counsel, in a court where I had never felt safe, separated from my husband and child. How could he thrust this onerous burden on me?

"I am perfectly aware of my responsibility," I informed him and I heard the cutting edge in my voice. "And I promise you, Fray Torquemada, heresy will not flourish should I wear the crown. But I will not punish the innocent. That is my final word."

I bowed my head, in deference to his spiritual superiority. "Now, you must excuse me. It is long past the hour when I should retire."

I did not wait for his response as I walked to my bedchamber door. As I turned the knob, I looked over my shoulder. He was gone, the outer door closed; a candle near it burned steadily, as if his departure had not stirred the air, as if he'd never been here at all.

It is your duty. . . . God has granted you a great privilege; with it comes great responsibility.

I shuddered, stepped into the warmth of the room beyond, where Ines had turned down the bedcovers and lit the braziers and was awaiting me with robe and brush in hand.

Yet even as I sought to forget, his words clung to me like a shadow.

CHAPTER TWENTY-ONE

An exhausting round of festivities, banquets, and excursions filled the next few weeks.

Despite his wasted appearance, Enrique was determined to make an occasion of our reunion, and so we had a program for every hour of every day. Bundled against the chill, we went to hear Mass in the cathedral, to visit important nobles in their palaces, to be entertained by choirs of children in the orphanages, and to meet with important merchants. Every night we donned our cumbersome regalia to dine with the court, as though the mere act of appearing together and sharing a trencher might somehow stifle whatever plots and schemes the grandees hatched in the shadows.

I evaded all business with Enrique's council, however. Though Carrillo had come to court, a brooding giant at the edges of our activities, I exchanged only pleasantries with him until he asked brusquely one evening, "Do you plan to have him declare for you in the succession before he drinks himself to death? If not, pray let me know so I can go home. It is the sole reason I orchestrated this meeting between you."

I gave him a pointed look. "As far as I'm concerned, he never declared against me. Joanna la Beltraneja was deemed a bastard and the queen is in a convent. I was sworn heiress at Guisando. And," I added, as he scowled, "Fernando is not here. I'll not make any arrangements without my husband's presence."

His smile was serpentine. "Ah, yes. I've heard your husband is still in Aragón, contending with the thorny issue of how to gainsay the French—though it seems he did secure that dispensation Borgia promised. I trust we'll soon have the pleasure of Prince Fernando's company. As important as his realm's affairs are, it is the future of the crown of Castile that should most concern us, yes?"

I refrained from comment, gritting my teeth. Carrillo still had an almost preternatural ability to sniff out discord, and I had no intention of informing him that I shared his sentiments. In fact, I'd recently received a letter from Fernando that had left me deeply disturbed, in which he explained that his recent triumph over the French had resulted in a short-lived treaty, which they broke as soon as he turned his back. Rather than peace talks, he was now engaged in wresting back vital Aragonese lands that the French had overrun and therefore he could not promise exactly when he might return. In the meantime, he warned me not to conclude any arrangements with Enrique or to entrust the archbishop with our affairs. *Carrillo does not care about protecting our interests,* he wrote. *All he wants is to curry favor with the king and get you back under his thumb.*

His distinct lack of sentiment or trust in my abilities galled me. I returned word that I had managed my affairs perfectly well until now and had no need to entrust Carrillo or any other with them as such. I also asked him to please conclude his own affairs as quickly as possible, for his presence was required here. But my discomfort must have been writ on my face, for the archbishop's smile turned savage at my silence. I knew he perceived my isolation, removed from my new family and at the mercy of my half brother's bizarre inclinations.

For bizarre they were. Enrique's copious consumption of wine—after having displayed near-abstention all his life—had made him a figure of ridicule; by the evening's end he was slurring his words, weaving through the courtiers with his Moors and pages in tow, demonstrating an intimate familiarity with those far below his rank. He was prodigious with aspiring favorites, lavishing gifts on all but paying marked attention to Villena's handsome, dissolute son, Diego, who, having inherited his late father's title and lands, was fast becoming a cause of concern for me. As I sat rigid on the dais, watching Enrique parade young Villena about like a new mistress, I was plunged back to those awful days when I'd been a captive infanta, powerless to affect my future.

I missed my home in Aranda, my belongings and servants. I detested the gilded deception of the court, the furtive whispers, barbed glances, and constant plotting that made the alcazar seethe like a viper's nest. I missed my child, Isabel, with a visceral ache. But above all, I missed Fernando. As I sat there watching my half brother make a mockery of love with his newfound friend, I could almost feel my husband's hands on me, lifting my skirts as we tumbled back onto the bed, laughing. And as desire rose in me, I had to dig my fingers into my palms, reminding myself that now was not the time to let my passions overcome me.

That night I became so despondent that I declared my intention to pack my things and leave Segovia within the hour. I was only dissuaded by Beatriz, who made me promise to stay until Epiphany.

"You must consolidate your status, no matter what," she said. "Remember, you've not come this far to discard it all in a fit of pique."

She was right, much as I disliked hearing it. I had not fought all these years for my right to call myself heir of Castile, to wed the man I'd chosen, and live as I saw fit to now turn tail and flee because I missed my home. But slowly, my compassion for Enrique began to curdle inside me, a sour taint that made me feel uncharitable and had me on my knees in the chapel more times than I cared to count. I knew he deserved my pity; he was still in mourning for Villena, and, as so many of us do, he sought consolation in the wrong place. Yet I could not abide the thought of a new favorite emerging to complicate my existence, one who carried the treachery of his father in his blood, no less. Nor could I comprehend how a king who had suffered so much by his own indulgence could have learned so little.

December roared bitter wind and snow, encasing the alcazar in an icy shroud. While the courtiers danced under silken banners hanging from the eaves, I kept my smile affixed to my lips, not displaying by word or gesture my growing horror at the sight of Enrique lounging on a quilted divan in a faux tent, with young Diego Villena at his side on spangled cushions, eating tidbits of spiced partridge from Enrique's own fingers. I saw everyone watching; I saw Carrillo's mouth twist in disgust, and I wondered how much longer it would be before the eruption came, before some grandee would declare he'd had enough of this disgraceful behavior, and whether out of envy, pride, or indignation, unsheathe his sword, as Villena himself had done years before.

Then, one fateful evening, as Enrique's habitual carousing began after supper and I rose to depart, a sudden hush fell. I glanced up, catching Beatriz's startled regard moments before her husband, Cabrera, rushed across the floor to the pavilion-like ensemble Enrique had established in the alcove.

The king was doubled over on his pillows, Diego Villena anxiously patting his back, as if Enrique were choking. Only Cabrera had gone to his aid; as I hiked up my skirts to better cross the floor, the courtiers drew back one by one, and I saw Carrillo by a sideboard, alone, goblet in hand, a contemplative look on his broad, weathered face.

Enrique was gasping, his entire body contorted. Cabrera inquired rapidly, "What did he eat? Where is the platter?" and as I neared, Enrique raised his ghastly white face and whispered, "Why now? Why, when I'd have given it all over to you soon enough?" before he grimaced and doubled over again. A protracted agonized moan erupted from him as bloody foam seeped from his mouth; he fell to his knees, groaning, "It hurts. God help me, it *burns*!"

As I made myself start to bend over him, young Villena thrust a hand at me. "Get away from him," he hissed. "You did this. You did it so you can steal his throne." He fell to his knees, gathered the writhing king in his arms.

I started to protest, horrified by his accusation. But before I could speak, a hand fell on my sleeve like a vise and I heard Carrillo say in my ear, "Go. Now."

A moan issued from Enrique. Cabrera stood helpless by the king. I met his solemn stare and said, "You will keep me informed."

He nodded. I knew that as long as he was involved, no one would seek to officially accuse me, yet as I turned to my ladies, who waited anxiously among the courtiers, I could almost hear young Villena's terrible words ringing in the air.

They believed I had done it.

They believed I had poisoned my own brother.

CABRERA FINALLY CAME to me hours later, after I had furiously paced my apartments declaiming my innocence to Beatriz and Inés. "His

Majesty shows some improvement," he said wearily, as Beatriz rose to offer him a goblet. "He was taken to his rooms to rest, but Villena insisted that they could not stay here. They departed for Madrid."

I stared at him in disbelief. "But he is ill and Madrid is almost a full day's ride away, over impossible terrain. Are they insane? Where is Carrillo? How can he have permitted this? How can *you* have permitted it?"

"Your Highness, the king himself commanded that his horse be readied. He would not hear a word of advice to the contrary."

"Madrid is part of Villena's marquisate," I said, turning to Beatriz. "They'll gather supporters against me. God save us: This is Diego Villena's fault. He's just like his father. He'll poison whatever rapport Enrique and I managed to establish."

As my fears tumbled out, I spoke the one word I should never have uttered aloud. My outburst was met with an awkward silence. I reeled back to Cabrera. "My lord, you've known me since I came here as a girl. Surely, you can't believe I'd ever . . . that I'm capable of. . . ."

He shook his head. "We are all aware that young Villena seeks to enrapture His Majesty as his father did before him, and that he fears Enrique's affection for you. I'd not worry on that account. Whatever was said in the *sala* cannot be taken seriously; the king was not in his right mind. But his health remains a grave concern."

He paused. I saw him exchange a resigned glance with Beatriz before he added, "We did not want to trouble you with this, but one of the pressing reasons we worked so hard toward your reconciliation is because His Majesty has been ill for months. He suffers a stomach malady much like Villena had, one that causes him to vomit blood and bleed from his anus. He's done himself no good by ignoring his physicians' advice that too much wine, meat, horseback riding, and . . . other excesses aggravate the condition."

Relief overwhelmed me. An ailment: Enrique was sick. He had not been poisoned.

Then I went still. "Are you saying . . . ?"

Cabrera met my eyes. "He could be dying as we speak. And he is not in Segovia anymore, where we can watch over him. Your Highness, we must prepare. Should he—"

I lifted my hand to stop him, turning away in a daze. I walked to the

narrow arrow slit overlooking the keep. My view was obscured by darkness and swirling snow; as I stared out into nothingness, I saw my half
brother's tormented face in that horrific instant before his legs gave way
under him.

Why? Why now, when I'd have given it all over to you soon enough?

I had thought it was an accusation against me but I was wrong. He
had known for months that he was mortally ill. It was not only his grief
over the loss of Villena that had convinced him to sanction our reunion. In his heart, he'd known time was running out, just as I knew in
my heart that the time I'd long anticipated, struggled, and suffered for
was fast upon me. And I was alone, with only a few trusted friends.
Fernando was hundreds of miles away in his embattled kingdom while
I was about to face the most critical moment of my life. I wished again,
with a fervent longing, that he was here. In that instant, I'd have self-
ishly let the French overrun Aragón if it meant my husband could be at
my side.

I heard the door shut. Cabrera had left.

Beatriz came behind me. "My lady, please listen to me. We cannot
afford to delay. If we are right, every hour counts. There are those who'll
do anything to keep you from the throne. Andrés and Archbishop Carrillo want to send a trusted man to Madrid to monitor the situation but
they need your permission."

I could not speak for what seemed an eternity. When I finally did,
my voice was calm: "Do whatever is necessary."

THREE DAYS LATER, on the evening of December 12, following a perilous ride during which he exhausted two horses, our spy brought word
that King Enrique IV was dead.

PART III

The Double-edged Sword

1474–1480

CHAPTER TWENTY-TWO

I awoke before dawn, after only a few hours of rest. Drawing my marten-lined robe about my shoulders, my newly washed hair plaited down my back, I went to the window and rubbed the frosted panes to catch a glimpse of the rose-colored dawn breaking over the keep. I was transfixed by the sight, the light so diaphanous and shimmering it seemed opalescent, as though refracted from within the interior of a perfect pearl.

It was going to be a beautiful day, I thought, as I heard my chamber door open. I turned to see Beatriz and Inés, carrying the sections of my gown and an enamel coffer.

"Did you sleep?" asked Inés, as they carefully laid out the azure velvet overdress trimmed with ermine, my favorite fur, the underskirt of mulberry satin and the gold-lined tabard, and embroidered pearl-and-gold-cord headdress which we'd spent feverish hours sewing, in between funeral observances for Enrique and arrangements for my accession.

"Not a wink." I neared the coffer Beatriz had put on my table. She unlocked it with a key, opening the carved lid to expose ropes of pearls, glistening emeralds, pink rubies, and brilliant diamonds, twined with breathtaking sapphires of every imaginable hue.

I regarded them with a catch in my throat, these esteemed symbols of royal prestige that had adorned many of Castile's queens, from Berenguela of León to the infamous Urraca.

"Every last one is there," said Beatriz. "Andrés made certain Juana did not get away with anything. He even sent officials to the convent where she is immured to retrieve whatever she might have stolen when she first fled the court. She didn't have much."

I picked up an emerald bracelet with intricate Moorish-style gold links. "I imagine she isn't happy with the turn of events," I said, recalling that I'd once seen this very bracelet adorning her wrist. Had Cabrera confiscated it from her as she ranted and railed in her seclusion behind hallowed walls, from which now only death could free her?

"She is . . . subdued. She implores mercy for her daughter." Beatriz eyed me as I clasped on the bracelet. It was heavier than I thought, its square-cut verdant stones gleaming against my skin. "What will you do? For now, la Beltraneja remains under custody with the Mendozas but her mother still insists she is Enrique's, and the child herself believes the same. You will have to contend with her at some point."

"Yes," I said absently, mesmerized by the emeralds' luster. "I will. But not today."

"Of course not," piped Inés. "Today is your coronation. Today, Your Highness will—"

"*Majestad,*" interrupted Beatriz. "Remember, she is a queen now."

Inés flushed. "Oh, I forgot! Your Majesty, please forgive me." She turned to me, flustered; I regarded her sternly before the smile I struggled to hide broke across my lips and behind me, Beatriz let out a guffaw.

Inés stamped her foot. "That wasn't very nice. I thought I'd offended!"

I clasped her hand. "Forgive me. I don't care how you address me in private." I smiled at Beatriz, outstretching my other hand. "I still can't believe this is happening. How can I be queen of Castile?"

"Well, you are," said Beatriz. "And you'll be a very tardy one if we don't start dressing you now."

While they bustled about me, removing my robe and commencing the process of layering my gown over me, I realized that the past two days had been such a whirlwind of conflicting emotion that a part of me had transformed into an impartial witness to my own upheaval. I'd experienced conflicting emotions over Enrique since his death, just as I had during his life. I had donned the white serge of mourning to attend his obsequies and heard in quiet from the newly elevated Cardinal Mendoza the dreadful account of Enrique's final hours. He had agonized in a freezing chamber in Madrid's old alcazar, with no one to attend him save his loyal Moors. His servants and intimates, including the faithless Diego Villena, forsook him the moment it was clear he would not survive. They left him with no more respect than for a dying dog, Mendoza told me; and he himself had to hire outsiders to prepare Enrique's corpse for entombment.

As customary, I did not attend my half brother's funeral. Instead I ordered a Mass sung in the Segovia Cathedral, while his cortege wound its way to the Monastery of Santa María de Guadalupe, where he was laid to rest. As I prayed for his soul, I made myself remember not the capricious king I'd grown to mistrust and fear, but rather the odd, timid man I'd met years before, who'd shown me affection. I couldn't honestly say I would miss him, not after all that had passed between us, but I felt his loss in some intrinsic part of me, a loneliness born of the knowledge that of the three of us who had shared our father's blood, only I remained.

But even if I'd wanted to mourn more, pressing decisions intruded. The most difficult had been whether to announce my accession at once or delay until Fernando could be with me. Carrillo argued we had no time to waste. Like Cabrera, he believed any postponement would threaten my hold on the throne. Moreover, we had no assurance that Fernando could come at all, given the ongoing trouble in Aragón. Still, I vacillated almost a full day until I had the chance to consult with Cardinal Mendoza upon his return from Enrique's funeral. I trusted the moderate prelate who'd supported me without ever betraying his loyalty to Enrique; he heard in silence my outpouring of doubt, my fear that I'd insult Fernando and bring harm upon our marriage if I proclaimed myself queen while he was absent.

Mendoza said quietly, "I understand how difficult these last days have been and how much you now must contend with, but you are the sole heiress of this realm. As your husband, Fernando of Aragón will hold the title of king-consort, but he has no other hereditary rights in Castile, as he himself agreed by his signature on your prenuptial Capitulations. The right to the throne, my child, is yours alone."

I spent the evening in an agony of indecision, anchored before the altar in my rooms. I implored guidance, an answer that would lift the burden of self-reproach from my shoulders. While Castile had had other queens, none had reigned successfully for long. Was I committing a sin of pride, believing I could accomplish what no woman before me had? The kingdom I stood to inherit was a cauldron of vice and duplicity; our treasury was near-bankrupt, our people sunk in calamity. Many, if not all, of the grandees—not to mention the Holy Father in Rome and powers abroad—would say Castile required the firm rule of a prince like Fernando, whose courage and vigor were forged in war, and thus tempered to the many obstacles we faced.

I had the uneasy feeling Fernando himself would say the same.

Yet even as I sought to persuade myself of my innate unsuitability, part of me rebelled. I'd not fought all this time to shirk my duty now. The crown was indeed mine to bear as a princess of Trastámara; in my veins ran the blood of a dynasty that had ruled Castile for more than a hundred years. My subjects expected me to assume the throne and would not suffer Aragón to reign in my stead. To delay or compromise could be seen as a sign of weakness. I must never let it be said that Isabella of Castile lacked conviction.

Even so, as Beatriz set the rounded headdress on my brow, carefully arranging the white silk veil that cascaded from it, and Inés knelt to slip the leather pattens on my feet, I wondered what would happen once Fernando read the letter I'd sent.

The cathedral bells tolled, summoning the crowds to the cordoned streets through which I would ride with my entourage to the *plaza mayor.*

"Quickly!" said Beatriz, and after she affixed the clasp of my black damask cloak, she and Inés lifted between them its long train and we made hasty progress to the keep. There, under a brilliant winter sky so blue it hurt the eyes, waited the clergy and the select lords invited to attend my accession. They bowed low, caps swiped from brows, exposing balding pates, thinning fringes, or manicured tumbles of locks to the morning chill. I recognized Carrillo in his signature scarlet cape, Cardinal Mendoza attired in gem-studded vestments, and Beatriz's beloved Andrés, impeccable as always in black velvet.

I paused. Except for me and my ladies, no other women were present. Though I knew that these men's mothers, wives, daughters, and even mistresses were arrayed along the route in all their finery, straining to catch a glimpse of me, I felt as if a shaft of light had pierced the sky to fall solely upon my person, marking me apart.

I made my way to Canela, who snorted impatiently under his rich caparison of damask adorned with the castle and lion rampant of Castile, his reins bedecked with silly tassels. He looked as if he had half a mind to munch on them.

Don Chacón was holding the reins. He wore a stiff green doublet and had trimmed his thick, dark beard; as his brown eyes met mine I saw pride shining in their depths. He'd remained steadfast at my side since Alfonso's death, a companion and trusted servant I could always rely upon. His presence bolstered my confidence. Today, in honor of his service, he had the privilege of leading me through Segovia's streets.

The procession assembled; ahead of us walked Cárdenas carrying aloft an unsheathed sword. The crowds went silent as he passed and I caught furtive astonishment in the faces of those nobles who held coveted positions along the route. The old blackened sword—excavated at my insistence from under piles of rusting armor in the treasury—was a hallowed relic of Trastámara kings, symbol of justice and authority; no queen had ever had it carried before her during her ceremony of ascension. I raised my chin, focusing on the central square ahead, where my throne awaited on a dais hung with crimson bunting in front of the Church of San Miguel.

Chacón carefully assisted me off my horse. Standing alone on the bloodred carpet of the dais, with thousands of Segovians arrayed before me, I listened to the royal pennons snap in the wind and heard the herald cry out into the diamond-crisp air, "Castile! Castile for Her Majesty Doña Isabella, proprietress of these realms, and for His Highness Don Fernando, her husband!"

In shouting unison that sparked sudden tears in my eyes, the crowd repeated the words.

Mendoza mounted the dais, holding the Bible. *"Majestad,"* he intoned, "do you accept the acclamation and vow to uphold the sacred duties that God has set before you?"

I put my hand on the Holy Book, opened my mouth to utter the speech I'd carefully rehearsed. But something stopped me. Among the thousands watching I caught sight of a spectral figure, standing apart, his pale eyes smoldering, his face white as bone. . . .

A knot filled my throat. I could not look away.

"Majesty?" murmured Mendoza. "The vows, if you please."

I blinked; when I looked again, the figure was gone. I tore my gaze from the spot, swallowed and recited in a slightly quavering voice: "I accept this great honor bestowed upon me and swear by these holy *evangelios* to obey the commandments of our Church, to uphold the statutes of this realm and defend the common welfare of all my subjects, aggrandizing these kingdoms in the custom of my glorious progenitors, and safeguarding our customs, liberties, and privileges as your lawfully anointed queen."

A rustle like the wings of an enormous falcon passing overhead whispered across the square as everyone went to their knees. The nobles came forth one by one to swear their oaths of allegiance. The court officials handed their wands of service to Cabrera, signaling a change in regime, and I knelt before Mendoza as he described the sign of the cross above my head.

"God bless Queen Isabella!"

And my subjects, the people of Castile, roared their approval.

IT WAS PAST midnight when I finally returned to my rooms. My feet ached. My jaw was sore from the constant smile I'd been required to keep on my face. I'd heard a solemn Te Deum, returned to dine in the alcazar, and then assumed my seat on the dais to receive for hours a long queue of well-wishers, including the wary grandees, who must have wondered as they bowed before me what my next move would be.

I'd seen myself reflected in their pupils as if I stood before a mirror. I beheld the white hand I extended, each finger decorated with rings, the shimmering gold fabric of my sleeve, draping the rounded arm of an inexperienced twenty-three-year-old woman. I saw their disdain in the twitch of their mouths, which turned their mellifluous greetings to sneers.

To them, I would not be a queen until I proved myself stronger than them.

The very thought exhausted me. As soon as my equally weary ladies undressed me and staggered out, bleary-eyed, dousing the candles as they left, I curled up in bed and shut my eyes. I must send for my child, I thought. I wanted my Isabel with me.

Before I drifted into sleep, I whispered, "Fernando, I am waiting. Come home."

SNOW-FLECKED WIND STIFFENED the colored pennants and carpets hung from balconies to welcome my husband. As soon as word came that he was on his way, I had requested that Archbishop Carrillo, Admiral Enríquez, and several high-ranking grandees meet him halfway and escort him to Segovia, with all the dignity and honor his status merited. He'd delayed a day to rest and don the new clothes I'd had made for him—a tunic of burgundy velvet trimmed in sable, half-boots of tooled cordovan leather, perfumed gauntlets, and a gold necklace that had belonged to Enrique, newly polished and adorned with our emblem of the arrows and yoke, crafted by the finest goldsmith in Toledo. Through these gifts I hoped to convey my pleasure at his return; now, I waited eagerly in the *sala,* seeing in my mind the wintry wind buffeting his passage and hearing the muffled cries of the crowds that had gathered to cheer him as he entered the city.

I wore violet silk, my hair plaited about my head in what I hoped was a fetching style. I tugged insistently at a loose thread on my cuff. I wanted to rush out into the keep, to welcome him with open arms after so long an absence—but a queen did not display her emotion in public. Moreover, as I was the queen, it was his duty to first come to me.

Sweat pooled between my shoulders, trickling down my back under my gown as I strained my eyes toward the far doors. The heat was stifling, cast from too many braziers and oil lamps lit to ward off the afternoon chill. Where was he? What was taking him so long—

I heard voices, the clatter of booted heels. I almost bolted forth as a collection of men burst through the doors. The courtiers bowed in unison. I recognized him at once, even from a distance—that compact muscular figure in his new doublet, striding toward me. As he neared, I stepped to the edge of the dais, my smile breaking free, unrestrained.

"My lord husband," I whispered, almost in tears at the sight of him so proud and strong before me. He removed his cap. His hair had grown; it now draped past his broad shoulders like a curtain of deep brown silk. A new, close-cut beard framed his square jaw.

He lowered his head. *"Majestad,"* he said in stilted formality, "it is my great honor to reunite with you at long last."

I faltered. The hand I held out remained untouched between us. "And mine, as well," I finally said. I stepped from the dais to embrace him. His body was lean, hard, toned from months of warfare against the French. He did not embrace me in return. When I drew back, he regarded me with icy focus.

He looked as if I were the last person he wanted to see.

"HOW COULD YOU do it? How could you do this to me?"

We stood together in my private chamber, to which we had retreated as soon as politely possible, following the interminable banquet during which I sat at his side, my apprehension a lump in my throat. He'd barely eaten from the fifty courses I'd ordered served; scarcely touched his goblet. When our little girl was presented to him, he greeted her with a perfunctory kiss and then he sat brooding as the court dined below us, his anger coiled about him like a tail.

Now, he unleashed it—without reserve.

"I am humiliated," he went on, his voice sharp as a blade. "I had to hear it from you in a letter, in the middle of my father's court in Zaragoza. I had to hear the news that my wife had had herself declared queen while I was miles away." He swerved to the table, where Ines had left a platter of dried fruit and a beaker of wine. He poured liberally, his hand visibly shaking.

His anger had caught me so off-guard that for a moment I didn't know what to say. Then I ventured, "But I thought you understood; I explained it all to you in my letter. The need for haste was due to the suddenness of Enrique's death. I had to act quickly, lest some grandee take into his head to foment rebellion in la Beltraneja's name. Carrillo, Mendoza, even your grandfather the admiral—they advised me it was the right thing to do."

He regarded me from over the rim of his cup. "So, that is your explanation? You blame your advisors for not taking me into account?"

His accusation stung me. "I blame no one," I retorted. "It was a decision I had to make. The circumstances were unprecedented. I acted in Castile's best interests."

"I see," he said and he set his goblet aside. "Castile is more important than me. I thought we'd agreed to rule together, as equals, so that the ancient divisiveness between our kingdoms would no longer apply. But it seems I was wrong."

"You—you are important," I quavered. "But in Castile, the right of the sovereign . . , it is paramount. I am required to proclaim myself queen first, before . . ." My explanation faded into uncomfortable silence under the impact of his stare. I realized, with belated regret, that while my intentions had been honorable, I had made a terrible mistake.

"Who am I to you?" he asked quietly.

I started in my chair. "You are my husband, of course."

"No. Who am I?" he repeated. "Am I to be co-ruler with you or do you, like so many others, believe that I, a prince of Aragón, should hold no rights here? Do you believe I should be content to be your consort, my sole concern to provide Castile with heirs?"

I jerked out of my chair. "How can you ask that of me?" I knew I should measure my tone, for he had not raised his. And his questions, much as they might hurt, were rational, but reason flew from my head. In that instant, the only thing I heard was his doubt of me, his indifference to a dilemma that had nearly torn me apart. "I agonized over what to do," I cried. "I prayed, for hours on end! I consulted everyone I could, but ultimately I had to—"

"You did not consult me," he interrupted. "You didn't even write to ask what I thought. You declared yourself queen and had the sword of justice carried before you. You made it seem as though there was no other monarch here but you."

I stared at him, outraged. After all these weeks of tumult and uncertainty, of working myself to exhaustion in meetings with my councilors, seeking to shore up Castile while he was fighting the French—surely, he did not expect my sympathy! But then I spied something in his expression, a fleeting vulnerability in his eyes. With a sinking of my heart, I recognized the emotion.

Fear.

Fernando was afraid. He thought I wanted to keep him from having as much power as me, and he'd be left, exposed, to the derision of my court—the Aragonese who bedded the queen but had no say in how she ruled. His pride of manhood was injured.

Relief flooded me. This, I could deal with.

"I did what I had to," I said, softening my voice. "I was loath to ask you to abandon Aragón in its hour of need. I had done it once before, when we married, and I knew how much it had cost you. I only sought to protect our kingdom until the time when you could be here to claim it with me."

I could see he didn't miss the emphasis I placed on "our kingdom," though he didn't acknowledge it. He would not surrender so easily.

"You might have waited," he muttered, lowering his eyes.

"Yes, I might have. But if I had, Castile might have been lost to us."

"So you say." He went quiet for a long moment. Then he said, somewhat begrudgingly, "I suppose this is also my fault."

I stood without speaking, waiting for him to continue.

"I signed those damned Capitulations," he said. "I was so eager to be your husband, to save you from Villena and Enrique, that I signed away my rights—as Carrillo just reminded me only hours ago, when I protested to him on our way here that he should have counseled you according to the law. He told me he had. By Castilian law you hold the superior right. You are the queen; upon your death, may it be many years hence, our eldest child will inherit Castile. I will never be king here in my own right. He suggested I remember it."

Inwardly, I seethed. Carrillo had gone too far! Did he not realize that a public rupture between Fernando and me at this crucial moment was the last thing we could afford? We were still vulnerable, our hold on Castile unsecured; the grandees would exploit any discord between us to further their own ends. They'd make a disaster of our reign before we'd even had a chance to commence it.

I had to find a way to resolve this rift and put an end to Carrillo's presumption. He was the one who held no rights here, not Fernando. "We can have the law changed," I stated, with more conviction than I felt, for in truth I wasn't sure we actually could.

He lifted his gaze. "What did you say?"

"I said, we can change the law." I thought fast, cobbling together a solution. "We'll convene a special inquiry, with counsel to represent us,

THE QUEEN'S VOW   229

like a court of law. We'll examine every precedent, every statute; we'll go over every clause in our prenuptial agreement. Wherever disparity can be rectified, we will do it." I paused. While I had no idea if what I proposed was feasible, I wanted him to know I was willing to go to any ends necessary to ensure that he and I were viewed, and treated, as equals.

He bit his lower lip. "You would do that, for me?"

"That and much more," I whispered. "You are always first in my heart."

My knees gave way as he swiftly crushed me against him, his lips on mine. He gathered me in his arms, carried me to the bed. He tore off his doublet, fumbled with his shirt, his hose. I watched him even as I tried to untangle my own jumbled skirts, the countless ribbons and laces. . . . I went still as I saw his nudity—that scarred, chiseled flesh that I had hungered for more than I had realized, that I had missed and longed to taste the way a parched wanderer longs for water in a desert.

"I hope you are hungry tonight," Fernando murmured, "like a *loba* at full moon."

I looked at him in utter surprise. Then I laughed. "Did you just call me a she-wolf?"

"Yes. You see, I like she-wolves," he replied, grinning with a mixture of boyish insolence and lasciviousness, making me laugh even harder. "I like to stalk them, hunt them, and skin their pelts, especially when they take themselves so seriously. *Grrr!*"

And he threw himself at me, growling and pawing as I felt my entire body go weak with desire and relief. He finished undressing me with expert hands, making my pulse race. As he passed my shift over my head, unraveling my braided coiffure so that my hair coiled loose about me, I let out a small moan—an unwitting but inescapable admission of lust that made his member thicken, harden against me.

"You are hungry," he breathed and then he was over me, inside me, teasing, shifting, moving, plunging. . . . I clasped my thighs about him and the world with all its troubles, with its fears and foibles and inevitable disillusions, melted away.

For the first time in months, I rejoiced that I was, indeed, only a woman.

I ORDERED OUR legal inquiry the very next week, selecting a choice panel of high-ranking grandees, including the admiral. I had my new confessor, the pensive and legally trained Hieronymite monk Fray Hernando de Talavera, appointed as our secretary; Cardinal Mendoza represented my rights, while, in a perverse pique of revenge, I appointed Carrillo to act for Fernando. I was furious at the archbishop for having spurred my husband's anger, and now I made sure he was aware I expected him to offer Fernando a spirited and logical defense for equality in our monarchial powers. To his credit, Carrillo did exactly as I commanded, gaining even the reluctant grandees' support of Fernando's precarious position. Most agreed that our Capitulations—the controversial document which Carrillo had spent months negotiating and which he considered one of his finest achievements—was unprecedented, indeed almost unenforceable, given Fernando's and my married state.

However, when the issue of our succession arose, it was I who came to my feet.

"My lord," I said, looking to where Fernando sat enthroned in his red-and-gold mantle of estate, "because of the union that exists between us, this realm shall always remain the inheritance of our issue. But as thus far it has pleased God to bless us with a daughter, Castile's succession must be invested in her. Aragón's law prohibits her to succeed to your eventual throne; yet one day, she must marry a prince who could command our patrimony for his own use, turning both Castile and even Aragón, upon our deaths, into vassal states, should God see fit to deny us sons. This would prove a terrible burden upon our consciences and a calamity for our subjects, as I'm sure you will agree."

His expression darkened; I'd been correct in suspecting he privately struggled with the intransigence of his own kingdom, where our daughter could not be named heir. It drove a wedge not of our making between us. I was willing to concede many points, including having his name precede mine on official documents and ceremonial addresses, granting him leave to act as supreme commander of our armies, and allowing him the ability to render justice, but on this point I stood firm. Isabel had to succeed in her own right. Castile must never become subject to Aragón's ancient exclusion of female rulers.

Finally, he nodded. "I agree. Let there be no more discussion of this matter." He gave me a weary smile and came to where I stood. He kissed my cheek. "You win," he murmured. "You should have been a lawyer, my moon."

Holding my hand aloft, he declared, "Let it be done! In honor of our agreements, Her Majesty and I command that a new coat of arms be forged, displaying the castles and lions of Castile with the gold and red bars of Aragón."

"And beneath it," I added, "let our arrows and yoke be entwined with the Gordian knot, as a symbol of the perpetuity of our union."

The grandees broke into applause. Fernando smiled, flushed with pride at their acknowledgment, and proceeded out with his gentlemen to change for the afternoon feast.

With a sigh, I started for the opposite doorway and my waiting ladies. Carrillo intercepted me. Behind us, the clerks began to gather the documents of the inquiry.

"You've made a grave mistake," the archbishop announced. "By allowing him these privileges you negate the precepts set forth in your prenuptial Capitulations and endanger the very sovereignty of Castile."

I regarded him coldly. "All I've permitted is that my husband command the respect due to him as king. I retain sole authority to appoint and promote ecclesiastics; I carry ultimate say over our fiscal disbursements and tax collection, and only I can declare war. Indeed, aside from a few concessions, the sovereignty of Castile remains intact. My daughter will inherit after me, and Fernando can never rule here in his own right. Is this not what you yourself advised him to submit to, my lord?"

He ignored my barbed tone, flapping his meaty hand with its massive ring in a disparaging gesture. "You don't know the Aragonese as I do; they recognize no boundaries. Should you die before him, without a son to succeed you, he'll never accept your daughter as queen. He'll deny her rights and turn this realm into Aragón's vassal."

"You go too far," I replied. "He is the father of my child and I am pledged to him. While I regret that his kingdom will support only a male-dominated succession, I do what I must to keep the peace in our marriage."

He snorted. "Well, that will take more than a few concessions, I can assure you."

I lifted my chin. I was growing heartily sick of his condescension and resisted the urge to dismiss him permanently. "What do you mean by that? Speak plainly, my lord."

"I mean," he said, with deliberate malice, "that His Majesty has been lying to you for months. He has a mistress in Aragón: that is why he delayed his return. Apparently, she is with child and she begged him to stay. Of course, it's not the first time he has strayed, as you are aware."

I did not react. I did not move a muscle. Within me, a wave of emotion was building, molten hot and suffocating.

Carrillo eyed me. "Or can it be you were not aware? I thought he'd told you about his bastard son by another woman before your marriage? It's not as if it's a secret. All of Zaragoza knows how much he dotes on the boy. Even King Juan has had the child at court and has lavished him with gifts. Why, they even seek to bestow an archbishopric on him."

My throat closed. I could not get enough air into my lungs. "Of course I was aware," I managed to say. "And now you say he has another . . . ?"

"Yes, by another woman, some minor noble's daughter." Carrillo shrugged. "Their morals are deplorable. No wonder the French are so eager to invade! Aragón has more in common with that nation of degenerates than it cares to admit."

My hands clenched at my sides. In that instant, even as I struggled against the wail that threatened to rip my very insides, I let myself feel what had been brewing for as long as I could remember, the tangled emotions that had dominated my interactions with Carrillo from the day he had come into my life—they finally resolved into one inescapable sentiment.

I had had enough. I wanted this man gone from my life.

"You will remove yourself from court at once," I said. "Go to your palace of Acuña or Alcalá de Henares, and stay there. I do not want you in my presence."

He blinked, startled. "You—you cannot mean that."

"Yes, I do," I replied. "Indeed, I've never meant anything more. No one, my lord, disparages my husband the king to my face. Not even you."

"But I am your advisor! I helped you win the throne. You cannot rule without me."

"I do not need anyone to rule for me, nor do I need an advisor who refuses to respect my decisions. Therefore, I order you to leave court. *Now.*"

"You—you . . . order?" His face turned ashen, his eyes bulging. "You dare dismiss me, the head of the See of Toledo, the man who has seen fit to pave your way to power? You dismiss me like some lackey? Were it not for me, you'd not be standing where you are today, Doña Isabella. You'd have been married off years ago, sent into exile to breed a parcel of Portuguese brats and sew your life away in some drafty castle by the sea!"

I refused to rise to his bait. "You give yourself too much credit. And accord me too little. I will not repeat myself. I expect you gone within the hour or I will send for my guard to accompany you."

I held out my hand for him to kiss in farewell. He met my gesture in silence before he deliberately ignored the respect he owed me and instead swerved away, tromping heavily to the door. He paused there, glaring over his shoulder. "You will regret this," he said, and marched out, bellowing for his page.

At my indication, the stricken clerks also scampered out, leaving me alone before the table. Moments later, Fernando walked in. "Isabella, *mi amor*, what happened? Everyone just heard Carrillo yelling like a muleteer—"

I turned to him. "Is it true?"

Before he could formulate a response, I saw the answer writ on his face—an unmistakable pallor, followed by a humiliated flush that cemented his guilt. I barely heard his next words: "So, he told you. I should have known. That old whoreson cannot bear for us to be happy. He never could. All he ever wants is to—"

"He is not the one who broke his vows." I had to lean my hands on the table, a terrifying emptiness cracking open inside me. "You did that. And you lied to me about it."

"God's teeth, I didn't lie. It happened before we wed." He moved to me. "I was going to tell you, Isabella, I promise. The boy . . . he is just two years old and—"

"I do not refer to the first child. I mean the one you are currently expecting."

He froze. I tasted blood in my mouth; I had bitten through the inside of my lip. "You do not deny it," I said. "Is she . . . this woman, do you love . . . ?"

"No. I swear to you, no." He looked at me helplessly. "It was a moment of weakness, of madness. I was so far away, from you, from our home; I was so tired of war, of those endless nights waiting for the French to fall on me. I felt as if the entire world watched, waited for me to fail. I . . . I needed comfort."

"And so you took another to your bed, while I was here, contending with my mother, with our daughter, with the crisis of Enrique's death? You betrayed our marriage because you were tired and needed comfort?"

"Yes." He paused, shook his head. "I'm not saying I did right. God knows, I regret it now, but I am only a man. I am not perfect, Isabella. I never pretended to be."

My gut twisted as if he had struck me. "You are sure the child is yours?" I asked, and the voice I heard coming out of my mouth was cold, impersonal, not mine at all.

He flinched; evidently he hadn't considered the alternative. "I believe so," he said quietly. "I have no reason to think otherwise."

"Very well. Then once the child is born, you must see to its proper upkeep. You will find a position for it—in the church if it's a boy, a noblewoman's service if it is a girl. I will not have it said that the king of Castile neglects his responsibilities." I summoned my fractured composure, forcing out a last question, the answer to which I didn't really want to know. Once I did, the reality would be undeniable.

"The other child, your boy. What is his name?"

"Alfonso," he said softly. "Like your late brother."

"I see." I searched his face, saw his love and guilt and sadness reflected there, his sincere remorse—and it undid me. I felt as though our entire existence lay in shards at my feet, broken like so much fragile glass. "All this time we sat here," I said, "seeking equality, extolling our *tanto monta* . . . well, here it is: We are equal now, on paper. But we both know there can never be true equality between us, not while one of us keeps such secrets."

"Isabella, please. It was an indiscretion! It meant nothing to me."

"Perhaps. But to me, it means everything." I started to turn away. I did not want him to see how torn I felt, how lost. I did not want to concede to him any more of my emotion.

"Isabella," I heard him say, incredulous. "You cannot be serious. Would you walk away from me when I have admitted my error? Will you not at least allow me the chance to make things right between us?"

With the room swimming in a haze about me, I ignored him, departing without another word. I was vaguely aware that Inés and Beatriz were suddenly at my side, steering me past the courtiers crowded in the passage, through the hall with its waiting grandees, and up the spiral staircase to my chamber. The moment the door was bolted, I wanted to give vent to the primal howl of wrath and sorrow pulsating inside me.

Instead, I heard myself whisper, "I must bathe."

"Bathe? But there's no hot water," said Beatriz, twisting handfuls of her gown in her anxiety. "We'll have to fetch it from the kitchens."

"It doesn't matter." I started to tear at my clothes, my fingernails catching on the ties, shredding the delicate fabric. "Get these off me. I feel as if I'm suffocating. I cannot breathe. . . ."

Beatriz and Inés surged forward, divesting me of my garments, yanking the ornate layers from my body until I stood trembling in my silk undergarments.

"Pour the water from that decanter on me," I ordered, and Inés gasped. "My lady, no, it's from the aqueduct, for drinking. It's too cold. Look at you: you're shivering."

"*Pour it!*"

Beatriz grabbed the decanter and I closed my eyes and outstretched my arms as she overturned it on my head, the water—drawn directly from the alluvial spring that fed Segovia's Roman waterway—drenching me in ice, drawing from me a small, shrill cry.

That sole unwitting sound, like the stunned protest of an animal caught in a snare, was all I could release. Though grief battered me, no tears came. My disillusion was too deep. There was no physical way to relieve it. Standing there, rivulets of chilled water dripping down my breasts and thighs, freezing that place where the memory of passion dwelled, I went silent as a tomb.

I let Beatriz strip off my sodden shift, envelop me in velvet and lead me to the chair before the fire, while Inés anxiously stoked the embers. I did not utter a word. I just sat there, staring into the flames.

I was queen of Castile. I had prevailed over every obstacle to fulfill my destiny.

And I had never felt more alone.

CHAPTER TWENTY-THREE

Time was my ally and my foe.

There was so much to do in preparation for the months ahead, the hours in the day were not enough. And yet, each night felt endless as I lay alone in bed, staring at the shadows cast by the guttering candles on the walls.

Together, Fernando and I organized our council according to competence, refusing to yield to any notions of aristocratic hierarchy. Noble blood meant nothing if it was unaccompanied by wholehearted dedication to the realm and a demonstrable lack of self-aggrandizement. Prominent Jews such as Rabbi Abraham Señeor assumed charge of our precarious finances. The loyal Cabrera was reaffirmed in his position as governor; Cárdenas was named my official secretary, and Chacón became our chief steward. Several of Fernando's trusted Aragonese servants, including his treasurer, Santángel, held coveted positions in our households.

Of course, none of this sat well with the grandees, who suspected that our ultimate aim was to curb their privileges. For centuries, they had been allowed to build fortresses at will and retain armies of vassals; thus, although the Cortes had approved us as monarchs, several cities remained uncommitted to us, and several lords—most notably the Andalucían marquis of Cádiz and Diego, the new marquis of Villena—contested our rule vigorously, saying that Joanna la Beltraneja's claim to the succession had not been disproved.

Indeed, the queen's bastard daughter was the thorn in our crown. I was particularly concerned about reports that Diego Villena had reputedly tried to steal into the castle where she was being held. I should have ordered her strict imprisonment in a convent, but despite the insulting moniker of la Beltraneja now firmly affixed to her name, to me she was still just a twelve-year-old girl, deprived of all status, without even her mother to guide her through the vicissitudes of life. Though we'd not seen each other in years, I still cared for her, still remembered the pretty babe she had been. Beatriz scolded me for my leniency, reminding me that Joanna was a threat, a figurehead around whom malcontents would rally. But I'd not have her suffer undue hardship, seeing as she'd done nothing to earn it. Besides, other influential grandees, like the admiral and the marquis of Santillana, head of the powerful Mendoza clan, willingly signed the oath of allegiance to us, recognizing that the chaos in Castile must be resolved before we slid into irrevocable ruin. And strategically important cities such as Medina del Campo, Ávila, Valladolid, and Segovia recognized my claim to the throne above and beyond any other.

I threw myself with steely resolve into each task, refusing to let my personal travails thwart me. I joined in Fernando's outrage over reports sent by our investigative officials that painted a picture of a realm riddled by corruption, with laxity and venality rampant among our clergy. Poor harvests and the tumult of past reigns had left our people impoverished, our coinage so debased by Enrique's wholesale approval of mints that merchants now refused to accept monetary payment for goods, collapsing our export markets and sending our royal rents into arrears. Fernando suggested we reduce the number of mints from a hundred and fifty to a mere five and revise our entire tax-collection system. It was a prudent, long-term solution. I approved it and he gained the respect of our Castilian advisors.

Yet even as our dream of restoring Castile took root, the pain of Fernando's betrayal calcified within me. Being close to him was agony, though I never showed it. I smiled and heeded his every word, behaving with impeccable propriety when we greeted the ambassadors who arrived from all over Europe at the behest of their curious masters. Every ruler was anxious to gauge our suitability, to seek an advantage over us or weaknesses to exploit. From the spider Louis in France to vile Afonso in Portugal, from the lofty eminence of the Vatican to the embattled Plantagenets of England—a dynasty to which I was related—they all smiled and watched and waited. Our success would be rewarded with treaties, alliances that would expand our influence and secure our standing. Failure would render us carrion.

With the entire world bearing witness to our first tentative steps as rulers, I knew enough to hide my pain. There was no room or time for personal indulgence. But there were still those moments after dining in the hall when Fernando would turn to me uncertainly, the question in his eyes. Every time, I wanted to nod, to forgive and surrender; I wanted to feel him again, the shape of his body molded against mine. Ashamed by my own carnality, I confessed to Fray Talavera; he advised that I must not let my husband's transgressions override the sacred obedience I owed Fernando as his wife. Fray Talavera did not go as far as to also remind me of my duty as queen, but his implication was clear: Although our daughter, Isabel, was healthy, I knew better than most how unexpectedly and swiftly tragedy could strike. Fernando and I must safeguard our bloodline; we had to solidify our hold on the throne with more than reforms.

We had to have a son.

But I could not give in. It was as though I dwelled outside myself, seeing and fearing my actions, knowing I accomplished nothing by denying him, yet unable to do otherwise. The fact that he did not implore, did not rage; that he merely turned away to finish his wine and retire to his rooms, became the excuse I hid behind.

When he apologizes, I told myself. When he says aloud he is sorry, then I will forgive; even as I knew that he could not do that any more than I could, that we were not the sort of people to abase ourselves, even to each other. Fernando would only come to me when I let it be known that I was willing to accept him—exactly as he was.

It might have gone on forever, this impasse between us, turning us into sudden strangers who shared nothing but the same roof, if stronger forces had not come into play.

But they did.

IT WAS APRIL 1475.

We had traveled to Valladolid to attend festivities held in our honor by the formidable Mendoza clan, whose intention was to openly proclaim their support of our sovereignty and stifle any simmering discontent that might be brewing.

Despite our treasury's sorry state, I emptied the coffers for the occasion, knowing that only by exceeding the grandees' luxurious tastes could Fernando and I entice them to our side. With our program of reform gaining momentum, we required every last bit of support.

I remained gracious yet watchful as the nobles clattered into the city to partake of our generosity. Though the Mendozas had the honor of hosting the occasion, I had composed the guest list and most had been deliberately invited because they'd not yet sworn allegiance to us. As they came before our dais, I hid my dismay; the wealth they openly flaunted was staggering, their cloaks lined in cloth of gold, wives and daughters emblazoned with enough gemstones to finance armies. Clearly, not everyone in the realm suffered penury, and I was relieved that I'd decided to risk the expense. It was shameful, a parade of useless extravagance, but one in which we, as Castile's new rulers, must not be outdone.

On the day of an outdoor joust, I donned an emerald-and-gold-shot brocade that I'd paid for with one of my necklaces, its hanging sleeves lined in crimson and edged in ermine, the cuffs banded with rubies. I added a pearled caul for my hair. Fernando had likewise taken his cue from his counterparts, galloping onto the field in a magnificent suit of Toledo-forged armor; its gold and silver inlay depicted our emblem of the arrows and yoke on the gleaming breastplate. My chest tightened as he bowed from his destrier before the dais, waiting for a token of my esteem, according to tradition. He looked like a knight of legend in his shining metal; biting back a surge of remorse, I proceeded to watch him charge his opponents with a fervor that toppled every last one.

As we rose to applaud, Beatriz said in my ear, "No matter what he may have done, surely you don't intend to refuse him forever."

I gave her a sharp look. Though I'd told her time and time again I must be shown deference at all times in public, for only then would the fractious nobility learn I was not a monarch in the mold of my late brother, Beatriz said what she pleased, when she pleased.

"Well?" she added, with hands at hips. "What more do you want?

He just shattered his lance for you. Now, I suggest you offer that lance a sheath, before some hussy does."

I froze. Then, to my disbelief, a sudden bubble of mirth rose in me and I had to clamp my lips shut lest I burst out laughing in full view of the court.

"Shall I send word to him?" she asked.

I lifted my chin with icy reserve. "Yes," I hissed. "But do it in private. I don't want everyone knowing my business."

THAT NIGHT, I dressed with painstaking care in azure silk and applied costly lavender oil to my wrists and throat. Inés then proceeded to light enough scented beeswax candles to illuminate a cathedral; finally, I had to tell her that unless her aim was to blind Fernando, she must desist.

I sat before the hearth anxiously, my ladies at my side. We pretended to embroider, but of course we were actually listening to every sound outside the door. When we finally heard his footsteps, we rose in unison.

I didn't know what to expect until I saw him standing on the threshold, clad in his knee-length tunic from the evening feast, his face in shadow.

My heart started to pound.

He motioned. "Ladies, I would speak with my wife in private."

Inés and Beatriz hastened out, leaving us alone for the first time in three long months—months that now seemed an eternity as I gazed upon his somber features. His eyes were dull, almost pained, as they rose to meet mine.

"Isabella," he began, and I nodded. I braced myself for his approach, for the reconciliation I had longed for, but only now realized I'd not been ready to accept because I had felt, somehow, that my surrender would mean I approved of what he had done.

His next words, however, caught me completely off guard, stabbing through me. "There is no easy way to say this. Afonso of Portugal has declared war against us."

I stared as if he'd said something incomprehensible.

"On us?" I heard myself utter. "But . . . why?"

"La Beltraneja." He regarded me without any visible judgment, though, like Beatriz, he had advised me several times to imprison her. "In exchange for Afonso's help to conquer Castile, she's agreed to marry him and make him king. According to them, she is the rightful queen and you have usurped her throne."

"But Afonso is her uncle! And she is in our custody."

Fernando let out a worried sigh. "I'm afraid she's not anymore. She escaped with Villena while we've been here, distracted. He has signed an alliance with Afonso, recruited Cádiz in Andalucía and the master of the military orders of Calatrava and Alcántara to join their cause. They have gathered an immense force against us, nearly twenty thousand strong."

I reached for the back of my chair. Twenty thousand . . . I could not even begin to fathom it. It was more than anything we could possibly hope to gather without the support of the grandees.

"I've spoken with Santillana and the admiral," Fernando continued. "Santillana of course blames himself; after all, she was supposedly being watched in one of his castles. He says he'll grant us as many retainers as he can muster. He and the admiral will also speak to the other nobles and urge them to lend us support, but, Isabella, we still need you."

"Me?"

"Yes. You are the queen. You must declare war in return. And you can rally the people. The undecided cities may heed your call. We must conscript as many men as we can if we are to defeat Afonso. We've very little time to mount our offensive."

I looked at my white-knuckled grip on the chair and instructed myself to let go. I must not give in to panic. I understood the gravity of this threat; we could easily be annihilated. Portugal was a small country but strong, untouched by the years of plundering and weak rulers we'd endured in Castile. And Afonso was a seasoned commander who'd routed the Berber Moors and accumulated massive wealth in the process. If we did not act quickly and garner enough support from the grandees to counter him and Villena, we would undoubtedly lose our throne.

"Of course," I said quietly. "I'll write to every city this very hour. I'll send out decrees, offers of full pardon for prisoners and other criminals who agree to join our forces, anything that is required."

He nodded in assent, as if he'd expected as much. "There is one other thing you should know," he said, and I went still.

"Carrillo is involved. He helped Villena gain access to la Beltraneja. The letter of conduct that Villena used to enter the castle—it was signed by the archbishop."

You will regret this. . . .

Rage boiled up inside me. "Then he shall answer for it. I will deal with him myself."

"No." He abruptly stepped to me, taking my arm. "Carrillo is dangerous. I do not trust him. I never have."

I paused. I could feel the heat of his touch through my sleeve. "He'd not dare harm a hair on my head," I replied, and though I meant to sound bold, I heard the catch in my voice, brought on by Fernando's proximity and not by any fear I had of the archbishop.

He looked into my eyes. "Isabella, you don't understand. If anything should happen to you, I . . . I could not bear it. I wouldn't survive."

His unexpected admission thawed the last of the ice in me. I reached up, caressed his clean-shaven cheek. "You would survive; you would have to. What would Castile do without you?"

It was as close to forgiveness as I could offer, and in that moment, my words freed us. Though I knew in a dark part of me that he might stray again, that a man like him might be incapable of doing otherwise, I could no longer hold myself aloof. I wouldn't go on wishing he were something he was not, nor pretend some miraculous change would overcome him as a result of my exigencies.

Whatever the future held for us, we must face it together, as husband and wife.

"I love you," I heard him whisper and I felt his tears falling, precious as gems, on my hand. "I didn't mean to hurt you. I never meant to hurt or deceive you."

"I know." As I drew him to me, his arms came about me. He wept, quietly, against my chest, and I soothed his hair, feeling the thinning on his crown, his fragility manifested in that one vulnerable place.

I was the stronger one, I thought, as his hands slid to my waist and began to undo the tassels of my robe. I had the conviction of my principles, which overcame the errant weakness of the flesh. Then I felt his arousal press against me and his lips at my bare throat, burning, ravenous. My own ardor engulfed me.

For a brief few hours, I did not think anymore.

♛

I SAT UPON Canela on the windswept plain outside the city of Alcalá de Henares. I'd ridden without stop, despite Fernando's protests and the admiral's concern that by physically separating, Fernando and I might weaken our stance. But we didn't have a choice. Someone of sufficient authority was needed to rouse the cities in person; who better than me, their queen? Meanwhile, Fernando—now fully vested with equal powers, granted by me—could issue the declaration of war and begin canvassing the land for the necessary armaments we required to do battle, none of which we possessed in sufficient quantity or repair.

We left Isabel in Beatriz and Cabrera's care, with strict orders that she be confined to the alcazar. And now I was here, outside Carrillo's city. If I could force a confrontation, he might submit. But as I watched Cárdenas, whom I'd sent to Carrillo's palace to announce my arrival, riding back to me through the city gate, I wasn't entirely sure what to expect. A gust of wind snatched his cap off his head, tousling his thicket of fair hair; he didn't react, galloping straight toward me as if hounds nipped at his heels.

I tightened my grip on my reins, causing Canela to paw the rocky ground.

"Well?" I asked, as Cárdenas came to a halt. I felt my company's eyes upon us—Don Chacón, Inés, my other secretaries, and the few attendants I'd brought: enough to enhance my aura of regality but not so many that they'd impede my progress.

Cárdenas said haltingly, "He says if you enter through one gate, he'll go out the other."

I sat still on my saddle. "He defies me?"

Cárdenas nodded, clearly discomfited to be the bearer of this news. "He told me that just as he raised Your Majesty to your current station, so will he take you down."

At my side Chacón rumbled, "That poltroon deserves a rope! He'll get what's coming to him, so help me God. I'll drag him to the gibbet myself."

"No." I held up a hand, maintaining a semblance of calm that I did not feel.

Chacón said, "*Majestad,* if we don't put him in his place now, he'll never cease. He's at the heart of this entire affair. His arrest will send a warning to the others."

I looked past them toward the city, to the bastions of the old castle, imagining the stork nests perched among the mortared battlements.

"It's too late," I replied. "Even if I order his arrest, the damage is done. Villena and la Beltraneja are at large; the Portuguese advance on my realm. I'll not waste time chasing down one man when it can be better spent gathering the many we need to fight."

Chacón frowned. "In that case, where do we go now?"

I turned Canela resolutely into the wind. "To Carrillo's see of Toledo. If we win the city, his revenues will be cut off. That'll serve as a warning not even he can ignore." Under my breath I added, "God Almighty made me queen. Now, let Him defend me with His favor."

TOLEDO RECEIVED ME with overwhelming acclaim, offering a large contingent for our forces as well as a significant monetary contribution for arms. I was relieved; as Castile's oldest ecclesiastic seat and Carrillo's main source of income, the city's capitulation represented both a strategic and a symbolic victory.

But my struggle had just begun. Several important cities had yet to be persuaded, including Burgos in the north, whose position as a royal patrimony was strategically vital to our defense. I had to personally visit every undecided city and gain its allegiance, on my knees if need be. Any town with a sizeable population must also be appealed to, for we still needed soldiers—lots of them.

Fernando sent urgent word that the Portuguese had crossed the border into our realm, armed to the teeth. The city of Plasencia in Extremadura had opened its gates to the invaders; there, in the lofty cathedral above the Jerte River, flanked by treacherous Villena and his accomplice grandees, Afonso V and la Beltraneja were betrothed. Fortunately, they couldn't actually wed until they received a papal dispensation of consanguinity.

Having learned something myself about the unreliability of said dispensations, I composed an impassioned appeal to the Vatican, stating the case for Joanna's illegitimacy (which negated any claim she might have on the throne) and requesting that His Holiness refuse to sanctify her union with Portugal. I added a personal note to Cardinal Borgia, who'd helped untangle my own marriage situation, promising him ample recompense and our eternal gratitude if he did his part to persuade the pope.

Using Cárdenas as relay messenger between us, we decided Fernando should start the offensive while I continued to scour the country for extra money and recruits. I would ride to Burgos, then to Ávila, and from there reconnoiter with Fernando in the fortress of Tordesillas, which was fortified and easily defensible.

I DEPARTED BURGOS under a violent downpour. I had won the city's allegiance after nearly a month of negotiation with stubborn officials, many of whom feared Fernando and I would usurp their archaic feudal rights. I was impatient, sleep-deprived, and anxious to see my husband. To worsen matters, after years of drought, the heavens had decided to break apart like an overripe fruit and release their pent-up waters on the parched land, inundating rivers and turning the roads into seas of mud.

Too much rain was nearly as disastrous as none; the scant harvest would molder, its tender roots suffocating and rotting in the saturated earth. There'd be another year of no grain, of starvation and uprisings in the towns. More immediately, in this deluge it would take me weeks to reach my destination. Looking straight ahead into the blinding sheet, my hood plastered to my skull and my skirts soaked through to my thighs, indignation rose in me, savage as the weather.

How could God do this? How could He turn from me? When would He realize that I was ready to lay down my very life to serve His cause, which surely must be the future glory of Castile? Hadn't I suffered enough? Hadn't this beleaguered land given enough blood, sweat, and tears? Hadn't we suffered the sacrifice of our sons, our women, our livelihoods, our very peace? What more did He want of us?

What more could He want from *me*?

I didn't realize I was actually shouting until I caught the echo of my voice in my ears, followed by a furious clap of thunder. Canela started underneath me, whinnying. I turned to gaze at my company, all of whom looked at me as if I'd gone mad.

"*Majestad,*" said Chacón. "You are overtired. Perhaps we should turn back."

"Turn back? Absolutely not! We're going forward and not stopping until—"

A savage cramp in my belly cut off my breath. I felt myself double over in my saddle, dropping my reins, my hands plunging instinctively to my abdomen. The pain was like talons, ripping me from the inside. I must have swayed, started to slip sideways, for in some distant but still cognizant part of me not yet hazed over by pain, I heard Chacón yell and leap from his horse, rushing to Canela to grasp the reins. Ines cantered to my side, grabbed hold of me before I slid off my horse. I summoned up enough will to right myself, though I could only clutch at the saddle horn, stunned by the viciousness of the onslaught.

Then I felt it—sticky warmth, seeping out of me. I looked down, watched in a daze as crimson petals unfurled in my lap. As the pain overcame me, I thought in a haze of disbelief that I hadn't known. I hadn't even suspected that I might be with child. . . .

Inés cried out. "The queen is bleeding! Quickly, she is hurt!"

Darkness roared over me. God had answered my question.

"YOUR MAJESTY MUST rest," said Doctor Díaz, our court physician. He had ridden posthaste to the town of Cebreros where we'd halted, only a few miles outside Ávila. "It will take a week or so to recover your strength."

"I . . . I cannot," I said, my voice raw. "Fernando . . . he needs me. In Tordesillas."

"His Majesty has been notified of the difficulty you've encountered. He would not wish you to risk yourself further." Díaz turned from me as if the matter were concluded, saying to Ines, "I'll leave you this herb draft. She must take the recommended dose as scheduled. If the bleeding returns, apply pressure as I showed you. I must go to Ávila to secure more medicine, but I'll be back by tomorrow eve at the latest."

"We won't be here," I told him.

Ines rose from her stool. She'd held vigil all night as I thrashed, delirious with fever; she was haggard but her voice was firm. Without taking her eyes from me, she said to him, "Yes, we will. *Gracias,* doctor. Go with God."

He nodded, setting his cap on his head and glancing once again at me with his knowing, kind brown eyes. He was a learned man, Díaz; a converso, as so many of our best physicians were, trained in both Jewish and Moorish medicinal techniques. He had treated my daughter for the occasional cold and other minor ailments. He had also just saved my life, even if he'd employed curing arts which the Church prohibited, the prevailing doctrine being that sickness of the flesh stemmed from sins of the soul that only prayer and repentance could heal.

"You must rest," he said again and he walked out.

Inés drew her stool close, wrung the warm chamomile-soaked cloth in a basin at her feet and set it on my brow. I closed my eyes. The saffron smell reminded me of my childhood, of the arid summers in Arévalo, where the hardy plant grew wild, like weeds.

At length I summoned enough courage. "Was it . . . ?"

Ines sighed. "It was too early. They could not tell."

CHAPTER TWENTY-FOUR

I paced my apartments in Tordesillas, where the windows, high in a turret, overlooked the hamlet that bore the castle's name, the broad flow of the murky Duero River far below, and beyond, as far as my eye could see, the dusty ocher expanse of the *meseta*. Somewhere on that plain, entrenched outside the city of Zamora, Fernando faced Afonso V and his army.

We'd had the briefest of reunions, after I defied Doctor Díaz's advice and departed Cebreros exactly two days after my miscarriage. Ines had fluttered about in distress; Chacón lifted paternal protest; Díaz warned of dire complications. None stirred me. All I wanted was to escape that terrible room that echoed with stillborn promise. I needed to ride hard and fast across my land and see my beloved's face once more.

He had been waiting for me in the keep. As I crossed the flagstones under a storm-rent sky, I had seen the sorrow etched on his face, in the hollows of his eyes. I'd flung myself into his embrace, not caring about the soldiers assembled about us, the officials and courtiers and grandees. With my face buried against his neck, which smelled of sweat and sun, I'd whispered, "I'm sorry. I am so sorry."

He had held me close. "Isabella, my love, my moon—what would I do without you?" He did not care about the child, not if it came at the price of my life; and together we had repaired to the rooms he'd prepared for me, decorated with my tapestries and furnishings, which he had ordered brought all the way from Segovia.

"You shouldn't have," I'd chided, even as tears pricked my eyes. "The expense . . ."

"Bah. What are a few more *maravedies*?" he'd smiled.

Isabel was fine, he assured me that night as we lay tangled in our bed, hearing the rain—that endless rain—driving against the castle walls. Beatriz and Andrés watched over her in the alcazar, where nothing could harm her. We had not spoken of the force bearing down on us, of the threat nothing could protect us from. We'd caressed and kissed; lost in the scent and feel of each other, we'd made tacit agreement never to mention again the loss we both so keenly felt.

He left me before dawn, arrayed in armor, at the head of the patchwork army we had assembled, composed of vassals and retainers, volunteers from remote villages, carters, pages, townsmen, minor nobles, and prisoners whose sentences had been commuted so they could fight for Castile. As he rode across the drawbridge spanning the gorge, under rippling standards emblazoned with our arrows and yoke, he looked over his shoulder and raised his gauntleted hand.

"Isabella, *mi amor*," he shouted. "Wait for me!"

And so I had, for weeks, as humid June dragged into sweltering July. I was kept informed of every event by the couriers racing to and from Fernando's encampment; from them, I learned of Afonso's craven entrenchment behind Zamora's unimpeachable walls, his refusal to come out and engage, though Fernando challenged him to single combat. Our men were forced to lay siege, to dig trenches and poison wells, until supplies dwindled and tempers flared and the offensive we'd painstakingly forged out of hope, loans, and force of will began to fall apart.

"Give us victory," I prayed. "Let us triumph. You took my child; now give me this."

I still hadn't learned that bartering with the Almighty only incites His displeasure.

On July 22, as I paced in the castle in Tordesillas, a missive arrived, scrawled in a hand I did not recognize at first. I read it, horrified. I raised my eyes to the exhausted messenger and said in a voice hard as stone, "Go back. Tell him I forbid it. Not a single tower in Castile must fall to them."

"*Majestad,*" replied the courier, with a cowering stance, "it is too late. The Portuguese commandeered Toro and cut off supply lines to our army. Our soldiers lacked fresh water and food. Then flux broke out; men fell sick and there began to be talk of abandoning our cause and going over to Portugal's side. Before the soldiers deserted, the king ordered our retreat. They're already on their way back here."

The missive, shredded by my fingers, dropped to the floor.

"Bring my hat," I cried out. "And saddle my horse!"

The heat outside was a demon, exhaling the fires of Hell. I could scarcely catch my breath as I rode across the drawbridge, down the steeply sloping road, past the hamlet, over the causeway across the river and onto the simmering plain. There, I ordered a canopy set up, and a portable chair and table were brought. As Canela panted alongside my secretaries and Inés, I waited. A goblet of water sat untouched on the table. Hours passed. As violet dusk crept over the plain, plunging us into twilight, I finally caught sight of the bedraggled men straggling over the red-rimmed horizon.

I mounted Canela and held up my hand, refusing all company. Alone I rode out to meet our returning army. Fernando was at their head, along with the admiral; their faces were scored by fatigue, sunburnt skin peeling off their noses, their hair matted and filthy. Their armor clattered in panniers at the sides of their trudging, foam-lathered horses.

It was the sound of that discarded armor, unsullied by the blood of our foes, that most enraged me.

Fernando looked up, startled, as I rode forward. Then he spurred forth, as if he sought to put as much distance as possible between us and the watching grandees and quarrelsome soldiers whose lack of conviction in our enterprise had doomed us before we'd so much as maimed a single Portuguese soldier.

"Isabella," he began, haltingly, "I . . . we had no other choice. They would not leave the city; they skulked behind Zamora's ramparts and pelted us with arrows, with rocks; with their own filth." His voice trembled with humiliation. "Afonso laughed at me from the battlements—he laughed and mocked me! He said he'd make a better king on his privy stool than I could ever hope to be on Castile's throne. He refused my offer of combat. He said he preferred to wait and watch us die slowly, like flies suffocating on his shit."

I held his gaze for a long moment. I tried to summon compassion, sympathy, any feeling from inside the vault where my heart used to be. Then instead I said coldly, "You should not have come back, not while he held as much as a single tower in Castile."

His eyes narrowed. "What was I supposed to do? We've no siege engines, no cannon, no powder. You knew that. We've been woefully unprepared for them from the start."

"None of that matters." I thumped my chest with my fist. "We have God on our side; we are in the right, not those who come to steal what is not theirs. With our faith and an army like ours, how could Afonso of Portugal's words rob you of the courage that moves men to battle?"

He flinched visibly. His voice hardened. "Isabella, I am warning you: Stop this. You were not there. You do not understand."

But I was beyond heeding him, beyond reason. It was as though every insult, every fear, every flight I'd ever taken since the perilous days of my childhood had coalesced into this vast, excruciating humiliation—this unbelievable moment when my husband, one of Aragón's most vaunted warriors, had turned tail and fled from the very enemy whose sole purpose was to wrench our throne from us.

"You may say I do not understand," I said. "So many men believe that women cannot speak of war because we do not risk ourselves on the battlefield. But I tell you, nobody has risked more than me, because I wagered my husband and king, whom I love more than anything." My voice broke. "I risked my heart for the good of these realms, knowing that if we failed, I too stood to lose everything!"

My words echoed around me, across the silent plain. Our army was immobile—miles of men, of faces I did not know. Fernando remained motionless on his destrier, his face an impassive mask.

"If you'd torn down the walls of Zamora," I added, "as you would have, if you had my will, Portugal and its sovereign would have been wiped from this realm and we would not find ourselves here in this shameful hour."

He clapped his hand to his saddle, making his horse paw the ground. "I don't believe this. After everything we've endured, you complain because we've returned whole? We may have not won a battle, but neither did we lose one."

"No?" I retorted. "You may think there is glory in defeat, but *I* will not be satisfied by anything less than victory."

The moment I spoke, I knew I had gone too far. His expression turned inward. "Well," he said softly, "then I fear we'll have a heavy task ahead, for it seems you cannot be satisfied by the efforts of any mere mortal man."

His voice cut through the haze of my anger, returning me with a jolt to the present, the stark situation before me—of our army, ragged and threadbare but, as he had tried to tell me, still intact; of Fernando himself alive, not lying dead or wounded under a heap of corpses. He had drawn himself up in his saddle and I saw before me the prince I had chosen for his tenacity, who had fought time and time again for his own realm. He was a king, who had made an impossible decision today in order to spare us potential devastation tomorrow. And he was my husband, who, out of love for me and my realm, had gone to war to battle our foes, prepared to die, if need be, for the good of Castile.

With sickening clarity, I gazed toward the plain. I saw for the first time the tired admiral regarding me from his horse in discomfiture, and the soldiers—all the brave men—crippled by flux, hunger, and heat. They regarded me with a heartbreaking mixture of awe and disillusionment. I was their queen, but rather than expressing my gratitude for their salvation, I had chastised them for their refusal to sacrifice themselves.

I felt like hiding my face. Was Fernando right? Would I never be satisfied by the efforts of anyone, most of all my own self?

"Forgive me," I whispered, and I forced myself to meet Fernando's eyes. I expected to find him remote, distanced from me, perhaps forever. I had attacked him before his men, the worst insult anyone could inflict on a commander; he had every right to hold me accountable for my actions. Instead he showed me reluctant comprehension, as though he understood all too well the fount from which my anger had sprung.

"There is nothing to forgive," he replied. "Henceforth, let us show humility before Him for whom even the most powerful are weak, so in our hour of need He may grant us mercy."

My throat knotted. I had no words. None seemed adequate to erase those I had so thoughtlessly strewn. I turned Canela about. Together, Fernando and I rode back to the castle, with our army marching behind us.

☙

WE SUMMONED THE Cortes to session in Valladolid, where I made a passionate appeal for help. We now had a foreign army on Castilian soil, intent on our destruction. But the representatives of the cities—drained by their past donations—voted us no new funds. All we had left, said Cardinal Mendoza as we sat bleary-eyed at our council table, was the Church. If I declared that the ecclesiastic authorities must donate half of their gold and silver for defense of the kingdom, we could melt it down for the money we needed. Otherwise, we'd have no other choice than to seek a parley with Afonso and Villena.

"Out of the question," said Fernando. He glanced at me. "Not one tower, you said. We cannot leave them a single tower."

I repressed my smile. Our confrontation in Tordesillas had marked a shift in our marriage. Though it had been too strident of me, too overt a demonstration, it had shown him I was ready to strap on armor and sword myself; that I too would live and die, if need be, in defense of my throne. That realization had inflamed his lust, so that he'd taken me in our bedchamber with a passion that left me raw. More interestingly, it had led him to accord me moments like these, moments where he left the final decision in my hands—hands he now judged as capable, as worthy, as any man's.

"Rome won't like it," I said warily. "His Holiness has yet to issue the dispensation Afonso needs to wed Joanna la Beltraneja, but if we confiscate Church treasure, he might suddenly see fit to do so."

Cardinal Mendoza's face registered his agreement. "He might, yes, but His Holiness will be advised that it's in his best interest that Your Majesties prevail, as you shall prove devout and generous champions of the faith in years to come."

The cardinal's implication was clear, though in his eagerness to gain this new source of funds, Fernando did not see it. "Yes," my husband said. "We shall, absolutely. Put it in writing." He searched my eyes. "Isabella, what say you? We need cannon, powder; all the modern accoutrements. We can buy them from Germany and Italy but they'll want the payment up front. This is our only hope."

I knew this to be true, yet I still shrank from the idea. I did not want to incur such a debt with the Church, for regardless of how assiduously we fulfilled our end of the deal, there would be hidden interest. But without fresh resources, we were as good as dethroned. We could harry the Portuguese, as we'd been doing since our retreat, cutting off their supply lines and torching the surrounding farmlands so they had nothing to forage; keeping them caged in Zamora, Toro, and the few cities in Extremadura they'd overrun. But we couldn't expel them. Like vermin, they would multiply, spreading their dissent like a disease. Eventually, they would wear down our people's resistance; in time, their presence would become acceptable; welcomed, even, if they promised enough in return.

And if that happened, Afonso and la Beltraneja would prevail. They would see Fernando and me captured or killed, and they would seize our throne.

Reluctantly, I nodded. "Let it be done. But only under these conditions: We will return whatever we borrow in three years' time. And every *maravedi* we mint is to be used toward our war effort. Not one goes into our privy purse."

Mendoza inclined his head, signaling his agreement. Fernando rose purposefully, leaning toward me to murmur, "This time I promise you I'll wipe those whoresons off the face of the earth."

He meant it, too. His shame and fury ran deep. Never had Fernando of Aragón found himself in a position of supplication, and he plunged into the requisitioning of our army tirelessly, tallying inventories, overseeing the purchases of weaponry, tracking the shipments as they arrived, and devising safe passage from the ports to our base camps.

In turn, I organized the food provisions, recruitment, and training. I made agreements with the grandees and even sent Cárdenas to the Moorish caliph of Granada, with whom I signed a treaty, promising the Moors free range within their kingdom and personal redress by me of any grievances, should their borders be invaded by our Andalucían grandees. In exchange, the caliph sent four thousand of his best archers, who could each shoot a hundred arrows from horseback without so much as a pause.

The hard work and long hours suited me; like Fernando, I was burning over the insult done to us. Any lingering affection I'd had for

Joanna la Beltraneja was extinguished in those frenetic months, as Fernando and I devoted every minute to defending what she so callously offered up to Afonso.

I did not see Isabel for months at a time, though I corresponded regularly with Beatriz. I did not read, embroider, or engage in any of the feminine pastimes I'd always enjoyed. I took a brief trip to Arévalo with a contingent of fresh guards, for I did not put it past Diego Villena to attempt to raze the castle. There, I found the staff gray as cinders, caught in an insular existence. They were barely aware of the tumult outside their walls, save for the perennial lack of goods. My mother behaved as if she'd seen me just the previous week before she forgot who I was, lost in her inescapable delirium. Gnarled and now clearly faltering, Doña Clara refused my offer of retirement; she insisted she would die on her feet, serving my mother as she always had. I had no doubt she would. Nevertheless, I hired extra women from the village to do the chores. I had nursed the secret hope that perhaps the time had come to bring my mother to court, where she could assume her role as dowager and where I could take better care of her, but during that painful visit I realized she would never be fit for public life. I couldn't risk it; I could never let it be said that the taint of madness ran in my family nor let it blemish my daughter's prospects for marriage. Though rumor would invariably spread, no one must see the proof for themselves. My mother would stay in Arévalo until her death, forgotten by the world; and I departed the castle with that sad sense of disorientation I invariably felt whenever I returned home, as well as the irrevocable guilt that I had condemned my own flesh and blood to an isolated existence, both for her sake and for the future of Castile.

Christmas was a quiet affair. Winter precluded any armed conflict, and while Fernando took advantage of the lull to go to Valencia to fetch a phalanx of soldiers sent from Aragón for our cause, I finally reunited with Isabel in Segovia. She was nearly five years old, startlingly lovely with thick burnished golden hair and turquoise-green eyes that were so like my mother's. I was content to do nothing but take wintry strolls in the alcazar gardens with Beatriz, wrapped in furs, while Isabel dashed about, enchanted by the magic of the snow; for a time, I pretended I had no other care in the world beyond whether or not the hearths had been lit.

But all too soon the New Year arrived; before the snows had even thawed, Fernando departed with our newly equipped force, pared to lean precision. The fierce Moors on their jennets were joined to our cavalry; the German cannon and Italian gunpowder were on ox-drawn carts; the oiled siege engines and catapults wheeled behind the serpentine procession of iron and blades like unwieldy giants.

Once again I took up residence in Tordesillas; once again I was receiving my news from couriers, waiting, always waiting, for the next dispatch.

The war began with promise. The Portuguese had grown slack in the intervening months, fatted on the plunder of our looted cities, and in a bold step, Fernando quickly seized Zamora. Afonso sallied forth from neighboring Toro in high temper, engaging us in a flurry of arms, all aimed at distracting us while his enterprising son managed to sneak past our border patrols. To my furious disbelief, he arrived with reinforcements from Portugal. Suddenly, the army we had spent eight painstaking months assembling was outnumbered, surrounded on all sides by an ocean of the enemy.

Fernando bid a hasty retreat behind Zamora's stout medieval walls. I immediately sent reserve squadrons to harass the Portuguese and send them scurrying back to Toro. I hoped to secure Fernando an opening salvo, but after three weeks of skirmishes and hot words flung at each other from across walls, it became clear that if Afonso—trapped in Toro, in unbearable cold—was not winning anything, neither were we. In fact, the last of the gold we'd borrowed from the Church was fast dwindling and Fernando, holed up in Zamora, which the prior Portuguese occupation had emptied of everything edible, was starting to feel the pinch. Communication between us was nearly impossible; but one or two of his couriers did manage to reach me.

We may have to start eating our horses, he wrote, *if something doesn't break soon.*

I knew this time he would indeed do just that before he gave up. I ordered every castle within a hundred miles of Zamora and Toro either occupied or demolished. I then posted garrisons at every crossroads, denying the Portuguese all escape routes other than the way they had first come. I also issued decrees threatening to hang any man, woman, or child, commoner or grandee, who dared offer so much as a crust of bread to the invaders.

At night, with the candles guttering and my fingers cramping from writing letters to the nobles, petitions to the cities, and declarations to the people, all aimed at staving off any thought of compromise with the Portuguese, I went to the chapel and anchored myself before the altar. I did not lift any pleas. I did not barter or promise. Shutting my eyes, I let the silence, encompassing and profound, wash over me.

I barely slept. When I did, I dreamed of our ancient battle cry of "Santiago!" drowned out by ringing swords, the shrieking of horses, the sucking sensation underfoot as the earth churned into a swamp of blood and mud. I awoke gasping, fists grasping the sheets.

I could lose him, I thought. Fernando could die.

On a blustery March morning, almost two months since Fernando had taken Zamora, Inés brought a messenger to me. He was just a boy, no more than twelve; as he fell to his knees at my feet, drenched to his skin from the rain outside, I noticed with sudden heart-pounding irrelevance that his cloak was so filthy I couldn't distinguish its color.

"Majestad," he whispered, in a voice of utter exhaustion. He extended a scrap of paper, flecked with mud and rust-colored stains.

As I took it, I had to remind myself to breathe.

There was no seal. Feeling Inés's anxious gaze on me, I turned to the pale light of the window and held the paper up to it. I let a moment pass. Whatever this missive said, I must not crumble. I must not faint or weep. I must be strong. Fernando would expect that from me, just as I would from him.

I opened the missive. I read three words:

Victory is ours.

I RODE OUT at once to meet him. By then I'd learned that Afonso had ordered a retreat because my cutting off of his supply lines and the razing of the surrounding castles had denied the Portuguese any chance of haven. Fernando pursued him; the armies clashed in a marshland pass, where our men fought with such a ferocity that, outnumbered as we were, we proved lethal.

Afonso fled across the border to his realm, bemoaning his losses. More than half of his men had perished, their weapons and other belongings purloined for our treasury. Later, I would discover that Joanna la Beltraneja had also escaped to Portugal to seek asylum at her betrothed's court; I vowed she would never set foot in Castile again unless she came as my prisoner.

When I saw Fernando on the raw wood dais near the battle site, haggard but smiling in his rich red damask, his chin lifted with the pride of one who has proven himself, I had to stop myself from rushing to him. This time, our reunion was imbued with the ceremonial regality he had earned as a warrior. After we clasped hands, we turned to the applauding soldiers to receive the tattered standard of Portugal, whose bearer had been hacked to pieces defending it. I promised to consecrate a new cathedral in Toledo with it to commemorate our triumph. Then we heard Mass for all those who had lost their lives and went home to Segovia, to reunite with our daughter and our court.

At long last, Castile was ours.

CHAPTER TWENTY-FIVE

The Moors have an old saying: Before a man dies, he must see Sevilla. I would add that the same goes for a woman, and in the summer of 1477, I finally got my chance.

The previous year had been one of ceaseless labor as Fernando and I contended with the aftermath of the Portuguese war. We traveled nonstop, chastising larcenous nobles who'd lent Afonso covert aid and tearing down their fortresses, thereby depriving them of the luxury of stout walls to hide behind. Too many private castles had sprung up in Castile during the lawless years of my father's and Enrique's reigns—some of the grandees still fancied themselves above the crown itself. They exacted tribute from surrounding villages like feudal warlords, studding the landscape with defensive aeries which they filled with retainers beholden only to them. Some had even refused our call to arms during the Portuguese invasion and, in the wake of the war, Fernando and I decided it was time to teach them a lesson they'd not soon forget. We declared that only those castles officially sanctioned by us could remain standing. If the lords did not take it upon themselves to demolish their illicit holdings, we would do it for them—and level a heavy fine on the owner as well, as punishment.

We also summoned the Cortes to further refine our fiscal and legal systems and to revive the citizen-led Santa Hermandad, a law-enforcement institution which, like so much in Castile, had fallen into disorder. Through the Hermandad, we sought to restore order in our far-flung provinces by hunting down renegade mercenaries and other assorted criminals and villains. Gradually, city by city, town by town, hamlet by hamlet—sometimes, it seemed, stone by stone—we subsumed Castile under our authority.

Chastened and deserted by his Portuguese allies, Diego Villena came to court to beg our forgiveness on his knees. He stood to lose everything, and unlike his father he did not have the fickle Enrique to rely upon. Though Fernando argued we should take his head, I reasoned that by restoring Villena's aristocratic privileges, we'd win noble support by demonstrating we were also capable of mercy even in the face of outright treason. It was a risky venture but it paid off; soon after, several of the noblemen who had resisted our order to reduce their holdings came before us, albeit grudgingly, to swear their allegiance.

As for Archbishop Carrillo, he expressed no remorse. He left me with no alternative than to order him to renounce all worldly vanities and take permanent residence in the Monastery of San Francisco in Alcalá, under pain of imprisonment. Broken by his own actions and deserted by all, including his servants, who fled into the night carrying off his few remaining assets, he did not disobey my order, going into the Franciscan cloister under guard, to live out the rest of his days in impoverished oblivion. As much as I regretted that so bold a churchman and warrior should have been brought so low by his own inability to conform, I did not spare him any pity. Unlike Villena, whose youth and brash nature had thrown him into reckless alliance with Afonso of Portugal, Carrillo's involvement had been a deliberate act of revenge against me because I had chosen Fernando's counsel over his. This time, there could be no forgiveness.

Nevertheless, even with Carrillo permanently removed and our plan to rebuild the kingdom proceeding apace, I continued to struggle with my own private turmoil. I'd not conceived again since my miscarriage and the expert physicians I had consulted were unable to offer a satisfactory explanation. They all advised that I should rest more and dedicate myself to pursuits better suited to the delicate feminine temperament; the supposition, it seemed, was that a woman who behaved like a man somehow proscribed conception—something I found absurd. Surely fulfilling my duty as a queen regnant did not preclude my ability to carry out my womanly functions as God intended.

Nevertheless, anxiety ate at me, especially when Fernando and I made love. With Ines's covert assistance, I procured foul-tasting verbena drafts to balance my humors. I doubled my quota of prayers. I even rode north to Burgos in a blinding storm to visit the isolated chapel of

San Juan de Ortega, which contained a primitive stone relief believed to depict a woman in childbirth. I knelt for hours on the icy flagstones in front of it, requesting succor. I donated funds to build a larger church in the saint's name. But my womb did not stir. My menses remained irregular, as they'd always been, but the blood inevitably came, often with such force I had to clench my jaw against the pain. I could not understand why God, who had granted us so much, who had steered us to victory over Portugal, would deny Fernando and me that one blessing we most craved—a prince who could inherit our crowns after our deaths, uniting Castile and Aragón forever.

Eventually, Fernando noticed my preoccupation. At night in our chambers after the audiences were over and our bejeweled regalia was discarded, he murmured reassuring words to try and quiet my anguish.

"It will happen when the time is right," he whispered as I lay in his arms, inert as stone. "My love, we will have a son when God wills it so."

I wanted to yell, cry, break things; anything to vent my sorrow and frustration. It did not help when I discovered that his liaison in Aragón had resulted in another boy; that even as he'd pursed his lips and sent the messenger off with a gift for the child, pretending it meant nothing, it confirmed his virility and my failure to give him what that other woman had.

By the summer of 1477, I could scarcely look at him, at anyone. I was so miserable that I almost rejoiced when urgent word arrived that another feud between Andalucía's most powerful noblemen—the duke of Medina Sidonia and the marquis of Cádiz—had broken out.

Fernando was taken aback when I informed him I wished to personally orchestrate a lasting reconciliation between the southern lords. We'd already decided to eradicate the last remnants of noble resistance in Extremadura, so it was out of the question that we should both be absent from Castile at this crucial time. But if Fernando could not go, I was determined to. He sought to dissuade me, citing the dangers inherent on traveling into the lawless, Moorish-plagued region of Andalucía, but I would not be swayed. I kissed him and my bewildered Isabel goodbye, packed up my household, saddled Canela, and fled south.

South, into the blazing white heat—into the profligate garden of Andalucía, where pomegranates, figs, dates, and lemons glistened on trees like gems on a sultana's throat; south, where whitewashed cities cradled aquamarine bays, and I could be alone with my grief.

I'd heard the tales of Sevilla, of course. Who had not? It was one of our oldest and largest cities, the former capital of the Moorish invaders before King Fernando III expelled them in the thirteenth century. Built on the banks of the emerald-hued Guadalquivir, where trade from Africa and the Levant, from far-flung England and the Low Countries sailed into its port every day, Sevilla was a white-hued confection of filigreed towers and lattice balconies that hung over winding streets; shaded by magnificent palms and the bitter orange trees whose thick fruit was inedible yet when distilled yielded an intoxicating fragrance. Here, violence and blood-debt—those twin coins of Andalucía—simmered under the city's gilded surface; here, in the heart of a world where long ago the Moor, Jew, and Christian had found a brief rapport, anything was possible.

I had expected to be awed by the famous city of reflections, to breathe in its intoxicating orange-scented air and be transported to a time when divisions between faiths and skin tones blurred. And I was. But I did not tell anyone as I first disembarked from my barge on the Magdalena Bridge, where the populace had gathered to welcome me with showers of rose petals and the strumming of guitars, that Sevilla's beauty did more than affect me. As I stood there before the city's magnificent open gates, I finally felt a feeling inside me that I had feared I'd lost forever—a fiery leap that quickened my very blood.

I felt alive again.

I took up residence in the opulent alcazar in the city's center, close to the unfinished stone cathedral that rose upon the razed remains of the great mosque. In the palace, the sound and feel of water permeated the senses, trickling in mosaic fountains, shooting in graceful arcs over placid pools in the gardens, and sitting in lily-shrouded ponds—water and heat, a seductive brew that made me want to cast aside my confining garments and stalk naked like a feral cat through my rooms, which unfurled into each other in a labyrinth of sandalwood and painted tile and marble.

I set up my official public chambers in the main *sala*. Here, enthroned under my canopy of estate, sweltering even in my lightest gowns, I received the duke of Medina Sidonia, who oversaw Sevilla and most of the surrounding region.

Tall, spare to emaciation, with silver-streaked black hair swept back from his narrow brow and a puckered scar on his temple, he personified our southern pride, regarding me with a faint condescension at odds with his impeccable manners, indicating that he was unused to submitting before anyone, least of all a woman.

Bowing with practiced elegance, he uttered, "I pay Your Grace homage and render unto your royal person the keys to this, my city, in which you must now reign supreme."

The words were of course symbolic; he had no actual keys to give. Indeed, he stood there quite empty-handed, as though words were sufficient proof of his loyalty, as if he hadn't spent the last ten years turning the south into his private treasury through his battles with Cádiz, confiscating lands and castles that rightfully belonged to the Crown, letting the region collapse into lawlessness while he garnered immense wealth and refused to pay his taxes.

I disguised my amusement at his rigidity. If he'd possessed an ounce of shame, he would have blanched. But he didn't. Instead he declared, "I cannot be expected to surrender anything else while Cádiz is left at large, *Majestad.* He takes no greater delight than in raiding my lands, carrying away my crops, my horses, my cattle, even my serfs."

"Then he too must atone for his actions and render homage to me" was my dry reply.

The duke laughed harshly, to my unpleasant surprise. "Cádiz, atone? He will never do it. He disdains all authority, even that of his sovereign. He is no better than a common criminal! You should order him arrested and disemboweled for his defiance."

"Should I?" I didn't appreciate Medina Sidonia's tone. I didn't appreciate his lecturing me before my court. He was evidently oblivious to the fact that neither he nor Cádiz had ever held any right to the myriad territories they'd usurped between them. In truth, the proud duke was no less a villain than his enemy and I had half a mind to inform him of it. Instead, I maintained my composure as I said, "I assure you, I am here to see justice served and to have this quarrel between you and the marquis settled. To that effect, my lord of Cádiz will be summoned to appear before me forthwith."

Medina Sidonia scoffed. "We'll see how long it takes for him to respond, if he responds at all."

I was not dissuaded. While I waited for Cádiz's answer to my dispatch, I decided to teach the duke by example. I ordered a dais set up in the hall so I could spend every morning receiving the populace. Once they heard of my willingness to entertain their grievances, the people lined up for hours to present themselves to me.

I required that Medina Sidonia attend these sessions as a warning, for, as I suspected, I'd not been told the half of the situation in the city. Beneath Sevilla's fabled luxuriance beat a dark and twisted heart. Everyone sought an advantage, and usually it involved another's death or destitution, such as in the case of a man who came before me to declare that his herd of goats had been stolen by thieves terrorizing his neighborhood. He had lodged a complaint with the local magistrates but instead of receiving aid, he was made to pay a fine. When he refused, masked men entered his home and beat him; his young daughter was also, to my horror, violated before his very eyes.

"No one would believe me," he said to me, twisting his cap in his gnarled hands, his gaze darting nervously to Medina Sidonia, standing like a granite pillar by my throne. "They say we all lie, every one of us, though I later found my entire herd being sold in the marketplace. *Majestad,* I implore you for justice. My goats are my livelihood: I need their milk to make my cheese and provide for my family. And my daughter—" his voice broke. "She has been despoiled. No man of honor will have her now."

"What's another despoiled Jewess?" cut in Medina Sidonia, before I could speak. As I turned my stare to him, he added, "This man blasphemes, like all his foul race. He obviously refused to abide by the law and keep to his ghetto. If he insists on peddling his cheese in the marketplace, how can our magistrates possibly be held responsible for what befalls him?"

Medina Sidonia's callousness didn't catch me unawares. He'd appeared at court every day clad in costly silk and velvet, accompanied by

266 C. W. GORTNER

a retinue worthy of a potentate. His sword was of the finest craftsman-ship, his gloves and sleeves adorned in jewels and gold; to live as he did, he required a substantial income. And as most grandees had done for centuries, he no doubt supported the magistrates, who, in turn, paid him a percentage of whatever their bands of larceners brought in. It was a time-honored method used to uphold a lavish lifestyle and achieve a stranglehold over large swaths of territory; and precisely the sort of de-spicable corruption I was determined to stamp out in my realm.

Without taking my eyes from the duke, I asked, "Are the Jews for-bidden from mixing with the Christian populace in the marketplace?" I already knew they were not. Unlike Castile, where tolerance had al-ways been uneasy, at best, Andalucía had enjoyed a more convivial his-tory. Segregation from the Christian population had not been required for centuries here, though many of the region's Jews preferred to remain within their old designated areas.

Medina Sidonia looked startled. "No," he said, "but common sense dictates—"

"Common sense? My lord, even if Jews were forbidden from the marketplace, which they are not, this man was extorted and assaulted, his property stolen, his daughter gravely dishonored. What sense can there possibly be in citizens of this city fearing for their livelihoods, for their very lives?" I turned back to the man, who cringed, as though he wished he could disappear. "Do you know the men who entered your home?"

He nodded, his voice barely above a whisper. "They are the same as the thieves. They . . . they've done such things to others, with the mag-istrates' full knowledge. They steal from us because we are Jews and cannot use arms to defend ourselves against Christians."

I motioned to Cárdenas, who acted as my chief secretary in these judiciary proceedings, overseeing a committee of legal experts drawn from the university. "Inform my secretary here of who the criminals are and where they can be found," I told the man. "I shall see they are ar-rested and"—I shot a pointed look at Medina Sidonia—"judged. If found guilty, as I am sure they must be, they will be disemboweled, their body parts hung on the city gates to warn others that Isabella of

Castile extends her protection to *all* her subjects, regardless of their creed or status."

His head bowed, tears slipping down his cheeks, the man whispered, "God bless you, *Majestad,*" and Cárdenas led him to the table to record his complaint.

"Your Majesty should not indulge the rabble," I heard Medina Sidonia say in a clipped voice. "It only encourages their defiance."

"It seems to me that it is you, my lord, who encourages the rabble," I retorted, fixing him with a glare. He bowed low, muttering an apology.

Tasting iron in my mouth, I turned my attention back to the line of waiting petitioners. Medina Sidonia knew what I expected, and when, several days later, I was told that the gates of Sevilla had been festooned with the torn and bloodied pieces of the condemned, I was encouraged. If the denizens of this cauldron of anarchy thought I would yield toward mercy or shirk the harsher aspects of my duty because I was a woman, they were mistaken. Come what might, I would not falter until I had restored full obedience. I proceeded to dispense justice without regard for rank or gender, not allowing anyone who had committed a crime to escape punishment. To instill fear of me, and of the laws so flagrantly flouted, I deliberately remarked aloud in the hall one afternoon that nothing gave me greater pleasure than to see a thief mount the steps to the gallows—which caused many of those waiting to see me to cower, even as others slipped furtively out of line and fled.

Finally, the bishop of Sevilla came to request a private audience.

I waved Medina Sidonia out and once I heard what the bishop said, I was glad I had. The bishop had a reputation for being a kind man, given to learning and compassion, but I did not expect the words that came out of his mouth.

"Your Majesty has proven herself a paragon of virtue," he began, "but the people of Sevilla . . . they grow afraid. Many are leaving the city for fear that your arrival has closed the door to all hope of clemency."

I frowned, glanced at Cárdenas. "Is this true?"

Cárdenas consulted a folder in hand before giving assent, his green-blue eyes sober. "It is, *Majestad*. Over a hundred cases we've heard thus far are unresolved because either the claimant or the accused have not returned to hear our judgment."

I returned my gaze to the bishop, discomfited. "I had no idea. I regret if I've instilled fear in my subjects, for that was not my intent."

"I never thought it was," he said hastily. "It's just that . . . well, men are more inclined to evil here in the south, where we've languished for so long under ineffectual lords and the constant threat of the Moors. Your Majesty's appearance is a blessing, a great honor; but, if I may be so bold, such wrongs as those that plague Sevilla cannot be righted overnight."

His words jolted me. With sudden clarity I realized that my zealous ardor to restore order to Sevilla was, in part, a vain attempt to somehow redeem myself in God's eyes, to prove I was still worthy of His favor. I had left my daughter and husband, my duties in Castile, on an ephemeral quest for redemption. Once again, I had let vanity overcome reason, just as I had on that awful day on the fields outside Tordesillas, when I had berated Fernando before our army.

"No," I said softly, "I suppose not. You are wise to advise me of it, my lord." I stood, my gem-encrusted gown pooling like liquid gold at my feet. My ornamental crown dug into my brow; I longed to retire to my rooms, to shed myself of these contrivances of power, which suddenly seemed so meaningless.

"Pray, tell the people I've no desire to deny mercy," I said. "All those who have transgressed will be granted amnesty for their crimes, providing they do not offend or break the law again—all save heretics and murderers, of course," I added.

The bishop nodded. "Thank you, *Majestad*," he said, and then, as I started to turn away, he added, "In regards to heretics, there is something I hope you'll consider."

I looked over my shoulder. "Yes?"

"The Jews," he replied, and it was as though with this one utterance, he darkened the room around us. "Here in Sevilla, the hatred toward them has increased. They are not technically heretics, of course, as they have not converted; but since your arrival, there have been several incidents in their quarter that I think you should be aware of."

I nodded that he should continue, though I dreaded what was coming next. I recalled the poor man whose goats had been stolen. I could only imagine how many more such terrible deeds had been committed that I had not been informed about.

"A family in the ghetto of the goat-herder whose case you heard was recently dragged from their home and stoned to death," said the bishop. "Several synagogues have also been vandalized, with one burned to the ground. Many Jews are being denied the right to buy or trade in the marketplace or are being severely taxed for the privilege." He sighed. "None of this is new, I'm afraid. It comes and goes, this hatred, like a pestilence. But now, some of the aggressors cite Your Majesty's presence as an excuse; they claim the queen of Castile will not abide Christ's killers in her midst and take the law into their own hands, even though you yourself saw justice served to a Jew."

I stiffened. "Anyone who claims to serve the law in my name risks grave punishment. The Jews of this realm are also my subjects and thus are under my protection."

"Yes. Unfortunately, not too long ago the Jews suffered extremities of forced conversion or death in Castile. I'd not wish to see such misery again. It is said they bring it upon themselves, because they hoard riches while Christians starve, and conspire with the conversos to undermine our Church. But I have seen no evidence of this."

He surprised me. I'd not expected a churchman to cite the horrors of the past, which had been sanctioned by our ecclesiastical authorities, or to plead the plight of the Jews.

"I'll consider this matter," I said, looking again at Cárdenas. "In the meantime, have a decree issued at once that any molestation of Jewish property or person will incur immediate retribution. Have it posted in every plaza in the city."

When I returned my regard to the bishop, I found unabashed admiration on his face. "I must admit, I was unsure of you at first," he said. "We've had rulers before who promised change, but you, my queen, exceed all expectations. Your decree will go far in helping to restitute wrongs perpetuated on the Sephardic people. However," he paused, as if considering how to phrase his next words. "There will be consequences. Few share your sense of justice."

I smiled. "Consequences are not something I fear. Let those who disapprove come to me and they'll learn soon enough where the queen of Castile stands."

He bowed and left. By the time I'd heard the rest of the day's petitioners and sat down for my afternoon meal, I was no longer concerned with my own personal travail.

I had caught a glimpse into a future I was determined to avoid at any cost. This simmering discord between Jews and Christians could spread and kindle a conflagration that would affect the rest of the realm. I could not afford to have our fragile, newfound unity threatened now, after so much strife.

"We must take further action in defense of the Jews," I declared at a morning council meeting the next day. "Though I don't share their beliefs, I'll not abide them being maltreated or accused of inciting conversos, who, by all accounts, are faithful Christians."

I paused, watching my confessor, Fray Talavera, exchange a knowing look with Don Chacón. My steward had grown grizzled, his hair thinning, his big, muscular figure softening with age. But his character remained as discerning as ever, and I'd come to respect those rare occasions when he offered his opinion.

"Perhaps Your Majesty should join us for a sermon tomorrow," he said.

"A sermon?" I frowned. "By whom? On what?"

"It's best if you simply came," explained Talavera, his dark eyes solemn. "No one need know you're there. I can arrange for you to sit behind a screen, above the pulpit."

"Why on earth would I wish to hide?"

"Because if the orator knows you are there, he might not be as candid," replied my confessor. "Trust me, *Majestad*, you'll be most interested in what he has to say."

The following day, I sat behind a celosia with Inés at my side, as a thundering voice belonging to a Dominican priest, one Father de Hojeda, sent cold horror through me.

"They deliberately cultivate a false face so they can practice their foul rites," Hojeda thundered. "They abhor our Holy Sacraments, the sanctity of the saints, and deny the chastity of our blessed Virgin. They go to Mass by day, these two-faced Marranos, but by night they refute the rites by which they were welcomed into our Holy Mother Church, communing with their foul brethren, who abet their defiance. They must be found, revealed, expunged in the flesh, before their infection rots us all!"

His words left me deeply unsettled. As soon as we returned to the alcazar, I queried Fray Talavera, who related that he had heard similar reports of Jews inciting conversos to secretly embrace their forsaken faith, even as they feigned conformity to ours. Indeed, many claimed it had been happening throughout Castile for centuries; only indolent priests looked the other way, mired as they were in their own ignorance and venality.

"Of course, it could be an exaggeration," he said, "but I also believe you should know all the facts before you take up this cause." He paused, with marked emphasis. "It is fraught with peril," he went on, uncannily echoing the bishop of Sevilla's warning. "Few will support the defense of those deemed responsible for our Savior's crucifixion. Though we've had a policy for many years of *convivencia* with Jews, it doesn't mean everyone agrees with it. In fact, I would venture to say that few Christians would have them in our midst, given the choice."

"I understand," I said. "Thank you, as ever, for your candor. I shall write at once to Cardinal Mendoza and seek his esteemed counsel on this matter."

That evening, after I sent my letter, I gazed out of my fluted windows into the sultry night. While I would condemn any harm done to the Jews, who served me at court faithfully and from whom many of my nobles, including my own beloved Beatriz, were descended, I couldn't afford to ignore the potential undermining of our already severely degraded Church. My ancestors' reigns had been less than exemplary as far as religious conformity was concerned. Years of civil warfare and struggle with the nobility had corroded the Church's foundations; it was common knowledge that many of our clerics kept concubines, while licentiousness and the lack of the most basic scriptural adherence ran rampant amongst Castile's convents and monasteries. I was resolved to restore our Church to its prior glory. But in the upheaval since my accession, I'd not yet found the time to dedicate myself to such a monumental task.

Con blandura had been my motto—with a soft touch. I did not want to repeat the past; the mere thought of persecution, of bloodshed and suffering, after everything Castile had undergone, only stiffened my resolve, even as I recognized I could not forever evade this potential threat to my kingdom's unity. In order to compete internationally, to forge alliances with foreign powers that would keep France at bay and establish us as sovereigns worthy of respect, Spain would have to present a united front—a Catholic front, from which no dissent could be kindled to undermine our strength.

I would have to authorize an investigation to verify the troubling claims surrounding the conversos, and, if found true, establish a remedy. As a Christian queen, I could do nothing less. The spiritual welfare of my people was as vital to me as their physical well-being, perhaps even more so, for while the body was a temporary vessel, destined to return to dust, our soul was eternal.

I longed for Fernando. I'd received letters from him, detailing his exploits in Extremadura, where he'd tracked down the pockets of rebel Portuguese and their sympathizers with fervor. I wanted to curl next to him in our bed and pour out my concerns, to hear his sage assessment and know I was not alone, that whatever occurred he was always there beside me.

I closed my eyes. I could almost conjure him, his hand at my waist, his voice, husky with the night's wine, at my ear. . . .

A knock came at my door. I started, pulling my robe closer about me as Inés hustled to open it, her tawny hair unbraided for the night.

Chacón stood silhouetted by the flickering torches set on the corridor walls. "Forgive the intrusion, *Majestad,* but the marquis of Cádiz has arrived. He requests audience with you."

"At this hour?" I started to refuse, then paused. If Cádiz was actually here, I'd best receive him. Given their mutual hatred I didn't want him running into Medina Sidonia before I had the chance to gauge Cádiz's nature for myself. "Very well," I said, "show him into my private patio."

When I stepped out through my bedchamber doors onto the alabaster patio, where the evening air was redolent with the scent of jasmine, I was completely taken aback by the man waiting for me. Medina Sidonia's complaints about Cádiz had conjured in my mind the image of an unruly predator. Instead, the noble who bowed low seemed impossibly young, little more than my own twenty-six years. He was of medium stature and lean build, with a shock of fiery hair, freckled skin, and verdant eyes fringed in long ginger lashes—gorgeous eyes that seemed to hold flecks of gold in their depths and that only the intermingled bloods of this region could produce.

He wore violet satin trimmed in silver; as he swept into his elegant obeisance, the silk lining of his cape rustled. It was an affected gesture, calculated to appeal, and I had to suppress my smile. If Medina Sidonia personified the stringency of Andalucía's aristocratic privilege, then Cádiz exemplified its flair for the dramatic.

But I stiffened my spine and my voice, for no man, no matter how well attired, should think he could flatter his way past my displeasure. "You were summoned a month ago, my lord marquis. I trust you have an explanation for your untimely delay?"

"*Majestad,*" he replied, in a dulcet tone that would have made a troubadour envious, "I have no excuse other than that it took your messenger many days to reach my castle in Jerez, seeing as he had to cross lands hostile to me because of the enmity of Medina Sidonia, whose patrols illegally infiltrate my borders. Likewise, I had to re-cross those same lands in disguise, in order to reach you with body and soul together."

I tapped my foot, loud enough so he could hear. "I sincerely hope you did not come all this way to tell me that. Lest you need reminding, I am your queen. I don't take kindly to those who flout my authority. Nobleman or commoner, when I send a summons I expect to be obeyed."

He dropped to one knee, lifting his beautiful eyes with such endearing humility that I heard Inés let out a small, unwitting gasp. Though I made no indication I was affected in any way by his posturing, secretly I had to agree the man was breathtaking.

"Your Majesty, I am in your power," he said, holding his hands out wide, "with no safeguard other than the declaration of my innocence against the wrath which my enemy, with his lies, has fostered in you. Nor," he went on, his voice lilting with a passionate resonance, "do I come to speak mere words—I come to act. Send, my queen, to receive from my hand your fortresses of Jerez and Alcalá, and should anything else in my patrimony serve you, I will surrender it, as I surrender my person to you in utter obedience."

Silence echoed in the wake of his lavish speech. I glanced at Chacón. He stood with arms crossed at his burly chest, his eyebrow arched in skepticism. Castilian to his marrow, he wasn't impressed by good looks or pomposity. But as I returned my gaze to the still-kneeling marquis, I was suddenly of a mind to accept his avowal at face value. Oh, there was expediency here, no doubt; he knew when to recognize his advantage. But if he'd caught wind of my intent to submit his lawless region to order, as I was doing throughout Sevilla, and had thus decided it would be wiser to comply than continue to engage in treasonous demonstrations of his might, it suited me like pearls. With his capitulation, half of western Andalucía—most of it appropriated illegally during my father's and late brother's reigns—would revert to my sovereign control, along with its numerous castles, cities, and vassals.

"My lord marquis," I said, "while it's true I've not heard the best accounts of you, your offer shows good faith. Deliver to me these fortresses and I promise to mediate your quarrel with Medina Sidonia, safeguarding both your honors."

His smile was exuberant, revealing perfect white teeth. "Your Majesty, I am your most humble servant. Everything I have is at your command."

I let myself smile in return. The man might be a rogue but he was an irresistible one.

"My secretary Cárdenas will draw up the deeds. Once the keys to these castles are in my possession, then we can discuss the terms of this humble servitude."

I extended my hand; he actually dared to press his lips to my fingers. It was blatant flirtation, almost outrageous, and I couldn't have been more pleased. Cádiz might have scored a victory over Medina Sidonia, who, once informed of this midnight meeting, would have no other choice but to submit as well, but in the end it was I who had truly won.

I had tamed Andalucía's most powerful lords without spilling a drop of blood.

AS I EXPECTED, Medina Sidonia hastened to outdo Cádiz by surrendering six of his fifteen castles; Cádiz then offered up ten more of his. Mediation between them proved simple enough, seeing that both their holdings were now severely reduced. I proportioned the rest of their contested domains equally, keeping the largest share for Castile. In return, Cádiz vowed to wage holy war for me against the Moors, a brash statement that made me chuckle, and Medina Sidonia offered to introduce me to a Genovese navigator he patronized, who had a scheme to bypass the usual Turk-plagued routes and discover the riches of Cathay, a proposition I politely refused until a more opportune time, even as I stifled a chuckle at his supposed largesse. Medina Sidonia might have been tamed, but he'd not willingly part with any more of his wealth or risk his person if he could avoid it, preferring instead to surrender a client he no doubt had decided was no longer worth the expense.

With the southern regions of my domain thus pacified, I began preparing for my reunion with Fernando, embarking on a thorough refurbishment of the antiquated apartments in Sevilla's alcazar. His triumphs in Castile were no less important than mine; he'd brought to heel the last of the recalcitrant grandees in Extremadura and pacified the area, strengthening our vulnerable border with Portugal against future attacks. He deserved a worthy reception, and I was determined to provide it.

I was weary of discord. I just wanted to be with my family again.

SEPTEMBER SMOTHERED SEVILLA with intense heat; by midday, an egg could be fried on the street and everyone retired to sweat away the afternoon hours behind closed shutters. It was unfortunate that Fernando made his entry at just this hour, but as he sailed down the Guadalquivir in a barge decked in velvet bunting and garlands, enthroned under a canopy, his crown on his brow and a new beard framing his broad features, the heralds' shrill trumpeting more than made up for the scarcity of the crowd.

I was almost unable to contain myself as he helped Isabel and Beatriz disembark from the barge. Though I believed in proper etiquette at all times in public (for how else could we instill in our unruly subjects a healthy respect for our authority?) I eagerly moved forth, obliging my equally overdressed and heat-struck entourage to follow me across the bridge.

Fernando's eyes gleamed. *"Mi luna,"* he murmured as he took my hands, "you look well. You've even got some color in your cheeks." He was teasing, as he often joked that the sun reflected off me like a shield. I'd not even noticed in the excitement of the past days, the mirror being one of my lesser vanities; but of course all my comings and goings must have bronzed my usually pallid skin. He, too, looked well. The months of campaigning had pared him to trim muscularity, his compact body exuding energy, like that of a tireless young steer.

As I tore my gaze from his mischievous smile, I saw my daughter drop into a curtsey. *"Majestad,"* she said, in a solemn tone that betrayed painstaking rehearsal, "I am honored to be here with you and to congratulate you on your victorious labors."

I had a lump in my throat. "Thank you, *hija mía*. Please, rise. Let me look at you."

She was so beautiful I found it almost impossible to believe she'd come from my womb. At nearly seven years she had already budded to a willowy height inherited from my side of the family. Her hair was a darker auburn than mine, her eyes flecked with amber, like gold-veined turquoise. Gazing into those eyes, still limpid with innocence, I was overcome by guilt. Isabel looked just as my mother must have at her age, before the ravages of solitude and widowhood had taken their toll. I had not been back to Arévalo to see my mother in nearly two years. . . .

"Look how pretty you are," I said, and Isabel beamed, revealing she had recently lost one of her teeth; as if she suddenly remembered this, her hand flew up to cover her mouth and she flushed crimson. I took her by the hand, holding her at my side as I smiled at Beatriz, who'd cared for Isabel in Segovia during Fernando's and my absence.

"You are well, my friend?" I asked softly, and she nodded, proud and beautiful as ever in azure silk, her olive-toned skin flushed with the heat, tiny beads of sweat on her voluptuous chest, and her black eyes sparkling. I had a sudden urge to clasp her hand and rush upstairs to share secrets, as we had when we were girls.

That evening, I sat on an outdoor dais in the alcazar courtyard with my husband and daughter beside me, dining and laughing, sharing anecdotes with Beatriz as the city outdid itself in its zeal to welcome their king and princess to Sevilla. Fernando drank more than habitually, his hand slipping under the tablecloth to fondle my thigh.

That very same night, I conceived.

A FEW WEEKS later, we sailed down the Guadalquivir for a much-deserved respite in the coastal castle of Medina Sidonia.

There, for the first time in my life, I beheld the sea.

From the moment I laid eyes on it, I was captivated by the way the sunlight cast spears of fire across the colors of its ever-changing surface, which the waves tossed aside like so many garments, from indigo to deep emerald to the amethyst of twilight. And the sound, so loud where it pounded against the rocks, yet becoming a mere whisper as it slipped, warm and enticing, between my bare toes on the sand. Hiking up my skirts while the breeze, tinged with salt (which I'd later taste everywhere, as if it had soaked into my skin), tugged my veil, I wanted to plunge into that rippling Mediterranean sheen, though I'd never learned to swim.

I felt its call in the deepest part of me, like some pagan yearning, strong as sin.

I knew then that I was with child, in that moment when the vast waters before me called upon the hidden water inside. I turned, exulted, to call to Fernando. He stood on the shore with Medina Sidonia, scanning the contents of a missive the duke had just given him. Before I could say a word, he turned and strode toward me, his grave features revealing his disquiet.

"What is it?" I asked him. "What has happened?"

He handed me the parchment. "From Cardinal Mendoza: He has reviewed your request for an ecclesiastical investigation into the state of the conversos throughout the realm. He writes that the reports you heard in Sevilla barely skim the surface. According to his officials, there are many incidents of conversos upholding proscribed Jewish practices while pretending to adhere to our faith."

My mouth went dry. I didn't even want to look at the letter.

"Mendoza asks our leave to request an edict from Rome to establish the Holy Tribunal of the Inquisition in Castile," Fernando went on. "This is serious, Isabella. He has the support of Torquemada, who apparently has been informed of your forbearance toward the Jews in Sevilla and is not pleased; he complains that we are less than diligent in our sovereign duty. Both he and Mendoza believe reviving the Inquisition can help root out the false Christians and pave the way toward your stated desire to reform the Church."

Standing with him on that endless beach suffused in dusk, our child's laughter floating in the spindrift that webbed the air, with the knowledge that another child even now grew inside me, I felt a profound chill.

I folded the parchment and shoved it, seal and all, into the silk pouch at my waist. "Their request is premature," I said. "The Holy Tribunal has not functioned in Castile for many years; it's in as much need of reform as the Church itself. And we've much to consider already. We still have to convene our Cortes to revise the legal codes and curtail the nobles' privileges, not to mention that, like every king before us, we'll be expected to take up the Reconquista against the Moors. This is hardly the time to assume another burden, especially one of such magnitude."

Fernando looked toward the crash and ebb of the waves, his aquiline profile softened by the lingering twilight. At length he said thoughtfully, "No doubt you're right, but it would be a mistake to ignore the cardinal's request. Since we assumed charge, the entire world has been watching, waiting for us to fail like our predecessors. I'd not want our own churchmen griping to Rome that we're less than devout, for if we're expected to take up the Reconquista against the Moors, as you say, we'll need Rome to sanction the crusade. His Holiness could deny us his blessing if we don't show willingness to rid Spain of heresy. Besides," he added, "how burdensome can it be to deal with a few lapsed conversos?"

I touched his arm. "Fernando, it may not be a few. Don't you understand? If what Mendoza and Torquemada say is true, it could mean subjecting hundreds, maybe thousands, of our subjects to arrest and inquiry by our authorities. It would create fear among our people at a time when we seek their trust."

"But that is how these things work. The Inquisition was designed by Saint Dominic to separate the defiled from the faithful, to salvage and purify those whose souls run the peril of damnation. I personally cannot believe there are thousands; but if such is the case, wouldn't it be better to contend with them now?"

He spoke as if it were a foregone conclusion, as though he had no doubt that reviving the Holy Tribunal was the only sensible solution. For a moment I didn't know how to respond. I knew he shared my piety; we were both unfailing in our attendance at Mass and private devotions. For us, there could only be one church, one faith. So how could I explain this baseless fear that overcame me at the thought of embarking down this path?

"Is that really what we want?" I ventured. "To authorize an institution answerable to Rome, whose jurisdiction over us will be absolute? If we request this edict from His Holiness, we must also accept his authority over this matter. I, for one, am not so eager to let Rome dictate how or when we should act."

His frown relieved me. Like me, he was loath to invite Rome into our affairs. While we did not seek quarrel with the Holy See, we did not want the fruit of our endeavors to be usurped by the bottomless need of the Vatican, not when our coffers were nearly empty. For our country to prosper, we must dictate our internal policies, even in such delicate matters as religious unity.

"What if we request that the Inquisition be placed under our control?" he suggested. "As rulers of Castile, we could supervise its activities, appoint its tribunals and overseers; we could devise a *new* Holy Office according to our requirements."

"We could," I replied, taken aback by his quick solution. Sometimes, Fernando had an uncanny way of cutting through a problem. "But will His Holiness agree? No monarch that I am aware of has ever been granted such license before."

"Perhaps no monarch has ever asked."

I turned away. The breeze grew stronger, whipping the water to gold-tipped foam. In my purse, the letter weighed like stone. Was this what God intended? Had He appointed Fernando and me as His vessels of fire, to purify our faith? I did not know; my own conviction, usually so steadfast, had deserted me.

"If I grant this," I finally said, without taking my gaze from the tumbling water, "we must proceed carefully, with due diligence. Cardinal Mendoza must promise to ensure that every effort is made to return those who've erred back to the Church by peaceful means. I will not authorize harsher measures unless left with no other choice. And I do not want the Jews harmed. Only those whose adherence to our faith has come under doubt are to be investigated."

I looked at Fernando. He met my searching eyes, his expression somber. "It shall be as you command," he said. "I will see to it personally."

"Then do it," I said softly. "Write to Mendoza and tell him we approve his request. But only to obtain the edict; I reserve the right to implement it in my own time."

He nodded and reached for my hands. "*Dios mío,* you're like ice." He glanced sharply at Inés, who tarried with my other ladies nearby. "Her Majesty is cold! Bring her cloak."

Within minutes, we were hustling back up the cliff-side pathway to Medina Sidonia's castle, the ladies chattering, my Isabel's cheeks reddened from the sun. She was elated, all decorum forgotten in the novelty of an afternoon spent in frolic.

"It's beautiful, isn't it, Mama?" she breathed, slipping her hand in mine as we paused at the crest to look out upon the sea, unfurling toward the horizon like endless silk. "But so big. Beatriz says you could sail across it forever and never reach the end. It must be lonely."

"Yes," I said, wistful. "I think it must be."

CHAPTER TWENTY-SIX

All the midwives—and there were far too many, in my opinion—assured us that I would bear a son. Everything indicated it, they said, as they hovered over the particulars of my various minor complaints, including the very odor of my urine. Of course, we'd heard all this before; we'd been told much the same when I was pregnant with Isabel. But as the days passed in Sevilla's alcazar, a luxurious haven in which to withstand the upcoming travails of pregnancy, I watched the crones' blandishments exert a powerful influence over Fernando. The more impatient I grew with the constant fussing over me, the more solicitous he became.

Despising the societal penchant for turning expectant women into useless creatures and determined to serve of some use while I awaited the child's birth, I began seeking a tutor to teach me Latin. I regretted my deficiency in this language of international diplomacy every day; I hated having to rely on translators, feeling it exposed me as a provincial queen, with no formal learning or training. But I was distracted from my quest when an envoy from England arrived bearing another extravagant baptismal font as a gift (we had dozens by now) and during its presentation, he mentioned that his king had authorized that nation's first printing press.

"Is that so?" I leaned forward in my throne, forgetting my swollen feet in my too-tight slippers. "I've heard of an astonishing renaissance taking place in Italy, where once lost or forgotten ancient texts are now being made available again through these presses."

The envoy smiled. "Indeed, Your Majesty. Painting, music, poetry, and sculpture are flourishing under the patronage of many learned rulers, from the Medici in Florence to the Habsburgs in Austria, who provide their artists with access to classical texts. His Grace King Edward

IV is determined that this unparalleled wealth, learning, and knowledge should also flourish in England."

"How marvelous!" I was enthralled. I had heard that the printing
press could produce hundreds of books in less than half the time required for hand reproduction by scribes; with a fleet of these remark-
able devices, I could begin to replenish our sorely depleted libraries,
neglected by the years of tumult and civil war. Literacy in Castile was
restricted to monks, enterprising scholars, and the very wealthy; few
ordinary people could afford books, much less read them.

Here, at last, was something important I could contribute.

I decided at once to set up charitable funds for education. I had
Cárdenas purchase twenty presses from Germany and ordered them
installed in Salamanca and other major university seats. In honor of my
efforts, the new press in Valencia sent me its first printed product—a
book of hymns to the Virgin, dedicated to me and my unborn child.
The exquisite volume, bound in calf skin and with a sharp tang of ink,
fascinated me. I couldn't quite believe a machine had made it, as I kept
repeating to Fernando, who chuckled and said, "I hardly see the fuss.
It's still just a book, yes?"

I regarded him in astonishment, my belly jutting before me. "Do
you not see that with these presses, we can begin to further the education of everyone in our realm?"

He eyed me in amusement over his goblet, the remnants of a greasy
partridge lying dismembered on his plate. We had taken to dining in
my rooms in the evening because it was more comfortable and didn't
require me to maneuver the treacherous steps of the dais now that I
entered the sixth month of my pregnancy.

His smile widened. "I assume by 'everyone' you also mean women?"

"Of course. Why not? In Italy, women are permitted to attend universities and receive degrees. Do you object to women having the freedom to learn something other than domestic arts?"

"Me? Object?" He spread his hands wide, in mock surrender. "God
forbid!"

I eyed him. "Are you indulging me because the midwives told you
to? Because I am well aware that many men share the widespread

belief—spread, by the way, by those who are barely literate themselves—that education weakens a woman's inherently frail moral fiber."

"I've never heard that," he replied, "though I suppose it bears some merit."

I hissed in a breath, controlled myself just in time as I caught the gleam in his eyes. He was doing his best to keep from breaking into laughter.

"Good." I settled against the cushions of my big padded chair, unreasonably annoyed that he was treating this important issue with a carefree air. "Because I intend to issue a mandate that will permit women to both study *and* instruct at our universities. In fact, I'm planning to hire a woman to tutor me in Latin."

"I wonder if such a miracle exists?" quipped Fernando.

"She will," I retorted, "if I have any say in it!"

He could not curb himself anymore; with a gush of delighted laughter that brought a begrudging smile to my lips, he got up and came to kiss me. "Then, by all means," he murmured, "issue your mandate, though I've no doubt not a few men in Castile will soon wish that Gutenberg had never invented his machine."

"You're impossible," I groused. But after he left, I retrieved my little book from the side table, caressing its gilded cover.

It was high time I showed the realm that women could serve a higher purpose through education. My own Isabel must wed one day and act as our representative in a foreign court. How much better might she fare if she possessed the advantages of the education I had lacked? She and Castile must reap the marvels of this new era; I wanted female scholarship, and the impulse to learn, to be a commonplace occurrence in this realm.

But my resolution was cut short by the end of my pregnancy. The moment of my confinement came—weeks later than scheduled, as I'd resisted being sequestered—and after only a few days of enclosure with my women, my water broke. Within hours, I found myself in full agonizing labor.

Sweltering under the sweat-soaked veil, I clenched my jaw and pushed with all my ebbing strength. The pain was enormous, tearing at my insides; I thought, in that moment of utter exhaustion, surely I would not survive, that this child, whom I had longed for, cared for so assiduously during the nine long months, would be my doom.

"Push, Isabella," murmured Beatriz at my ear, her hand cool as a blessing through the dripping veil. "The midwife says the head is visible. Just a little more . . ."

"Sweet Mother of Christ," I whispered as I rallied my muscles for one more push. "Let it be a son. Please, let it be a prince."

Everything I knew, everything I aspired to, was reduced in that moment to a single shuddering breath; a painful gasp and agonizing contraction of flesh, and then the welcome gush of hot blood.

"It's here!" I heard the midwife cry. "The child is born!"

Through the flurry of skirts, I gazed up desperately from my stool and watched as the hunched midwife sliced and tied off the cord, swabbed the tiny white body clean of gore, turned and dripped honey in its open mouth. I waited, my body throbbing as if on fire, until I heard the first bewildered wail and the midwife lifted her triumphant face to me.

"Castile," she declared, as if she'd personally orchestrated the event, "has a prince."

WE NAMED HIM Juan, for both his grandfathers and our patron saint, the Baptist.

I heard later that Fernando presented him to the court with tears in his eyes. Recovering in my apartments, I would make my official appearance after the Baptism and my churching. But Beatriz kept me apprised of every development, from the pride in my husband's stance as he held our little infante aloft to the court's acclaim (prompting Juan to burst into tears) to the cacophonous revelry that seized the entire realm. In Segovia, people danced around bonfires and a hundred bulls were slaughtered in Salamanca—a horrid spectacle I was furious to hear about and refused to sanction. From Aragón, old King Juan sent us an enormous gold baptismal font; it took six men to carry it into the Church of Santa María. He also sent a private note asking us to grant Carrillo a pardon for his past offenses and restore his income, both as a gesture of compassion for our son's birth and out of respect for the archbishop who'd fought so hard to gain us the throne and was now "a sad and ruined man."

I agreed. I had no room left in my heart for anger. I'd been vindicated; after eight years of marriage, I had safeguarded our dynasty with a prince who would inherit both Castile and Aragón upon our deaths. I had earned the admiration of our most unrepentant subjects, and within days of Juan's birth, the last remaining criminals in Sevilla fled for refuge in the Moorish-held port city of Málaga. Bells tolling throughout the realm prompted priests to hide their concubines and bastards and clutch at their Bibles, fully aware that with the arrival of a male heir, I would soon be free to turn the full force of my attention to the reform of our Church.

On the Feast of Santa Marta, six weeks after the birth, Fernando and I appeared together to formally present our son to Sevilla. We rode into the congested streets, cordoned to allow us passage on our horses, under a sun so hot it bleached the sky. Sweat pooled underneath my pearl-encrusted *brial* and crown. My stalwart Canela, bedecked in equally excessive finery, pranced nervously, his hooves ringing sparks from the steaming cobblestones.

The crowd's cheering scattered pigeons from the tile rooftops. Juan rode before us in a canopied carriage, cradled by his godmother, the duchess of Medina Sidonia. The marquis of Cádiz escorted the infante, basking in the acclaim with a handsome man's insouciance; Medina Sidonia rode before us with our standard, a privileged position that denoted our high esteem.

Then, all of a sudden, the cheering faltered and faded to silence. As the people looked up in unison, a pall came over the day, tinting it opaque, lengthening our shadows. At my side, Fernando drew rein. He peered upward, his ruby-studded gold coronet tilting on his brow.

He froze. *"Dios mío,"* I heard him whisper. *"El sol se apaga."*

"What? The sun can't go out," I exclaimed, craning my face to follow his fearful gaze, though the weight of my headdress and crown hurt my neck.

In the scorched sky, I saw a shadow slicing across the edge of the sun like a black scythe.

Around us, I heard terrified gasps. People collapsed to their knees.

But I remained calm; during my scavenging in the library of Segovia as a princess, I'd come across several writings describing this phenomenon—eclipse, I believed it was called. I informed Fernando of it as he sat frozen on his horse.

"Eclipse?" he echoed, as if the very word were incomprehensible.

"Yes. Sometimes, the moon slips over the sun, eclipsing its light, but then it goes away and everything returns to normal," I said in irritation. It was blistering hot. I was drenched in perspiration. I wanted to reach the dais in the main plaza, fulfill our obligations, and return to the shelter of the alcazar before we all broiled to death in our finery. I also was worried for my son, who'd surely break out in a rash in this infernal heat.

"But, it . . . it's an omen," stammered Fernando, to my disbelief. "On the very day our son is to be presented, this—this eclipse occurs? It cannot be a good sign."

I resisted the urge to roll my eyes. For all its far-flung territories and holdings, Aragón was still a land steeped in superstition, much like Andalucía.

"It's not an omen," I said, more tartly than I intended. "Our son has been christened already, blessed by God. This is just the moon forgetting her proper place." I smiled, lowering my voice to a quip. "You, of all men, should know something about that."

He tried to return my smile but I could tell he was truly frightened, as though he believed this insignificant celestial event presaged the future.

I gestured impatiently to Medina Sidonia, who appeared utterly contemptuous of the collective fear around us. "My lord duke, if you would . . . ?"

He barked at the immobile retainers, arrayed like statues around us as they stared up at the half-covered sun. "Onward! Her Majesty commands it!"

Our horses' passage made a disconcerting echo on the now silent streets. By the time we reached the plaza and the crowd had assembled there, the light had begun to return, the moon's intrusive sliver already ebbing away.

I mounted the dais, taking Juan from the duchess and staring upon the anonymous mass of people, compelling them to stop looking to the sky, to turn their eyes instead to me and the child in my arms.

I put no trust in auguries. I did not believe in any force stronger than God.

And God would never let any harm come to my son.

IN THE EARLY spring of 1479, we left the gardens of Andalucía and returned to Castile.

We made the journey in slow stages because of little Juan, whom I kept with me at all times due to his alarming propensity for colic. I had changed his wet nurse twice in the last six months, to no avail; I was so concerned for his welfare that this time I allowed myself to be persuaded to not nurse him myself, though the change in nurses didn't help. I also consulted a host of learned physicians, Jewish and Moorish alike, and donated a small fortune to Sevilla's Virgin of Antiquity and her Christ Child, known for their curative gifts. Fernando tried to reassure me that many babies suffered colic and outgrew it, but I felt my son's distress with every fiber of my being and could barely pay heed to anything else. Isabel rode with me, Beatriz, and Ines in our carriage, enduring the teeth-rattling jolts over pitted roads as she crooned and dangled silver rattles in front of Juan to keep him distracted from the pains in his stomach.

Shortly after our arrival in Segovia, I discovered I was once again pregnant. As I looked up from the pail where I'd just retched out my morning meal, Beatriz gave me a long compassionate look. Fernando had insisted on resuming his rights in our bed well before I felt ready to accept him; he'd not been rough, but neither had he been accommodating, and I'd complained to Beatriz in a rare fit of candor that he seemed unable to accept "later" as an answer. Now, her one look told me why; Fernando wasn't as immune to Juan's fragility as he feigned. Babies died every day, of colic and other maladies. Our succession was still vulnerable; we needed another son.

This need was reinforced when word reached us that, after years of failing health, Juan of Aragón had died. Fernando immediately departed for his realm to attend the obsequies for his father and to meet with his Cortes, which remained separate from those of Castile by our prenuptial Capitulations. I wanted to go with him; with his father's passing, our kingdoms were now truly united under one rule. But I couldn't make the journey, not with a babe to care for and another on the way.

My third pregnancy proved troublesome from the start. I was constantly at odds with myself, missing Fernando from the moment he walked out the door yet too exhausted to even walk across my chamber, plagued by constant nausea that made me dread the months of restrictions ahead.

My temper hardly improved when I was informed of yet another uprising in Extremadura in Joanna la Beltraneja's name, masterminded by that old goat King Afonso, whose defeat at our hands—and Rome's subsequent refusal to issue him the dispensation he'd requested to wed Joanna—burned in him like brimstone. He'd bribed a pack of discontented minor nobles to spring their revolt the moment Fernando's back was turned.

"What am I to do?" I exclaimed to Beatriz. I sat at my desk, reading the latest reports sent by the admiral, whom I'd dispatched at the head of an army to quell the revolt. "Don Fadrique writes that he's arrested all the nobles involved. They'll be deprived of their estates and executed, of course, but he had to set torch to the fields, round up villagers, and chase the Portuguese back across the border like wild dogs." I waved the paper at her, my fatigue incinerated by my temper. "Those miscreants fled with sacks of treasure looted from our churches slung over their backs! They pillaged what we can ill afford to lose and wagged their fingers at our men from across the border!"

I flung the paper on my desk, making the candle flames dance erratically. "I cannot let Afonso get away with this. Clearly I've been too naïve to think that being exiled in Portugal would keep Joanna quiet. Fadrique says that, under questioning, most of the nobles admitted they rebelled against my rule because Joanna calls herself Enrique's true daughter and Castile's only queen! How dare she question my right to my throne, when everyone knows she is Beltrán de la Cueva's love child?"

Beatriz paused by the bed, where she scented my linens with lavender and anise before folding them into a coffer. "Maybe you should offer a peace treaty," she suggested.

I snorted. "I'd rather offer a barrage of cannon fire."

She chuckled. "No doubt, but gunpowder is expensive and Afonso is a coward. He'll hide in his fortress and make you do all the work. But if you offer a treaty and insist on negotiating with your own mother's sister, Princess Beatrice, then you—"

"—could request that la Beltraneja's custody be strictly enforced," I cut in and smiled. "Beatriz, you should have been a diplomat. It's perfect: Afonso will not dare refuse me, especially if I sweeten the offer with the promise that once my Isabel comes of age, we'll consider a marriage alliance with the son of his heir the crown prince, whom he has not wed to la Beltraneja because of the age difference. I can trump him at his own game and still give him what he wants: pride of place, and a healthy dowry through Isabel to boot."

Beatriz nodded, picking up my stack of linens. "Get to work then," she said. "Anything's better than watching you mope and drag your feet for the next eight months."

I laughed, turning to my desk to ink my quill with renewed purpose.

King Afonso returned word that he would meet me at our border to discuss my proposal. It was time we put an end to this quarrel, once and for all, he wrote. Yet after I'd undertaken the two-day journey by litter to the windswept castle of Alcántara, leaving my children in Beatriz's care, I was informed that the king had fallen ill. I was left stewing for two weeks before I received word that he was dispatching Joanna herself, along with my stated preference for a representative, my maternal aunt Beatrice of Portugal.

I embraced the tall, elegantly dressed blood relative I'd never met till now. Her blue-green eyes and oval face were achingly reminiscent of my mother's. I sensed at once that Beatrice was an ally, and indeed, as soon as our pleasantries were dispensed with, she stated that she wanted lasting peace between our nations.

"We are neighbors. It hardly benefits us to be at each other's throats," she said, with a lift of her fair brow, "seeing as we share a border and family ties."

"I couldn't agree more," I replied. "And is the king also in agreement that the child's care should be transferred to you?"

"He is." Beatrice paused. "I fear the child's opinion is another matter," she added, and she rose from her upholstered chair to open the doors. Joanna appeared. She came before me, stiff as a pole in her rich dark velvet.

I forced out a smile. "My child, how lovely to see you again; you're a woman grown."

And she was—most alarmingly, in fact. I had forgotten she wasn't the little girl I'd escorted about the gardens of the alcazar, not a plump underage pawn to be molded by my will. At sixteen, Joanna might have been beautiful, had she not a prematurely embittered cast to her features. As I covertly searched her for any resemblance to my late brother, I found only her mother, Queen Juana, in her features. She was slim as yew, with the same seductive black eyes, lustrous hair, and sullen lips. I tried to overlook her pointed refusal to curtsey or show me any other sign of deference, but the sight of her coiled thorns about my heart. She was a sworn foe, fully capable of making herself some other troublesome prince's wife, if not Afonso's queen; the last thing I needed was a rival shadowing my every move, a figurehead behind which malcontents, such as those in Extremadura, could rally.

"Do you remember me?" I asked her, and I could tell by the flash in her eyes that she did, though it suited her to feign otherwise. She did not reply.

"Answer Her Majesty," snapped Beatrice, sharply nudging the girl.

Joanna's eyes narrowed. "I see no queen here," she intoned, in a high nasal voice meant to carry. "Unless you would prefer that I answer my own self?"

Beatrice gave her a withering look before turning to me. "The child has cultivated airs at court that ill suit her. She's spent too much time absorbing others' suppositions."

"Evidently," I said. I did not remove my stare from Joanna, but to my disconcertion, she did not avert her gaze, returning my regard with such calculated effrontery I found myself clenching my fists under my sleeves.

"So, you believe you bear more right to the crown than me?" I asked bluntly.

Her slight flinch revealed she wasn't as contemptuous as she'd have me think. She did not answer at once; her mouth was pinched, as if she gnawed at the inside of her lip.

Then she blurted, "I believe I am King Enrique's sole heir. I believe you, Princess Isabella, have usurped my throne and let it be bantered about that I am a bastard. But in my veins runs blood as pure as yours, for I too am of the royal houses of Portugal and Castile."

"Is that so?" I did not shift a muscle. Inside me, cold certainty took hold. She must be disposed of. I could no longer afford to disdain the threat she posed.

I said to my aunt, "In this case, I believe we have much to discuss. Clearly my original plan was too lenient." It was an unmistakable threat and Joanna reacted just as I hoped.

"I will not be denied!" she erupted. "You cannot fool me with your arrangements and petty lies. I am the rightful queen of Castile! I will never renounce my claim to you. *Never!*"

Spittle sprayed from her lips, her entire body taut. I watched Beatrice's expression shift from discomfited embarrassment to resolution.

"The child obviously needs a calming tonic," she remarked, and she rose and came to me, linking her arm in mine to draw us toward the gallery. We left Joanna standing there, rigid, aware that all her scheming, all the indignities she believed she had endured, were about to be ignored.

Though I didn't look back, I felt her eyes boring into my back.

A MONTH LATER, I bid my aunt a fond farewell. The winds buffeted me where I stood on the drawbridge, sending my cloak swirling as I watched the Portuguese retinue lumber off. It had been an exhausting four weeks of negotiation, during which I'd gamely fought off my daily malaise. Beatrice had proved a canny spokeswoman for Portugal, certainly far abler than the blustering Afonso in her eloquent support of her nation's cause.

Nevertheless, I prevailed. I steadfastly refused any concessions to lost territories or monies, citing the fact that Portugal had invaded us, not the other way around. While I agreed to the original proposal in which my daughter Isabel would be sent as a bride for the son of Portugal's crown prince, and ceded crucial exploration rights on the open sea, on one point I was immutable: Joanna must renounce all claim to my throne. If she liked, she could wait a requisite number of years under guardianship in a convent until my son came of age, at which time a union between them would be considered. Or she could take holy vows now. To preempt further conspiracies in her name I stipulated that under no circumstances was she to continue to make unfounded assertions about her paternity.

I allowed her six months to reach a decision. As the litter drew away I saw its curtains flick back and I was treated to a last glimpse of her face. The hatred in her eyes pierced me where I stood; but in her bitter pallor, I already read defeat.

She would die before she submitted to my terms. Like her mother before her, she had too much conceit and not enough sense. She'd delay as much as she could, staving off the inevitable, but in the end she'd have no other choice. Immured in a convent, she would live out the rest of her days as an unwilling bride of Christ, forgotten by the world.

Still, as she vanished forever from my life, I shuddered to contemplate the havoc she might have wreaked, had she been able to prove what she so fervently believed.

FOLLOWING THE SIGNING of our treaty with Portugal, Fernando and I repaired to Toledo. There, on November 6th, I delivered my third child.

This time, my labor was brief, a mere few hours of discomfort. As the midwife set my newborn child in my arms, I thought without doubt she was my most beautiful—a perfect infant in every way, down to the fuzz of reddish curls on her still-soft crown, her milky skin, and her languid amber-tinted eyes. She did not fuss; rather, she was content to lie cradled beside me, as if her abrupt entrance into the world had left her unaffected. Though I should have been disappointed that she wasn't the boy we had hoped for, a fierce protectiveness overcame me as I held her, coupled with sudden sorrow.

Like my Isabel, she would grow up, and one day leave for a distant court as a bride. I'd schooled myself not to let my emotions get the better of me when it came to my daughters; unlike Juan, who would stay and inherit our kingdoms, I knew from the start that an infanta's duty lay elsewhere.

Still, there was something so compelling about this child, as if the bond severed with the belly cord had not actually separated us. I kept her with me until Fernando tiptoed into my chamber to stand at the foot of the bed, regarding me with a quizzical air.

"Rumor is you'll not surrender her to the wet nurse. The ladies are scandalized. They think you'll nurse her yourself."

"She's not hungry yet." I peeled back the edge of fleece swathing her face. "Look: she's fast asleep. She's been like this since they gave her to me. She's so at ease, it's almost unnatural. Have you ever seen a newborn so quiet?"

He came around the bed to gaze at her. "Her hair is red, like my mother's."

"Then we must call her Juana," I said, "in honor of your mother." I craned over to kiss her warm forehead, upon which life had yet to inscribe any lessons.

"Infanta Juana," echoed Fernando and he smiled. "Yes, it suits her."

"YOUR MAJESTIES, WE must put the edict into effect."

We sat in the council chamber of Toledo's alcazar; outside, a chill evening rain plunged winter's veil over the streets. It was late. We had just finished another long day of negotiations with our Cortes, comprising thirty-four procurators from Castile's seventeen major cities. Fernando and I had directed our joint efforts toward the strengthening of our authority, setting into motion an ambitious, years-long agenda for revision of our legal codes and taxation.

Now, bleary-eyed and fatigued, we faced Cardinal Mendoza and the ecclesiastic committee we'd authorized two years earlier to investigate the allegations of converso heresy in Castile. Beside me, Fernando sat sunk in his chair, his ringed hand at his chin as he regarded with shadowed eyes the stack of papers heaped on the table before us—an assiduous collection of scandalous indictments of priests who had counseled students against the Virgin and the cult of saints; furtive testimonies of neighbors who'd seen friends eat unleavened bread and place coins in the mouths of their dead, like the Jews; reports of converso parents who'd washed away with spit the oil of Holy Baptism from their babes' brows; even unsubstantiated, horrific rumors of the torture of Christian boys during Holy Week, in mockery of our Savior's passion. They all pointed to the same, inescapable conclusion.

"You're certain?" said Fernando, his voice hoarse from the day's sessions. "You believe without any doubt that these false conversos subvert our Church and even gain profit by it?"

"Yes, *Majestad.*" Mendoza motioned to Fray Torquemada. I tensed in my chair as the ascetic Dominican friar stood, his black robe clinging to his jutting shoulders. He'd become even more emaciated since I'd last seen him, so much so that at first I thought he was mortally ill—a skeletal figure of sinew and bone, without any color in his gaunt face. It seemed impossible he could move at all, malnourished as he was; yet his pale eyes smoldered with undeniable fervor. Here, at long last, was the moment he had awaited.

I concealed my dread as he began to speak.

"It is all true," he said, in his low, passionless voice. "And there is more—much more than even we can imagine. In addition to their secret Judaizing, these filthy Marranos ally with the Jews, extorting loans from good Christians at exorbitant interest and controlling the monies available. Not one Jew breaks the earth or becomes a carpenter or laborer; all seek comfortable posts with the ultimate goal of gleaning profit at others' expense. Their wealth exceeds the Crown's. Like the infidel, they dine on gold while many starve."

His words were not particularly novel; I'd heard similar disparagement for years in my late brother's court. But now Torquemada spoke to a new audience; he sought to spark a response not in me but in Fernando. He had studied my husband from afar, with that uncanny prescience he'd once shown me. He'd discovered Fernando's twin vulnerabilities—fear of rampant heresy and fury at the perennial poverty dogging our heels.

"You say their wealth exceeds ours?" Fernando straightened. All semblance of reflection was gone.

Torquemada inclined his tonsured head. "Yes, my king. And by your leave, in sanctioning His Holiness's edict establishing the Inquisition, we can begin God's work and separate the pure from the defiled, restoring glory to both our Church and your treasury."

"How so?" I said, preempting Fernando. "How exactly will this Holy Tribunal benefit our coffers?"

Torquemada slid his gaze to me, with uncomfortable intimacy. "The properties of the condemned will revert to the crown, Your Majesty. It was part of the terms you yourself set forth before His Holiness, was it not? You asked that all functions of the Holy Inquisition, from its appointees to punishments exacted, should remain in your hands?"

I clenched my jaw, resisting the urge to look away. As if time had paused and turned back, I saw myself as I'd been that night long ago when I had first met Torquemada in Segovia—a troubled adolescent with the weight of the world on my conscience. Then he had read my innermost desires, brought me a solace that helped me marshal my strength. Now I was not so sure of him anymore. Since the day he had come to extort a promise from me, while Enrique lay dying, a seed of doubt had been growing.

Doubt is the Devil's handmaiden, sent to lure us into perdition.

"Surely, there can't be as much wealth as you describe," I replied, feeling Fernando's stare on me, almost as intense as Torquemada's. "And I did not authorize any policies taken against the Jews. Only conversos, I said: only those who have erred in our faith."

Torquemada stood quiet, unblinking. I finally looked past him to my confessor, Fray Talavera. He nodded at me quickly, in encouragement. Like me, he'd grown increasingly troubled by Torquemada's relentless quest to expel the Jews from the realm. Though the commission we had appointed was overseen by Cardinal Mendoza, the friar had slowly come to dominate it with his fiery rhetoric.

"And what of my educational program?" I went on. "I asked that we send trained and experienced prelates throughout the realm to preach the principles of our faith; they were charged with ensuring that all those who misunderstood or had been brought up in error were gently corrected and returned to our fold."

"Indeed, and our prelates did as Your Majesty bade," said Cardinal Mendoza, clearing his throat. "You'll find in those papers reports from eighty prelates, all of whom unfortunately concur that these converso heresies are, in the majority, too ingrained to ever be expelled by doctrinal education. In Andalucía, the situation is particularly grievous, with many of the Marranos defiant of or even impugning the Church. Their souls risk everlasting damnation. It is your obligation as God's anointed monarch to save them."

Torquemada said abruptly, "Your Majesty seems to forget you promised to devote yourself to the extirpation of heresy once you became queen. To deny the promise now is tantamount to committing heresy yourself."

As I clenched my hands about my armrests, Talavera interjected, "With all due respect, I am Her Majesty's confessor. I assure you, she's a devout servant of the Church, who takes these allegations most seriously—"

"These are not allegations!" roared Torquemada, his voice reverberating against the wood-paneled walls of the enclosed room. I'd never have thought his lungs capable of such volume; clearly, neither had Fernando, who visibly recoiled. "These are truths!" The friar flung out his hand, his thin fingers curled as if he cradled invisible flames. "To deny it is to deny Christ himself! Better to enter Paradise with one eye than to suffer in Hell with two."

I glanced warily at Fernando; he stared at the friar, awestruck. He had his own confessor from Aragón, on whom he relied, but I could tell he felt the hypnotic draw of Torquemada's conviction. It disturbed me to witness the friar's force wielded on my husband because in the moment, I realized that I no longer felt it. I no longer believed in Torquemada.

Fernando spoke: "But we've always had conversos in these realms, and they've served us well. How can we know who is a heretic and who is not?" As he spoke, he reached out to take my hand, something he rarely did in public. His palm was warm, his fingers reassuring as he squeezed mine. He may have felt Torquemada's power but he was clearly not going to let himself be swayed by it. His practical Aragonese nature required unassailable evidence before he would act.

"There are true conversos, sincere in the faith, who abjure those who deliberately practice foul rites," answered Torquemada, his voice once again placid, as if he hadn't just shouted before his sovereigns, "and there are those who lie. They cannot be easily distinguished, especially in Andalucía, where they have dwelled so close together for so long. This is why we request that the first Tribunal of the Holy Inquisition be appointed in Sevilla; it is hallowed work, best undertaken by those with stout hearts. However, once we eradicate this evil, God will show mercy. He will pave the road to glory and the kingdom of one—one crown, one country, one faith. He will help you drive out the heretic, the Marrano, and the infidel, so you can build a new world in which Spain reigns supreme and the righteous can rejoice."

Fernando sat still. Something in my face must have conveyed my discomfort, for he said, without warning, "The queen and I must seek our own counsel." Helping me from my chair, he guided me with a hand at the small of my back to the adjoining chamber, where braziers and candelabra were lit to ward off the dark and cold.

A window with fluted columns offered a sweeping view of the city. In the distance, thrusting high above the steep cobbled streets, was the elaborate tower of the Cathedral of Santa María, the oldest in Castile, founded by Fernando III, scourge of the Moors.

I stepped to the window as Fernando busied himself pouring wine at the sideboard. I thought of all the holy edifices in my realm, many of which had fallen into neglect during my father's and brother's reigns. Were their disrepair and the clergy's licentiousness to blame for the canker now eating away at our faith? I'd recently issued a decree enforcing clerical celibacy and appointed a commission of bishops to oversee reform of all monasteries and convents, as well as the appointment of new prelates. I'd also coerced the Cortes to set aside funds for the restoration of dilapidated churches, including Toledo's Church of Santa María, as well as the construction of our new Monastery of San Juan de los Reyes, to commemorate our victory over Portugal.

"Everything I do," I said aloud, hearing Fernando come behind me,

"I do for the exaltation of God and our country. So why do I feel as though this turmoil has no solution, no answer, no end?"

"It has an end. It just isn't the one you want to hear."

I turned to him.

"The time has come, Isabella. We cannot equivocate any longer. As Catholic sovereigns, we must set an example. Heresy can no longer be tolerated in our realms."

"Are you so certain this is the way?" I asked.

"Yes. We are God's appointed sovereigns. He would not lead us astray." Fernando leaned in to me, his strong features softened by the candle glow. "It's our sacred duty, Isabella. You know it and so do I. Sometimes, we must act against our hearts, because it is the right thing, the only thing, to do."

I searched his eyes. "If we proceed, our subjects will die."

"Only the guilty, only those who refuse to repent. True Christians have nothing to fear." He caressed my cheek. "My moon, you mustn't doubt. You always wonder if we do God's will and I tell you, we *do*. We can do nothing else. Torquemada is too bold but he speaks like a prophet: one crown, one country, one faith. We have no place for anything less. We are building a new nation for a new age; it's what we dreamed of, all those years ago. This is our time. And once we purify Castile and Aragón, we'll turn our sword on Granada. We'll take up the Reconquista and rid the land forever of the infidel."

I wanted to surrender. I wanted to submit to his steadfast belief in our destiny, which never faltered or wavered, despite the odds. I suddenly despised my own frailty, my impractical feminine heart so easily deceived, so fallible, I no longer trusted my own self.

I whispered, "Why do these false conversos defy us? Why deny God's truth and condemn your immortal soul? I can't believe any person would do this willingly. They are misguided; they just need time to understand how they sin, so they can repent."

He pulled me to him. Against his chest, I could feel the tempo of his heart. Lost in this sea of doubt, he was the one thing I could cling to.

"The heretic is a stubborn sinner," he said. "You mustn't let their defiance torment you. We are king and queen. Whatever we ordain, we do for the greater good." He cupped my chin, lifted my face to his. "Let

Torquemada assume this task. He can start in Sevilla, show us what he can achieve. If we don't agree with his methods, we'll intervene. Though he'll oversee our new Inquisition, by our papal edict he is answerable to us—and us alone."

I did not speak. The moment stretched between us, taut with my hesitation. I recalled my own words of defiance years ago, when Torquemada first came to me about this: *Yet even if I were crowned tomorrow, the last thing I'd condone is the persecution of my subjects.*

Since the day on the beach two years before, when I first sanctioned the inquisitorial edict from Rome, I had known it would come to this. It had been building like a storm in the distance, the inexorable price I had to pay for everything God had given me.

"I will agree," I said at length, "but only on these conditions: First, whatever is confiscated from the condemned must be used to further our efforts toward unity. Second, the Inquisition must restrict its activities to lapsed conversos only."

"Bien," he murmured. "I'll see to it. Now, are you ready to go back inside?"

We joined hands again, returned to the chamber where Torquemada stood patiently, hands folded before him, as though he already knew what we would say.

"We are deeply disturbed by everything we've heard," I said, "and as Father Talavera has assured you, we take this matter most seriously." I paused, passing my gaze over the assembly. "Prepare the order for signature. We will authorize the Inquisition in Castile."

I turned on my heel and left quickly, so they could not see my sorrow. In my rooms, I had Ines extinguish all candles save the votives on my altar, and I went to my knees before it.

"My Lord and Savior," I whispered, "hear now the supplication of Your humble servant. Show me the truth. Manifest through me Your will. Let there be no room for me to err through ignorance; lend me the strength so I may achieve my charge and cast Your light upon these kingdoms, which have suffered so much evil and destruction."

I bowed my head, waiting.

But God did not answer me that night.

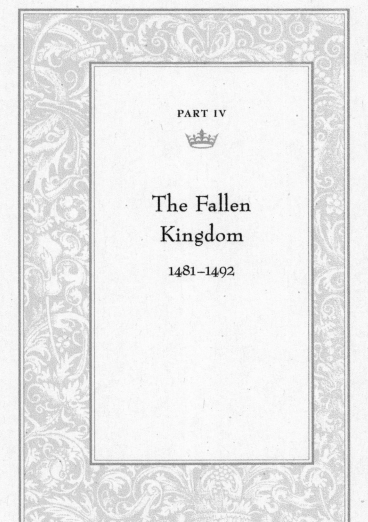

PART IV

The Fallen
Kingdom

1481–1492

CHAPTER TWENTY-SEVEN

Clamoring crowds gathered at the sides of the road. The men were dressed in fresh-laundered tunics and hose, waving caps upon which they'd pinned carnations; the women wore embroidered shawls and clutched eager children by the hand as they watched us pass in lumbering procession. The entire court was on caparisoned horseback, the nobles in damask stiffened with gold tracery, the ladies in ostentatious cloaks and swirling veils, the liveried servants and grim guards riding alongside the endless line of mule-drawn carts bearing our entire household.

From my carriage window I looked onto the assembly of people framed against an unfamiliar landscape of sharp verdant vales. This was the fertile land of my husband's birth, which I was seeing for the first time. I tried my best to summon a smile. His subjects had been waiting for hours, days even, word having gone out in advance that we were on our way to his capital city, Zaragoza, to have our two-year-old son sworn in as heir by Aragón's Cortes. It was to be our dynastic milestone, the symbolic union of our realms under one heir.

My gaze strained toward the front of the procession, where I knew Fernando rode with Juan in front of him on the saddle, waving and smiling. I had to clamp my lips to stop myself from ordering that my son be brought to me this instant.

"His Highness the infante will be fine," said Beatriz from her mass of pillows opposite me. Ines and my daughters rode in a separate litter; Beatriz had recently confided to me that she was finally with child and I'd insisted she share my transportation, knowing well how hard travel can be when in that state. "Just listen to the Aragonese acclaim him! And His Majesty and Chacón are right there in case the infante tires."

"I know." I lifted my hand to wave, realizing the crowds had seen me. I'd wanted to ride on horseback as well, to be close to Juan, but I'd tripped on the staircase as we left the alcazar in Segovia and hurt my ankle, so now I was confined to this carriage, which was probably just as well. After fretting over the long hours of journeying from Castile; of the cleanliness of the various places along the way where we had to stop; of the need for fresh water and foodstuffs, not to mention my son's health, I was not at my best. Moreover, I thought, glancing at the leather portfolio beside me, bulging with grievances and petitions, I had more than enough to do before we reached Zaragoza.

"His colic has improved," Beatriz added, as I reluctantly let the window curtain fall back in place. "And he hasn't had a fever in over a month. Surely, this means the physicians are right and his health is improving."

"They should be right," I muttered, "considering how many of them I've hired and how much they charge." I paused, seeing the pained look of understanding that crossed my friend's face. "Isabel never suffered as much as Juan did in her childhood," I said, my voice catching, "and at only a year old, Juana has a vigor that's almost insulting. Why does God test us so? We've done everything we can for Juan; his household is devoted to him, and that crowd of physicians has nearly bled him dry with their leeches and potions. And still he has those rashes, that dry cough, and awful fever—" I shuddered, recalling the many nights spent in sleepless vigil at my son's bedside. "It's as though we're being punished."

"Stop that, no one's being punished," said Beatriz. "Why would God seek to punish you or your son? Juan is just delicate. But he will grow strong, you'll see."

I nodded, distracted. I could hear the welcoming cries and knew it was good for Juan, who was rarely allowed out in public, and for Fernando, who reveled in the opportunity to show our son to his realm. It was also good for the people of Aragón themselves, who were fiercely independent and would have to be coaxed into union with Castile. But all I could think of was the hidden threats lurking everywhere, from unseen stones in the road that might throw a horse, to pestilential scabs on someone's reaching hand.

I took a deep breath and forced myself to turn to the portfolio. As I took out the first batch of reports, my stomach sank. Beatriz must have noticed the change in my expression, for she chuckled. "From Torquemada, again? What does our crow have to say this time?"

I resisted laughter. Incorrigible as ever, Beatriz had taken to calling my chief inquisitor this in private, because she said he was forever caw-cawing doom wherever he went.

"What else?" I skimmed the first paragraph of his dense handwriting. "He needs more money to pay his informants. He says that since he first set up our Tribunal in Sevilla, over eighty suspects have been arrested, with six more condemned this week, may our blessed Virgin have mercy on their souls." I crossed myself, sickened by the thought. While I knew it was the only way, that only fire could save those who refused to recant—for by suffering the torments of Hell on earth might their souls be saved in Heaven—I could not abide imagining the stench of burning flesh fouling that fragrant city.

"That makes how many he's burned so far? Twelve, thirteen?" asked Beatriz, picking at a stray thread on her bodice. I did not answer, reading onward, flabbergasted.

"Listen to this," I exclaimed. "He reports he needs the money because hundreds of conversos are fleeing into the kingdom of Granada, where the Moors promise them refuge." I looked up at her. "They actually prefer to live among infidels? But the Holy Tribunal has only been in Andalucía for six months; surely so few deaths aren't excessive? Torquemada says the exodus could affect the south's economy. Trade is fast coming to a halt as conversos abandon their homes and businesses, often without notice."

"And what does he expect you to do?" said Beatriz. "It's not as if you can ask the Moors to refuse the conversos entry into their kingdom, though I'll wager they're fleecing every last one of their wealth as soon as they cross the border."

With a frown, I set the report aside. "Well, I must do something. It's unacceptable for our subjects to flee rather than abide by our dictates. I'll send him the money and as soon as we reach Zaragoza, issue an order with Fernando forbidding all unauthorized departures from those cities where the Inquisition is at work. As Fernando says, true Christians needn't fear, for they have nothing to hide."

"Indeed," said Beatriz, evidently relieved that my distress at the news had overtaken my worry over my son. I opened the next report and was soon immersed in my work, which, as always, proved an all-engrossing task that kept other concerns at bay. At least here I could direct my path; here, in the minutiae of my kingdom, I was the ultimate arbitrator after God, rarely prey to the helpless anxieties that motherhood often caused.

WE REACHED ZARAGOZA two days later, arriving under a luminous northern sky that shimmered like silvery canvas over the breadth of the Ebro River, the spindle spires of the Cathedral of San Salvador, and the alabaster bastions of the Aljafería Palace, birthplace of my own ancestress Saint Isabel of Portugal. This would be our official residence for the duration of our stay. The people of Zaragoza celebrated our arrival with days of festivities; several weeks later, exhausted by a schedule of events that included offering piles of flowers to the city's patron La Virgen del Pilar, Fernando and I proudly watched our son sworn in as heir by Aragón's Cortes.

We tarried in Zaragoza until November before returning to Castile and our palace of Medina del Campo, where we planned to stay for the winter. Here I discovered that, like Beatriz, I was with child. It was also here, one chill afternoon, that we received the news that would decide our fate.

Fernando lounged by the fire with his hunting dogs at his feet as Isabel and I embroidered an altar cloth we'd been making for the local cathedral. I kept one eye on the group of ladies sewing nearby; with her pregnancy advancing, Beatriz had elected to return to Segovia to be closer to Cabrera and had left in her place a parcel of local noblewomen, most of whom were young and gauche, and therefore in need of constant supervision lest their foolish airs got the better of them and they succumbed to improper behavior. The last thing I needed was to be forced to arrange hasty marriages as reward for wantonness. Among them was one of Beatriz's distant cousins, María de Bobadilla—a dark-haired, curvaceous beauty with startling green eyes. More sophisticated than the other girls, María understood the value of her assets and had excited interest among our men within days of her arrival. However, only one man in particular concerned me and I now watched as María coyly directed her gaze at my husband only to find herself pierced by my basilisk stare.

Inés came hurrying in; accompanying her was a cloaked youth, so coated in dust and mud that his livery was almost unrecognizable. He fell to his knees before me, drawing forth from his soiled doublet an equally soiled envelope. "I bring urgent word from the marquis of Cádiz," he gasped, his voice croaking with exhaustion. "The city of Zahara has fallen to the Moors. My lord fought back and seized the Moorish citadel of Alhama de Granada, but he needs reinforcements urgently, if he is to hold it and avenge Zahara's fall."

At my side, my ten-year-old Isabel went still, her beautiful blue-green eyes wide. Fernando sputtered awake, having caught the messenger's last few words. "Impossible," he said. "Zahara's impregnable as a cloister. And Alhama has those famous hot springs; it's a favored retreat of the caliphs, close as it is to Granada. King Abu al-Hasan Ali would fall on his own sword before he let anyone take Alhama."

"Yes," I added, even as my heart started to pound, "and since our war with Portugal we've a treaty with King al-Hasan. He'd never break it so flagrantly."

"Though he's yet to pay us one nugget of his promised tribute," remarked Fernando sourly, staggering to his feet to swipe the missive from the messenger. I motioned to Inés, who poured the poor man a goblet of wine while Fernando cracked the parchment's seal.

He read in silence, his brow furrowed. He lifted astounded eyes to me. "It's true," he said, cold fury in his voice. "Zahara has fallen to al-Hasan; that Moorish dog seized it in retaliation for the border skirmishes he's been having with Cádiz. The Moors slaughtered every man; the women and children are enslaved, taken to the mountain city of Ronda. In return, Cádiz stormed Alhama in a stealth attack. God save him, he has struck at the heart of the Moors' domain!"

He thrust the paper at me. I took it with trembling hands, my eyes racing over the lines. "'*Ay de mí,* Alhama!' al-Hasan wailed when he heard of Alhama's fall," I read aloud, to the now-silent chamber. A gasp

rose in my throat. "Cádiz claims al-Hasan has leveraged terrible retribution on him and his men, assaulting them with such force that he had
to send to his wife and the duke of Medina Sidonia for help."

The messenger, throat wetted now, said hoarsely, "*Majestad,* my
master has kept al-Hasan and his curs at bay thus far, but he'll need
more men if he's to hold on to Alhama and reclaim Zahara. He also bid
me tell you that al-Hasan is estranged from his son Prince Boabdil,
who's thrown al-Hasan out of Granada and claimed his throne; the
entire Moorish kingdom is vulnerable because of their quarrels, my
master says."

Isabel whispered, "Are the Moors going to hurt us, Mama?"

Her tremulous voice jolted me out of my horrified daze. "No," I
said quickly, turning to her, "of course not, *hija mía.* They are in Andalucía. We have no Moors here."

"But we did." Her wide, frightened eyes met mine. "The Moors
once held parts of Castile, didn't they? What's to stop them from coming here again?"

I went still. I had no idea how to answer her startling, and horrifying, question.

"We will stop them," said Fernando. "Your mother and I will drive
that entire filthy horde into the sea if it's the last thing we do." He
looked at me. "Isabella, we cannot delay. We must help Cádiz. And al-
Hasan's discord with Boabdil could work to our favor if we're quick
enough to take advantage of it."

"Advantage?" I echoed. "Are you saying we . . . that we should . . . ?"

He nodded; María de Bobadilla clapped her hands in excitement.
"*Sí, Majestad!*" she exulted, with no more restraint than a fishwife. "The
Moors are vermin. If you don't exterminate them, they'll overrun us!"

Isabel blanched; I could see her nights haunted by dreams of turbaned demons, despite the fact that for centuries Granada had been a
fractured kingdom, weakened by its own internal discords and sheltered only by its geographic position in the Sierra and lucrative trade
with the Turks and other eastern neighbors.

"You are frightening the infanta," I snapped. María dropped into an
apologetic curtsey, treating everyone to a full view of her enticing cleav-

age. As I caught Fernando's eyes lingering on her breasts, I said with more sharpness than I had intended, "My lord husband and I must discuss this in private. Inés, see our messenger attended to; the rest of you, please accompany the infanta to the gallery. I will join you as soon as I can."

They left Fernando and me alone. Jealousy coiled in the pit of my stomach. I had to force it aside, giving Fernando my full attention as he said, "We must declare the Reconquista, Isabella. I know it's not the way we hoped it would come about, but we can't let the infidel claim as much as a single stone on Christian soil. My ancestor Fernando I wrested Zahara from the Moors four hundred years ago; now we must go to its defense."

A shudder went through me; this was the last thing I'd expected, the last thing I wanted to contemplate. "You know as well as I do that our history is strewn with the mistakes of our ancestors. For every gain made by fighting the Moors, something was lost. The reconquest is always more easily embarked upon than won."

"We still must try." He came to me, set his hands on my shoulders. "It is our sacred duty as monarchs, but more than that, it is time we ended eight hundred years of infidel arrogance, of bad treaties, false tribute, and lies. The Moors know, as we do, that this stalemate could not last forever. For centuries, they've held on to the best lands in Andalucía, the Mediterranean ports, and the city of Granada itself. Now we must reclaim what is ours."

I met his fervent gaze. "Can't we simply side with Boabdil against King al-Hasan and send reinforcements to Cádiz?"

"Yes, that's exactly what we'll do! We will use Boabdil to drive a wedge into the heart of the Moorish kingdom, and then, once we've weakened them, we will destroy them, utterly. Granada and its riches will be ours." He let out a crack of laughter, of sheer exultation. "Think of it, *mi luna*—all of Spain will finally be united under one crown, one country, one faith. This is our destiny; we must rise to the challenge and show the world what Isabella and Fernando are made of."

Everything warned me against this costly, potentially catastrophic enterprise which we had no guarantee of winning. Few kings had ever succeeded against the Moors, and never completely. But Fernando expressed such fervent impatience to prove our mettle in this, the most important venture of our lives, that I kept my misgivings to myself.

Whatever I said would fall on deaf ears. The uproar at court once news spread of Zahara's fall was unstoppable; regardless of the immense practical considerations that this enterprise entailed, we had to respond. Besides, Fernando was right: The holy war against the Moors was our destiny. We could not allow them to remain on our soil as rulers, holding in their thrall a rich and coveted portion of our southern domain. I had wanted the war to come about on my terms, after our coffers were full and the rest of our realm was in order; I had wanted to make the decision as to when and where we would fight because I knew from history that such a crusade would be costly, disruptive, and extremely trying.

But the Reconquista had begun, with or without me.

As I embraced Fernando, he whispered, "Not one tower, my love: We'll leave them not one tower to hide in," and so I let myself surrender to God's greater plan.

✦

IN JANUARY 1482 we petitioned the Cortes for funds for the war and dispatched our request to Rome for the papal edict of crusade. After attending Mass in Toledo to pray for the enslaved taken from Zahara and thank God for granting us the liberation of Alhama, Fernando and I stood together on a gold-draped dais and declared our intent to travel in person to the south and install our court there to oversee our enterprise against the Moors.

While I refrained from expressing my doubts, our Cortes was not so politic. It voted us only enough funds to address the immediate issue at hand, refusing to sanction any more until we proved the effort was worth the expense. I remained steadfast at Fernando's side as he gave up sleep and sometimes even food overseeing our initial plans and covert alliance with Boabdil, fully aware that I must leave my children with Beatriz and Cabrera in Segovia. I couldn't take them to war in the south, not while I myself was with child and uncertain of the situation awaiting us. The very thought of leaving them behind for months made me feel as though my entire existence had been overturned.

In addition to being separated from my children, I had to pare down my household, servants costing money we could ill afford. It wasn't easy to decide who stayed and who would go, but I took cold pleasure when it came to expelling María de Bobadilla from my service. I had no proof she'd done more than bat her seductive eyes at my husband but I seized the opportunity to arrange her marriage to our new governor of the Canary Islands and dispatched her forthwith. When I offhandedly mentioned her departure to Fernando, he didn't pay any mind, to my relief. The thought of bloodying his sword with Moorish blood had swept all other considerations aside.

By mid-April we were installed in the Andalucían city of Córdoba, once the celebrated capital of the Moors in the south, with its magnificent red-columned mosque and fortified alcazar. Here, Fernando and I met with our southern lords and captains, and decided our first move would be to take the city of Loja, as its proximity to Alhama and Granada would shore up our defenses and send a clear message to the Moors.

"We can't allow al-Hasan to think we'll falter," Fernando told me when I joined him in his rooms to review the plans. "Taking Loja will leave Granada even more vulnerable and he'll know we mean business. It will also help relieve Cádiz's garrison, which has held on to Alhama almost single-handedly. This is Loja here," he added, pointing at the map. "It's like most cities in Andalucía; it sits on a crag over this ravine."

I peered at the sketched terrain. "If that ravine is as steep as it appears, we can't surprise the city as Cádiz did with Alhama, can we? We'll truly have to lay siege to it."

He nodded. "And that, my love, is where you come in."

"Me?" I smiled, placing a hand on my bulging belly. "You expect me to don chain mail and ride with you in this advanced state?"

He chuckled. "Now, that would be a sight, wouldn't it? But as appealing as that is, I actually need you to organize the provision of our troops. No one is better at economizing than you, and we must stretch that paltry sum our Cortes saw fit to give us as far as we can. Our men must be as well prepared as possible. Remember, that wolf al-Hasan has had all this time to anticipate us and rally his support; while Boabdil has promised by the terms of our alliance to refuse his father all assistance, al-Hasan will still have men and lances to spare."

I was deeply moved by Fernando's confidence and delighted to be able to help, despite my lassitude and bulk. As I entered my eighth month of pregnancy, I was exhausted from the moment I awoke. I donned only the loose kaftans worn by the local populace to accommodate my massive belly and profuse perspiration, for Córdoba was a veritable cauldron in the summer, hotter even than Sevilla.

In the alcazar patios lavender, jasmine, and roses flourished, so redolent that the mere brush of a hem against the bushes released clouds of fragrance. But I passed by without noticing, my hours filled from dawn until midnight. With the limited funds we possessed, I had to improvise, restricting our court expenses so I'd have enough to barter with merchants for weapons, armor, and tents, for cattle, chickens, and other livestock, as well as wine, barley, and other grains—all of which was needed to feed our men during a prolonged siege. At night I pored over my accounts with the diligent Cárdenas, checking and rechecking every sum, borrowing from my own wardrobe purse to add to the war chest, knowing that unexpected events would require extra costs.

My efforts were cut short when I went into sudden labor on June 28, during a council session. One minute I was presenting my inventory list; the next, I doubled over as the pangs overcame me. The lords went quiet as Fernando rapidly assisted me to my feet and my women led me to the birthing chamber where my water broke, splashing over my embroidered red leather slippers.

The next twenty-four hours were a blur. Fernando refused to leave my side, defying the custom that men were not allowed in a birthing room. He mopped my brow with cool mint water and barked orders at the harried midwives, who didn't know how to react to his presence. Though I was scarcely aware of anything but my pummeled body, I sensed him near, his hand on my forehead, his voice whispering, over and over, "*Mi luna,* push. Push with everything you've got. I'm here. I will not leave you."

Finally, in the early morning hours, I straddled the stool and, with a guttural cry, released my fourth child—a girl. As she was cleansed and delivered to the wet nurse I continued to strain, seeing and not believing the torrent of blood coming out of me. The chief midwife muttered that there was another child, a twin, lodged inside me. As night swallowed day, the shadow of death hovered near; through my narrowed eyes I could see its spectral visage, black wings outstretched. The midwives finally forced Fernando out into the corridor, where the nobles had gathered. Inés took his place, coaxing me to impossible efforts, for by this time I was so drained I could barely whimper.

Finally, the twin slipped out in a viscous gush. The midwife swiftly gathered it; as I saw her turn away to wrap it in cerements, covering its face, I released a howl that reverberated through the alcazar.

With tears in her eyes, Inés worked my numb limbs out of the sopping shift and into a clean bed-gown. As she tucked me into lavender-scented sheets, I clutched at her, whispering, "I want to see her. I want to see my baby. . . ."

She shook her head. "No, *Majestad*," she murmured. "You do not. Rest now, for the love of God. Your daughter is well; she is nursing. The other is with the angels."

But she wasn't. She had died unshriven, an innocent soul condemned forever to dwell in Purgatory. I was disconsolate, unable to rest, until Fernando brusquely ordered Cardinal Mendoza to perform last rites over the body and dribble holy water on our lost child's tiny misshapen skull.

Then my husband enfolded me in his arms and held me as I cried myself to sleep.

CHAPTER TWENTY-EIGHT

Fernando departed with an army of eleven thousand men under a July sun so hot it cracked the soil like boiled leather. I had to bid him farewell from bed; my recovery from labor was frustratingly slow. Our newborn daughter, christened María in honor of the Virgin, was placid, fair-haired, and healthy. I knew I was fortunate indeed that she exhibited no ill effects after such a difficult birth, but I felt little connection to her, as if all the anticipation I'd nurtured had perished with her twin. In time, the midwife assured me, I'd come to love her, but as my breasts ached and my milk dried I felt only a disturbing emptiness, and the shame gnawed at me because of it.

While I waited for news of the siege on Loja, forcing myself to take slow walks around the patio in the cool hours of dusk, word arrived from my aunt Beatrice in Portugal. Joanna la Beltraneja, frustrated by the impasse I'd imposed on her, had decided to take her holy vows and live out the rest of her days in the convent. I was relieved. Soon after came the news that my old mentor and foe, Archbishop Carrillo, was dead.

The sorrow his passing roused in me was unexpected, though his death didn't come as a surprise. I'd known for some time his health was in decline, ever since I'd ordered him to assume the life of a monastic. His circumscribed existence in the cloister must have been harsh on a man with his passion for life. For days after I received the news, I kept seeing him as he'd been in his glory, the barrel-chested warrior-priest whose bravura had propelled me to the throne only to turn against me like a jealous lover. Though I was no longer the trusting infanta he'd so fiercely sought to mold to his will, the world seemed smaller, somehow, without him in it.

My preoccupation soon shifted when the first couriers brought news from Loja. The terrain, Fernando wrote, was impossible, rocky and perilous; our forces had been obliged to separate and camp in different areas, while Fernando, Cádiz, Medina Sidonia, and the other grandees surveyed the remote city on its crag for some weakness to exploit.

They waited too long. As they sought to shift the army to a less vulnerable position, the Moors of Loja swarmed out with a ferocity kindled by weeks of deprivation. In the ensuing battle, several of our knights were killed. My hands trembled as I read the missive detailing that Fernando had found himself cornered by a scimitar-wielding Moor intent on taking his head as a prize. He had been saved only by Cádiz's savage defense.

I stood at the alcazar's gates with the court about me as the survivors straggled back. Fernando was riding at their head; sunburnt, bearded, and blood-spattered, he clutched our royal standard in tatters in his fist.

I made myself smile as he dismounted; the lesson I had learned years ago at Tordesillas was still seared in my mind. Though I wanted to rail at the injustice of our defeat, the months of planning and expense wasted, venting my frustration would resolve nothing. We had miscalculated. We had forgotten, in our zeal and pride, how tenacious a foe the Moors could be. Now we had to contend with the consequences. I saw in Fernando's haggard features his relief at my demeanor, though I also could see his acute humiliation at the fact that he would have to publicly acknowledge his defeat.

"We will try again next year," I said, as he dismounted before me.

"Try?" He gave me a bitter smile. "We'll do more than that, my moon. I'll tear the very seeds from this Moorish pomegranate one by one. Next time, it is we who will give no quarter."

Proud words; but in the meantime we had a decimated army to reassemble, not to mention laying our dead, which numbered in the thousands, to rest. Burials had to be arranged, relatives notified, widows' pensions paid. Córdoba quickly became a place of grief. When Fernando suggested I return to Castile to oversee our business there—we had to petition the Cortes for more funds—while he stayed behind to safeguard the border, I readily agreed. I wanted nothing more than to go home.

IN SEGOVIA, I found my children busy with their studies. Isabel was serene as ever. Juan remained too thin and pale, still prone to fever. Juana was a vigorous child with a mass of coppery curls and "a temper to match," as Beatriz often teased. My friend had delivered a healthy boy whom she and her husband adored. They had christened him Andrés, after his father, but with the distraction of having to care for her new babe, Beatriz had indulged Juana's whims. My second daughter displayed early talent when it came to languages and music, but she was rebellious as far as her daily regimen was concerned, far too much so for a three-year-old.

I had a stern discussion with her about her unseemly penchant for throwing off her slippers to wade barefoot in the garden ponds. "Infantas should not behave thus," I informed her when she pertly replied that her feet swelled in the heat. "Decorum at all times is essential."

Juana pouted and proceeded to do exactly as she had been doing, so I decided to take her with me on a long overdue visit to Arévalo to see my mother. I reasoned that time alone with me, away from the distractions of court, would instill in her a modicum of behavior. To my disconcertion, she proved entirely unmanageable during the two-day trip, leaping up on the litter cushions to peer out the window at the passing *meseta,* and pointing and chattering excitedly about everything she saw, from the swooping eagles that stalked the plains to the crumbled watchtowers pockmarking the barren ridges. I watched her with bemusement, thinking of the fables I'd heard about changelings. Of course such tales were nonsense; but though she resembled Fernando in her coloring and disposition, there were moments when she caught my regard with those penetrating eyes of hers and suddenly she would seem years older than she was, as if another being dwelled in her skin.

She quieted down once we reached Arévalo, however. The isolation of the castle under its brooding sky seemed to affect her, and she stared, wide-eyed but silent, at the old servants moving like ghosts about the halls, treating her with the stiff discomfort of those who'd lived for years without ever seeing a child. I tried to reassure her that there was nothing to fear, that this had once been my home, but she only brightened when one of the castle dogs, descendants of my brother's beloved Alarcón, snuffled up beside her. She had a way with animals, just as Alfonso had had.

She displayed an unexpected reticence at the sight of my mother, ensconced in the faded splendor of her apartments, which she now refused to leave. Dressed in the antiquated fashions of her brief tenure as queen, so gaunt her wrists poked like bones from her frayed sleeves, my mother peered at Juana for a seemingly endless moment before she crooked a finger at her, motioning her forward. Juana refused to budge. I felt her hand clasp at my skirts, resisting my murmured urge that she go and kiss her grandmother.

Then my mother whispered, "*Tan desgraciada*. So beautiful and so unfortunate, like me."

Juana gave a frightened gasp; even at her age she understood the tenor of this pronouncement, uttered with the eerie assurance of a prophecy.

"Mama, please," I said. "You mustn't say such things. She's only a child."

"So was I, once." My mother's watery eyes turned distant. "So were you. Youth is no protection; in the end, life scars us all."

After that, I wouldn't let Juana see my mother again. I stayed long enough to ensure that the household was in order; old Doña Clara was an invalid now, near-blind with cataracts and crippled by gout, so I hired a new matron to oversee my mother's care before I bundled up Juana and my bags to return to court. I was ready to do battle with the Cortes over the funding of our next Moorish offensive; to summon nobles to enlist retainers in our army; to write letters to Germany and Italy for reduced prices on large quantities of gunpowder and artillery; and to meet with my treasurer, Rabbi Señeor, to arrange low-interest loans through his usurers, in case the Cortes's funding fell short. As usual, my time at Arévalo had left me restless, eager to move forward.

Soon after my return to Segovia, my confessor, Fray Talavera, came to see me. "Torquemada has sent this," he said, setting a parchment on my overflowing desk. "He'd heard you seek coin through the Jewish moneylenders, and he is outraged. He claims that while he fights to purify the Church and obtain divine favor for your crusade against the infidel, you ignore the very devil in our midst."

I picked up the letter, crowded with line after line of Torquemada's habitually dense handwriting. With a sigh, I set it aside. My head ached; if I had to read through each one of his complaints, I'd need a tonic. Better just to hear them.

"What else? Our head inquisitor never remonstrates without offering his solution."

Talavera's lean, white-bearded face creased in a smile. He was not fiery, not like Torquemada; his was a tranquil steadfastness I'd increasingly come to rely upon and trust.

"More of the same, I fear. He insists that while the Jews remain at large, their influence will obstruct all attempts to eradicate heresy among the conversos. He says we can no longer turn a blind eye. He demands that you issue an edict: Either the Jews convert or they must be expelled, on pain of death."

"He says all that, does he?" I said flatly. "Anything else?"

Talavera sighed. "He claims there is precedent. England and France expelled the Jews centuries ago. Few Christian countries tolerate them."

"And he's advocating that I take this stance now, in the middle of a crusade?" I forced in a calming breath. "He overreaches his duties. You have my leave to inform him as much. As I've stated before, the Jews have served us faithfully and we have a long history of coexistence with them. This is not a decision I can take precipitously, nor do I intend to."

"Yes, *Majestad*." He turned to the chamber door. He paused, looking over his shoulder at me. "The hour of reckoning must come," he said quietly. "It is unavoidable, much as we may regret it."

I went still, meeting his somber gaze. "But it is not here yet," I answered, though my reassurance sounded hollow to my ears. "And when it does come, they may convert. They are a misguided people, lost to the light of our Savior, yes, but worthy of redemption. As their queen, I owe them my protection even as I strive to guide them toward the one true faith. I need time. I cannot perform miracles."

He bowed his head. "I fear you may need one, to save them all."

AS WINTER CHILLED the air, Fernando and I were reunited in the Monastery of Guadalupe in Extremadura, site of Castile's most cherished shrine, that of the black Madonna carved by Saint Luke. Here, among shaded cloisters and colored brick patios, with the rugged cordillera swathed in mist in the distance, we tarried as a family.

I was spending as much of my time as I could with Isabel; at twelve, she was fast becoming a svelte beauty, her immaculate complexion and fair tresses giving her the appearance of an angel. All the younger ladies of court eyed her in covert envy and she never seemed to notice, as if she were immune to her own reflection. She preferred to occupy her time studying, and perfecting her Portuguese, in preparation for marriage to that country's heir.

When she practiced it aloud, Juana would peer at her suspiciously. Once, she blurted, "You act as if you're looking forward to leaving Spain," then she wrinkled her nose in distaste.

"That's my girl," chuckled Fernando. "A Spaniard to her core, she is." He swung Juana into his arms; as she squealed and pulled off his cap, revealing his now near-bald pate, I resisted a frown. He favored her too much. He even had a nickname for her, "Madrecita," because she reminded him of his late mother. I'd told him countless times she must not grow up thinking she was more privileged than our other daughters, for she too must one day take her assigned place in the world, but Fernando would just chuck her chin and say, "My Madrecita will be an envoy for Spain no matter where she goes, eh?" And Juana's emphatic "Sí, Papa!" did not reassure me, either. At this rate, Fernando would spoil her so much she would think no prince worthy of her, nor capable of living up to her father.

We celebrated that Christmas season together, serenaded by minstrels, slicing pies out of which flew flocks of startled sparrows, dressing the manger with carved ivory figurines. The snows were light, a mere frosting that lent the season glamour without its habitual biting chill. On Twelfth Night we went in candlelit procession to the cathedral in Segovia to hear midnight Mass while the Dominican choir of Santa

María lifted a haunting paean to the Nativity. Surrounded by my children, with my husband at my side and my lifelong friend Beatriz behind me, I knelt for communion, in heartfelt gratitude for everything God had given me.

Little did I know how much would be exacted of me in return, in the days to come.

CHAPTER TWENTY-NINE

I was awoken in the middle of the night. Though we kept separate apartments as monarchs, Fernando and I had managed to dine together that night, and in a moment of rare intimacy, given all the recent demands on our time, he had turned amorous. Later, he fell asleep in my arms. I lay with his head resting on my breast, as I caressed the wiry hair of his chest. I noticed a few stray white hairs; the sight roused tenderness in me.

Hours later, insistent knocking startled me awake. Fernando grumbled, burying his head in a pillow as I eased him aside. I pulled on my robe and padded hastily to the door. Though it was March and winter was almost over, the night's chill emanated from the alcazar's stone, so that I was shivering by the time I cracked open the door. Ines peered at me from the passageway, her hair in a plait under her bed-cap, her own robe clutched about her.

"What is it?" I whispered, so as not to wake Fernando again. "Is it Juan? Is he ill?"

"No, no, His Highness is well, fast asleep. It's the marquis of Cádiz. He's here. He asks to see you. He says it's urgent."

Alarm rippled through me. "Cádiz is here? But he's supposed to be overseeing our latest offensive in Andalucía; Fernando charged him with the task until he goes there himself."

As I spoke, I glanced back at the bed. Fernando did not move, sunk in slumber. He'd been working for weeks on end, organizing the new battle strategy, traveling all the way to his own Cortes in Aragón to harangue them for extra money. We were almost ready; in a few weeks' time, while I saw to the cumbersome move of our court back to the south, he was due to ride ahead and take up the reins of the crusade.

"I'll be with him in a moment," I said, passing a hand over my own unbound hair. "Go now, before we wake the king."

I dressed in a dark gown, tying my hair back in a net and throwing a wool mantle over my shoulders. As I descended the stairs in the torch-lit cold, I heard men's voices echoing from the hall. Squaring my shoulders, I entered the room to find Chacón, Fray Talavera, and several important men of our court surrounding the marquis of Cádiz.

He dropped to one knee at the sight of me. In disconcerted surprise, I took in his appearance: his black clothing filthy, his cloak and boots mud-spattered, as if he'd ridden nonstop from Andalucía. He also looked as if he'd aged years, his entire countenance haggard.

"*Majestad,*" he whispered, as the other men stared, "forgive me."

I thought irritably that he must have had another quarrel with Medina Sidonia. This time blood must have been spilled, or he'd not have ridden all this way.

"You have come a long way for my forgiveness," I remarked. "Pray, what is the cause?"

Cádiz did not speak; as I watched his eyes fill with tears, I looked, bewildered, to Fray Talavera. My confessor said quietly, "There has been a terrible defeat."

"Defeat?" I looked back at Cádiz, still prostrate before me. "What defeat?"

"Near the city of Málaga," Cádiz answered in a low voice. "In the pass of Ajarquía. Medina Sidonia, the master of Alcántara, and I . . . we decided to lead a raid into the passes to scorch the fields and prepare for His Majesty's arrival and the taking of Málaga. But El Zagal learned of our intent and he attacked us without warning."

The previous alarm I'd felt uncoiled in me like a snake. El Zagal was al-Hasan's brother and rival—a fearsome Moorish chieftain who held the fertile passes to Málaga, as well as the coveted seaside city itself. Fernando had been planning for months to take Málaga, as its fall would cut off Moorish supply routes and remove an important obstacle in our quest to isolate Granada.

Cádiz's voice took on a hard edge. "Boabdil must have warned him. We were counting on his silence but he double-crossed us, to join forces with El Zagal, likely because he thought that together they could defeat al-Hasan. El Zagal pinned our men in the gulch. It was nightfall; we could barely see anything. The infidels poured down the gulch on horseback from either side, while their peasants hurled stones from above. In the confusion, we were trapped."

"Dear God." I crossed myself. "How . . . how many are lost?"

Cádiz let out a broken sob. "Over two thousand, including three of my brothers. God have mercy, those Arab dogs cut off their heads and took them on spikes to Málaga. I managed to make it out on foot after my horse was shot from under me, but I saw so many injured, so many left to die without a word of consolation, the gypsies and peasants creeping in to search and dismember them while they still gasped for breath. . . ."

I reeled in disbelief; Chacón hastened to my side. "My husband the king," I stammered. "He—he must be told."

"We now have Boabdil," added Cádiz, forgetting in his anxiety to ask for my leave to rise to his feet. "I heard it just before I came here; they captured the miserable traitor. He rode out from Granada to conduct a raid, thinking we'd been so severely hurt we'd not fight back. But the count of Cabra learned of it and fell on him. He's being held in Córdoba's alcazar. His mother the sultana is frantic; she's willing to pay anything for his release—"

"And we must consider her offer," said Fernando, from the hall entrance. Everyone went still as my husband, bareheaded and clad in his robe of scarlet and gold, walked in. I watched his expression as he approached Cádiz, who'd collapsed again to his knees. I expected to hear a torrent of abuse hurled upon the marquis's head. It was a disaster for us; in a single ill-fated stroke, we'd lost more than half of Andalucía's garrison army, which we had fortified with an influx of new recruits and funds only weeks before. But Fernando merely came to a halt before Cádiz and said quietly, "You may rise, my lord. You have suffered the torments of Hell in our name, it seems."

Cádiz did so, unmistakable fear on his face. "Majesty, please, I beg your—"

Fernando lifted a single finger, silencing him. "There is nothing to forgive. God, who knows better than we the reason for His actions, has taught us a lesson in humility. The good are punished for a time; but He always returns to succor us. Indeed," he said, with a taut grin, "has He not already dropped al-Hasan's treacherous pup into our lap?"

As Cádiz pressed a quivering hand to his mouth, overcome by emotion, Fernando half-turned to me, holding out his hand. I felt his strong fingers enclose mine. Standing at his side, I was never prouder of him than in that moment. I heard him say, "We must learn from our mistakes. We will mourn the fallen and console the survivors, and never forget that God is on our side. By all that is holy in us, the infidel shall not prevail."

BY APRIL, THE month of my thirty-second birthday, we were back in Andalucía. There, in Córdoba's magnificent alcazar, with its red porphyry pilasters and horseshoe archways, Fernando and I sat enthroned under our cloth of estate—the knotted cords and yoke vividly displayed—as Boabdil, king-usurper of Granada, came before us.

He'd enjoyed a luxurious confinement at our command, with every privilege he could want at his disposal, save his freedom. The prince was sleek, with the olive skin of his mixed blood, tumbling dark hair, a full beard framing his sculpted mouth and long nose, and a subtle, lucid stare that belied his vacillating nature. After heated deliberation in our council, we had agreed to release him, on the condition that henceforth he must be our vassal and ally, obliged to pay an annual tribute of twelve thousand gold *doblas,* release all Christian captives, and permit our troops free passage through his domains. In exchange, we would support his claim as king of Granada over that of his estranged father, al-Hasan.

I did not think he would agree, or if he did, that we'd encounter stiff opposition from his mother. The sultana might have made extravagant offers for her son's ransom but she was also a former Christian captive turned odalisque, renowned for her skill in games of power. If anyone would see through our terms, she would and she'd be certain to extract a heavy recompense before she agreed; but to my astonishment the sultana consented at once, not even pausing to consider the ultimate ramifications of our alliance.

Thus, this farce of a reception—the prince in a billowing silk robe and tasseled fez, kneeling to kiss Fernando's and my hems, acknowledging us as his overlords before signing with a flourish our new treaty—brought a caustic smile to my lips.

Rising to our feet, we each embraced Boabdil; Fernando even kissed him on both cheeks, as if they were brothers. When my turn came, I held the Moor's lean body a moment longer than required, whispering in his ear, "I expect you to honor your agreements. If you dare betray us again, I promise you'll not find refuge in all this land."

He started, drawing back to meet my stare. I didn't know if he understood Castilian; all our negotiations had been made through his interpreter. The sudden falter in his regard made me suspect he understood far more than he had let on.

I gave an incline of my head, saying loudly, "Thus may we find harmony between our faiths." Fernando clapped his hands and the brass-studded double doors of the hall were flung open to reveal servitors laden with departing gifts for our esteemed guest.

Fernando and I exchanged a knowing glance as Boabdil let out a gasp, rushing over to examine the rich leather saddles for the eight white horses we'd prepared for him outside; the coffers of sarcenet, velvet, and damask; the embossed plate armor from Toledo. He turned, his face aglow, to babble excitedly at his interpreter, who translated, "His Highness is overwhelmed by your Majesties' generosity. Surely, he says, there are no greater monarchs in all the Christian world."

Fernando guffawed, waved a dismissive hand. "Mere tokens of our esteem. Her Majesty and I believe my lord Boabdil will keep his word as befits a true prince."

"Indeed," I added, smiling graciously at Boabdil, "I believe we understand one another."

We accompanied Boabdil to the alcazar gateway amidst the blare of horns and flurry of banners. An escort of two hundred Castilian knights handpicked by us would see him safely to the sierra of Granada. As we watched him ride out with his head held high, the route lined with cheering citizens and strewn with flowers, as I had instructed, Fernando said through his teeth, "God willing, before the year is out, I'll see him lick the dust off my feet as I kick in the doors of his precious palace of Alhambra."

"Amen," I said and I lifted my chin.

The time had come to give the Moors a true taste of our might.

AFTER I RETURNED to Sevilla to set up my court, I summoned my children to my side. It promised to be a long year of war. I wasn't about to be separated from them for so much time, particularly as María was still nursing. Fernando brightened when he saw the ostentatious train lumber in from Castile; he loved our brood and the inevitable uproar they brought wherever they went.

I would allow no idleness, however, even in my children. I organized the ladies and the noblemen's wives accompanying the court into efficient corps to oversee the inventories of wine, bread, livestock, and other supplies. I set Isabel and Juana to sewing portable tents for ambulatory infirmaries to treat our wounded, an innovation I'd decided upon after hearing Cádiz's horrific reports of those left to die in Ajarquía. I provided sacramental vessels for the consecration of mosques. And as I'd heard that the tolling of bells distressed the Moors, whose summons to prayer was by voice only, I imported large bells from Galicia to be carried in portable towers with our army, as well as smaller bells to bedeck the soldiers' sleeves and the harnesses of the mules and horses.

Throughout Andalucía, forges were set up to craft guns and siege weapons, which would be fueled by the vast amounts of gunpowder I imported at reduced cost from Italy and Flanders and stored in vaults located along our borders for easy access; my aunt Beatrice even sent me a thousand barrels as a gift. Our old enemy King Afonso V had died, and Portugal's new king, Juan II, supported our crusade wholeheartedly, seeing as Isabel was promised to his son.

Four times a day, every day, I heard Mass in the chapel and prayed for victory. Every night, I sat up late with Fernando, Cádiz, and our military leaders to review our strategy, which consisted of the siege of hundreds of castles and cities we must take in order to isolate Málaga— that glorious port which opened like an oyster onto the Mediterranean and supplied the Moors with their life-sustaining trade. Only by capturing this city and destroying El Zagal in the process could we avenge the carnage of the Ajarquía, now known to every Christian as Cuesta de la Matanza, the Hill of the Slaughter.

I refused to even entertain the thought of defeat. There wasn't an hour of the day that I didn't wish I could take up a sword and ride at the head of our army; it seemed impossible I'd ever believed that a woman should sit at home while men risked their lives. But my lot was patience, it seemed, for I discovered I was once again with child, even as Fernando marched upon city after city, felling them in quick succession at great cost of life and limb; always with the goal of pushing the infidel further out of his domain, cutting away, piece by bloodied piece, at the pomegranate of the Moorish emirate.

By autumn of 1485, we'd claimed ninety-four castles and more territory than any Christian monarch before us. But Málaga was still under the Moors' control, as was Granada itself. We had no illusion these would be easy victories; cornered as they were, the Moors were tenacious. But we held the upper hand; the infidels' world was crumbling all around them. Leaving a garrison force to guard the cities we'd conquered, we returned to Castile for the winter, pleased with the progress we had thus far made.

In December, in the frescoed apartments of the Palace of Alcalá, once the domain of the late Carrillo, I took to my bed to deliver my fifth child. As always, we hoped for a son, but our disappointment soon turned to concern when our daughter emerged so small that everyone feared for her life. I braced myself for another loss, but my new daughter surprised us all. She not only survived but she soon thrived. Within weeks she seemed an entirely different babe, her skin pale as an owl's underwing, her hair the same gold-auburn tint as my own, only with a thicker curl.

Fernando whispered to me that he thought her our prettiest child yet.

We named her Catalina, in honor of my English paternal grandmother.

I FIRST MET the Genovese navigator in the monastery of Guadalupe in Extremadura, where we'd come to stay shortly after the New Year celebrations.

Preparations were under way for our spring thrust against the Moors; we had severely weakened their front, but then news had come of our foe King al-Hasan's death. The field was left open to his brother, Zagal, who at once made overtures to Boabdil. The faithless prince took his bait and covertly sided with him, even as he feigned continued alliance with us; with al-Hasan's demise he could claim Granada as his own and saw no further need of our support. Though the loss of our copious gifts to him—which might have been better used to bolster our treasury—rankled me, Fernando assured me that Boabdil's breaking the treaty now would only serve us later, once we had him cornered in Granada and at our mercy. I had warned him he would find no refuge if he betrayed us, but betrayal can yield unexpected benefits, as Fernando said, and I intended to reap them in full. Invigorated by these developments, Fernando declared that this was the year to take Málaga, as the city's fall would weaken the tenuous grip Boabdil held on our ultimate prize—Granada.

That afternoon, he stood at the main table in the monastery hall, his breath showing in puffs, though the January weather had been mild. He pored over the battered maps with his chancellor Luis de Santángel and Cardinal Mendoza, detailing our strategy.

I sat near the brazier, warming my feet (they felt perpetually chilled since I'd given birth) and reviewing my correspondence, which had piled up during the Christmas festivities. Inés and Beatriz were watching my children: Catalina snug in a cradle while Juana rocked her; María playing with her dolls; Isabel quietly reading from the psalms with Juan. As often happens in families the closest in age were not the closest in affection: While Isabel and Juan had grown close, Juana gravitated to Catalina. María seemed unaffected by her surroundings; at three years of age, she was so placid she astonished her attendants, who declared they'd never cared for a less troublesome child.

As I kept an eye on Juan, who'd recently recovered from a tertian fever, Chacón strode in to inform me one Master Cristobal Colón was requesting audience. "He brings this," said Chacón, and with a disapproving frown, he handed me a letter of introduction, sealed with the emblem of the powerful Castilian grandee the duke of Medinaceli.

"He requests to see us now?" I asked. I was starting to feel drowsy and had been considering putting aside my letters to indulge in a rare afternoon nap. Moreover, I wasn't dressed to receive visitors. I wore my simple black velvet house-gown belted at the waist, my hair coiled under a white veil and fillet.

"Yes," growled Chacón. Now in his seventies, he'd grown fat and extremely protective of our family, standing guard over us like a mastiff. "He says he's come all the way from the south and insists on seeing you in person. He's stubborn as a mule, that one; he's been waiting in the outside gallery for over three hours. I told him you were at council and then dining, but he's not moved from his spot the entire time."

I nodded, scanning the parchment. I now vaguely recalled that this navigator had once been a client of Medina Sidonia's. In his letter, the duke of Medinaceli explained that Medina Sidonia had tired of the Genovese's demands and sent him packing. Colón went to Medinaceli, who believed in the navigator's claim that he had a viable plan to circumvent the years-long Turkish blockade of the Mediterranean and cross the Ocean Sea instead to discover an uncharted passage to the Indies. Medinaceli was willing to partially fund him and furnish ships, but Colón wanted our royal sanction. Without it, he would leave Spain and present his enterprise to the French king instead.

"Interesting," I mused. I folded the letter, handing it to my secretary Cárdenas. Suddenly I felt quite awake. "Fernando, did you hear this? The navigator is here."

My husband glanced up. Red tinged his cheeks; he was evidently in the midst of heated debate with Mendoza over battle schemes. Even at fifty-nine years old, the urbane cardinal was an experienced general who'd led our troops in battle, and he had firm ideas about how best to bring about Málaga's downfall.

"Navigator? What navigator?" Fernando glared at Mendoza, who sipped from his goblet, unperturbed as ever by my husband's temper.

"The one patronized by Medina Sidonia, remember?" Even as I asked, I knew he didn't. He scarcely recalled what we'd eaten for supper; these days all he thought about was the crusade, as if our past year of victory was not enough to erase his one defeat. He'd never rest until he had Granada on its knees.

"Yes, yes," he said impatiently. "And . . . ?"

I smiled. "And he's here, in Guadalupe. He wants to see us."

Fernando flicked his hand. "Fine, see him." He returned to haggling with Mendoza; I nodded at Chacón. "I shall receive him. But warn him, I expect him to be succinct."

Chacón returned with a tall, broad-shouldered man wearing a plain black doublet. He'd removed his cap, revealing a thatch of sandy hair with glinting strands of silver; as he bowed, I noted arrogance in his stance, his obeisance executed with the inbred pride of a noble.

When he looked up, I was startled by the intensity in his pale blue eyes.

"*Majestad,*" he said, in a deep voice. "I am honored."

Honored he might be, but he offered no apology for his uninvited arrival. I had to curb my chuckle. He'd indeed spent time with Medina Sidonia. Only close contact with a man of that caliber could have engendered such confidence.

"They tell me you've been waiting a long time," I said. "Perhaps you'd like some mulled wine?"

"No, if it pleases you." He didn't remove his gaze from me; even my ladies began to take notice, shifting to stare at him. Most men wouldn't have looked up without my leave, much less refused my offer of refreshment. "I have much to tell you," he added, and I was pleased to see a slight flush in his sculpted, otherwise pale cheeks. "I've indeed been waiting a long time—over two years, in fact."

"In the cloister gallery?" piped Beatriz, and he turned his solemn regard to her.

"I would have, if that would have given me resolution," he said, and I had no doubt he meant it.

"Very well, then." I settled with deliberate poise against my chair, even as my blood quickened. He was undeniably magnetic; some might have said too much so. With his well-built frame and stark aquiline nose, brooding eyes, and resolute air, he lacked humility for a common-born man, convinced, as usually only nobles are, of his intrinsic worth.

He stood before me with his chin lifted as though I should have been expecting him, as if everything that had come before was but an interlude to this crucial meeting between us.

For a breathless moment, I shared the sentiment.

He launched into his appeal. He had the resonance of an orator; he'd obviously practiced his speech, declaiming his absolute conviction of the world's spherical shape, of secret maps entrusted to him, and his belief that the Ocean Sea—that vast unexplored expanse—was not nearly as vast as everyone believed. He had no discernible accent, which made me wonder at his claim that he was the son of Italian wool carders, but my doubts faded as he transported me with his tale of being shipwrecked in his youth on the shores of Portugal and of his years spent in Lisbon in the company of mariners and geographers, where the writings of the Egyptian astronomer Ptolemy and Greek mathematician Eratosthenes had opened his eyes to the possibility of distant lands, bursting with spices, jewels, and silk, waiting to be claimed. I found myself swept back to my adolescence in Segovia, where I'd huddled over ancient tomes and marveled at the spirit of adventure that propels men to brave the unknown. It was as though he instinctively knew how to stir those chords in me, employing his bold intent to dissolve the barriers of rank between us.

Of course, his claims were unproven, far-fetched; his demands for putting them into action outrageous; his request for titles and bounty from his discoveries almost delusional. No man had ever come before any monarch asking for so much, while offering so little in return.

Yet when he finished, standing with arms extended and his voice echoing about us, there was utter silence in the hall; even my children had paused in their games to hear him, and I realized I'd unwittingly leaned forward in my chair, so that now I sat with my chin resting on my folded hands, regarding him with rapt attention.

Then I discerned a faint drumming of fingers on wood and turned to see Fernando, his hand rapping the map-littered table. Beside him, his chancellor, Santángel, was wide-eyed and oblivious; Mendoza had a faint smile on his thin lips, as if he were amused.

Fernando snorted. "That was quite a lot of hot air. Perhaps you could put it to better use blowing up Moorish fortifications for us, navigator."

I cringed inwardly as Mendoza chortled. To his credit, Master Colón merely inclined his head, as if he understood that he had nothing more than theories to commend him.

"You are aware we are at war, yes?" Fernando went on, betraying that while he'd seemed otherwise preoccupied, he had overheard everything. "Yet you expect us to fund this impossible enterprise on your word alone?"

"Your Majesties' war is one that will bring the light of God to thousands," replied Colón. "I can help you bring the same to thousands more, and build you a lasting empire for your children the infantes, one on which our sun will never set."

"*If* you are right," said Fernando. "*If* you don't end up falling off the edge of the world and disappearing forever with our money and ships."

Colón assented. "There is always risk. But Your Majesties have never seemed averse to such. In fact, some might say your attempt to evict the Moors after centuries of their dominion over Granada, when so many before have failed, constitutes the height of folly."

"Folly it might be," retorted my husband, "but we'll prove them wrong." He turned his gaze to me. "We've important business to attend to. This is not the time for dreams."

I had to agree. What Master Colón requested, given our circumstances—it was too much. But I didn't want to send him away unrewarded; deep inside, I shared his passion. I believed that what he said had merit, though I had no justifiable reason why.

"I would speak with him more," I heard myself say, coming to my feet, and Fernando gave me a terse nod, swerving back to the table to snap his fingers at Santángel, who rushed to refill his goblet. The spell Colón had cast was broken; all of a sudden, daily life resumed, with Catalina waking up and starting to cry, Juana hushing her as Beatriz went to attend them; María playing with her dolls, and the ladies whispering amongst themselves as Isabel resumed her reading and Juan stifled a yawn.

I heard it all and did not heed any of it. Inés fetched my cloak.

Colón kept his eyes fixed on me as I folded the lynx-lined brocade about my shoulders and motioned to him.

"Come," I said. "We'll walk in the gallery."

THOUGH INÉS TRAILED at a discreet pace behind us, she ceased to exist as I walked with the navigator, subsumed by my keen appreciation of his presence. His height obliged me to crane my eyes toward his strong, aquiline profile. The silence in the gallery magnified the *clack* of his boot heel on the cold flagstone, the rustle of his well-worn velvet breeches; the hall's subdued lighting had flattered his costume—in the harsh glare outside, I could see his clothes were not new. Again, I was struck by his confidence. Few men I knew would have dared come before their queen in anything but the most costly garb, even if they had to mortgage their estate to buy it.

The cloister gallery enclosed a private garden, filled with topiary and now-bare flower beds. Around us, the enameled spires of the monastery cluttered the azure sky. A lone stork circled a nest high above; as I paused to watch it, Colón murmured, "It is truly a miraculous thing, that they may go so effortlessly to where not even we, for all our superiority, dare venture."

I glanced at him. "Do you speak of flight or sail, Master Colón?"

He gave me a subtle smile. "To me, they're one and the same." He paused. "The Italian artist Leonardo da Vinci believes that one day we can construct machines that will enable us to take to the sky. He says that we will surpass even the birds in our ability to navigate the world."

"That would indeed be wondrous," I said. "But won't it make everything smaller?"

"The world is only as small as we see it, my lady. Imagination knows no limits."

I wasn't quite sure how to respond to this, or to the fact that he'd dropped my royal title in favor of a most informal, and improper, mode of address.

"My husband the king is right," I eventually said, as we turned a corner and proceeded down the vaulted corridor. Outside, a light snow began to fall, the swirling flakes dissolving before they reached the ground. "We are in the midst of a great and arduous crusade, into which we have poured all our efforts."

My innuendo lingered; I hoped I wouldn't have to state the obvious: Our treasury could not possibly support a plan as ambitious as his, not while we were at war.

He let out a resigned sigh. "It is not unexpected. Abroad you are hailed as a visionary warrior queen, who, by the strength of your will, shall raise this once-beleaguered nation to power." He paused, staring out toward the dancing snow. "However, I was warned by some that your vision does not extend beyond your realm's borders."

I laughed shortly, though his comment stung. "Gossip was never a concern of mine."

He turned to me. He did not speak, and I felt inexplicably compelled to fill his silence with my defense. "However, those who criticize me fail to understand my purpose. Indeed, though I have not made it public, I'm in the midst of arranging a match between the Habsburg emperor's daughter and my heir Prince Juan, as well as one with the Habsburg heir and my daughter Juana. My eldest daughter, Isabel, is already promised to Portugal and I hope to see one of my other daughters wed to England. So, as you can see, I do look beyond my borders, even if for the moment my main concern lies within. I would not be a good queen were it not so. But Castile must come first. That was my vow on the day I took the throne."

He bowed his head. "I meant no offense. I am privileged beyond words that you consented to see me today, given the circumstances. I realize you have much to do and that time spent with family is a rare luxury."

All of a sudden, I wanted to touch his shoulder, reassure him somehow. Instead I said, "I do not wish for you to take this proposal elsewhere. Though it is not within our means at this time to grant your requests, I will appoint a committee to look into your claims, headed by my confessor, Talavera, a man of great wisdom. And I would grant you a stipend, enough so you needn't be dependent on others. Are you alone?"

"No, *Majestad*. I have a son, Diego; he is being taught in the Monastery of La Rábida."

"And your wife . . . ?"

A shadow crossed his face. "She died years ago, before we left Lisbon."

"I am sorry," I murmured. "God keep her. Then I shall make the stipend such that you have enough to care for your boy." I extended my hand; as he leaned over it, faintly touching his lips to my ring, he said, "Thank you, *Majestad*. You are indeed a great queen, whom I'd be honored to serve with my body and heart."

To my disconcertion, I felt heat rise in my cheeks. What was it about this man, that he could rouse such emotion in me? If I hadn't known myself better, I would have feared I was attracted to him, though I knew that physical appeal was too simple an explanation for the depth of feeling he evoked in me. I now believed he was indeed someone I'd been destined to meet, an act of fate I could neither resist nor evade.

I withdrew my hand, took a step back. "You are welcome to travel with our court when we return to the south. But I should warn you, it is hard business we are about; it requires all of one's faith and endurance, for it is God's work."

"I have never been afraid of God's work," he replied.

When he turned and walked away, a swagger in his step, without so much as a by-your-leave, I had to smile. He was not one to shirk divine challenge. I'd assumed as much.

Though he had offered nothing save his word, I'd been captivated by this enigmatic stranger, who had given me a glimpse of the world's larger mystery.

And I vowed that were it ever within my power, I would see to it that he had his voyage.

CHAPTER THIRTY

I paced the colonnade, sweltering in Andalucía's unremitting heat, my every sense attuned to the officials and other court servants bustling through the alcazar patio around me. I was waiting for news from the front.

"Where is he?" I asked, for no doubt the hundredth time, as my poor Inés tried to keep up with my erratic perambulations, perspiration dripping off her brow onto her damp bodice. "How long can it take for one messenger to arrive? Fernando and our men left for Loja over two weeks ago; surely, there must be some news by now."

"My lady, His Majesty warned the siege on Loja might take time," Inés said, as she had so many times before. "It is not so easy, he said, with my lord Boabdil determined to hold on to the city as part of his kingly rights."

"He has no rights," I snapped, "not after he turned on us to unite with that wolf, El Zagal." I paused, immediately contrite about taking out my anger on her. "Forgive me. I'm at wits' end, it seems. I long to *do* something; I can't bear to be kept apart from the reconquest of my realm anymore."

She nodded in sympathy; the fight for Loja was particularly symbolic. It was the site of Fernando's first shattering defeat at the hands of the Moors, now taken over by that worm Boabdil as part of his new alliance with El Zagal. Our decision to wrest it back and send Boabdil packing to Granada with a taste of what was yet to come could have important ramifications, not the least of which being that if we failed, we would give El Zagal and his roving bands of warriors the incentive they needed to challenge all our previous accomplishments. It would ignite sieges and sweep attacks on several fronts.

I was about to regale Inés with all my worries again when I heard the sudden clatter of running footsteps, accompanied by the clamor of courtiers. As I turned, I caught sight of a messenger in our livery rushing toward me, an excited crowd in his wake. He fell to one knee, extending a square of parchment.

I was unable to move. I couldn't even reach for the paper. My gaze was fixed on the bowed man's head, so Inés took the missive in my stead and, at my near-imperceptible nod, cracked the seal.

"What . . . what does it say?" I whispered, feeling the eyes of every courtier watching me.

Inés replied with a catch in her voice. "Loja has fallen, *Majestad*!"

"I'm going to Loja and that's the end of it."

My councilors greeted my declaration with a stunned hush, followed immediately by an anxious outcry. "Your Majesty cannot! Think of your safety, of the risks. A Moorish assassin, any mishap on the road, not to mention the conditions at camp—none of these are conducive to a gentlewoman's state, let alone that of a sovereign queen."

I allowed myself a smile. "I cannot account for mishaps on the road or conditions at camp; these are in God's hands. As for assassins, if they pose such a threat, I shall have a light suit of armor crafted especially for me, to protect my person."

"A suit of armor?" they gasped in chorus, as if I had said I would don a codpiece.

I resisted a roll of my eyes. Chacón eyed me in amusement from his position in the corner of the chamber, arms crossed at his burly chest.

"Fine," I conceded, "no armor. It's too hot anyway. Just a breastplate and sword," I added, "in case I should run into one of those mishaps you seem so concerned about."

The lords couldn't conceal their dismay, but I felt it was less for me and more about the possibility that they'd be obliged to accompany me; older nobles all, they would not set foot near the front if they could avoid it. They preferred to dispatch their retainers, sons, whomever they could find to fight in their place. Their cowardice made me want to laugh. All of our younger nobility had flocked to our standard; indeed, even middle-aged lords such as Medina Sidonia had waded knee-deep in infidel blood for our greater glory.

"As you remind me, I am their sovereign queen," I said. "If I go to my husband's side at his hour of victory, it will inspire our men to greater feats of courage. And I intend to go not as a timid woman, but as a warrior, ready to fight and die, as they do, for Castile."

Chacón broke into a grin as I walked past him to the doors; a week later, the royal goldsmith delivered to my rooms the beautiful embossed breastplate, crafted of tempered iron and embellished with black-and-gold trellis tracery, its interior padded with fustian-stuffed crimson velvet shaped cleverly to accommodate my bosom.

As he helped me into it and fastened the straps, I felt as if I were encased in stone. "It's so heavy," I said, turning awkwardly to my mirror. "Are they always this heavy?"

The goldsmith shifted forward to adjust the fit. "This is one of the lightest I've ever crafted, *Majestad*. The armor that our lords and His Majesty wear is almost double this weight, as it's composed of more sections to protect the body."

"Double?" I had a newfound appreciation for our men. I wondered how it must feel to be surging up a steep escarpment in the blazing heat while wearing one of these things. I turned to retrieve the sword—a slim, shining length of blade with a ruby-and-emerald-studded hilt shaped like a crown. It too was heavier than I expected. As I returned to the mirror, the sword held aloft in my hand, I vividly recalled the moment from my childhood when Beatriz and I had watched the sun ebb over Ávila, arguing over the merits of our gender.

Who said a woman can't take up the sword and cross, and march on Granada to vanquish the Moors?

"She was right," I mused aloud, and Inés met my eyes in the glass.

"Who, my lady?"

I smiled, shaking my head. Beatriz was in Castile, finishing up the packing of my household and preparing my younger children for the trip south to join us.

Oh, but wouldn't she be furious when she heard she had missed this!

EXHAUSTED AND BLOODIED as they were, the soldiers lifted a deafening cheer at the unexpected sight of me riding into camp on my white steed, clad in my breastplate, with my ornamental sword strapped to my waist. The men's welcome resounded across the gaping fortifications of the shattered city, and I saw by their joy that I had been right to come as one of them, rather than as the lofty queen arrived to reap their hard-earned laurels. The captured infidels fell to their knees in supplication, scraping the dirt with their foreheads; their women scooped up handfuls of burnt earth and poured it, wailing, over their heads in abject grief.

"Look at them," said Fernando, in awe. "They're terrified of you."

"They should be," I replied. Ascending a dais to face our men, I declared, "I commend you this day, because as knights you've defended our faith from the infidel danger that threatens our land. God knows our cause is just and will not forget the hardships you have endured. He shall grant us our reward in Paradise. As for me, I thank you with all my heart for your sacrifices!"

I swiped off my broad-brimmed, tasseled hat, exposing my hair—darkened to deeper auburn in my maturity—to the glaring sunlight, as a sign of deference to their courage. The roar of acclaim that ensued caused the captive infidels to fall into cowering silence. In elation, I clasped Fernando, holding our twined hands aloft as I cried, "*Tanto monta, monta tanto!* Onward to Málaga and to victory!"

That night, Fernando took me with such a passion. "You are my warrior-queen," he whispered, thrusting inside me. "Now, make us a son, my *luna*. Make us another prince."

But within weeks, my menses had returned. When Beatriz arrived with my other children, I confided to her that since Catalina's birth, my bleeding had become sporadic, sometimes accompanied by harsh cramping, though I was not yet forty.

As I paced Córdoba's alcazar, restless as a caged lioness, without even the excuse of needing to safeguard a child in my womb, I knew what I must do. As soon as I heard that our army had entrenched itself before Málaga, I donned my breastplate and sword, left the younger children in Ines's care and rode out with Beatriz and Isabel to inspire our troops.

My first sight of Málaga, fringed by the Sierra Blanca and lapped by the sapphire sea, took my breath away. The sultry May wind rustled the spiked fronds of palm and date trees; above the city's high ramparts hung a succulent thickness of smoke, incense, and that rich, indefinable musk of herbs and spices.

The Moors knew what we intended; they'd had ample warning since Loja. The rotted heads of our fallen stared sightlessly down from the battlements as we approached; we were now an army of fifty thousand strong, spreading onto the scorched plain like avenging angels.

With its one hundred and twelve fortified towers, the city crouched at the foot of the crenellated sierra like a magnificent lion. I hid my distress at the thought of the devastation we must wreak, reviewing our ranks and supplies, dining with our commanders and ensuring that Fernando's armor and sword were properly oiled so he'd suffer no mishap in battle. While our new cannon and catapults would inflict most of the damage, breaching the walls and destroying the battlements from which the Moors might pour hot oil, boiling pitch, or shoot poisoned arrows, hand-to-hand combat was inevitable, and I always worried, watching from my distant vantage spot with Isabel and praying for my husband's safety.

For days we pounded Málaga's walls. The dust of pulverized stone and mortar wafted on the air in suffocating gusts, so that we had to tie cloths about our noses and mouths. The dust settled on everything, in everything; our clothes chests, our beds, our utensils; even our food and drink tasted of grit. We had known it would not be easy, I reassured my daughter as we sat in our pavilion listening to the ceaseless clangor of the bells I had ordered to be rung day and night. The sound mingled with the keening of our wounded and the shrieks of despair coming from Málaga's trapped inhabitants. Yet even I had begun to wonder at the Moors' preternatural tenacity; with the port blockaded by our ships, and no way to relieve the city, starvation and disease must have started to take an insidious toll.

Finally, three months after the siege began, word came that the Moors wished to parley with us. By now it was evident no reinforcements would be forthcoming from Granada. The denizens sent a holy man of theirs, who claimed reverence for my status as queen, and I agreed to meet with him in my audience tent while Fernando rested after another long day of overseeing the siege. I had dressed carefully, in my purple robe of estate, gold-lined caul, and sapphire diadem, but at the last minute, just as we were about to enter the tent, Beatriz snatched the diadem from my brow and pushed her way ahead of me.

"What do you think you're doing?" I hissed. She did not reply and I watched, aghast, as she sauntered into the richly appointed chamber and assumed my throne, leaving me open-mouthed and furious. Had she lost her mind? Had the heat and all this dust stirred some madness in her?

The red-haired marquis of Cádiz strode in moments later, accompanying a cloaked, turbaned man. This man lifted glowering eyes at the sight of Beatriz on my cushions; before any of us could react, he lunged forward with a howling cry, pushing Cádiz aside and reaching into his cloak. I froze when I saw the curved dagger raised in his hand.

Beatriz let out a piercing scream. The guards posted outside rushed in, almost throwing me to the ground. Tackling the Moor—who bellowed words none of us could understand—they gripped him by his wrists until he released the dagger. As it fell to the carpeted floor, I moved to take it.

"No!" cried Beatriz. "Don't touch it!" With the edge of her skirt, she gingerly retrieved the dagger by its hilt. She showed it to me. My skin crawled as I stared at the engraved blade, on which glinted a faint green film.

"See?" she whispered. "Poison; he meant to stab you with a poisoned dagger."

"*Dios mío.*" I looked at her in disbelief. "You saved my life. How did you know?"

She shrugged. "I had a feeling." She gave me a tremulous smile. "Forgive me for snatching your crown like that. But if he'd succeeded, better he had killed me than you."

"He will die," snarled Cádiz. "Drawn and quartered on the *vega* before the entire city, so his foul masters can watch!"

I turned to the assassin, held fast by our guards. He met my regard without discernible fear, though he must have known what awaited him. I doubted he spoke our language and was startled when he uttered words in a passionless voice that sent ice through my veins.

"This time, your crucified god has protected you. But from this day forth, know that every hour you breathe, Christian queen, is an hour you borrow against death."

I lifted my chin. "Take him away," I whispered.

Awoken by the commotion, Fernando staggered into the tent moments later, grasping me and pressing me to him. "My *luna*, my love, when I think of what could have happened . . ." He tightened his arms around me. "Filthy Moorish dogs, they do not know the meaning of honor, to send an assassin under the guise of negotiation. I will kill him myself, with my bare hands. I will rip out his foul heart. And then I will pull that miserable city down about their heads, so help me God."

"No, please." I drew back from him, mustering a weak smile as I waved everyone else out. Once we were alone, I said quietly, "We've lost nearly two thousand already and there are countless others dying in my infirmaries. Our supplies are nearly finished. We cannot endure much longer. Fernando, I fear we must seek accord, even if it means withdrawing from Málaga. There will be other years, other opportunities—"

"No." His voice was flat. "There will be no withdrawal. No one threatens my wife."

He marched out, crying for Cádiz. As I followed him, I heard him tell the marquis, "Send a herald to the walls of the city. I want it proclaimed that if Málaga does not surrender unconditionally within three days, we will raze the city to the ground and put every person inside to the sword."

"Fernando," I said. He turned to me, his eyes black and unyielding in his ashen countenance. I bit back my protest; I knew I had to cede to his judgment.

Within three days, the frantic citizens of Málaga had mobbed their leaders and sent us their offer of surrender. Fernando tore it up before their messenger's terrified eyes. "I said, no conditions. None."

"But Your Majesty," implored the kneeling man, "there are Christians and Jews in the city, as well. My lord El Zagal says he will kill them if you do not come to terms."

"If he touches one hair on a Christian head, he'll regret it," my husband said. "You will all regret it." He leaned close to the man, so close I almost didn't hear his next words: "I'll execute you one by one, in front of your families; I'll make your wives watch before they too are killed. I won't leave a single Moor alive, not a man or woman or child. Tell that to your lord."

The messenger gasped, swiveling to me in mute appeal. At my side, Isabel choked back a sob. The siege was taking its toll on her; she had lost weight, grown so pallid that veins could be traced under her skin. Her marriage date approached; we could not send her to Portugal in this sorry state. We could not allow this untenable situation to continue.

I lifted my voice. "We promise to spare you, if you do as my husband the king asks. Surrender within the week or I cannot be held responsible for what befalls you."

The messenger scampered back to the smoldering city. Before, Málaga's denizens had heckled us from the ramparts. But since we'd catapulted the mangled headless corpse of their would-be assassin over the walls, they'd gone silent. No one was visible now as the messenger slipped back under the massive outer portcullis.

Two days later, Málaga capitulated.

I couldn't say the claiming of Málaga as a Christian possession of Castile was worthy of celebration. Our casualties numbered nearly three thousand. Within the city itself the surviving populace had hardly fared much better. Forced to eat their dogs and cats, and then their horses, after having endured months of ceaseless bombardment, they regarded us from the rubble of their homes in tormented submission, aware they'd been abandoned to their fate.

Cádiz and the other nobles argued for mass executions. They insisted that the people of Málaga must pay for the crime of attempting to murder me; moreover, El Zagal had escaped before the surrender, no doubt abetted by these same people, which further enraged the grandees. But I refused to allow such savagery in my name. I persuaded Fernando that everyone should be sold into slavery, although those who could pay ransom must be freed. It was the best I could do under the circumstances; Fernando had gone rigid at my request, and it took me several hours of reasoning before he finally gave his consent.

Still, many would suffer on our galleys; many would die. It was the terrible price of the crusade and I took no pleasure in it, even as the silver cross sent by the late Pope Sixtus was hoisted with pulleys over

Málaga's mosque, which was now consecrated as the Cathedral of Santa
María de la Encarnación.

In the midst of this, I received a letter from my treasurer, Rabbi
Señeor, who had made the arrangements for the loans that financed our
crusade; a committee of Castilian Jews wished to ransom their brethren
in Málaga. After careful consideration, I accepted their payment of
twenty thousand *doblas,* and four hundred gaunt Jewish men and
women were released to melt into Castile.

It was a small mercy, practically meaningless; but one I insisted
upon, all the same.

CHAPTER THIRTY-ONE

Though we were within striking distance of Granada, the final tantalizing jewel in the broken Moorish diadem, where Boabdil skulked behind the Alhambra's vermilion walls, our men were exhausted. We decided to retreat to Castile for the winter.

Congratulations on our recent successes had poured in from abroad; even France, our perennial foe, saw fit to send us a set of figurines of the saints to place in our newly consecrated churches. Fernando snorted when he saw them: "Only gilt, of course, not gold. The French are nothing if not cheap, even when it comes to God's work."

Still, I was intrigued by our new prominence, especially by the offers of marriage arriving for my children. In addition to the Habsburg alliances I was already negotiating, the new English monarch, Henry VII—who'd established his Tudor dynasty after killing the last Plantagenet king—expressed an ardent desire to have one of my daughters for his newborn son, Arthur. Such alliances would expand our power and encircle France in a web of familial relationships that could prove that rapacious nation's undoing. All the offers required attention and the appointment of ambassadors in each of the courts abroad, as well as gracious deliberation. With our treasury, as ever, near empty, I arranged for another set of loans from the Jewish moneylenders of Valencia, offering up several more of my jewels as surety; they would hold them in symbolic safekeeping and in return provide me with the funds I required to hold dazzling receptions at court for the visiting envoys, in order to impress upon them the splendor of our realm.

I also dedicated myself to the continuing education of my children, as well as my own instruction, which had lagged far behind my initial hopes. When I received word through Cárdenas of a gifted female scholar known as La Latina, I was intrigued. Born Beatriz Galindo to a minor noble family, she had been chosen from among her sisters for the cloister, but at an early age she showed such talent for reading and for Latin that she was sent instead to study at the University of Salerno in Italy, one of the only universities in Europe that accepted women. After earning degrees in Latin and philosophy, she returned to Castile to gain a professorship in the University of Salamanca—a direct result of my edict that women be allowed all the benefits of higher education. She had so exalted herself by her proficiency in languages, as well as her erudite discourse on rhetoric and medicine, that she had become a prodigy among her peers.

I decided to summon her to court.

When she came before me in my study, a small woman clad in a plain brown wool gown, her linen headdress concealing her hair and emphasizing her gentle blue eyes and rosy cheeks, I could not help but stare in disbelief.

"You . . . you're so young," I said, as she rose from her reverential curtsey.

"*Majestad,* I am twenty." Her voice was soft but authoritative, as if she'd never had the need to raise it in order to be heard. "I was entrusted to the convent at the age of nine, where I might have stayed, had my love for learning not caught the attention of my superiors. I studied in Salerno, but since your edict I returned to teach and learn under the guidance of my patron, Don Antonio de Nebrija."

I must have shown my bewilderment, for she added, "Don de Nebrija is famous in scholarly circles, both here and abroad. He's currently preparing a compilation of Spanish grammar which he hopes to dedicate to Your Majesty."

"A book on Spanish grammar?" I said thoughtlessly, as I glanced at the bulging leather satchel she'd set on the floor by my desk. "What would be the need? I know our language."

"*Majestad,* the ancient Romans used language to build their empire. They made Latin so widespread that to this day we continue to use it. Could we not do the same with our language? It would surely benefit our country if more of our people could read and write in their own tongue. Much as I revere it, Latin is not nearly as accessible."

I went still. Without so much as a tremor in her voice, she had just reminded me of my ignorance. I was not offended, however; I could tell she meant no insult. She'd also noticed my wandering gaze, for she motioned to her satchel and said, "Do you want to see?"

I nodded. As she hoisted the satchel onto the desk and unlatched it, I had to resist the urge to clap my hands in glee. I felt like a child at Epiphany. Beatriz Galindo had brought a bag of books with her from Salamanca!

"This is *De Finibus*"—she handed me a slim leather-encased volume—"an important treatise about ethics by the Roman philosopher Cicero. And this," she added, selecting another beautifully tooled calfskin book, "is *Carmen Paschale*, a fifth-century epic by the poet Sedulius, based on the Gospels." She paused. "Many deem him a shameless imitator of Virgil, but I find his interpretation of the Bible rather original. I thought we might start with him, seeing as Your Majesty is such an upholder of our faith."

My hands were itching to open the books but I felt sudden shame as I met her contemplative regard. "These books are in Latin. I . . . I fear I do not understand Latin very well. I've been studying as much as my time permits, but I've made little progress." I gave a short, embarrassed laugh. "As you just said, I find it's not very accessible."

She reached over to pat my hand, as if we were the best of friends. "You soon will," she said, "if you grant me the great honor of instructing you. I am very familiar with Latin, as my nickname attests." She smiled, revealing perfect dimples in her round cheeks. "And perhaps in time, we shall see more splendid, and modern, works written in Spanish too, and Your Majesty hailed as the patroness of our very own renaissance in the arts."

She could not have spoken words dearer to my heart. I longed to be known as such; I wanted to bequeath a legacy that went beyond warfare. Though I strived for spiritual and physical unity in all of Spain, I believed a truly great country, one that would endure for centuries, must be built on the foundation of a literate and well-rounded society.

Breathless now with excitement, I opened the book as she drew up a chair beside me. When Fernando came in hours later, he glanced in pointed interest at Beatriz Galindo as she sank into a puddle of skirts at his entrance.

When I explained who she was, adding that she'd also agreed to oversee our daughters' instruction, he smiled. "So, at long last you found your lady tutor," he said.

His indulgent chuckle as he waved Beatriz to her feet and then proceeded to light extra candles—"You'll go blind in this light"—before leaving us to our studies showed he was pleased. A well-educated wife, he had learned, could only benefit our realm.

THE NEXT TWO years passed swiftly. Cádiz, Medina Sidonia, and our other Andalucían nobles held the frontier, withstanding the numerous attacks by El Zagal's Moorish raiders. Though he had escaped from Málaga, leaving the city to its fate, El Zagal was fueled by his desire to avenge the loss of the city which he had once ruled over with impunity. And his actions only enflamed Fernando's resolve to put the rebel Móor's head on a spike.

Thus, after assembling a new force of munitions and men, we returned south to focus on our next target: El Zagal's fortified city of Baeza.

Protected by mountainous ravines and valleys of *huertas,* or orchard land, Baeza's denizens were among the most entrenched of the Moors; their hatred for us after years of relentless crusade had been brought to fever pitch by the fall of Málaga. Cádiz told us that El Zagal had gotten wind of our plans and dispatched ten thousand of his best warriors to the city in anticipation of our approach. The people had stockpiled over a year's worth of supplies, strengthened their battlements, and stripped the surrounding land of all crops, leaving only denuded orchards and thickets of dense trees, brambles, and bracken to thwart our passage. Moreover, the city itself sat on a steep hillside encircled by forested ravines. To lay siege to it, Cádiz warned, was certain to be difficult and prolonged.

We had heard such dire predictions before and we had succeeded, but still I found myself torn in two as I anxiously bid farewell to Fernando when he left at the head of our army of forty-three thousand, which he would lead into the Guadalquivir vale that fed Baeza's *huerta.* For while I was left behind at court, at the mercy again of couriers to bring word between us, I faced an even more difficult task: I had to turn my attention to preparing our beloved Isabel for her departure to Portugal.

I had delayed for as long as I could, citing the war, our perennial paucity of funds, Isabel's youth and her need to stay close to her family. But she was entering her twentieth year and the Portuguese king's patience had reached its limit. My aunt Beatrice wrote to say that we'd best seal our agreement before another monarch offered up a bride for his son, Prince Afonso.

"Portugal is just across our border," I told my daughter, as we packed her belongings. "We can visit every year, or more, if we like."

"Yes, Mama," she said, her delicate bare fingers—for she could not don jewelry until she had her wedding band on first—meticulously folding the multitude of embroidered linens and lace-hemmed chemises, thick mantles and hooded cloaks, and sumptuous gowns trimmed with my favored ermine that I had ordered made for her. I'd lavished a fortune I didn't have on Isabel's trousseau, borrowing against outstanding loans to furnish her with everything she might need for every possible climate and season, as though she were not going just across our border but rather across the ocean to a land I didn't know or trust.

I kept swallowing against the lump in my throat as I beheld her stoic acceptance of her fate. I had planned for this day with painstaking care and yet the very thought that she would soon be far from me, in her own court, wed to a prince I had never met, made me falter; I had to resist the urge to clutch her to me and never let go. She was the first of my daughters to leave; how could I do this three more times? How would I bear it?

Beatriz knew how distraught I was; she stayed by my side right to the final farewell at the border between Spain and Portugal, where amidst fanfare and billowing silk banners, I surrendered Isabel to my aunt Beatrice and her entourage. Portugal had sent hundreds of ladies, nobles, and officials to accompany my daughter to Lisbon with all the appropriate distinction, but according to ancient custom dictating that royal grooms did not fetch their brides, her husband-to-be was not present.

As I embraced Isabel in that windswept field, she asked tentatively, "Do you think he'll love me as Papa loves you?"

It was her first admission of the fear she had kept from everyone, hidden behind her serene visage. Holding her face between my palms, I whispered, "Yes, *hija mía*, he will. I promise you."

She tried to smile; I would have promised her anything in that moment to ease her anxiety, but I couldn't possibly predict whether her husband would care for her, and she knew it. Meeting my gaze one more time, she stepped back, turning resolutely to the hundreds of strangers awaiting her, and crossed those few paces of grass into her new realm.

Beatriz stood beside me as I watched my child being swallowed by the Portuguese. They surrounded her and led her to her waiting mare for her journey; all she had left of Castile were the clothes on her back and the coffers filled with her trousseau.

I thought my heart might break as I returned to Sevilla. I was unable to utter a word despite my ladies' anxious inquiries; I feared any admission of sorrow would set me to crying in front of everyone. I missed my Isabel with a silent, aching helplessness in the ensuing days; even the dented cushion on the window seat, where she used to sit and sew or read with me in the afternoons, served as a stark reminder of her absence. My other daughters were still too young to fill the void left by Isabel, and at eleven, Juan was immersed in his impending manhood, his princely activities taking up all of his attention and time. Even the weather reflected my low spirits: a rare spate of intemperate storms inundated Andalucía, causing rivers to flood, spoiling the harvest and sweeping away entire hamlets as if they were children's toys.

A few months after Isabel left, I received word from Fernando, entrenched in his siege on Baeza.

We are beyond despair. The city withstands us with the fiend's own obstinacy and infidel ambushes fall upon us in the middle of the night only to retreat like mist, leaving our dead in pools of blood. The storms have turned our camp into a sea of mud, so we can scarcely pitch our tents, nor care for our few remaining beasts. Because of the rain, the fodder rots, as does everything else in this forsaken place. I set the men to cutting back the miles of woods and *huertas,* as the ground is so sodden we cannot scorch it, but it will

take months of labor and rations run low. Now flux threatens to take
hold, our wells having been poisoned by corpses dumped into the
source waters by the Moors. The horses are dying and many of our
men are so despondent, they threaten to desert. They say God has
turned His face from us. . . .

I summoned the council. "We must send aid to my lord husband
and his men at once. They need livestock, supplies, medicine, and food.
The Moors have everything in Baeza to withstand months of siege, so
we cannot hope to starve them out. We must be as well-provisioned as
they are, if we are to win."

The council greeted my declaration with grim silence; it was Cardinal Mendoza who finally said, "*Majestad,* we allocated everything we
had when His Majesty first embarked on this expedition. And with the
recent expenses for the Infanta Isabel's trousseau . . . I fear there is nothing left."

"Nothing left?" I echoed, incredulous. "Whatever does that mean?"

"Exactly that: There is not enough in the treasury to meet the sums
you require."

"Impossible!" I said, unwilling to believe what he was telling me.
But as I regarded the grave faces of those seated around the table, my
heart sank. I knew I had spared no expense on Isabel's leave-taking; I
had been so concerned for her well-being, I'd not let myself give thought
to the possibility that Baeza might resist us for as long as it had.

"But surely there must be something we can do," I said to Mendoza.
He sighed. "There is always the option of increasing taxation, but
the nobility will no doubt resist, and the Cortes must approve any additional requests—"

"That'll take months! Am I supposed to leave the king and our army
outside Baeza without any aid while we plead with the nobility and wait
for the Cortes to make up their minds? My lords, you are our appointed
council. You must have better advice to give."

None of them replied, but the way they uncomfortably averted
their faces gave me all the answer I needed. They had no other advice.

"So be it," I declared. "I'll resolve the matter myself." I waved them
out angrily, disgusted by their lack of initiative. I didn't even look up as

they filed out; when I finally lifted my eyes, I was met with only Mendoza's steely gaze. Now in his early sixties, leather-skinned and wiry from his own considerable participation in our crusade—which had including charging into battle numerous times at the head of his retainers—he was a guiding force for me in Castile not only through his passion for architecture and education, but also in his dedicated administrative oversight of our new Holy Office. He shared my desire to shape our nascent kingdom into a power as grand, as enticing, as any in Europe, an accomplished realm celebrated and courted by every nation.

"I know what Your Majesty is thinking," he said, "and I beg you not to consider it any further. You've ventured down that path too many times, and they hold too much of your patrimony already. Would you hand over the entire kingdom to the Jews to win this war?"

"You know I would. I'd pawn my very petticoat, if that were what was required."

"You cannot." He stepped to me. "Torquemada watches every step you take. You refused him before when he asked you to expel them and he will ask again as soon as the Reconquista is over. You cannot grant them so much power over you that they would be able to consider mounting resistance."

"The Reconquista is not over yet" was my reply, "and if the council cannot help me, then I have no other recourse. Please tell Rabbi Señeor I will see him."

"*Majestad,* I implore you. What else do you have to give?"

"Better you do not know, if it causes you such distress," I replied and I looked pointedly at the door. He left without another word. While I waited for Rabbi Señeor, Ines slipped in to see if I needed anything.

"Yes," I told her. "Fetch my casket with my nuptial necklace."

She stared at me, stunned, and I clicked my tongue impatiently. "Must I repeat myself? Do it. Now."

When she returned, I unlatched the casket lid and took a long look at the ceremonial ruby-and-pearl collar from Aragón that Fernando had sent to me before our wedding. I had flaunted it many times to the envious admiration of our court; it was the tangible symbol of our love, my most treasured possession after my crown.

I shut the casket with a resolute click and closed my eyes.

"Let my sacrifice be worthy of Your divine favor," I whispered.

I entrusted the casket for safekeeping to Rabbi Señeor that very evening, in exchange for a substantial personal loan. Then I gathered my entourage and, without further ado, I embarked the next day through a blustering storm to Baeza.

The viscous mud in the passes sucked at my horse's hooves; the roads crumbled away entirely in parts, forcing us to build makeshift bridges over streambeds that raged with torrential waters. As I huddled on my saddle, narrowing my eyes against the needles of sleet and rain, I too began to doubt God heeded us anymore. Never had I witnessed such misery as what I saw when I finally reached the encampment.

Fernando emerged from his tent to meet us—haggard and soiled, with sleeplessness engraved in dark circles under his eyes. The mess about him was evidence enough for his despair; the few living horses that remained stood covered in sores, bones showing. The livestock pens were broken and empty. The camp itself was mired in muck, with half-naked men wandering about with listless faces, while others crouched moaning in the open, emptying their bloody bowels. A miasmic stench assaulted me, the putrid odor of death curdling the very air.

As Fernando kissed me wearily and led me about the camp, I knew the situation was the worst we had ever faced. Over half of our army was dead. The other half was ill or slowly dying from the flux. As I made my visit to the crowded infirmaries, where men lay on file after file of sagging, louse-infested cots, they gazed up at me and wept like children.

That night, I told Fernando that I had secured us more money. "We will import grain and dig new wells," I said. "Rebuild the washed-out roads and summon every man in Andalucía. If necessary we'll send to Castile for additional recruits and raise whatever extra funds we need. We will not give up." I clasped his hand from across the table. "Never."

"As always, your strength brings hope," he said. "But hope will not win this city, my *luna*. Winter is coming. How are we supposed to survive it? Once you counseled me to retreat from Málaga but I resisted. Now, I fear, retreat is our only choice."

I'd never heard him so dejected, as if all his zeal had been sapped from him. I understood at that moment that he'd reached the limit of his seemingly indefatigable reserves; he was thirty-seven, an age when most kings looked forward to reaping the rewards of their youthful exploits. He had not known more than a few isolated months of peace in our entire marriage, forever at war or preparing for it. Now here he sat, battle-worn and heartsick, believing himself responsible for the collapse of our seemingly unattainable dream of a united Spain.

"No," I said quietly, "hope cannot win this city. But we can. We *must*. You've done so much. Leave this to me."

He sighed his assent. "If anyone can conquer Baeza, my *luna*, it's you."

I had never thought to hear such words from him; though I had known in my heart that he appreciated and respected my fortitude, I had not imagined he'd voluntarily entrust such an important task as the downfall of a city to my hands alone. If I failed, we would likely lose the crusade. We would spend the next ten years engaged in minor skirmishes, lengthy sieges, and abortive battles, taking back with blood and sweat and expense in the spring and summer what the Moors would filch from us in the winter. Eventually, our funds and the ability to raise them would dwindle; the pope, our fellow Catholic monarchs abroad— while all wanted to see the infidel herded back over the Strait of Gibraltar and cornered, none would part with so much wealth as to ensure that our crusade could continue indefinitely.

If we were to take Granada, Baeza must be ours. And though it came with some risks, I had an idea of how to accomplish it.

Leaving Fernando to rest for a few days, I met with the other commanders to review our situation. While we lacked almost every supply imaginable, I pointed out that we certainly had enough lumber left from the early efforts of cutting back the forest that surrounded us, which acted as a natural bastion between us and Baeza. My plan was to stockpile the wood and cut even more; while we did that, I would send for supplies and specialists who knew a thing or two about bringing down stubborn citadels.

Marshaling all the men who were well enough to work, I set them to chopping down everything. They had trimmed the woodlands around the camp, carving a labyrinthine opening toward the insolent city on its hill, but they had spared the fruit-bearing trees, for we were still a people who had known famine. Now I had them demolish every tree, scorching and razing without discrimination until we had cleared vast swaths of land. With all the newly felled wood, I ordered palisades erected, high walls and towers—a new fort to confront Baeza, standing on the shorn vale like a monstrous toadstool.

Here we dug in for the winter, the fort offering protection from the Moors' raids. While it was too cold and snowy outside for the army to engage in physical assault, I would not be dissuaded by mere weather. I ordered all the livestock, rations, extra cannons, and siege engines I had bought with my necklace to be lugged up in tarp-covered wagons over the treacherous passes. We would assemble our munitions in the spring before Baeza's disbelieving eyes.

"We'll need even more men, especially harquebusiers, gunners, and archers," remarked Fernando, who had recovered from his ordeal and was helping to oversee the camp's restoration with his usual penchant for detail.

"I've already sent for them," I assured him, "but hopefully we will not need them."

I turned to my cluttered portable desk and handed him the letter I'd spent the last six weeks composing, laboring over every word, every phrase, until I was confident I had it right.

Fernando read it in utter silence before lifting his eyes. "Isabella, what you propose," he said carefully, "is nothing short of treachery. Boabdil is faithless, yes, with no more sense of honor than a cur, but not even he would agree to these terms. There's nothing in it for him, except the promise of his life, which for now he needn't worry about."

"Oh?" I eyed him. "Boabdil sold himself to us before, did he not? And he's not such a fool that he cannot know by now that we'll come to him again eventually, either with a pact or with troops storming his gates. And he has no one left to betray us to once we take Baeza. Under the circumstances, I think my proposal is quite reasonable."

"Reasonable?" Fernando let out a guffaw. "You're asking him to give up everything, to turn on his own kind. If he agrees to this, he's even more of a craven idiot than I thought." He paused. An admiring grin spread across his face. "I didn't think you had it in you."

"When it comes to our kingdom," I said, "I have this in me, and much more."

I sent my letter off in secret to Granada. We did not wait for an answer long; within a few weeks, I received word from my envoys that Boabdil had readily accepted my terms, just as I knew he would. Once I had his response in writing, I sat down to compose a letter to El Zagal, who I knew had spies in Granada and was watching everything I did from his citadel, powerless to affect or alter my course.

My offer to him was concise: Unless he wanted to suffer another crushing defeat as he had in Málaga, he must surrender. I warned him that if he did not, this time I would give no quarter. I would order my army not only to raze but also to salt the very earth on which Baeza sat and to kill everyone in it. But if he accepted my terms, I would be merciful. I would spare his life and grant him refuge in a specially appointed domain in Las Alpujarras, where he could live with his people in peace, retaining all his customs without interference. I added that he must realize by now that, in the end, we would prevail; even if it took a lifetime, we would never give up. Moreover, I took pleasure in pointing out that his nephew Boabdil would not come to his aid, and to prove it I enclosed a signed copy of our new treaty with that traitor, which stipulated that once El Zagal was defeated, Boabdil promised to relinquish his realm in its entirety to us, in exchange for his own safety.

It took a month, during which I had our weapons assembled right below his walls and cut down the last of the magnificent forest. Finally, El Zagal returned his reply.

He was weary of the fight. He appreciated my offer but he preferred to leave Spain for North Africa. As for his nephew Boabdil, he wrote: *Let Granada fall.*

♛

WE FIRST SAW Granada in the spring of 1491, after our wholesale devastation of the surrounding *vega*. Once again I ordered the orchards, wheat fields, and olive groves to fall beneath our scythes and torches, so there could be no possibility of relief for the entrapped citizens.

Despite the blackened fields, never had any city looked as beautiful as that sprawling metropolis we'd coveted for so long—a fantasy framed by the snow-tipped sierra, the honeyed towers of the Alhambra encircled by garlands of cypress and pine. Streets cascaded in twisting mazes, crowded with thousands of refugees, Jews and Moors and false conversos, all of whom had fled the devastation of our crusade.

Boabdil, at the last moment, had reneged on our treaty; reality had come crashing down on him when he heard of Baeza's fall. Clearly, he had not expected his uncle El Zagal to surrender and he hastily manned his own walls with cannon, vowing to defend Granada till his dying breath. I was outraged by his blatant disregard of the terms we'd set, but after Baeza, with the fragments of the once-supreme Moorish emirate at our feet, Fernando and I decided this final victory must be bloodless. The time had come for the pomegranate to yield its fruit without any coercion from us, and so we set up our silk tents and pavilions as if we were on holiday, bringing our children with us to witness the historic occasion.

Tragedy had struck our family; only nine months after their marriage, Isabel's young Portuguese prince had died tragically from a fall from his horse, and she had returned home a widow. I had ridden all the way to the border to escort her home, and had been sadly shocked by the change in her. Thin as a twig in her black widow's weeds, her beautiful hair shorn to stubble, she went about either weeping or declaring her desire to enter a convent. To my consternation, she claimed that God must want her for Himself, to make her suffer so. I tried to tell her that while I believed God instilled in some of us a vocation to serve Him alone, hers seemed more a response to overwhelming sorrow, but nothing I said moved her. She refused all consolation, so much so that I had to appoint physicians and a special household to ensure that she ate and slept, and to restrict the time she spent on her knees in the chapel.

Alone in my rooms with my women, I vented my dismay. "I sent a golden infanta to Portugal and she's come back a phantom! What on earth has happened to her? That a daughter of mine should want to lead a religious life is admirable, but she has a role to fulfill in this world, and it cannot be in a nunnery."

Inés sighed sadly. "The poor child must have loved her prince very much."

Beatriz met my eyes, and in her silent look, I read my innermost fears. My eldest daughter was behaving like my mother, indulging a melancholic penchant for drama that chilled me to my very bones.

The realization bolstered my resolve: I ordered everyone to refuse to entertain any talk of convents, even if it made Isabel feel comforted. Everyone complied, but Juana, in characteristic fashion, goaded Isabel mercilessly. At eleven years of age, my second daughter was unwilling to concede any weakness in herself, much less in others.

"You look like a crow," Juana remarked as we sat in my pavilion after dinner one evening, the warm wind flowing through the tent's open flaps. Outside a thousand campfires glittered on Granada's *vega* like fallen stars as our men settled in for the night. "Always in black and moping about; it's unseemly. After all, you were married less than a year. You can't possibly have loved him *that* much."

Isabel stiffened on her stool, the altar cloth we embroidered between us tightening in her fingers. "And who are you to judge? What do you know of love or loss, spoiled selfish child that you are?"

"I might be spoiled," retorted Juana, "but at least I know I'd never love anyone so much that I'd forget myself."

As Isabel gasped, I said sharply, "Enough. I'll hear no more recriminations from either of you. If you must argue, do so elsewhere than in my presence. Honestly"—I shot a reproving look at them—"what has come over you?"

Isabel averted her eyes; Juana stuck out her tongue. I set my embroidery aside. I did not believe in corporal punishment but Juana was too impudent for her own good. I had a mind to—

I paused. "Is that smoke I smell . . . ?" I started to say, as Juana leapt to her feet, tossing her hopelessly tangled yarns to the floor and rushing to the pavilion entrance. She gasped. "Mama, look! The camp is on fire!"

Pandemonium broke out. As the duennas and other ladies raced to the back of the pavilion to gather sleeping Catalina and María from their beds, I hurried with my older daughters outside. To my horror, I beheld flames leaping like nimble devils from tent to tent, incinerating the velvets and silks and brocades, consuming everything within their path in minutes. All around us courtiers and soldiers were shouting; horses whinnied in terror and tore loose from their tethers, galloping about in panic as the dogs bayed. I didn't know where to turn; the smoke was already so thick I could barely draw in a breath. Suddenly, the marquis of Cádiz materialized out of nowhere, smut on his face and his clothes. "*Majestad,* come quickly!"

"Where are my husband and son?" I cried as he led us around the burning encampment, toward a nearby hill that offered protection.

"They are safe," he said. "The fire started in my tent, where they slept, but they got out in time. The king's hounds started barking the moment they saw the flames."

"*Gracias a Dios.*" I clutched Catalina to me. In the eerie interplay of fire and darkness, I caught sight of Juana's face. She was pale and wide-eyed; her mouth ajar in an expression I could only describe as exultant, as if the catastrophe had been staged for her amusement. I was appalled. Did she have no fear, no sense of the destruction and loss happening around us?

As if she read my thoughts, Isabel said quietly, "She doesn't care. She thinks it's a game. She has no respect for anything."

I hushed her. With Catalina in my arms and María held by Beatriz, we reached the hill's summit, which offered a terrible view of the conflagration. Fernando came running out of the darkness, his loyal hounds at his heels. I glimpsed our son, Juan, nearby, still in his nightshirt, his sword in its jeweled scabbard gripped in his hand. He'd recently been knighted in honor of his thirteenth year and refused to be separated from his weapon, even while in bed. At the sight of him, his white-gold hair tangled, his face blackened by soot but otherwise unharmed, tears of relief sprang to my eyes.

Juana plunged into Fernando's embrace. Encircling her with his arm, he drew the rest of us close and we turned to watch our great cloth city, proof of our vanity and the whimsical folly of fate, burn entirely to the ground.

LATER, JUANA INSISTED the Moors had shot a flame-tipped arrow into the camp to start the conflagration, though a remorseful Cádiz had assured us that someone or something, perhaps one of the dogs, had upset an oil lamp, setting his tent on fire. Whatever the cause, we'd lost most of our belongings, including our wardrobe, and the court ladies had to lend us gowns and other items of apparel while I sent to Sevilla for new things.

From Granada's ramparts, the denizens jeered. They clearly believed the fire would be our undoing, but we remained undaunted. Our possessions may have turned to cinders, but our will was intact. I ordered a new city built on the camp's charred remains, this time made of stone. We would name it Santa Fe, in honor of our hallowed faith, which had saved us from a fiery death and guided us to safety.

The sight of our masons at work silenced the taunts from Granada. More than a city, Santa Fe was a statement of our resolve. Here, we might live for years if need be, the only place in Andalucía unsullied by the Moors. Boabdil's reaction was to fire his cannon and send out raiders to harass our troops. But as winter swept in and the city began to go hungry, riots began. With his people growing increasingly desperate and angry, Boabdil realized he had no option but to honor the terms we offered—full amnesty for his people, who would be allowed to maintain their customs, language, and dress. Anyone who wished to leave would be free to do so; we would even provide the means. And any who wished to convert would be welcomed into our Church, their past sins washed away by Holy Baptism. In addition, as our vassal, Boabdil would be granted the same domain in the Alpujarras that his uncle El Zagal had rejected. But under no circumstances could he ever return to Granada. On that point I was immutable.

By January 1492, his envoys had submitted his surrender.

WE ENTERED THE fallen city, last bastion of the Moor, as snow drifted down about our cortege like fine ash. The people stood in eerie silence, gathered at the sides of the road to watch us pass, the heraldic standards of our nobility fluttering in the frigid morning air. Many of our courtiers had donned traditional embroidered tunics in Moorish style, as a sign of our respect for the magnificent civilization which had left its indelible mark on our land, but an occasional bereaved lament from an unseen woman gazing at our advance from behind a latticed window conveyed the people's awareness that the world as they had known it was gone.

We accepted Boabdil's surrender in person at the city gates, where he threw himself on his knees before us. Fernando dismounted to embrace him as a fellow sovereign; now that we were triumphant, my husband knew how to be magnanimous.

With quivering hands and tears in his eyes, Boabdil offered up the keys to the city. "These are the last relics of our empire," he said, his voice quavering. "To you go our trophies, our realm, and our person; such is the will of Allah."

Behind him, seated on a beautiful Arabian horse, a heavyset woman swathed in black veils lifted vicious kohl-lined eyes to me. I had my daughters around me, each clad in a new scarlet brocade and veiled in the Moorish tradition, though Juana had already lifted her veil to see more clearly, entranced by the events around us. As I returned the woman's stare, I didn't need to be told that she was the sultana, Boabdil's mother, who'd fought for her son's freedom. In her defiant regard, I found a pride that had nothing left to feed on save itself; and I knew, without doubt, that it had been she who'd sent the assassin to my tent, the dagger poisoned by her own hand.

As she rode away with her son, she cast a final look at me over her shoulder. There was no despair, no contrition; only furious regret that I had succeeded where she had failed.

We ascended the road to the Alhambra. As we neared the infamous palace, built on legend and blood, I found myself leaning forward in my saddle, longing to kick in my heels and gallop straight to the massive vermilion gates. But I was a queen now, not a brash young infanta like Juana. I'd grown stout in my middle age, as had my beloved Canela, my favored horse whom I'd retired from service years ago due to his advanced age, but today I rode proudly, his thin form covered in a billowing gold-threaded caparison. While he no longer possessed the muscular fleetness of his youth, he had been with me from the beginning and he held his gray-flecked head high, a spry lift to his step, as if he understood the importance of this occasion.

The palace came into view, lounging on its plateau, its honey-brick walls seeming to reproach our advance. The same architects who had built this place had worked on Sevilla's alcazar at the command of one of my ancestors, adhering to the Arabic custom that rulers must not display their wealth to the world lest it incite envy. I knew that within lay a realm of incomparable beauty—chambers of alabaster hung with stone pediments and arches of lace; patios and arcades ringed by pilasters graceful as dancing women; lily-strewn pools where the reflection of the sky turned the marble walls azure, and gardens smothered with roses, lavender, and jasmine, their fragrance drifting into cedar-vaulted halls cooled by ingenious wind-catchers and high arched apertures that captured and softened the light.

I knew all this and still not even I was prepared for the magnificent emptiness of the place. Divans and quilted pillows had been left in disarray, as if their occupants had only just fled, and the scent of incense lingered like a lament.

Juana floated about perched on tiptoes, clutching little Catalina by the hand, mesmerized. Later, she'd spin fanciful stories of doomed concubines leaping from the towers and spectral reproaches from departed caliphs, but what most struck me in that moment as we moved through rooms that flowed into each other, where the glint of winter sunlight scattered over the ceramic walls, was the silence—so absolute that I could hear my own heartbeat in my ears, loud as the clack of my heels on the marble floors.

It was as though no one had ever lived here. After all his glory and thunder, the Moor had ceased to exist.

Outside, our battered silver cross was lifted over the palace. Cannons fired thundering volleys, followed by the heralds' cries: "Granada! Granada for our sovereigns, Don Fernando and Doña Isabella!"

Fernando reached for my hand; his palm was hard, permanently callused from years of wielding his sword. Gazing at him, I saw passion ignite in his eyes.

"We did it, my *luna*," he said. "We have won. Spain is ours."

Together we knelt to offer our gratitude to God.

So it was.

CHAPTER THIRTY-TWO

Congratulations on our conquest arrived from every major power in Europe; in Rome, the newly elected Spanish pope, Rodrigo Borgia, known as Pope Alexander VI, held a special procession and Mass in the basilica of Saint Peter and bestowed upon us the honorary title of the Catholic Monarchs, Defenders of the Faith.

Grateful as I was for the accolades, I wanted life to return to normal as quickly as possible. Ten years of war had come to an end; it was time to begin the process of healing and consolidating our nation, of seeing to our children's futures and upholding the Church's glory. Ensconced in the Alhambra, I turned my attention first to my children. It was imperative that they resume their interrupted studies, in order to prepare for the roles they would one day assume.

Juana, in particular, required firm oversight; her impressive educational accomplishments were overshadowed by her rebelliousness and her penchant for eccentric outings in the gardens, where she rushed here and there, dragging little Catalina along by the hand. Isabel likewise continued to worry me; she had recovered from the worst excesses of her grief, but she still insisted she was best suited to a holy life. She did not welcome any discussion of another marriage, though Portugal had again offered her a husband, this time in the form of her late husband's uncle.

María, however, was proving the balm to my troubles, a docile child who neither excelled nor failed in any of her undertakings. And Juan, my precious boy, became my primary focus, for I suspected I'd never bear another child. My menses had almost ceased. On Juan's slim shoulders now rested all of our dynastic hopes; he would be the first king to rule our united realm, and I oversaw his schedule personally, so he could master the complex art of being a monarch.

But my domestic respite was brief. Only weeks after we claimed Granada, we received word that our Jewish financiers were requesting urgent audience with us.

As they walked into our presence, their bearded faces careworn, their robes dusty from the long ride, I braced myself. By now, rumors must have reached them of Torquemada's claim about a widespread seditious Jewish plot to stiffen converso resistance and overthrow the Inquisition; they must have also heard of the riots in Castile and Aragón over the alleged crucifixion of Christian children, and other horrors supposedly perpetrated by their brethren. And as Mendoza had predicted, along with these vile reports, Torquemada had sent his renewed request that I issue an edict demanding the conversion of every Jew in the realm, on pain of forfeiture of goods and expulsion from my land.

I did not believe the half of it, though in public I'd expressed appropriate consternation. In all my life, I had never seen a Jew harm anyone, much less kill babes in mockery of our Savior. But I could not deny any longer that the tension built on centuries of mistrust toward the Jews—always simmering like poison under the surface of our much-vaunted tradition of *convivencia*—had, with the fall of Granada and the uniting of our realm, reached its boiling point. All over the kingdom, declared Torquemada, devout Christians rose in demonstrations to storm the Jewish ghettos, pillage their businesses, and throw them bodily out onto the roads. They would have no Jews in their midst anymore, my head Inquisitor claimed. The time for tolerating Christ's killers in Spain was at an end.

While I had no proof, I presumed these alleged spontaneous uprisings were part of Torquemada's quest to force Fernando and me into an impasse. His agents, now spread throughout the realm under the aegis of the Inquisition, brewed a cauldron of fear designed to push me into a decision I'd thus far refused to make. It infuriated me to think Torquemada believed he could manipulate me thus, but, manipulated or not, I had to face the ultimate consequence. I couldn't ignore the potential civil disorder in Castile to protect a people who did not share our faith.

Still, as I beheld these six huddled men who had come all the way from Castile to see us, who had lent us millions for our crusade and still held some of my most valued jewels as collateral, I felt the weight of their fears as if it were my own. I remembered when I'd faced this di-lemma years before and failed to heed it; then, it had seemed foolhardy to reverse our centuries-old policy of tolerance.

And as elderly Rabbi Señeor bowed, the azure velvet casket contain-ing my nuptial necklace cradled in his knobby hands, I remembered what Talavera had said:

The hour of reckoning must come. It is unavoidable, much as we may regret it.

Rabbi Señeor lifted his voice, a mere thread of sound, all but ex-hausted by his journey. "We come before you to beg Your Majesties not to heed the Inquisitor General's petition to expel us from this kingdom. As you well know, we've always supported your endeavors with every means at our disposal. Please tell us now, what do you want from us, your most humble subjects? Ask for anything and it shall be yours."

Fernando gave me a sharp glance. He had tensed as the men ap-proached our dais, his face adopting the inflexible expression he some-times wore when he felt challenged. He had supported the implementation of the Inquisition; I suspected he bore the Jews no particular love, though they'd acted as our treasurers. How would he react now?

"We want nothing more than subservience to our dictate," he sud-denly said. "Much as we may regret it, the time has come to prove your loyalty beyond material goods."

His uncanny echoing of Talavera's phrase startled me; I had not ex-pected it and neither had Señeor, who visibly blanched as he turned to me. "*Majestad,* we beg you as our queen. We are so many and so power-less; we appeal to your greater wisdom."

It was a mistake; nothing could rouse Fernando's ire more than to be disdained in favor of me. Before I could reply, Fernando pointed his finger at the rabbi. "Do you think to deny me?" he said, his voice soft with menace. "I too am ruler here; my heart is in the hands of our Lord, and it is to Him—and only Him—I need answer."

"Fernando," I murmured. "Please, let us hear them out." As my husband leaned back in his throne, his face white, I said to the rabbi, "What would you have us do, Don Señeor?"

He motioned hastily to the black-robed figures behind him; from their midst stepped a youth with angular cheekbones and careworn brown eyes. He was Rabbi Meir, Señeor's son-in-law, and another trusted financier of our court.

"Go," Señeor said to him. "Fetch it."

Meir and two of the others hastened out; they returned moments later with a large chest, which they lugged to the foot of our dais. Rabbi Meir unlocked the sturdy hinged lid. Within were several sacks, fastened with twine and sealed with red wax.

"Thirty thousand ducats," explained Señeor, as the others drew back. "Collected from our brethren to defray your Majesties' debts; our usurers have also agreed to cancel all loans to you and return your jewels as delivered, without expectation of recompense."

My throat went dry. I looked again at Fernando; saw by the twitch of a nerve in his temple that they'd touched him. Religious considerations aside, we were impoverished, more so than we'd ever let on. Indeed, only these men knew the full extent of it. Only they understood how far thirty thousand ducats would go toward restoring our treasury, not to mention the cancellation of the numerous loans we'd accumulated over the years.

"My lord husband," I said. "Does this meet with your agreement?"

He sat silent, still; that near-imperceptible twitch the only sign that he was considering the offer. Then he exhaled, opening his mouth to speak. But a commotion at the entranceway silenced him. To my dismay, the gaunt figure of Torquemada was striding toward us, his cassock swirling like dusk about his ankles, his eyes like agates in his emaciated face, which had grown even more arresting, and frightening, with the passage of the years.

His gaze fell on the open chest; as my heart capsized, he reeled to our dais. "I heard that you entertained these foul liars in your presence but I never thought to see this. Judas Iscariot sold our Lord for thirty pieces of silver; now, you would sell Him again for thirty thousand. Here He is, then. Take Him and barter Him away!"

Yanking his crucifix from his chest, he flung it at our feet and stormed out. In his wake he left a terrible hush. Looking down at the crucifix, Fernando whispered, "Leave us."

With a broken gasp, Rabbi Señeor started to stagger to his knees.

"No!" roared Fernando. "Now!"

They retreated; as the double doors of the hall closed on them, Rabbi Meir looked over his shoulder at me, with unmistakable resignation.

I sat without moving. They had left the chest and nuptial casket on the floor, but I did not even look at them. I had failed to anticipate this rage in Fernando; it was as though the very sight of Torquemada wielding his crucifix had awoken something feral, instinctual, but until now hidden, in my husband.

Finally he spoke in a trembling voice. "It is blood money. Torquemada is right: We bought our triumph with blood money and now we must atone for it. We must issue the edict, Isabella. No Jew can stay in our realm, lest we too are damned for it."

I swallowed. My mouth and throat felt as if I had just drunk a cup of sand.

"We bought our triumph with loans," I managed to say, "like countless kings before us. The Jews have always managed our finances; you know that as well as I. They have been valued advisors, treasurers, and counselors to us. What will we do without them, if they do not choose to convert?"

He passed his hands over his chin; the touch of his fingers bristling his beard was loud in the silence. "Are you saying you can live with it?" He turned his stare to me. "You can live with the fear that we might burn in Hell for eternity because we succored them?"

I did not tremble. I did not look away or evade his question. I met his eyes and I let myself fall into the chasm; I made myself see, feel, and taste the torments he posited, which might be ours if I heeded the reluctance in my heart.

"No," I whispered, and I bowed my head, as though the burden of the choice had already fallen upon my shoulders. "I cannot live with it. I cannot ask Spain to live with it. But it may mean the exile of their entire people. How can I be responsible for that?"

He reached across our thrones, taking my hand. "We have no other choice." He lifted my hand to his lips. "Do you need time?" he murmured and I nodded, fighting back a surge of sudden, bitter tears.

"No matter what you decide, I will abide by it," I heard him say. "It is your decision; it has always been your decision. You are Castile's queen."

THAT NIGHT IN my rooms, where the musk of vanquished odalisques clung to the enameled walls, as the nightingales of Granada keened outside my window, I went before my altar, with its illuminated Book of Hours, wrought gold candlesticks, and soft-faced Virgin with the Christ Child in arms, her mauve robes floating about her as she stood, posed, upon a cloud, ready to ascend. . . .

The Jews had children; they had daughters, sons. They were mothers, fathers, grandparents. Families. Could I do this? Could I, with one stroke of a quill, banish centuries of tradition, of *convivencia*?

It's always been your decision.

I remained anchored before the altar all night, until the last of the votives sputtered and extinguished in molten wax, until my body was numb and I could scarcely rise. I struggled against this final act, wondering how it would define my reign, fearing it would destroy my peace of mind and haunt me for the rest of my days. I had always resisted it because of the implications; I had made concessions, sought out any other means at my disposal to resolve the growing abyss between them and us. But now, I no longer had that choice.

If I protected the Jews, I risked alienating the very kingdom I had spent my life fighting to protect; I would deny the very God that had led me to this triumphant hour, the God that had allowed me, a mere woman, a frail vessel of bone and dust, to do what centuries of my ancestors had failed to accomplish—expel the infidel and bring Spain together under one crown, as one country, in one faith.

I risked my immortal soul, which would be all I had in the hour of my death.

Dawn came, limpid and wary as dawn in the mountains is apt to be. That morning after I bathed, broke my fast, and allowed Beatriz to tend to my bleeding knees, I sent word to my ministers to draw up my edict, known as the Alhambra Decree.

By royal command, every Jew who did not convert to the Catholic faith must leave.

"WHAT?" I LOOKED wearily up at Chacón. My old steward's enormous belly ballooned below his loose-cut doublet, and his gait was much slower now, pained by recurrent gout. Yet his mind remained keen as ever, and he still watched faithfully over Juan, shadowing my son's every move. His appearance at this hour of the afternoon, when most of the court slept away the heat and I attended to my correspondence, signified something of import.

"That navigator," he repeated, his bushy brows furrowing. "He's here again. He's outside, waiting. Apparently he doesn't understand the meaning of the word 'no.'"

I sighed, glancing at my ink-stained fingers. "Very well, give me a moment."

As I rose from my chair, Cárdenas glanced up. He was working with Luis de Santángel to devise a lasting solution to our disrupted finances. Though our decree of expulsion would not go into effect until May, its early promulgation throughout Castile had roused widespread chaos, and the payment of taxes and other required tariffs had suffered accordingly.

I'd been personally besieged by appeals from lord mayors and officials from every corner of the realm, all unsure as to my ultimate intent, obliging me to create a systematic method for how the edict would be implemented. Those Jews who chose to leave the kingdom would have to depart by the first of August from one of several designated ports. They were forbidden to take any gold, silver, or minted coin, though other valuables were allowed; they must sell or transfer homes and businesses to verified Christians. I had reluctantly authorized that everyone who chose to leave should be searched at the ports, with any proscribed items hidden on their person confiscated; the potential economic devastation from the loss of taxes and other revenues was a consequence of the decree I was determined to mitigate.

Santángel, a converso himself, had proven of immeasurable assistance. He'd already convinced Rabbi Señeor and his family to accept Holy Baptism, but other influential Jewish leaders, who had collaborated with me for years, supplying my armies and financing my efforts, resisted my decree, prompting many in their communities to do the same. This exposed the Jews to extortion and other forms of abuse from those officials charged with promulgating the decree and ensuring conformity, though all Jews were, by the same edict, under our royal protection until their departure. I had hardened my heart to the expressions of horrified disbelief, the fear and panic, the wailing in the plazas and implorations for mercy, for I still held out hope that, as in the past, such harsh measures would prompt mass conversions, preventing an actual exodus of these people who had for so long called this land their home.

Nevertheless, regardless of the outcome, Castile was my priority. My realm must survive.

Inés bustled up to me, attentive as ever to my needs. "Shall I fetch Your Majesty's shawl? It's still a bit cold outside."

I nodded gratefully and passed my dirty hands over my rumpled gown, attempting to smooth out the wrinkles. I let Inés drape the length of thick wool about me and walked with her into my antechamber, thinking as I did that the navigator certainly had a knack for catching me off guard. Fortunately, Fernando was not here; he'd gone hunting. The stifling inactivity of court life after years of crusade had made him surly and impatient and he'd been difficult at best these past few months. I did not want my husband to direct his temper against Master Colón, who, after all, was not to blame for our continued indecision regarding his enterprise.

As I entered the hall, Colón went to one knee. I motioned for him to rise, noting as he did that he was thinner than the last time I had seen him, though his doublet and cape were of much finer quality—costly black velvet that would have suited any grandee. His pale blue eyes were arresting as ever, as was his voice.

"*Majestad,*" he declared, without preamble, "I've waited six years for your answer."

"Answer?" I gave him a vague smile. "But I am told that my committee had assured you that, while admirable in intent, your plan to sail the Ocean Sea is too unfounded and too risky. Indeed, it might ultimately cost you your life."

"Danger, as you know, does not scare me" was his reply. "And you've continued to provide me with a stipend, despite your committee's rec-ommendations to cease. Perhaps I am mistaken, but I was of the belief that the queen of Castile makes her own decisions."

I gave him a pensive look. Beatriz sat sewing in an alcove nearby with Juana; both eyed us with undisguised fascination. Beatriz had always found the navigator an object of curiosity, and I could tell that Juana, a fellow adventurer at heart, shared her interest.

"Come," I said. "Let us walk in the garden."

We exited through the Patio of the Lions, toward the fountain ringed by the carved stone beasts. He seemed at ease walking beside me, as if we were alone, without an entourage of attendants at our heels. I was again struck by his effortless carriage; he had the air of a man who believed he was entitled to an important place in the world.

The spring day was brisk, as often happened in the mountains, but at least there was none of the torrential rain that inundated Andalucía this time of year. I was glad of the wan sun, even if it provided little warmth. I shut my eyes, lifting my chin to let the light touch my face. I felt an age had passed since I had been outdoors, away from my responsibilities.

When I started to attention, I found Colón regarding me with be-musement.

"You will not do it," he said.

I shook my head. "I cannot. It . . . it is still not the right time. I know I told you this before, but we've pressing commitments, so much yet to do. It's not feasible. Even if we could afford it, many who advise us think the idea would be madness."

"I should think you can heed whatever advice you choose," he replied, "seeing as some would also say your own actions from the beginning are a form of madness."

My voice hardened. "Do you dare reproach me?"

The sun highlighted his balding pate as he inclined his head. He was losing his tawny hair; like me, he had aged. This poignant reminder of our shared mortality moved through me like a presentiment.

"I would never presume," he said. "What I meant was, you act according to your conscience and have proven a worthier monarch than any of your predecessors because of it. I have no doubt your reign will become legendary. I only wish I could play some small part in it."

My anger melted away. "I too wish for it," I said softly. "You are welcome to stay with us; I can secure you a position of influence at court. I'm certain you'd be of value to us."

His smile did not touch his eyes. "Thank you, *Majestad*, but I fear that as your heart belongs to Castile, mine seeks the sea." He bowed low, though I'd not given him leave to depart. Before I realized what he was doing, I felt his strong fingers pry my own apart, setting something small into my palm.

He left swiftly. I stood there, silent. Only after he disappeared did I lower my eyes to see what he had given me, the object still warm from the heat of his hands.

A miniature galleon sculpted of pale rose gold.

My vision blurred. I heard myself call out, "Stop him. Bring him back."

Chacón hustled off. Beatriz remarked archly, "I do believe my lady has a secret."

Turning away from her, I pressed the tiny galleon to my heart.

And I smiled.

ON FRIDAY, AUGUST 3, 1492, Don Cristóbal Colón—newly entitled as High Admiral and newly appointed a noble of our court—departs the port of Palos. He travels with three ships—the *Niña*, the *Pinta*, and the *Santa María*. Serenaded by his crew, he stands at the prow of the *Santa María*, the wind ruffling his silvery hair. He looks ahead, always ahead, to the horizon.

I imagine him sailing downstream, past the monastery where his son studies his letters, crossing the River Saltes to reach that first expanse of salt-steeped water, whose currents will guide him past our Canary Islands into the immensity of the Ocean Sea.

I have no way of knowing what he will find, if anything; whether he will succeed in discovering his elusive passage or encounter endless storms and enormous white-capped waves, where ships flounder and sea dragons roam. He goes armed only with his faith and his dreams—

much as a young infanta did many years ago when she first left her home in Arévalo for a destiny unknown.

No, I cannot say what Colón will find. But of one thing I am certain: He will return. We are alike, he and I; once, long ago, no one believed I was destined for greatness.

Now, I am Isabella, Queen of Spain.

AUTHOR'S AFTERWORD

Anyone who researches Isabel of Castile (known more familiarly to English audiences as Isabella) will find themselves both fascinated and challenged. Isabella defied categorization with her heroism and contradictions; awesome in her resolve to forge a united nation, she was often misguided in her devotion to her faith, which gave rise to that infamous system of persecution known as the Spanish Inquisition.

Isabella's reign set the foundations for an empire that would grow to immense power under her grandson Charles V and reach its apogee with her great-grandson Philip II. The statutes and legal codes implemented during her rule; the universities she helped found, where the first female scholars in Spain were allowed to teach; the many cathedrals, monasteries, and convents she restored and patronized; the dark strain of bigotry and sway of the Holy Office—all are part of her legacy. So much did she influence Spain that her era became a byword for glory: the Época Isabelina, remnants of which can still be appreciated today in surviving examples of art, music, architecture, and nascent literature which flourished during her reign.

Isabella was never expected to become a ruling queen and she inherited an impoverished, fragmented, and deeply divided country, brought low by rapacious nobles and ineffectual kings. Together with her equally formidable husband, Fernando of Aragón, she forged a modern Renaissance state poised to assume its place on the world stage. Moreover, she had the vision to believe in the claims of a relatively obscure Genovese navigator, which led to the so-called discovery of the New World, expanding Europeans' knowledge of lands far beyond their own.

Centuries after her premature death at the age of fifty-three, Isabella continues to garner both the esteem and disdain of history. For some, she is a much vaunted queen who succeeded against all odds to mount the throne and lead Spain past the shoals of war to victory; for others, she remains a narrow-minded fanatic, who unleashed a wave of persecution responsible for the destitution of thousands of Jews, the deaths of her own subjects, and the rapine of the Americas.

It is important to remember that like all of us, Isabella was a fallible human being, both a product of, and an exception to, her times. She ignored convention yet adhered to it; choosing her own husband in an era when few princesses dared and believing in a God who would personally punish her for failing to do his will are examples of her dichotomy. Neither saint nor victim, she did what she thought was best for her realm, though some of her actions, viewed in hindsight from more enlightened times, are reprehensible. In her defense, she cannot have known Columbus's discoveries would end up destroying a rich and vibrant civilization, nor that her successors would pillage the very countries they'd conquered. Isabella left in her testament provision for the indigenous peoples of those far lands she never saw; she wanted them "treated gently" and converted to Christianity, not condemned to slavery. Her behest was ignored.

The expulsion of the Jews in 1492 is an equally calamitous act that has darkened her name. Hundreds of years later it is impossible to ascertain the queen's private feelings about the immense tragedy caused by her decree. That she was unaware of the consequences seems unlikely; nevertheless, nothing in the extant documentation indicates that she nursed a vendetta against the Jews, several of whom, such as Rabbi Señeor, had served her faithfully at court. That she did not believe in the rights of any faith besides the Catholic one is certain; no European monarch of her era did. We also have historical indications that she faced a myriad of external pressures, including violent uprisings against Jews throughout Castile, which compelled her to act after the conquest of Granada. Of particular interest is the opinion that Fernando urged her to order the expulsion for his own reasons. Isabella may indeed have hoped that with the edict she would achieve mass conversion rather than exile for her Jewish subjects; if so, she gravely underestimated the resiliency of a people who had for centuries survived while cleaving to their own beloved faith. Nevertheless, it is doubtful she planned on banishment from the start, as her most vehement critics claim, using the Jews for their wealth and biding her time until she saw the way clear to expel them. Most likely, she resisted the idea at first and was only gradually convinced of its inevitability. Once she made the decision, however, as in everything else she undertook, Isabella was implacable.

Her establishment of the Spanish Inquisition is another aspect of her character that has stymied even her most ardent admirers and fueled her detractors. In this novel, I depict one possible interpretation of how she reached this momentous decision, relying on intensive research into her personality and the ways in which she viewed her world. While I offer no apology for her actions, her aversion to cruelty is well documented. She did, in fact, abhor bullfighting and forbade that corridas be held in her honor, though her order was often ignored. I also found no evidence that she ever personally attended an auto-da-fé where heretics were burned. I also think it important to note that the Inquisition had existed in a weakened form for centuries before her. What made her particular Inquisition unique was that she narrowed its focus to so-called false conversos—those suspected of secretly practicing Judaism while outwardly feigning obedience to Christianity. Of course the Holy Office cast a far wider net of terror than she could have foreseen, but given Isabella's general disposition, it is safe to assume she did not take lightly the persecution of her subjects, though evidently she felt that the ends justified the means. This is once again an example of her contradictory nature, one which we may find difficult to reconcile with her humanity. It bears reminding that for Isabella and many others of her time, faith was a matter of survival of the soul and the precepts she embodied were not simply the result of extreme piety. Her fellow sovereigns shared her adherence to Catholicism and usually forbade, by law and other means, any deviation from sanctioned doctrine. Ironically, these very prohibitions paved the road to the Protestant Reformation.

It is impossible to confine a life as complex as Isabella's within a finite number of words. While I've strived to depict her as accurately as possible and remain true to historical fact, I admit to taking certain liberties with dates and events in order to facilitate this fictional interpretation. Among these liberties is Isabella's first meeting with Fernando. Tradition dictates that she and her future husband did not actually see each other in person until the night before their wedding. Nevertheless, as I felt it was important to establish Fernando as a character integral to Isabella's formation earlier in the novel, I set the scene in Segovia shortly after she arrives at court. I also changed Joanna la Beltraneja's birth year (she was born in 1462, not '64) to coincide with Isabella's summons to court, truncated the ten-year crusade to conquer Granada, and altered the death of Isabel's first husband in Portugal (he died after the fire in the encampment). Likewise, I shifted the date of the papal entitlement of Isabella and Fernando as "Catholic" monarchs, which actually took place in 1494, and streamlined other minor events to facilitate narrative flow. Inés is the sole fictional person in the novel. While Isabella did have an attendant of this name among her ladies, there is no evidence that the queen developed a relationship with her. Likewise, while Isabella's favored mount's name has been lost to us, I dubbed him Canela, in honor of a brave Arabian horse I rode in Spain in my youth.

Lastly, I have employed later terms for addressing royalty—i.e., "Majesty" for the monarch, "Highness" for princess or prince. In reality, the use of "Majestad" in Spain began under Isabella's grandson Charles V, who deemed "Highness" inadequate for his rank.

Readers interested in finding out what happens after this book may wish to read my first novel, *The Last Queen*, which tells the story of Isabella's daughter Juana. For those who wish to learn more about Isabella and her times, I recommend the following select bibliography. Please note that not all of these books are in print or available in English:

Álvarez, Manuel Fernández. *Isabel la Católica*. Madrid: Espasa Calpe, S.A., 2003.

Azcona, Tarsicio. *Isabel la Católica: Vida y Reinado*. Madrid: La Esfera de los Libros, 2004.

Hume, Martin. *Queens of Old Spain*. London: Grant Richards Ltd., 1906.

Junta de Castilla y León. *Isabel la Católica: La Magnificencia de un Reinado*. Valladolid: Lunwerg Editores, 2004.

Kamen, Henry. *The Spanish Inquisition: A Historical Revision*. London: Weidenfeld & Nicolson, 1997.

Liss, Peggy K. *Isabel the Queen: Life and Times.* New York: Oxford University Press, 1992.

Miller, Townsend. *The Castles and the Crown: Spain 1451–1555.* New York: Coward-McCann, Inc., 1963.

Miller, Townsend. *Henry IV of Castile.* New York: J. P. Lippincott Company, 1971.

Prescott, William H. *History of the Reign of Ferdinand and Isabella the Catholic.* New York: J. P. Lippincott Company, 1872.

Rubin, Nancy. *Isabella of Castile: The First Renaissance Queen.* New York: St. Martin's Press, 1991.

Val Valdivieso, M. Isabel de. *Isabel la Católica y Su Tiempo.* Granada: Universidad de Granada, 2005.

A Special Note from C.W.

Every year, thousands of Spanish greyhounds known as *galgos* are abandoned, maimed, or killed after a brief hunting season. Many dedicated rescue groups and individuals, both in Spain and abroad, are fighting to end the abuse of the *galgo,* one of Spain's most enduring symbols of nobility. To find out more, please visit www.galgorescue.org and www.baasgalgo.com. Thank you for caring.

ACKNOWLEDGMENTS

My heartfelt appreciation goes first and foremost to my partner, Erik, who never ceases to encourage me, as well as our beloved corgi, Paris. My agent, Jennifer Weltz of the Jean V. Naggar Literary Agency, Inc., is ally, friend, and warrior, without whom I'd be lost. She and her colleagues—Tara, Laura, Jessica, Elizabeth, and Alice—are the best representatives an author could hope for. I'm very fortunate in my editor, Susanna Porter, for her ongoing belief in me, as well as my assistant editor, Priyanka Krishnan; their careful insight has enriched this novel. Likewise, I owe a debt of gratitude to my copy editor, Kate Norris, for her meticulous attention to detail, and to the marvelous creative team at Ballantine. In the United Kingdom, at Hodder & Stoughton, I'm equally lucky to have my editor, Suzie Dooré, and assistant editor, Francine Toon.

I can't speak highly enough of the many bloggers who've been part of my virtual tours, especially Lizzy Johnson of Historically Obsessed. I'm also grateful to my tireless virtual tour guides, Cheryl Malandrinos of Pump Up Your Book Promotion, and Amy Bruno of Historical Fiction Virtual Tours. Marketing is always fun with these ladies at my side.

Book groups have honored me with invitations to chat in person, over the phone, and via Skype. I enjoy chatting with readers from around the world and sharing perspectives on these fascinating historical characters. In the Bay Area, I'm especially grateful to the many clubs who have hosted me with wine, laughter, and continuing support. I'd also like to thank the staff at Bookshop West Portal for keeping my books front and center.

Last, but never least, I thank you, my reader. Your feedback and messages often enliven the long hours at my desk. I hope to entertain you for many years to come.

To learn more about my work, please visit me at www.cwgortner .com.

THE Queen's Vow

C. W. GORTNER

A Reader's Guide

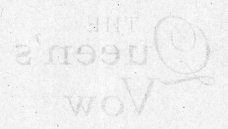

A Conversation with C. W. Gortner

Random House Reader's Circle: Why did you choose to write about Isabella of Castile?

C. W. Gortner: I initially became entranced by Isabella while writing my first novel, *The Last Queen*, about her daughter, Juana. In that book, Isabella is the triumphant, middle-aged queen of legend who has just conquered Granada and set the stage for Spain's emergence as a modern Renaissance state. Of course, in order to depict her accurately, I researched her, but my focus was more on the woman she became after she'd won the crusade against the Moors. Nevertheless, I got so many emails from readers telling me they'd first learned about Isabella in school because of her connection to Columbus and had fallen in love with her in my book that I realized—even hundreds of years after her death, she still exerts a powerful influence. Thus, for *The Queen's Vow* I decided to explore *how* Isabella became the queen she was.

Much of what we know about her is controversial; I was less interested in exonerating her deeds than understanding her motivations. To my surprise, I found myself captivated by her unexpected defiance and courage. She had a rather ignominious beginning as the ignored daughter of an exiled royal widow; no one expected her to become queen, let alone the sole monarch in Spain's history to unite the country. Her love affair with Fernando of Aragón is a rarity in history, as well; she chose her husband in an era when princesses rarely, if ever, did and defied everyone to marry him, sparking a civil war. As I researched her, I realized that, as with most legends, there's far more to Isabella than we think. She was both extraordinary in her determination yet fallible in her mistakes, and her dramatic early years are not well known outside of academic circles. She was, in essence, a perfect choice for me.

RHRC: How long did it take you to write this book, and what special research was involved?

CWG: It took about two years to write. As with all my books, the research began several years before that; for the novel itself, I took several trips to Spain, including one in which I followed in Isabella's footsteps, from the magnificent alcazar in Seville to the mountain city of Granada and the coveted palace of the Alhambra, site of perhaps Isabella's most famous triumph. The alcazar of Segovia, though much transformed over the years, also carries a strong echo of Isabella's early trials, as does the walled city of Avila and several other sites in Castile. I also read her extant correspondence and that of her contemporaries, as well as ambassadorial accounts of her and her court. Isabella has left relatively little in her own hand that reveals her inner thoughts—she was not given to inordinate displays of her feelings—but careful examination of what does exist, together with the aforementioned documentation and her actions during her lifetime, offer a framework from which to begin building an idea of the flesh-and-blood woman she may have been and the challenges she faced.

RHRC: How do you place yourself into the time period that you are writing about?

CWG: I read voraciously before and during the writing anything and everything I can find about my characters and their era. My bibliography for a novel includes countless biographies, social and cultural accounts, art books, architectural books, costume and music and gardening books—in short, anything that fuels my imagination and inspires me with details of a vanished world. I also travel extensively to as many extant sites related to my character as I can; though the places and the landscape have usually changed a great deal, for me there's no substitute to experiencing the countries that my characters once walked in. And I'm always rewarded by these trips. I had a memorable experience in Seville while researching this novel that shifted my perception of Isabella and her stay in that city significantly. You uncover nuggets of treasure when researching in the actual places that nothing else can substitute, not even the Internet. The libraries and archives in the cities I visit are always invaluable for locating little-known contemporary documents such as letters and eyewitness accounts that can change, sometimes dramatically, my take on a particular event. I also listen to period music, and when I can seek out period re-enactors to try on the clothing of the era. Though again this has changed (the Renaissance didn't have synthetic fabrics). The very act of donning a doublet, a gown with a train, a hooded cloak, or of moving within the weight of these unfamiliar constructions, helps me get a feel for how my characters felt when they were dressed—and, conversely, when they were not. It's also practical: you discover that perspiring in velvet is unpleasant, that riding or dancing in a costume embedded with jewels is a test of strength, and that it's impossible to wear most of the outfits we see in the portraits on a daily basis. The day-to-day clothing was less ostentatious; what has survived, what we see, is the ceremonial appearance.

RHRC: What is one of the greatest misconceptions about Isabella of Castile?

CWG: It must be the accusation that she was a fanatic who relished burning heretics. Isabella was deeply Catholic, as were most of her fellow sovereigns. She may have been more devout in practice but it's important to understand that religious persecution existed throughout Europe long before she came into power. The Jews, for example, had been expelled centuries before from England and France, and were barely tolerated in other countries. The suffering imposed on them and other non-Christians is a historical calamity, but not one unique to Isabella or Spain. What is unique is Isabella's revival of the dormant Inquisition to resolve issues of nonconformity to Catholic doctrine among Spain's vibrant and plentiful converso population (those who'd converted to Christianity over generations, often as a result of past persecutions). However, it's less well known that Isabella resisted this action at first and, even after she finally bowed to myriad pressures, insisted the Inquisition confine its investigations to suspected conversos only, thereby exempting practicing Jews from arrest and prosecution by her authorities. What Fernando and Isabella sought to do was utilize a time-honored mechanism of the Catholic Church to impose conformity of faith upon a people who, in truth, shared an amalgam of Christian, Jewish, and Moorish beliefs, due to centuries of coexistence. Isabella's first mistake was her belief that conversos would repent their nonconformity if only they were apprised of it; her second, more critical mistake was to trust that the Inquisition would abide by her dictates. In essence, she gave rise to a monstrous system of torture and death she could not control, even if her alleged fanaticism was in truth a sincere but misguided attempt to impose religious unity and thus safeguard her realm from heresy. Most enlightened people today don't really think about heresy; it's one of those archaic concepts from the past we barely comprehend. But to Christians of Isabella's world, heresy was real; they believed it threatened the very salvation of their souls. Isabella certainly believed this and consequently she made a grave error in judgment, though she would not have seen it that way. She was motivated by her divinely appointed duty as queen to impose the only faith she deemed valid, rather than a heartless desire to terrorize her people.

RHRC: Tell us about a discovery you made that most surprised you about Isabella.

CWG: I had no idea she was so forward-thinking in terms of women's education. We have to remember that Isabella came to power in a Spain fragmented by many years of ineffectual monarchs; bitter antagonism and private feuds had sowed near-total disorder, and on top of this, the country itself was divided, with the kingdom of Aragón holding much of the north, Castile most of the rest, and the kingdom of Granada, the Moors' last foothold, dominating part of the south. Once, Spain had been heralded for its erudition and advanced learning; by the time Isabella was born, even the wealthiest or most noble-born of men were barely literate, and women scarcely at all. She herself had no formal education, save for rudimentary basics. Comparing her educational schedule, as it were, with that of Elizabeth Tudor's, born eighty-two years later, offers startling contrast. Here we have two of history's most famous queens, each of whom became a symbolic personification of her land, yet while Elizabeth enjoyed an impressive upbringing that prepared her, even if accidentally, to be a monarch, Isabella had none. She lamented all her life her lack of education; in her early thirties, she dedicated herself to mastering Latin, and she championed a decree that facilitated women's entry into universities. She was the first queen in Europe to mandate that women could earn degrees and become professors; she also imported and made available the first printing presses in Spain. Isabella was so intent on promoting women's intellectual equality that she insisted her own four daughters be educated in the new Renaissance style; consequently, the infantas became paragons of learning, and were highly praised and coveted as brides.

RHRC: How do you strike a balance between depicting the reality of the times with modern-day sensibilities? Do you think issues Isabella faced in her era still resonate today?

CWG: It's always challenging to depict the past in a way we can both understand and sympathize with. Issues of religion, race, sexuality, gender, as well as how animals were seen and treated, are fraught with controversy when filtered through the prism of the past, because people then barely recognized these issues at all, much less debated them. Many of the freedoms we take for granted were unknown to denizens of the fifteenth and sixteenth centuries, while deprivation, disease, prejudice, and inequality were part of their daily lives. Unfortunately, all of these problems remain part of our modern landscape. While we are in many ways a more enlightened society, we carry vestiges of the past with us, and leaders throughout the world grapple with some of the same issues that Isabella did, in terms of providing safety for their citizens, mitigating violence, and assisting the sick, the hungry, and those whose lives have been torn apart by war and suffering. That said, I must take into account the needs of my reader to be engaged by my story. While historical accuracy remains a primary obligation, I do sanitize certain aspects of the reality of life in the fifteenth century. We romanticize the past; we forget the lack of sanitation, dry-cleaning, antibiotics, etc. While I strive for authenticity and avoid a tendency to convert a brutal, quixotic era into "costume drama," it is necessary to remember we can only take so much "reality" in novelized form. In the end, I write fiction. My principal function is to entertain.

RHRC: You're a man who writes historical novels about women. Do you find it difficult?

CWG: No, oddly enough. Though I am male, I was raised in a family of strong women. I grew up hearing their stories, their secrets, the various ways that women communicate. I was the little boy under the table when my aunts sat down for cigarettes and coffee; I absorbed their language in the same way that children absorb any language. So, it doesn't feel strange to me to write in a woman's voice. In addition, our emotional makeup isn't defined by gender: men and women feel the same emotions. We're just taught by society how we should or should not express them. The challenge is to not inject my personal bias or opinions onto my character. While I often don't agree with what she thinks or does, it's who she is that matters, not who I think she should be. In a way, I must restrain my own personality in order to inhabit the character I'm writing. The reader shouldn't see me, they should see Isabella. Another challenge is to build an emotional portrait that is true to what is known and expand on the often few facts in a realistic manner, so that she becomes to you, the reader, complex and plausible, with her particular strengths and flaws. I never want my characters to be carbon copies of one another: they must each have their own voice, because these are distinct women, with different personalities. I work hard to ensure that each one stands on her own.

RHRC: What do you hope readers take away from your work?

CWG: I seek to reveal secret histories, and in some small way restore humanity to people whose legends have overshadowed them. I also hope readers will come away from my work with the experience that they've been on an emotional journey. I want them to feel the way these people lived, their hardships and joys, and differences and similarities with us. Though a Renaissance queen's life was very different from our own, love, hatred, power, intolerance, passion, and the quest for personal liberty are all part of the human experience.

RHRC: What is your latest project?

CWG: I am currently working on my next historical novel about Lucrezia Borgia, tracing her so-called Vatican years, from her youth as the illegitimate child of an ambitious Spanish churchman to her sudden thrust into notoriety as the pope's daughter and brutal, dangerous struggle to define herself as a woman even as she battles the lethal ambitions of her family. Lucrezia is my first nonruler, so to speak, though it could be argued that she was regarded as royalty in her particular milieu. Once again, I've found myself drawn into the opaque life of a woman vilified by history as a poisoner and incestuous adulteress—immoral and promiscuous, the sole female in the notorious Borgia clan. Who was she, really? How did she survive those dramatic, blood-drenched years when Pope Alexander Borgia held sway over Rome and dreamed of uniting Italy under his rule? What was her true relationship with her powerful father, whom it was said she adored and may have slept with, and with her brother Cesare, that enigmatic warrior who came to personify the very best and worst that the Borgias had to offer? I'm just beginning to explore Lucrezia and her world, and I'm completely enthralled by it, as I hope my readers will be.

Questions and Topics for Discussion

1. In his new novel, C. W. Gortner presents a little-known account of Isabella of Castile, a figure who is controversial in history. His goal is to present her as a complex and multifaceted human being—one who faced difficult choices. Does he succeed? Is Isabella sympathetic to you? If not, why?

2. History cites that Isabella was the first sovereign to rule over a united Spain; her reign set the structure for the powerful force that Spain would become. In what ways was Isabella instrumental in creating a nation beholden to her? Do you consider her methods to be ruthless or pragmatic?

3. Isabella was one of the Renaissance's first ruling queens, but as she herself says at the beginning of the novel, no one believed she was destined for greatness. Talk about how Isabella became queen. What does it show about her personality? How does she feel before her sudden emergence as heir to the throne? How do these same sentiments evolve over time? Do you think she wanted to be queen or was she beholden to what she believed was a sacred duty?

4. Discuss Isabella's early life. What kind of childhood does she have and how do you think it shapes her later decisions? What are her expectations of her future compared to what actually happens? What kind of prejudices does she face as a princess?

5. How would you describe Isabella's relationship with her half-brother, King Enrique? In what way do their positions change?

Do you think Isabella loved her brother? Did you like Enrique? If so, why? If not, why not?

6. The Spain Isabella inherited was very different from the country we know today. Discuss these differences. As separate kingdoms, what kind of strife existed between Castile and Aragón? How did many of the people live? Are there any parallels we can draw today? Discuss the ways in which Isabella both seeks to unite the kingdoms and addresses social inequities.

7. Discuss Isabella's marriage with Fernando of Aragón. What brought them together? How was their union different from the norms of the era and how was it similar? How did Isabella see herself as a wife? Did anything about their relationship surprise you?

8. How does the novel present Isabella's role in the establishment of the Inquisition? Did you understand the events and decisions that led up to this controversial act? Do you think she deserves the full blame for the Inquisition? Do you think it could have been avoided? If so, how?

9. How does the novel address Isabella's war against the Moors? Do you think she went into the war willingly or unwillingly? What were the difficulties and challenges she faced as a warrior queen?

10. Discuss Isabella's children and her relationship with them. How true to her times was Isabella in terms of raising her children and how was she different? Do you think she was a caring mother or did she place duty first? Which of her children seemed most like her? Which one was most different?

11. Isabella's account is in her own voice. Does she express any doubt or regret for the actions she's taken or sacrifices she makes? How does she evolve as a person, from her early youth to her triumph

as queen of Castile? Do you think she is shaped as much by external influences as by her own emotions?

12. Do you think Isabella deserves her reputation in history?

13. What part of this book most surprised you? Which part did you find most engaging or most interesting? What have you learned from reading *The Queen's Vow* about the fifteenth century, Spanish history, and Isabella herself?

PHOTO: © STEPHANIE MOHAN

C. W. GORTNER's historical novels have garnered international praise and been translated into more than twenty languages. He divides his time between Northern California and Antigua, Guatemala. To find out more about his work and to schedule a book group chat, please visit cwgortner.com.

Facebook.com/CWGortner
@CWGortner

Chat.
Comment.
Connect.

Visit our online book club community at
Facebook.com/RHReadersCircle

Chat
Meet fellow book lovers and discuss what you're reading.

Comment
Post reviews of books, ask—and answer—thought-provoking
questions, or give and receive book club ideas.

Connect
Find an author on tour, visit our author blog, or invite one of
our 150 available authors to chat with your group on the phone.

Explore
Also visit our site for discussion questions, excerpts, author
interviews, videos, free books, news on the latest releases,
and more.

Books are better with buddies.
Facebook.com/RHReadersCircle

THE RANDOM HOUSE PUBLISHING GROUP